KT-523-706

The Weight of Angels

Catriona McPherson

Constable • London

CONSTABLE

First published in Great Britain in 2017 by Constable

1 3 5 7 9 10 8 6 4 2

Copyright © Catriona McPherson, 2017

The moral right of the author has been asserted.

A CIP catalogue record for this book is available from the British Library.

ISBN: 978-1-47212-528-6

Typeset in Minion by SX Composing DTP, Rayleigh Essex
Printed and bound by CPI Group (UK) Ltd, Croydon, CR0 4YY

Papers used by Constable are from well-managed forests
and other responsible sources.

Constable
An imprint of
Little, Brown Book Group
Carmelite House
50 Victoria Embankment
London EC4Y 0DZ

An Hachette UK Company
www.hachette.co.uk

www.littlebrown.co.uk

Terri Bischoff
With love and thanks

Prologue

The anger was long gone, doused in vodka and tamped down to a sour thud. But the memory of it wouldn't fade. For a few hours there, everything had been clear. The rage was a high, pure note sounding in your ears, slicing through the junk of life. It was a white light, vicious and merciless, showing the truth if you dared to open your eyes. It was a flashing blade, quicker and cleaner than anything.

A high note, and a white light, and a quick blade.

Then suddenly it was dark. Or maybe not suddenly at all because time had stopped its steady ticking. It lurched and yawned and slabs of it slid out from where they belonged and shoved in where they didn't.

But, sudden or not, there was darkness. And cold mud. The slop of stone-cold mud skidding under your heels as you dragged and staggered. Colder than ice, that mud. A sly, filthy cold.

And the smell of it. Not like earth at all. No mushrooms and leaf mould. No life. Just the tang of iron and the sulphurous seep of cold clay and the suck of the mud at your feet.

It dried like a carapace. Waking, hours later, feeling it like armour. Like an extra skin. It flaked off your fingers when you moved them and rubbed in crumbs on the pillow below your cheek. Under the sheets, last night's clothes were caked and streaked, clay-yellow and iron-red. Rusted iron, was it? Those red streaks. And that tang last night? That metallic reek.

Someone was moving. Someone was coming. The door opened and the silence lasted so long that sleep stole up and around again. Then, at last, screaming.

'No! Oh God, oh God, oh my God, no! What have you *done*?'

Chapter 1

'I been broke but I never been poor,' said someone on Facebook, in loopy writing, over a picture of a beach at sunset. It sounds great, and fair play to you if you can hack it. Me? At half past ten in the morning, on Tuesday, 16 February, after I'd dropped off my husband but before I'd got to my interview, on the A711 between Palnackie and Auchencairn, I became poor. Here's how.

Like a lot of broke people, I'd changed jobs and moved house in the last year. Also, like broke folk everywhere, I was praying as I drove along: Please, God, don't let the car break down. Please make that funny noise just because of the rain and nothing to do with the engine. Please make the petrol gauge be on the stingy side. Let there be plenty of fuel to get me there and back again.

I took the main road through Palnackie, trying not to think about the nice man in the garage shop on the side street. No one with an important appointment to keep would make a detour to hand over eleven pounds twenty for bread and milk.

But by the time I'd gone the five miles to Auchencairn, two things had happened.

First, this time I veered off the through road and went round by the back-street, a slalom of parked cars and sharp turns, not to mention an extra few yards using an extra few drops of petrol. Thing is, the shop in Auchencairn happens to be on the main drag and I owed the nice man in *there* closer to twenty, for bog roll and Tampax and a tub of margarine I'd scraped out that breakfast time, working a sharp knife right round the ridges where the lid snapped on, for Angel's pieces.

I wasn't paranoid. I didn't think he'd be out the front watching for me, setting up a road block for his nineteen quid. But if the funny noise wasn't just puddle water splashing up and I did break down, right under his nose, I couldn't laugh it off and buy a coffee from him while the AA came.

So that was one thing. But then came the clincher. Working my way round the back of Auchencairn, old ladies frowning through their nets to see who it was, I decided to do something only poor people do.

I decided to lie my way into a job. And not just a bit of spit and polish on the old CV, like everyone does – sole responsibility for day-to-day running, cash handling, managerial experience. I decided to tell big fat dangerous porkers, to defraud people who needed to count on me, to short-change people who needed more than I could give them. I reached over, took the thin green folder with my true life history in it and threw it onto the back seat, leaving the plump, buff folder, with the résumé that was going to land me this job, sitting there under my good black handbag, ticking like a time-bomb.

I heard my husband's voice in my head, laughing at me. *You*

4

hate it when I'm right, don't you? How long had it been since Marco had laughed in real life?

Actually, three weeks. He laughed when he found the job advert. 'God Almighty!' he shouted. 'Ali! Ali, get in here and see this.'

He was in Angel's room, on the computer. The kitchen timer was going and Angel lay on the bed with his hands laced behind his head, staring daggers at his dad, counting along with the ticks, grudging every lost minute.

I stopped in the doorway and put the tea-towel up to my face to breathe through its sweet folds. The room was tiny, to be fair. And Angel – Angel – is fifteen, with all his trainers under his bed and the sheets weeks past changing, a dark ghost of hair gel blooming on the pillowcase and God knows what under the duvet. But it was Marco too. Forty-eight years old and rank with the tension that never left him these days. Even now his face was shining and his hair, still dark at the back although his temples were silver, sat against his neck in wet spikes like shark-teeth. At least recently he'd started having it trimmed again. He'd even updated the style, making me hope we were turning a corner.

'I'll just crack the window,' I said, fumbling through the gap in the curtains and wrenching the catch on the metal frame.

'Mu-um,' said Angelo. 'It's freezing.'

'You need some air in here,' I said. 'Get under the covers if you're cold. Or go out for a walk and get your blood moving. The road's clear. Just stay off the verges.'

The shutter came down over his face and took a swipe at my heart on its way. I know, I wanted to tell him. I know. A walk, when none of your friends are in walking distance and you can't make new ones. Not with that phone and those jeans.

'Ali, will you listen?' Marco said, twisting round and beckoning to me. I stepped into the curve of his outstretched arm and he hugged my hip against his shoulder as he traced the text on the screen, moving the cursor like a karaoke ball.

'Full-time, flexible hours, excellent pay and advancement for the right candidate.'

'A job!' I said. 'Where?'

'Here!' he said. Yelped, really. 'Right here!'

Angelo snorted at the sound of his dad's enthusiasm and my heart healed. Wee shite, I thought, and turned to scowl at him.

'Where here?' I said, turning back. There had been long nights of working out petrol costs to Glasgow and Carlisle, calculating the take-home from the top line, with tax credits and me still signing on.

'Right bloody here,' Marco said. 'Townhead. Five minutes away.'

'Town*head*?' I said. 'That's the arse end of nowhere. What job is there for you at Townhead?'

Marco squeezed me harder against him and that was when he laughed. 'Not me,' he said. 'You, ya plank. It's for a beauty therapist.'

I had caught a little bit of his excitement, and the slump as it left me felt like the bathwater draining. Townhead was two farms and a phone box, and even the phone box wasn't hooked up these days. 'Oh, darlin',' I said, 'it'll be one of those franchise things. Make money in your own home. Pay this shyster in Townhead to get your starter pack and hand over a chunk of your takings.'

'Ye of little faith,' Marco said. 'It's not a franchise. It's a full-time position for a qualified beauty therapist to work at Howell Hall.'

6

'A-oooooooo!' said Angelo. 'Ow-ow-aoooooooo. Howl Hall? Go for it, Mum. You can wax their knuckles at the full moon.'

I said nothing. Marco let go of me and started fiddling with the cables to hook up the printer. The kitchen timer went off and Angelo leaped up, flat to standing in one move. 'Time's up,' he said.

'I'll just—' said Marco.

'Time's up, Dad. Twenty minutes. A deal's a deal.'

I looked up at him, trying to think what to say. *Up!* Up into the bum-fluffed face of the little boy I had been singing to sleep in my arms, seemed like ten minutes ago. I had only thrown out his shampoo shield when we moved out of our real house last summer. I found it in the bathroom cabinet and remembered him bolt upright in the shallow bath. 'Don't let the soap get in my eyes, Mummy. Promise me.' Sitting there looking like an old lady in a sunhat, with that floppy brim all over his face and his little ears bent down under it, while I lathered up his hair.

I threw out the shield in one of the extra-sturdy, extra-large black bin bags. Seventeen of them it took to downsize us into this place. No point saving money on the mortgage and handing it over in storage fees.

Marco had finished anyway. He gathered the pages from the printer tray, then took my hand and pulled me out, as our loving son nearly clipped my heels shutting his door.

'Marco, listen,' I said, back in the kitchen. 'They don't mean an ordinary beauty therapist. A commercial one like me.'

'You haven't even read it,' he said. He brushed the day's junk mail back against the bread bin and hitched himself up on the bunker. There was no space for a table. No space in the

7

so-called living room either. We'd turned into one of those families that eat in a row on the couch with the telly on. Angel and Marco were thrilled. I kept my mouth shut.

'"Howell Hall,"' he read, '"is an independent psychiatric hospital situated in the peaceful Galloway countryside."'

'Peaceful?' I said. 'What a pile of shite!' The headland round Howell Hall was owned by the army. When it was quiet it was very, very quiet, but when they were training, it was guns and tanks and soldiers shouting. DANGER AREA, the signs said. No kidding, I always thought when I passed by.

'"Its twenty-three beds, in private en-suite rooms, and individually tailored *therapy* programmes cater for clients with a wide range of health and social needs." See?'

'See what? They mean occupational or what-do-you-call-it. Like a proper trained-up . . . that can do psychology about body image. There was a talk about it at the college, like an option module?'

'Full-time, flexible hours, excellent pay,' Marco said again. 'And I'm looking and "qualified beauty therapist with relevant experience of special-needs clients" is all it says.'

'Well, there it is,' I said. 'I don't have any experience of special-needs clients.'

Marco was rubbing his jaw with the side of his hand. 'What about Oz?' he said.

I was draining the pasta and didn't answer, concentrating on pouring without scalding myself or slopping any of the strands over the edge of the sieve.

'You could make up anything about our year in Australia,' Marco said. 'How would they check? You could say you worked at an old people's home or a residential school for . . . whatever you call them . . . kids.'

8

'But I didn't,' I said. 'I don't know the stuff I'd have learned there.'

'Aw, come on, Ali,' said Marco. 'Google it. You could google yourself to being a brain surgeon, these days.' He hesitated, rubbing his jaw again. 'And you do know *something* about it, don't you?'

I tipped the sieve and sent the pasta sliding into the pan full of sauce, concentrating hard on the year in Australia. We'd had a last fling, the three of us, before Angelo started at the school. Temporary managers in our two businesses, temporary tenants in our house, and me sitting on a white beach watching them: Marco casting for sharks and Angel poddling about, with his baby doll under his arm, looking like a fish finger with all the sand stuck to his sunblock.

'Make your mind up, eh?' I said, keeping my voice light. 'Either I can tell tales about our gap year and no one's the wiser, or everything's on the internet for the world to see. Can't have it both ways.'

'So you're saying no?'

'I'm saying I can't believe you're even *asking* me!' I dropped my voice. Still a habit even though Angel would have earbuds in. 'You want me to go and work in a loony bin? Go inside that bloody abbey every day for hours on end?' He pulled his chin back into his neck and frowned at me. 'Hall, I mean, not abbey. Shit!'

'Don't upset yourself,' Marco said.

Truth be told, Howell Hall and the abbey and the Danger Area were all mixed together in my head and I tried not to think about any of them. I tried not to *look* at the abbey, even though it was practically hanging over us, right outside the living-room window, the bare bones of its vaults and arches

9

sharp against the sky, all the glass and wood gone, like a dead thing picked clean and left there.

Thank God the flood had drained at last. When the grounds were knee-deep for a week, and the wind rippled over the water, the abbey had looked like a ghost ship floating endlessly closer yet never landing. And that one still night the moon had come out, every arch was reflected to make an O, like a ghost mouth screaming. It was back to normal now, marooned in a sea of rotting yellow grass. But it was there. It was nearly dark already, of course, teatime on a day like this at this time of year, but I would still see its outline if I turned. It was always there.

I shouted over my shoulder, 'Ange? Tea's ready.'

He was moving. Food was the one thing that got a response from him. He filled the kitchen doorway. 'Pasta again?'

'You're welcome,' I said.

'Any garlic bread?'

I handed him his dinner and watched him as he took the five paces through to the couch and plopped down, swivelling the plate to keep it level and hitting the buttons on the remote with his free hand. Canned laughter broke out before his bum touched the cushion.

———————

I was used to driving past the army checkpoint – no more than a hut, really, with dusty windows, old phonebooks and *Yellow Pages* slumped on its windowsills, and yellowing posters adorning its walls, but this was the first time I had tried to get in. Half of me thought they'd turn me back. And half of *that* half hoped for it. But when I wound down the window and gave my name to the guy on the gate, he just glanced at his clipboard and tapped my name with his pen.

'Ms Alison McGovern,' he said. 'Here you are in black and white. You know where you're headed, madam?'

'It's just straight down, isn't it?' I squinted ahead to where the road dimmed and disappeared, as if the trees on either side had swallowed it.

'One road in and one road out,' he said. 'If you start to float you've gone too far.' He smiled and patted the roof of the car to send me on my way.

Strange job, I thought, looking at him in my rearview mirror as I drove away. When he'd joined the army, he couldn't have expected he'd spend his days standing in a kiosk on a back road in the middle of nowhere, keeping tourists and birdwatchers off the training range.

'It's got to happen somewhere, pal,' Marco had said. 'Sewage treatment, nuclear power, army training.'

Mental illness. He didn't say it, but I heard it anyway.

'Middle of Sauchiehall Street would be a bit daft, eh?'

Of course, he was right. Galloway is empty and this little corner of Galloway, a bulge in the coast with no beaches, is even emptier than the rest of it. And, Marco said, there were unforeseen benefits. Rare orchids, fragile mosses and shy nesting birds flourished there with no ramblers to flatten them or picnickers to scare them. It wasn't just a training range, he told me. It was a site of special scientific interest. It was a haven. A sanctuary.

All I thought of was how those shy birds would feel when the tanks started. And how those even shyer birds, those rare and fragile residents of Howell Hall, must feel on gun days.

Within a minute or two I drove out from under the trees. The army must have left them there – or even planted them

– for privacy, to stop geeks gawking from the roadside when the troops were on manoeuvres. But fifty yards inside the gate, and as far as the eye could see, everything had been cleared. There was nothing but grassy dips and swells, and those lumps of concrete, like at paintball. What were they called – bunkers? pillboxes? – but these had pockmarks blasted out of them instead of the splatters of colour.

One dark smudge, straight ahead, like the soldier said, had to be the hospital grounds. Yew trees, I thought, from the height of them and their black bulk.

It hadn't flooded up here, but still the tussocks were battered flat and sopped into clods, like hairballs, with all the rain. Grey-yellow grass and grey-white concrete and a gun-grey sky.

'Blasted heath,' I said to myself. I couldn't remember where that came from, didn't even know what it meant exactly, but it felt right. Imagine, on the worst day of your life, when you finally gave up and gave in and let yourself be taken where everyone told you you had to go . . . imagine coming here, to this.

The sign for Howell Hall helped a bit. It was a chunk of granite, polished on the front but rough round the other three sides, set into the grass at the side of the gateway. The name was chiselled, like on gravestones, and painted gold. It looked permanent and reliable and safe to lean against. Looked, in fact, like a country-house hotel. Like the website promised. It was nothing like any hospital I knew. Nothing like the memory, the one I squashed down every time it started to rumble, of a white enamel sign on tubular steel legs, the words in a trendy font unveiled at a meeting along with the logo.

I was doing about five miles an hour as I made my way along the drive so I had loads of time to take it all in. First glance, there was nothing remarkable. Just another big house, built on a wave of Victorian money. Marco was a history buff. Anything from a standing stone onwards was enough to have him parked up in a gateway and hacking his way through brambles for a closer look, but the Industrial Revolution was his darling. That was when his mother's family had left Naples and come north, and when all the murky deeds were done that had earned bewhiskered gentlemen houses like this one.

With a closer look, you could tell Howell Hall was something different. The keypad entry at the front door, the reinforced glass in the downstairs windows, the bars over the plain glass on the bedroom floor, and round the corner, a high chain-link fence separating the garden, with its many benches and its spacious gazebo, from the open drive.

There was someone in that gazebo. I didn't stare but I could tell even from the corner of my eye that they were dressed in night clothes. No one wore pale pink trousers and a pink fluffy mackintosh. Those were pyjamas and a dressing-gown, so that was a patient. One of the special-needs clients of my so-called wide experience.

As I slid the car into a free space between two BMWs and climbed out, I saw the figure start to move. I leaned in for my bag and folder. When I turned back she was halfway over the grass, fluffy dressing-gown and wild orange hair flying out behind her.

'Help me!' she yelled. 'Get me out of here. You've got to help me!'

I stood behind the car door as if it could protect me.

'Ten years!' she screamed, grabbing hold of the chain-link fence and shaking it, her hair over her face and her fingertips purple from how she'd shoved them through the mesh. 'Ten years and I'm the only one left now. I don't want to die!'

Chapter 2

I slammed the car door and scurried to the front of the house, my mouth tasting bitter and my heart beating in big, sickening gulps at the base of my throat. I'd meant to wait and gather myself before I rang the bell but the door was already opening when I approached and the woman who came to greet me saw me stumble as I looked over my shoulder.

'Ms McGovern?' she said. 'Alison? I'm Dr Ferris.'

She was definitely a doctor. She wasn't wearing a white coat or anything but there was no doubt. She had a soft green jumper on, cashmere probably, and dark green trousers. Not jeans or cords: slacks. Turn-ups and creases. They hung a perfect quarter-inch off the ground, just skimming the toes of high-heeled brown court shoes. She probably wore them all day and claimed they were comfy.

She held out a hand to shake and, when I took it, put her left hand on top. I had only ever seen men do that, and only on the telly, but it gave her a chance to show me her wedding rings: the solitaire, the half-hoop and the platinum band. And the pearl-pink manicure. Her skin was cool and silken and I was sure the hangnail on my thumb scratched her as she let go.

'Come inside,' she said. 'Welcome to Howell Hall.'

'Oh!' I said. 'Is that how it's pronounced? How-*well*?'

'Exactly. I can't think of a better name for a place of this kind, can you? It's like a good omen.'

It was like the worst case of denial I'd heard since I'd met someone called De'Ath at work one day. Mrs De'Ath, she told me, with a straight face.

She led me into an office facing the gardens and went to sit behind a desk with her back to a French window. I squinted out past her and saw that the woman in the pink dressing-gown was back in the gazebo again, smoking.

'I met one of the patients,' I said, nodding at the window. 'She seemed quite distressed.'

Dr Ferris twisted in her seat and looked, giving me a chance to admire her profile. Her neck was about twice as long as mine and her jaw made me think of swans. I lifted my chin and poked it forward. Her hair was held back in a silk scarf patterned in exactly the green of her jumper, the green of her slacks and the brown of her shoes. I didn't even know what shops still sold those scarves, like the ones the Queen used to wear with the knot on her chin that daft way.

'Ah,' she said. 'That's Julia. Well, yes, she can be rather mischievous. What did she say we were doing to her this time?'

'Nothing!' I blurted out. 'She just implied that she needed my help for some reason.'

Dr Ferris laughed – such a surprising clear bell of a laugh that I found myself smiling too. 'Spoken like a diplomat,' she said. 'And I don't mind at all that you call her a patient, by the way. We're plain speakers here at Howell Hall.'

15

My smile died.

'So,' she said, opening the folder on her desk. I recognized the form that Marco had filled in but there were three extra pages attached. Just as well I'd decided to go with the fake CV if Marco had already sent it. She flicked through all the wonderful things I had done in Australia: the special school where I'd volunteered; the memory-care end-of-life facility where I had been the resident therapist. 'Memory-care' and 'end-of-life'. He had found all the right words on the homepages of other nursing homes and hadn't missed a single one.

'This is all marvellous,' she said, 'but quite a while ago. Am I right in thinking that for the last . . .'

'Ten years,' I supplied, and felt an echo in my head from that patient screaming.

'You've been working in the commercial sector?'

'Yes,' I said. 'I had the salon in Dalbeattie. Face Value?'

'I pass it every week,' she said. The smile was there again. 'But you decided you'd rather return to a care environment?'

'I did,' I said. Marco had made it sound like a calling.

'Very brave of you to sell up before you had a job to move to,' she said smoothly.

'I knew I needed to refresh my skills,' I said. 'It's not the sort of thing that can be done by halves.'

'Refresh and *extend*!' she said. 'It was your art-therapy experience that made your application stand out from the crowd, if I'm perfectly honest.'

I tried hard but I knew a quick frown must have passed across my face before I managed to smooth my expression again to match hers. *Crowd?* The *crowd* of beauticians with psychiatric-care experience who'd applied to work here?

Her smile was as calm as ever but I was sure her eyes glinted.

My art-therapy experience was a free night class on landscape painting I had signed up for after Marco's mum gave me a watercolour pad and a set of paints at Christmas. I had stared at the half-opened parcel and wanted to weep. She must have spent fifty quid on that thick, creamy paper and the rainbow of paints, with the soft little brushes clipped to the lid. 'Because how could you live there with that glorious view and not want to paint it?' she said, meaning the abbey. She gushed on and on about the abbey the one time she came to visit us. As if the view of a crumbling ruin could make up for the galley kitchen and the metered electricity, for our car parked on the road and Angel's bike under a tarp round the back because there wasn't a shed to store it in.

'Don't write that down!' I had said, looking over Marco's shoulder as he filled in my recent experience. *Intermediate landscape painting.* 'It's about as relevant as my swimming badges.'

'Little faith,' he told me. And when he was typing the covering note, he went into a ton of detail about my long interest in 'both the diagnostic value and healing potential of art for all patients on the care continuum following my experience in Australia'.

Dr Ferris turned a page and kept reading. I could feel a flush beginning to flood my cheeks. 'Would you be willing to do the odd night shift?' she said.

'Night shift?' I stared at her. Why would the patients need beauty treatments or painting classes at night?

'Emergency cover. Would that be a problem? There would be overtime, of course.'

'Well,' I said, 'there's my son, you see. Angel's only fifteen

17

and he's going through a bit of a . . . challenging spell, if I'm honest.' This was my escape. If I said no to the night shift, I wasn't going to have to do this after all.

'Angel?' she said. For the first time, she sounded sharp. 'You called your child *Angel*?'

'It's a nickname,' I said. 'From Angelo. He's— My husband's half Italian and it's a family name.'

'Interesting,' she said. 'Did you know, Alison, that "Angel" is the most popular name for a still-born child?'

I couldn't speak. I leaned forward and peered at her. Silhouetted against the window like she was, I couldn't see anything of her expression. Her eyes weren't glinting now. It was like they had receded somehow.

'But I digress,' she said, and sniffed. 'What would you say to a starting salary of forty?'

I blinked, trying to work it out. Forty pounds a day was two hundred a week, eight hundred a month, not quite ten thousand a year. It wasn't the excellent pay I'd been imagining. And at eight hours a day full-time it wasn't even legal.

'I'm not sure I could actually agree to that,' I said. The relief was making me bold. 'It's a lot less than I was expecting.'

'Forty-five?' she said. 'Forty-five thousand, four weeks' paid holidays, as well as your statutory days and overtime for the night shifts we mentioned?'

She had heard me gasping but she kept talking without a hitch. She definitely knew. She had said it that way to catch me out.

'That sounds fine,' I said, on a fall. 'Forty-five is fine.' I had never taken that much home, not even in Face Value's best year.

'And I'm assuming you can start straight away,' she said.

'Of course.'

'Excellent. Shall we say by the end of this week you'll have your care plans ready for the staff meeting and a timetable drawn up for your first month? And you'll start as soon as your PVG comes through. You can meet the residents accompanied over the next few days and get a feel for things.'

I nodded dumbly. Care plans? PVG?

'You do understand,' she said, 'that a disclosure, even an enhanced disclosure, won't be enough.'

I added a smile to my nod, but I was sure she knew I had no idea what a disclosure – enhanced or otherwise – might be. And she didn't call them patients, after all.

'I can start now,' I said. 'If any of them are free.' Because if I met one and showed Dr Ferris I didn't have a clue, she would be less surprised when I phoned her and told her I'd changed my mind.

'Excellent,' she said again. She stood up and walked around the desk, her heels clicking smartly on the polished floor. 'Unless, that is, you have any questions?' she said, smiling down at me. 'Anything you want to ask about our methods, intake, CC status?'

'CC?'

She crinkled her nose. 'Clinical care,' she said. 'My goodness. You *are* rusty.'

My cheeks were flaming again as I followed her.

The biggest downstairs rooms were set up as lounges – that country-house hotel again. The silky-striped wallpaper, the spindle-legged furniture, even the flower arrangements – professionally bland – said here was a place to hold a golden-wedding party, not somewhere to kick a drug habit or learn to eat again.

19

A couple of women sat over a jigsaw at a long table in the dining room. They turned to us and watched our approach but said nothing. Dr Ferris put a hand on a shoulder of each and gave them one of her smiles. They looked back dead-faced. They were nothing like one another, really, but their pallor, the dark shadows under their eyes and the downward turn of their mouths were so identical they could have been sisters.

'This is Alison,' Dr Ferris said. 'Alison is a beautician. She's going to be working here. She's going to take care of your skin and give you lovely back rubs, aren't you, Alison?'

'Ali,' I said. 'It's nice to meet you.'

They just kept gazing up at Dr Ferris as if I hadn't spoken and, with another squeeze of their shoulders, she turned away. 'Let's go up and see the bedrooms,' she said, as we moved off. Not a word about either of the jigsaw-puzzle women. Upstairs, yet more of the country-house hotel, but with keypads on the bedroom doors and little sliding shutters at head height so staff could look in. Dr Ferris kept walking, silent now on the nap of the pale green carpet, until we came to a door propped open with a painted wooden wedge in the shape of an alligator.

'This is one of our nicest rooms,' she said. 'Vacant at the moment, although we're expecting an old friend to rejoin us in the next day or two.' She waved a hand. 'Look around, Alison.' I wandered this way and that, pretending to be interested in the suite of antique furniture and the view of the blasted heath. 'Bathroom,' said Dr Ferris, opening a door.

I peered in and nodded. 'Very nice.' It was better than nice, in all honesty. The bath stood in the middle of the floor, facing the window, and the pile of fluffy sea-green towels heaped on the towel rail at its side matched the selection of sea-green soap and lotions arranged on the shelves. 'They don't bring stuff from home?' I said, pointing to the bottles.

'Depends,' said Dr Ferris. 'Of course,' she added, with that smile again.

'Right,' I said. 'Drugs.'

She blinked. She might even have started with surprise. 'I don't think we've ever had anyone cunning enough to dissolve drugs in a bottle of Pantene,' she said. 'How would they ever precipitate them out again in a usable form?' She laughed musically.

I turned away to give myself some thinking time and noticed too late that she could still see me in the mirror above the basin. I met her eye. 'I don't have any experience of drug-abusers,' I said. 'Is that going to be a problem?'

'Not at all,' she said. 'Did you foresee them coming to art and beauty therapy while they're in active detox?'

I was frozen, couldn't nod or shake. Certainly couldn't break eye contact. She was absolutely on to me. Why was she keeping at it, like a cat toying with a mouse long after it died of fright?

'They won't rotate into your programmes until they're past the need for acute medical care. Of course,' she said, 'our usual concern regarding toiletries is one of our ana-mias glugging the stuff to purge. And, actually, the returning guest who's coming here tomorrow would think nothing of a little . . .' She raised her hand and mimed drinking, then gathered up the collection of bottles and smiled at me.

'I'm surprised you'd put them in a room like this, actually,' I said. I tried to sound casual, not too proud that I knew what 'ana-mia' meant. 'With these lovely carpets and everything.'

She raised her eyebrows and twisted her mouth. 'I'm very surprised that none of your teenaged clients in Australia had eating disorders,' she said. 'In fact, didn't your statement say that you had considerable experience?' I was frozen again: a little scrap of a mouse, clawed up into the air for fun, then dropped again. 'They're so incredibly cunning,' she said. 'The pukers. You could share a two-berth caravan with one and never know a thing. There's not the slightest chance one of them would ever stain a *carpet*.'

Suddenly I was exhausted. Whatever she was playing at I wanted out. Marco would flay me if I just walked away, though. I decided I'd make her get rid of me.

'I do have one question,' I said, turning back to face her. She gestured me out of the bathroom. I didn't start speaking until we were in the corridor, resuming our tour. 'I wondered if I could have an advance on my salary. Well, expenses really, I suppose. To buy some supplies. A couple of hundred should do it.'

I waited for her to laugh, or to grab me under one elbow and march me out of there, then phone through to the gate to make sure I left the grounds. Instead she answered me in that same smooth tone. 'Shall we say a round thousand?' she said, stopping with her hand on the fire door. 'I can write you a cheque when we get back to my office. Unless you'd prefer cash. For any reason.'

'Either,' I said, and I was shamed to hear the rasp in my voice. 'Cash or cheque. It's all one to me.'

'Cash, then,' she said, almost purring. 'Now, as you see, here we are in the newer part of our facility.'

Funnily enough, the wipe-clean area was less creepy than the renovated manor. It was bright and purposeful. An orderly in a green overall was mopping the floor in one of the rooms. And there was a nurse with a big, rattling bunch of keys, busy doing what looked like a stock-take of a drugs cupboard. Although I supposed it couldn't really have been a drugs cupboard since she was on her own, with no one checking. It must be bandages and kidney bowls.

Best of all, there were patients. Three of the rooms had young men in them, dressed in sweatpants and T-shirts, lounging on their beds, thumbs busy, their doors locked open with steel clips. They wore the mulish expressions of teenagers who weren't getting their own way. Maybe their way was heroin or glue, instead of new trainers or a later curfew, but they weren't so different from Angelo as far as I could see. In fact, looking at the angry rash of acne on one of the faces, I wondered if Angelo had taken something that put those spots on his baby face – he looked exactly like that sometimes, a cue for days of hiding behind a hank of hair and rummaging in the skin treatments bit of my product case, then swearing blind he hadn't.

I shook the thought away, as we headed back to the carpeted corridor. Spots were nothing to do with drugs and Angelo didn't even smoke. I sniffed everything he put in the washing basket to be sure.

We were at the head of the staircase when, corner of my eye, I saw a flash of pink. The woman from the garden flew up the stairs like a bat, swooping right up in front of me to whisper urgently into my face. 'She's not a doctor,' she hissed. 'Don't let her operate on you. She's not a doctor.' She was just a girl, really, aged by her weight and that terrible frizz of hair.

'And this,' said Dr Ferris, 'is our Julia.'

'Ten years!' hissed Julia.

'Julia has been lighting our lives for ten *weeks*. This is Alison, Julia. She's coming to work here and you should be nice to her because she's got a lot to offer you.'

'I killed him and they'll never let me go.'

She was close enough for me to smell her breath – cigarettes and mints – so I put my hands on her arms, just above the elbows and moved her back about a foot. I didn't care if that counted as assault. I was never coming back and I didn't want to leave with this maniac's spit on my face. 'Nice to meet you, Julia,' I said. 'When I've got my treatment menu printed out you could be my first client.'

'Treatment *menu*?' she said, not hissing now. Her normal voice was the same as Dr Ferris's. Posh Scottish that sounded English except for the *rs*. 'What the hell kind of quack are *you*?'

'Beautician,' I said. 'And art therapist.'

'You don't do acrylics, do you?' Julia said, holding one of her hands out in front of her and showing me a set of nails bitten down to the quick. 'I've wrecked these trying to scrape a tunnel out of my padded cell, haven't I, Doc?'

'Why don't you go and get dressed?' said Dr Ferris. 'Pop that dressing-gown into the wash.' She wrinkled her nose and Julia tucked her head down to the side and sniffed at her armpit.

'Gad, you're right,' she said. 'Ah, me! I don't know whether it's the meds or the panic attacks but I'm riper than a Stilton rind.' Her voice had changed again. Now she was drawling. 'Delighted to make your acquaintance, Alison. I'll be one of your first customers.' She swept past me. She did smell a bit, actually. But it wasn't the sharp tang of adrenalin. I knew what that smelt like. And it wasn't the sweetish fug that comes from being marinated in strong drugs either. It was just someone who hadn't bothered to change her clothes for a few days and needed to wash her greasy hair. I could have helped her, if I'd been coming back.

'Oh, Alison?' she said, spinning round and lunging towards me again.

I raised my eyebrows and smiled, managed not to take a step back.

'When you do a bikini wax,' she said, 'tell me you don't try to work round a pair of knickers like a bashful nun. I really need it done but only if you'll make a proper job of it. Arse crack to clit hood. Those long arse hairs are a bitch.'

I opened my mouth and shut it again without speaking. With a whoop of delighted laughter, she spun back and this time she really did leave. I turned to Dr Ferris, hating the way my cheeks had stained. 'What exactly is wrong with her?' I said.

'Of course, you'll be brought up to date at your first staff meeting,' Dr Ferris said, 'but as I'm sure you'll appreciate, we can't discuss confidential patient information in the communal areas of the house.'

'God forbid,' I said. 'I'd hate to embarrass her.' Dr Ferris simply shook her head and laughed softly. 'Are we done?' I asked. 'I might just get going, actually.'

Dr Ferris got a speculative look in her eye. 'One more,' she said. 'I'd like you to meet Sylvie. Now, Sylvie really *has* been here for ten years. Well, goodness me, almost fifteen now. This way.'

I fell behind as she clip-clopped her way along a side hall. I was fully ten paces back when she stopped at a door, knocked lightly and walked in. She held the door open and beckoned to me.

I don't know what I was expecting, but the room behind the door was a sort of summer parlour, by the look of it, halfway to a palm house or orangery or whatever they called conservatories in the old days. Apart from a single bed, hidden behind a printed-silk screen, there was nothing to suggest that the woman sitting by the window gazing out wasn't the lady of the manor, waiting for a maid to bring her tea or help her dress for dinner.

As I drew closer I saw that she was much younger than I'd thought, younger than me. The hair that looked white was really just faded and dry, bolls of thistledown behind and wisps as light as cobweb on her brow. Her skin, what little I could see since she was facing away from us, was dry too, pale and crumpled, and she looked as soft as raw dough inside her loose clothes.

Did she ever move? Her ankles, bare above her bedroom slippers, were purple with oedema and the skin was scaly and sore. The hands that rested bonelessly in her lap, their untrimmed nails curling round like ram's horns, looked as if they'd been discarded there and forgotten. There was a book lying face down on the table beside her – Maya Angelou, with a bookmark tucked into the pages, claiming it was half read. I didn't believe it.

'Sylvie, darling,' said Dr Ferris. 'This is Alison McGovern, a new member of staff. Alison's going to be joining us and she'll be helping to look after you.'

I walked in front of her armchair and bent down to stroke her hand. 'Hello, Sylvie,' I said. She kept her gaze lowered. I could only just see the glint of her eyes through her lashes. But it wasn't her eyes that struck me. She was breathing through her mouth and her top lip had dried until it had snagged on one of her teeth and puckered. The tooth was dry, too, furred with plaque. I couldn't help myself. My training took over. I crouched down and rummaged in my bag, finding the little pot of salve I always carried there. I snapped open the cigarette case that Marco had given me for my thirtieth birthday. I never carried cigarettes in it – I'd never smoked in my life – but it was perfect for a few cotton buds. I twirled one in the salve and touched it to her lip, swiping it free of her tooth. I dabbed it into the corner where the skin was broken and then I cupped her cheek in my hand, rubbing her temple with my thumb. 'There,' I said. 'That's better, isn't it?'

She took a deep breath, like a baby waking, and looked at me. Her voice made no sound but her lips moved. 'Better,' she breathed.

As I stood, she followed me upwards with her eyes, moving her head in three creaks.

'I'll see you next week,' I said, and I thought I saw the ghost of a smile.

Then I looked at Dr Ferris. Her face had drained and there was a flicker at the side of her neck where her pulse showed in a soft place between the sinews, like the fontanelle of a newborn. By the time I managed to drag my eyes away from it, she was on the move again, padding across the carpet, then clip-clopping on the parquet.

She had recovered before we got back to her office. 'You *are* honoured,' she said. 'Sylvie doesn't make eye contact.'

'What's wrong with her?' I asked.

'Hysterical catatonia,' said Dr Ferris. I nodded, as if I understood what that meant, and tried to commit it to memory to look it up when I got home. 'She hasn't spoken a word or interacted in any way with another person – client or team – since she got here.'

'But . . .' I began, and stopped. Probably mouthing echoes of

27

words she'd just heard didn't count. I'd find out when I looked up . . . Oh, God. I'd forgotten already.

'Now then,' Dr Ferris went on briskly. 'About that cheque.' She waited but I didn't bite. 'Or no – forgive me. I think we said cash, didn't we?'

I like to think it played no part. I would want to believe that I changed my mind about going back because of Sylvie and that whisper of a smile. But it's hard to deny that ten one-hundred-pound notes in my bag didn't make a difference as I drove off to the nearest petrol station and planned what easy, tasty junk to have for tea.

Chapter 3

Back at home, sitting outside in the car, I looked across at the abbey. A thing I don't often do.

When I was ill, before Australia, I met this one girl – Anne, she was called – who was scared of dying. She had found her friend after an overdose and it had got right into her bones, like a cancer. She was scared to sleep at night and scared to move in the daytime in case she died. In case being awake or falling asleep or even just living somehow killed her.

But every time she felt herself get better, you know what she did? She went to the cemetery to look at her friend's grave. She was in my group and, after a while, I got sick of listening to her. She'd had a bad experience nearly a year back – that much was true – but she wouldn't help herself. I said so.

'You've got very clear ideas, Ali,' the group leader said. And the rest of them just looked at the floor. I never could work out if they agreed with her. But being there wasn't some kind of hobby for me, like it was with some of the others. I wanted to get better and get back to normal, and that is what I did.

I learned what things to steer clear of and I cracked it in six months. My intake appointment was in July and by Christmas I was off their books. Back home to Marco and little Angelo, and we all had the trip of a lifetime to Australia before the start of school.

That was the beginning of the good times. Marco had turned a small-town chippy into the kind of business he could be proud of and he was sure it would thrive and flourish. Soon he'd be a local celebrity, he told me, pretending he was kidding. I knew he meant it and I knew there was even more that he didn't say. I knew he looked at telly chefs and then in the mirror. And dreamed and dreamed. I was happy with the salon. I had all the chairs and beds rented out, a receptionist and a shampoo girl, a book of clients that came back every month and used me for their weddings. We bought the house before it was even built and chose every last light switch and doorknob to suit ourselves. Put a pool table in the playroom for Marco and never minded how many of his pals we ended up feeding.

How smug we must have seemed to the people around us, who were already leading the lives we led now. They were surely there. I just didn't see them.

Just like I didn't see trouble the first time I looked at the abbey. We came to pretend to make our minds up about the cottage. Truth was, we had no choice. The rent was cheap – mates' rates from Marco's pal – and it was out of the town. That was the main thing. I wouldn't see Face Value lit up and bustling, somehow doing just fine without me. Marco wouldn't see the fliers pile up on the floor behind the glass door of McGovern & Son, lying there empty.

Of course, as soon as Angelo clapped eyes on the abbey, he

wanted to go exploring and I went with him, big lunk of fourteen though he was. Too many things had gone wrong and I was holding on pretty tight, grabbing any chance of him showing an interest in anything – even this – to see if I could get him talking.

The grass around the ruin had looked like velvet from a distance but it was lumpy and uncomfortable to walk on. Fallen masonry, I told myself, but I couldn't kick the thought that it was coffins, or even bodies with their coffins long rotted away. Angelo read from the information boards: "'The abbey was home to a thriving community of Cistercian monks from its foundation in 1142 until it fell into disuse after the Reformation." When was that, Mum?'

I shrugged. How many monks in all those years? Too many to be buried side by side. There must be bodies under bodies under bodies, crammed in like a junkyard. And then it was used for sheep. Angelo was reading it out, laughing: "'A shelter for sheep and cattle,'" he shouted to me. I thought of the rams nudging at the soft earth with their horns. They didn't de-horn sheep then, did they? Grubbing up bones and . . .

But sheep were vegetarians, so my thoughts turned to dogs. A pack of wild dogs, scrapping and snarling over the bleached bones of all those abbots and friars.

'Mary Queen of— Mum? Are you listening?' Angelo had shouted. 'Mary Queen of Scots spent her last night in Scotland sheltering here, before taking a boat across the Solway to seek protection from her cousin Queen Elizabeth.' He made a harsh noise, like the horn on a game-show. 'Bad move, Mary.'

I gave him the best grin I could muster. It wasn't good enough. Not by half.

'What's wrong?' he said.

'Absolutely nothing,' I said. And, really, there *was* nothing wrong.

When I was a wee girl, we used to make daisy chains, and if we had any daisies left over we'd pinch them in the crook of our pointing fingers with our thumbnails and we'd sing 'Mary Queen of *Scots* got her *head* chopped off'. And we'd flick and then giggle as the daisy head fell. Harmless. And once in the Museum of Childhood I saw a peepshow of it. The guillotine, the red satin of her dress and the sacking hood of the executioner. You put in a token and watched the show. The executioner raised his axe in three jerks, the figure in the red satin gown shook. Then the axe fell and the head dropped into the basket, its pale face turned up, its black hair rubbed off where it had hit the basket every time over the years in exactly the same spot. I shovelled in another token and kept watching. I wanted to see how they put it back together. But discs fell over the eyeholes and turned everything black. All I could see was my own eyes reflected there, and when the discs lifted, her head was on again.

I wouldn't even have said it made much of an impression. But it came back to me. When I was ill. Before we went to Australia. In my memory, those painted bystanders around the back walls of the peepshow were all singing, the jingle as tinny and fake as the axe falling. 'Mary Queen of *Scots* got her *head* chopped off.'

Then I learned how to keep away from things. Of course, sometimes it caught me unawares. Those faceless angels. Those bloody ceramic faceless angels. I didn't see that coming. Pam at my work collected them. She was a hairdresser and she had one at her chair. Then she had two and seven, and I got her in the Secret Santa and suddenly I had one. I sat it out on the mantelpiece in the lounge and went to bed. Never gave it a thought.

It was half past three in the morning when I heard it calling to me. Of course it didn't have a mouth – didn't have any features at all – and so it couldn't really shout. It just sort of moaned, with its clay face stretching and bulging. 'Mmmmmm,' it called. 'Mmmhmmm.' I woke up sweating.

'You mixed wine and cocktails,' Marco muttered beside me. 'You did, didn't you?'

I said nothing, just sat there panting.

'Sit tight and I'll get you an Alka-Seltzer.' He started to swing his legs out of bed. 'You don't need a bucket, do you?'

'I'm not drunk,' I said. 'I just need a pee.'

'Ssh! You'll wake the wee man.'

I hadn't even realized I was shouting. I went downstairs and picked up the angel. It was cold and still in my hands. Of course it was, now I was awake. But I threw it in the bin anyway. Felt relief as it shattered. And I turned the other way when I had to pass the growing collection by Pam's chair.

Only once more they got me. I was alone in the salon late one night, working on my tax return. I didn't even know what the noise was at first. I was concentrating hard and the humming might have been the fridge or the heating. Except, of course, I knew the shop's noises and this was new. It was faint, because they were far away, down on the haircutting floor, but Pam had ten of them by then so the chorus reached my ears.

I cocked my head and listened to that high-pitched thrumming chord. 'Mmmhmmm.' Then I jumped up, left all my papers out, left my cheque book sitting there, didn't even lock my office door. I just ran. I told them in the morning that Marco had phoned to say Angelo was poorly and asking for me. And, of course, they all understood. If someone's calling for their mum, you don't ignore it.

33

Those were the days. When Angelo called for me. Now he skulked at the abbey every chance he got as if he knew it was the one place I'd never follow him. The flood had scuppered him for two weekends and all the nights after school, but as soon as the water went down he was back.

The rapping on the window made me start so hard I felt my seatbelt bite. It was Angelo, stooping down to look in at me. He mimed for me to open up, then slid into the passenger seat.

'What you waiting for?' he said.

'Not waiting,' I said. 'Just thinking.'

When Angelo started conversations with me, these days, I was careful to match him, tone for tone, as offhand as he was. And I didn't ask questions beyond what he wanted on his sandwiches or whether he had any clothes to add to a dark load. It had taken him days to forgive me for trying to send him on a walk that day.

'No good, then?' he said. I turned and shook my head, not following. 'Never mind,' he said. 'Prob'ly best, eh?' He reached out and brushed the back of my sleeve with his knuckles and I tried not to let my mouth drop open. He was comforting me for not getting the job.

Right then I could have called a halt to the whole stupid caper. I could have shrugged and said, 'Thanks,' and we could have limped on a bit longer. But who said it was simple? The very fact of him trying to make me feel better was like a punch in the neck. He was fifteen. He should be selfish and carefree, looking to Marco and me for lifts and favours, not stifling his hopes and telling me it didn't matter. And what would it do to Marco to see 'the wee man' being brave? It would crush him. So I gave him a cheesy grin and waggled my eyebrows.

'Major plot twist,' I said. 'I got the job. I start on Monday.'

Angel did a big stagy jaw-drop, then screwed up his face and narrowed his eyes. 'And you're sure it won't land you in the . . .?'

'Doo-doo?' I suggested, and felt a warm surge inside me as he smiled. 'Nah, it's fine.'

'You sure? Because Dad made me read it over for grammar and that. What he wrote, you know? And it's pretty inventive.'

And there was *another* chance to rewind and stop this nonsense before it started. I had only spent sixty-odd pounds of the thousand. But I wanted him happy. And, more than that, I didn't care if he was proud of *me* but I wanted him proud of Marco. I didn't like him thinking his dad had got this wrong.

'I smoothed all that over,' I said. 'I said in my interview that your dad helped me and I admitted he'd gone a bit over the top, and you know what?'

Angelo gave me that narrow-eyed look again.

'They think it shows he's in my corner. Got my back kind of thing. They think it's a good sign that an employee's husband is so supportive. Well, you know, they're psychiatrists. So they see past the surface. They see through to the real stuff underneath.'

Angelo turned and faced the front. The day was fading and we could see the light of the television shining out from our front window.

'But don't you need accreditation and everything? Certificates, qualifications?'

'Nope,' I said. 'I need a police background check done, but I'm not *treating* the patients. I'm just offering . . . What did she call it? Extra-therapeutic recreational and personal services. It's really, really fine.'

'Minty fresh,' he said. He was still staring straight ahead, slumped down so far that his knees didn't fit behind the dashboard. 'What's the pay like?'

I knew that tone. He wanted something: jeans or a phone or a hairdo.

'Pretty fantastic, actually,' I said. I had to bite my tongue to stop myself adding, *Why?*

'Mouthwash,' he said. He clucked his tongue a few times but he still didn't say what it was he had his eye on.

'Talk English!' I said, to break the mood. There. I was Mum again, nagging him about his slang. He wouldn't ask me now. He just snorted, opened the door, uncoiled himself and went slouching over the road.

I got out and shouted across to him. 'Oy, Shorty!' He stopped. 'I've got two big bags of shopping here. Give us a hand, eh?'

He looked out of the side of his eye at the bag I handed him and managed not to smile when he saw the thick pack of bacon and the big bag of frozen pizza bites, but he stepped up his pace and was bouncing as he went up the short path to the front door.

Marco was home. Must have got the bus. But for once he wasn't watching the telly. It was on but turned to a radio channel, classical music blaring out loudly enough for him to hear in the kitchen.

He was wearing an apron, one of the flowered ones. I tried not to react. It was a code between us. One time when we were first married I came back to the flat and he was cooking skate wings, wearing one of my flowery aprons and nothing else. So, once Angelo was old enough to understand his parents flirting, Marco sometimes put it on to make me squirm. He was always home before me. McGovern & Son closed at half past four and my last client slot was six. For years I'd come home to tea on the table. All my girlfriends were jealous.

I sniffed. 'What's for?' I asked.

'It's only salmon,' he said. 'But I've made a herb crust.'

'Mu-um!' said Angelo, shaking the bag of bacon and frozen crap at me. 'No way! Fish? No *way*!'

'I'm starving,' I said. 'I'll eat yours.'

'You're having chicken pockets,' said Marco. 'I'm not a sadist.'

'You're pretty sure of yourself,' I said, coming up to look into the pan of rice he was frying. 'How did you know we'd be celebrating?'

Angelo was halfway out of the room but Marco called him back. 'I didn't,' he said. 'Are you ready for this? You sure you're ready?' He waved his spatula. 'I don't want to steal your thunder or anything, Als, but I . . . have got a job.'

'What?' I said. 'Since when?'

'Since today.' He was still grinning. But maybe 80-watt instead of 120.

'Why didn't you call me?' I said.

Even Angelo quirked a look at me then.

'What – like, to run it past you?' Marco said, down to 40-watt.

'Of course not!' I said. Then I stopped. How could I tell them what was wrong? I was just after saying to Angelo I'd squared away the lies on my CV. I could hardly turn round and argue to Marco that, if he'd landed a job, I was off the hook at Howell Hall. I could hardly chew him out for not phoning me as soon as he knew so I could get myself out – before Mad Julia had had a go at me, before I had seen that ghost woman sitting there

37

with her Maya Angelou, before Dr Ferris had given me those crisp hundreds and I'd split one.

'Sorry,' I said. 'It's been a stressful day. You just took the wind out my sails. But it's brilliant news, Marco! Fantastic!' I put my arms round his neck and planted a kiss on his mouth. Angelo fake-retched and walked away.

'It's only part-time.' Marco turned back to the cooker and shook the pan. The two little squares of salmon didn't move. He had burned them.

'Tell me all about it,' I said.

'Over dinner,' he said. 'You tell me and I'll tell you. Go and get changed.'

The staircase to our room was awkward, nipped out of the living room that didn't have the space to spare, and it led to a glorified attic, with a ceiling that sloped right down to the floor. We slept on the futon that used to be in the playroom, a patch of floor on either side for our bedside tables. 'Like students,' Marco had said, not that he or I had ever been students. We had left home, straight into a house full of wedding presents.

I stripped off my interview clothes, put my suit back in its zip bag – all my good clothes were in them because our 'wardrobe' was actually the airing cupboard with a rail added and the cladding on the tank was crumbly – then clawed my tights down and walked myself out of them. I had just picked up the Juicy velour I'd been sleeping in (it was cold up here) when I heard the siren.

The only window was the original attic skylight, single-glazed with a metal frame and a rusted prop to hold it open. We had to remember to shut it whenever the rain came on. I stood on tiptoe but couldn't see anything lower than the tips of the trees in front of the car park and the very top of one gable-end of the abbey. But even as high as that I could see the wash of red and blue light and I could hear the car slow and turn onto the access road. I grabbed my dressing-gown from the back of the door and went downstairs.

Marco and Angel were standing at the front window, all the lights off the better to see. I joined them, huddling up close. It was a police car, and I felt the relief like a fairground swoop in the pit of my stomach. An ambulance is always bad news for someone, a fire engine too, but a police car might just be cops getting their knickers in a twist over nothing.

Hard on that thought, another one struck me. What a good girl I'd always been. What a straight and narrow path I'd led for my forty-odd years that a police car was the best of the three.

Two is different, though. As the first pulled off the track onto the tarmacked square another came from the other direction, this one silent although its lights were on. I heard the door of the next cottage along bang shut and saw the neighbour hurrying down his path, fumbling his gate open, then trotting across the road so fast his walking stick nearly tripped him.

'I'm going over,' Marco said. 'Ali, put some clothes on in case they come to the door.'

'The cops?' I said, clutching at the neck of my dressing-gown, even though I knew it made me look like a scaredy. 'Why would they come here?'

'Because something's obviously kicking off,' Marco said. 'And they'll want witness statements. You were sitting parked out there ten minutes ago.' He took his Barbour jacket from the back of his armchair and went out, flipping the hood up against the beginning of a drizzle. I hated that jacket. He said he'd found it cheap in the charity shop and it kept the rain off him

39

but I hated the thought that whatever county-type had chucked it out might see him in it and recognize their cast-off.

'Was that where *you* came from?' I asked Angelo. 'Just now? Were you over there?'

He nodded. He was staring at the cars, his eyes gleaming. Except no. It was just that the lights were making his eyes gleam. Obviously. 'And *was* there anything going on? Kicking off?'

He shook his head.

'I'm not stupid, Angelo,' I said. 'Was there anyone else over there with you? Is there anything . . . Is there any reason for you to be worried?'

'Me?' he said.

'If your pals dob you in? To get out of trouble.'

'Mum, what are you talking about? What pals? Dob me for what?'

'I know you drink,' I said. Then I said again: 'I'm not stupid, Angel. But is it just drink? Are there roaches over there? Baggies?'

'Thanks, Mum!' he said. Then he laughed, but with his mouth closed so it was just his breath. 'Two candies with the lights and music for a "roach", eh? Naw, you're not stupid, are you?'

'What's a candy?' I said. My mouth was suddenly dry. 'Pills?'

He laughed properly now. 'A candy *car*, Mum. A cop car.'

'Oh.' I let my breath out and he laughed again, hearing me. 'I'm going to put some clothes on in case Dad's right. About a door-to-door? Because that was a good point. They wouldn't be making this much fuss over kids' stuff.'

'They'd send a couple of chimps if we're lucky.'

'Chimps?' I said.

40

'Community support officers,' said Angelo. 'Completely hopeless in most policing situations.'

'Where'd you learn that?'

'From – you know – being alive and going outside,' he said. The words were soothing: that drawl with the little scornful laugh at its back, just like always. But the way he was staring, tensed like a runner waiting for the gun, nothing moving but maybe his nostrils as the flight-or-fight breaths surged in and out of him? That was anything but normal.

'Are you sure there's nothing going on over there?' I said.

'Not a thing,' he said, looking away at last. 'Been a *long*, long time since that place saw any action.'

I moved to the bottom of the stairs and started climbing. I had my bare feet so there wasn't much of a racket, but I was hurrying a bit so I wasn't silent either. I could have sworn I heard him say: 'I'd just about given up, as it goes.'

Chapter 4

Marco came back when I was halfway down the stairs, dressed again. He did that little song and dance people do when they get in out of the rain, shaking himself and huffing like a hen resettling after an upset. When he'd got his coat off, he shook it out the front door before hanging it up but I could still hear drops falling, in flat-sounding blats, onto the square of plastic spread under the coat pegs.

'Well?' I said. 'What's happening?'

'Nothing we need to worry about,' he told me.

'Marco,' I said. 'What the hell? Tell me.'

'Don't upset yourself,' he said, like he always did.

He went back into the living room to stand beside Angelo, the pair of them like twins in the dark. Angelo was Daddy's boy from day one. In the hospital, he had fixed those milky blue-black eyes on Marco's face and stared. Marco had tried to hide the swell of pride. He had looked up and wiggled his eyebrows at me, sharing the moment. And he was a great dad. He never said a word when Angelo went through that phase with the baby doll. And certainly he always shared Angelo now.

'You're really not going to tell me what's happening?' I said, then grabbed the Barbour and went out, banging the door behind me. I scuttled across the road, hopping clear of the black puddles at both kerbs and keeping to the crest along the middle of the track that led to the car park. The neighbour was still there, along with a huddle of other people. They must have come from the rest of the cottages in the row since there were no cars except the two pandas – the candies, Angel had called them – parked up in a V-shape with their lights still flashing. They blocked most of the view of whatever was going on and the copper planted just inside the fence did the rest. He was standing like one of the guards at Buckingham Palace, staring over the heads of the little clutch of nosy-parkers, trying to look dignified, even with rain dripping off the peak of his cap.

'Does anyone know what's happened?' I said.

'Mrs McGovern!' the neighbour said, glancing away long enough to identify me, then training his gaze back on the distant view of swinging torch beams. They wheeled and shuddered, filled with dashing raindrops, giving the old abbey stones the leathery gleam of toad skins. 'Your husband was just here,' he said. 'Wouldn't he tell you anything?'

I bristled at the judgement and an easy lie sprang to my lips. 'The phone rang,' I said. 'He didn't get a chance.'

'I never heard it,' said the neighbour, glancing over the road. 'I've been meaning to have a word about your phone, as a matter of fact. I wonder if you could turn the volume down and set the machine to catch it a bit quicker.'

'His mobile,' I said, ignoring the rest of it, refusing to think about our back-to-back fireplaces, the gurgle of his hot tank in

43

our bedroom in the early morning, and the flush of his toilet three or four times in the quiet night. It was too easy to imagine him with a glass to the wall and a notebook open. 'So what happened?' I said again. I looked at the silent policeman, standing there less than four feet away. 'Can you tell us what's going on? Do we need to be worried?'

'Nothing to worry about, Mrs McGovern,' he said. I didn't know if he was taking his cue from the neighbour or if he recognized me. I didn't recognize him – at least, not with his hat pulled low and his face screwed up against the rain.

'They've obviously found something,' one of the others said. 'There's been no one put in a car so no one's been "surprised in the act". But they've found something that shouldn't be there, haven't they?'

We stood in silence for a moment and watched. The torch beams had stopped wheeling and were pointed at the ground now, the little glow of light making me think of nativity scenes. The rain fell steadily, pattering onto the brollies and mackintoshes of the onlookers, and bouncing off the Barbour hood. I breathed in the waxy stink from the waterproofing. He had definitely said it was second-hand but he must have bought a can of spray-on stuff to reseal it. Either way, he'd spent more than the price of a cheap cagoule.

'Could be stolen goods,' said a woman's voice, cutting in on my thoughts.

But we all knew better. We knew exactly what they'd found. Even the silent policeman knew we knew and, as we all stood there thinking about it and wishing it wasn't true, another engine sounded and a high-sided van pulled off the road, dazzling us all with its headlights at full beam.

'SOCO,' said one of the men.

The silent policeman unbent enough to say, 'At bloody last,' under his breath and went to direct it towards the gate.

'I just hope it's not a baby,' that same woman said. 'I heard a funny noise a few days back. I thought it was a kitten but I couldn't find it. I checked under all the cars.'

I left then. When I was halfway to the road I had to swerve off the track, jumping deep into the muddy verge, to let another car go by. It had a light on its roof too, but one of the sort they keep in the glovebox and just reach out the window to stick on top when they need to. A sign propped on the dashboard said 'PATHOLOGIST ON POLICE BUSINESS', and all doubt was gone.

The neighbour caught up with me when we were at our gates. He put a hand on my arm and looked up into my face, his eyes enormous behind the smeared lenses of old-fashioned glasses. 'You all right, Mrs McGovern?'

'Well, upset,' I said. 'Naturally. Mr . . .?'

'That's right,' he said. 'We haven't been on what you'd call neighbourly terms yet, have we? It's good to see you beginning to settle in and be one of us. It's a nice place, if you give it a chance.' I stared at him. Anyone would think we'd been admiring the municipal flower-boxes. I pulled my arm back but his hand came with it. 'I'm just going to get a tray of tea for the lads,' he said. 'Would you like to give me a hand?'

I shook my head and, with a more determined tug, I managed to free myself.

He watched me as I went up the short path to the front door. 'There's no point trying to pretend you're not really living here,' he said. 'You'll need people one of these days.'

Any other night it would have stung me, finding out he knew my story, hearing the relish in his voice as he predicted more trouble to come. Tonight it barely registered. I got the door open and shrugged out of the jacket, letting it fall to the floor behind me.

'I see you had a quality moment with Yoda,' Angelo said. They were still where I had left them, still in darkness.

'Was that a doctor's car?' said Marco.

I took Angelo's arms and shook him until he drew his gaze away from the window and looked down at me. 'What is it?' I said. 'Tell me what's over there.'

'Ali?' said Marco. He prised my hands off Angel, then curled his big ones around them. 'You're freezing,' he said. He reached over and clicked on the lamp on the table in front of the window. I winced as what seemed like a spike of brilliant light stabbed me. 'Jesus, Ali,' Marco said. I peered past the orb of light out into the dark again. I couldn't see anything over at the abbey, between the reflection of the lamp and every raindrop acting like a prism, but the neighbour was still out there looking in, his face sharp with delight. Then, suddenly and deliciously I found myself wrapped inside a cool grey cuddle that fitted me perfectly and filled the whole world.

———

I didn't want to come back, not to wet hair and the corkscrew tug of tights too hastily pulled back on and the food smell in our living room. But, hard as I screwed my eyes shut, the cool grey was gone, in its place the leathery bulk of the couch arm under my head and Angelo and Marco whispering.

'Get some whisky.'

'She hates whisky.'

'I don't need whisky,' I said, sitting up a bit. 'Did I *faint*? I've never fainted in my life.'

'What's wrong, pal?' Marco said. He was chafing my hands. Where the hell did he learn how to chafe hands? It was something the capable wife did in black-and-white films.

'Someone's dumped a dead baby,' I said. I heard Angelo start to say something, bitten off before it got going. 'I might have that whisky,' I added, and he went through to the kitchen, to where we had a bottle on top of the fridge. Budget or no budget, we needed one bottle of something in the house.

My parents, typical farmers, had ended every long day with two whiskies at the fireside. Slippers and sleeping dogs. My first taste of drink was a chubby finger stuck in the dregs and sucked while I was doing the dishes. It made me shudder. It tasted worse than earwax or the flecks of a drilled-out filling, and after that I remember looking at my parents as they sat taking their first sips, while the smoke belched out from among the logs and thinned to a ribbon. I'd wondered if they were just pretending.

They retired to France, to a villa with balconies and patios and someone coming in to do the garden. My dad's toast at their leaving party was 'never cut another blade of grass in my life'.

'Ali?' Marco said softly. He was on his knees beside me, his face so close I could see all his pores and the spikes of beard he always missed at the right corner of his mouth until I told him.

'I was thinking about Mum and Dad,' I said. 'Home. Everything always seemed so set in stone. And then how much it changed. I wonder now if any of it was real.'

'Hey,' said Marco. 'Where's this coming from?'

They passed the farm to my brother, like farmers do. It was fine by me. They'd helped me out when I bought my own business and I knew enough about farming to be sure I was well out of it. My brother, two years younger, looked ten years older and his wife was long gone, taking the kids with her. And it was fine by me that they went to France. Why shouldn't they? A bit of warmth and ease after forty years' grubbing a living from between the stones.

'How could they stay away?' I said. Marco shushed me. 'And how could someone throw a baby away, like an old sweetie wrapper? Leave it lying there.'

'Is that what happened, then?' said Angelo, coming back and putting a glass into my hand.

'Let's not dwell on it,' Marco said. 'The cops know what to do.' He nudged the glass towards my mouth, making me think of a mother hyena pushing a cub's snout down into the carrion. I needed to get a grip, I told myself. Where had *that* come from? I swallowed a mouthful and let the shudder pass through me.

'Not that,' said Angelo, jerking his chin towards the front window. 'I mean, Gran and Granddad. You're not speaking, just because they moved away? Cos Billie said they've got a pool now?'

Billie was my brother's wee girl. It was news to me Angelo was in touch with his cousins, like it was news about the pool. 'Not because they moved,' I said. 'Because they didn't come over to see me when I was ill and needed them.' I tried to laugh. 'They were probably too busy digging out the pool.'

'Needed them for what?' said Angelo. 'They're not doctors and nurses.'

'Let's not dwell on that either,' Marco said. 'Water under the bridge.'

I threw back the rest of the whisky. 'You don't need your mum and dad *for things*. If you ever need *me*, Angel-boy, you call and I come. Right?'

'Jesus, Mother,' he said.

'I'm serious,' I said. 'You need me, you call me, I'm there.'

He gave that mouth-closed laugh and shook his head at how lame I was. So, when the knock came at the door, he was looking right at me. There was nothing. No eye flash, no flare of fear. His smile widened. 'What's this *now*?' he seemed to say, before he pushed himself up from where he was squatting and went slouching through to the front door.

———————

She looked about twenty, the girl Angel ushered in ahead of him, and I would have recognized her as Galloway if I'd met her on the streets of Rio or crossing the tundra. She was short and sturdy, a series of cylinders joined together, like a balloon animal. Her fair hair was so thick her ponytail stuck straight out like a spigot and she had fine fair eyebrows and a velvety covering above her top lip that would start to be a nuisance when she hit her forties. She'd put concealer on her spots about six shades too dark for her milky skin. She could have been me before I learned better.

She undid her coat before she sat down and I thought either she had put on weight recently or the Dumfries and Galloway police uniforms didn't come in half sizes, because everything was a struggle for her: wedging herself back onto the couch; reaching her notebook out of her pocket; managing the teacup that Marco brought her.

'Just routine,' she said, smiling round the three of us. 'Can you give me your full names?'

Marco reeled them off, head-of-the-family style.

'And can you tell me when you were last in the abbey

49

grounds?' she said. 'Do you have a family dog you walk over there, kind of thing?' It was a line she'd been given and told to use. No one says 'family dog' spontaneously.

'I avoid it,' I said. 'It gives me the creeps.'

'I don't think I've been over there since—' Marco was saying, when her phone rang. She answered it without excusing herself and we heard the quack of someone's voice speaking urgently to her. Her head jerked up and she shot a look at me, the milky skin on her neck turning the boiled pink of sunburn.

'Right,' she said. She hung up. 'I'm just going to wait for my . . . colleague,' she said.

Through the thin wall to next door, we all heard someone leaving and we sat there, dumbly listening to the footsteps as they went down one path, and came up the other. Then there was a sharp rap and Angelo went to answer.

The sergeant was a burly fifty-year-old, Northern Irish, I thought when he spoke, with a broad, ruddy face and cold little eyes, belying his smiles. He could have been the sarge in some American telly series, handing out wisecracks and setting mavericks straight again.

'Now then, Mrs McGovern,' he said, as he settled down, tweaking his trouser creases and nodding at the constable to take notes. 'Your neighbour tells me all this across the way has upset you.'

'Of course it's upset her,' said Marco. 'You'd be worried if it *didn't*.'

I was sure the sergeant flicked a look at Angelo before he spoke again.

'How about if you talk me through what happened?' he said.

'We heard the sirens,' Marco began, but the sergeant held up his hand.

'Your wife first, sir,' he said.

'We heard the sirens,' I repeated. 'And Marco went over to see what was happening while I went and got changed. And then Marco came back and I went over. Then I came back and the constable arrived.'

'Well, that all sounds very ship-shape,' the sergeant said. 'And why did you come back, Mrs McGovern?'

'Like what Mr . . . what Next Door said. Someone over there told me what had happened and I was upset.'

'Who's this someone?' the sergeant snapped. Maybe he thought one of his men had been blabbing.

'One of the other neighbours,' I said. 'A woman. I don't know her name.'

The sergeant took a deep breath and looked around. 'Quiet place like this,' he said, 'I always imagine you'd be tight-knit. But it doesn't sound like it.'

'We've only been here a few months,' I told him.

'McGovern!' said the sergeant, snapping his fingers. He swung round to face Marco. '*Paulo* McGovern?'

'Was my granddad,' said Marco.

'That's right,' the sergeant said, his broad grin creasing his cheeks into puckers and his little eyes glittering. 'You're Tony and Maria's boy, aren't you? You're the one that sold up. You didn't have many friends in the D and G after that, son.'

Marco said nothing. Not even to the 'son'. Paulo's Fish had been open from lunch till the pubs shut, seven days a week, for fifty years, serving the Dumfries and Galloway coppers on the day, back and night shift and pretty much everyone else too. When the fair Maria, Paulo's daughter, married Tony McGovern, he gave up his apprenticeship at the motor works and took to frying. He was still in charge when I used to go in, one of a giggling crowd with our skirts rolled up, hoping to see his son, the boy who'd got Maria's black curls and a name to match them. We met *officially* at Sandy Pearson's twenty-first and Marco didn't remember me. Or, at least, he didn't connect who I'd become with one of the quieter girls from the waves of gigglers who had passed through the shop over the years.

Even that first night, he was already full of his plan. He told me all about it, sitting on the bonnet of his car outside the function room in the quiet and the cool, looking at a star-filled sky. 'It'll be a fishmonger's, with some café tables where people can eat freshly prepared food – they'll come in and choose it on the slab and ten minutes later they'll be eating it . . . Thai prawns in ginger, a skate wing in *beurre noisette*. And I'll have evening classes too. A cooking school. It's going to change people's minds about good food. I'll cater weddings and parties. Teach folk there's life beyond steak pie and chicken breasts.'

I'd quite enjoyed my dinner, so I didn't say anything. I certainly didn't say no one would want to sit and eat in a fishmonger's with the smell of it all round and people queuing for a pound of haddock. And, besides, I had my own dreams and no one who'd listen to them.

But the difference was that my dreams came true. Face Value was a solid business and I was good at it, cautious and tireless. I didn't mind the second-hand dryers and the home-made gowns, didn't mind washing my own towels at home on Sundays. Truth is, when I had enough money to use a towel service, I missed seeing them dancing in the breeze on the washing rope. And when I finally fitted out the salon properly, everything matching and new, I was sad to see it all go. I was jealous of the girl who came down from Glasgow with her brother in a rented van and bought it to start her own place.

Marco did things differently and explained it all: you had to get people through the door. You had to entice them. When you were trying to get people to eat your food you had to show some panache. I didn't argue. I didn't say that when people were letting you dig in their pores and put chemicals on their eyelashes you couldn't afford to look like a hole in the wall.

And, anyway, his corporate Christmas cards and all the carrier bags with the logo on them, the auction prizes he donated and the gift hampers he handed out reassured me. Everything looked fine so it was fine.

When he commissioned a designer after Angelo was born, adding '& Son' to the sign, I said maybe he was jumping the gun. He told me I was the evil fairy at the christening, showering curses. But he was smiling when he said it, and he had his arms round me.

For a few years after that I was too busy to notice, and then I was ill. And then I was busy again. I said nothing when he refinanced, when he started selling sandwiches and put in a drinks fridge to try to keep the café tables turning over. I said nothing when he sold the café tables and put a preserves display up instead, on a franchise basis. Fish and jam, I thought. But I said nothing. It wasn't until Angelo was twelve that I finally spoke up.

We had that conversation against the din from behind the Monster poster on Angelo's bedroom door, the bangs and thumps as he let us know what he thought of us. Marco had just told him he couldn't go to New York on a school trip.

'New York?' he said to me. 'Broadway? Gimme a break, Als. We went to the panto in Ayr and thought ourselves lucky.'

'All that's wrong is he doesn't know why,' I said. 'Tell him why. Tell *me* why.'

And out it all came. The second refinancing, the overdraft, the unsecured loan, the credit-card balances.

'How about a van?' I said. 'Take it to them if they won't come to you.'

'A fish van?' he said. 'Why don't I refit the fryers and extractors and start selling battered burgers to school kids?'

Because you couldn't get a loan to buy the fryers, I wanted to say.

'Why don't *you* get a van?' he went on. 'Do *you* fancy touting round the farms and schemes in a wee van?'

'I would if I had to,' I said.

'Good to know,' said Marco. And out came the rest of it. Out came the news that Face Value and McGovern's were in it together. That I'd been propping him up for years.

'But how?' I said. 'It's mine. How did you manage to borrow against it when it's mine?'

'You signed the papers, Ali,' Marco said. 'I did it on advice. Years back, when you weren't so great, you know. In case, things went bad and I had to step in.'

I couldn't even laugh. I just sat there gaping at him, trying to take it in. He had put papers in front of me when I was a zombie, drugged to my eyeballs and hauling myself through each unwelcome day. I could still remember exactly what it felt like, even though Marco didn't understand when I tried to tell him. It felt like the past was quicksand sucking at me and I had to grapple my way out of every hour and into the labour of the next one.

'I did it for you,' he said. 'So I could prop you up and you'd never know.'

'And then what? It just came in handy when things turned out the other way?'

54

'I wasn't thinking straight. You were happy again. I wanted you to stay happy. I thought I could ride it out and you'd never know. I couldn't face seeing you go back down.'

'Oh, no!' I said. 'You don't lay this at *my* door. I am fine. I was ill and I got better and I'm *fine*. You don't put this on me.'

Then I cleared off the dining-room table and we sat down together with every scrap of paper and every statement printed out, to put it right.

And he blocked every single one of my suggestions. I told him I didn't care which way we went – him working for me or me working for him, but we had to pick one basket for the few cracked eggs we had left. I told him it was time to swallow our pride and start again. And he would have none of it. He wanted to hang on.

I let him. But deep inside I thought bitter thoughts I'd never tell him. I'd never tell him he had taken his grandfather's hard work and thrown it away on some stupid pipe dream because he thought he was too cool to make chips and shake a bottle of sauce. I'd never tell him about giving full-body cleansing massages to fat women in their fifties who still had back acne or painting over some bloke's yellow toenails when he was headed to Ibiza. I'd never tell him to look at all the *other* men who gave away auction prizes and hampers at Christmas: mechanics and publicans and newsagents. Dirty overalls and dirtier fingernails and buckets of sawdust for puddles of sick and getting up at four o'clock hoping the pigeons hadn't pecked the rolls and no one'd pissed on the *Radio Times*.

'You don't understand, Als,' he said. 'It's different for men and women.'

I shook my head at him, no idea what he was on about.

'Me losing the business, or even me losing you your business . . . it goes deep. It's different for men.' He took a deep

55

breath before what he said next. 'Different things hurt most of all. I understood that when it was you.'

I didn't want Marco struggling in quicksand till he ached all over. And, even if I hardened my heart about *that*, I didn't want Angelo seeing it. And we couldn't all take off to Australia for a treat this time. What else could I do but stand beside him and keep hoping?

Finally, tail end of last year, we lost everything. We lost Face Value and McGovern & Son and our lovely house. We kept the cheap car and sold the good one. We rented what we could afford and ate off our knees in a row in front of the telly. We looked for jobs and lied to get them. And now here was this cheery-faced sergeant saying, 'You're the one who sold up,' and calling him 'son'.

'So where are you working these days?' he was asking Marco.

'Is that relevant?' I found myself saying.

'Just in case we need to follow up,' said the sergeant. 'Or are you here most of the day?'

'T&C,' said Marco. It was the Castle Douglas builder's yard, trade and commercial. None of Marco's skills would have got him a job there, so he had to be serving customers or stocking shelves.

'What's the number?' the sergeant said. 'Or do they let you keep your mobile switched on?'

I stared hard at the young constable, wondering if she'd started out sweet, if watching this cherry-cheeked man operate would turn her. 'Or are you here most of the day' meaning he looked unemployed and 'do they let you keep your phone on' meaning he'd got a job one step up from McDonald's.

'I'll find out and let you know,' Marco said. 'I've only just been taken on and I don't really start for real till Friday.'

He sounded cocky enough, but what did I know? Maybe being younger and taller and having all his hair made him the alpha here. Men were different, like he'd told me.

'Follow up what?' I said.

The man made a sort of pout as if he was reviewing all the things that might be worth following up. He shrugged. 'Am I right in thinking you're a minor?' he said, suddenly swinging round to face Angelo.

Angel put his feet down on the floor from where he'd been resting them on the edge of the coffee table, his boot soles an inch from the dinner plate abandoned there, scraps congealing. 'Me?' he said.

'He's fifteen,' said Marco. 'Why?'

'Well, since you spend so much time over there and since you were there tonight and since both your parents went over separately, leaving one of them in the house with you at all times, once the discovery was made, I think you're a very interesting person to us, Master McGovern. Wouldn't you say?'

Angelo started to speak but the sergeant interrupted him: 'Anyway, Mrs McGovern, as you were saying?'

'What?' I said.

'You were telling me your neighbour informed you what had happened. Carry on.'

'She told me a baby had been dumped,' I said. And at last I saw some of the merriment die down in the sergeant's little eyes. 'Wait,' I said. 'No, she didn't, she said she heard a noise that might have been a kitten, that she hoped it wasn't a baby. It's such a horrible idea, as cold as it's been, so lonely and dark.' The constable looked up at me and gave me a tiny smile. If it was just her she might have said something kind but, with a glance at her boss, she went back to taking notes again.

'Your neighbour was right, Mrs McGovern,' the sergeant said, still grinning.

My stomach started to churn. I had eaten a Toblerone in the car, then missed my dinner and a high sourness prickled in me. 'How old?' I said.

'Not as old as we'd like,' he said. 'Not old enough to be one of the monks.' I could feel the room start to slide and roll, making me think of dark wine swirled in a stem glass.

'Wait a minute – what?' said Marco. 'Why would you think it's a monk, if it's a baby?'

The sergeant gave a fake frown. All of his faces were fake, I was beginning to see. Grins and winks and this the biggest act of all. 'It's not a baby,' he said. 'Like I just told you. Your neighbour hoped it wasn't and she was right. So.' He beamed at us all. 'That's a relief, eh? Not that it's ever a happy day when you find human remains where they shouldn't be.' He sobered briefly, then turned back to Angelo and gave him a wink. 'You're fifteen, eh? Well, we need to wait and see what the pathologist says about how long it's been in the ground. But I'd say you're off the hook, boy.'

Chapter 5

'Although the youngest child killer I can think of offhand was – what – eight? Eight and a half? So, unless the body's older than seven years, all bets are off.'

I stared, speechless. I had come back to Howell Hall the next morning to look over the treatment room that was going to be mine and to see where I thought would be good for art therapy. Dr Ferris, on her way out, had introduced me to her husband, the other Dr Ferris, and all he could think of was the drama at the abbey. When he heard we lived across the lane from it, staring at it, and that the cops had come and questioned us, he sat me down in the staff kitchenette and got everything out of me. Even managed to make me repeat what the sergeant had said to Angelo. He'd be fantastic in a counselling session.

'But no child of eight I've ever come across in the literature has buried their victim and kept it quiet for years,' he said, tapping his temple with his pen as if he was trying to shake a memory to the surface, like when you want the good bits in the muesli.

'You're freaking Ali out, Dr F,' said the kitchen assistant who had come in, supposedly to get a cup of tea, but really to look me over.

'Oh, you'll soon get used to me,' he said, sticking his tongue out the side of his mouth and batting his hand down. 'I'm harmless, aren't I, Hinny?' He gave me an impish smile and a little shoulder shrug, then spun round, the lino squeaking under his trainer soles, and marched off. I gazed after him. He was short and shaped like a pouter pigeon, his chest straining at the buttons of his shirt so that tufts of chestnut hair poked through the gaps, his bottom sticking out so far that the flaps of his hairy tweed jacket gaped. His corduroy trousers swished like *Star Trek* doors with every step.

I was still watching the corner he'd disappeared around when Hinny snorted. 'Say it,' she said. 'Just say it. I know what you're thinking.'

I turned and looked into her dancing eyes. She was bubbling with laughter, hugging her cup of tea to her chest as she leaned against the counter. 'They're an odd couple, aren't they?' I offered.

'*Say it!*'

'I'm no expert, but I've hung around enough hairdressing salons,' I said. 'That is not a heterosexual person.'

Hinny beamed at me. 'You'll fit right in here, Ali,' she said. 'It's one of the great mysteries. They've got a kid, you know. Dido.'

'Ha!' came a voice from the other doorway. The little kitch-enette sat between the two wings, a long way from the catering kitchen where the meals were prepared and where Hinny could have got a perfectly good cup of tea. The newcomer had arrived from the modern side, what I thought of as the hospital side.

He had a green tunic on, short sleeves showing off an array of amateur tattoos and a couple of stretchy bandages around each wrist.

'This is Lars,' Hinny said. 'Lars, Ali. "Ha" what?'

I nodded at him. The tunic looked like a uniform but Lars had the scrawny look of a user, and when he smiled I saw that most of his molars were missing.

'Ha – that's the face of someone who's just met Dr F,' he said, sitting down. 'What do you reckon, then?'

'Are you . . .?' I said.

'Charge nurse,' Lars said. I thought he'd missed me glancing at the bandages but he peeled them off and showed me his forearms. I tried to take it in my stride.

'Misspent youth,' Lars said.

Hinny snorted. 'Yeah. I reckon he got that to help him in his gynaecology exams.'

'Can't you get them removed?' I said. Female genitalia were bad enough but the other tattoo was a swastika dripping blood from its sharpened points.

'They help some of the right wee radges believe I know what I'm on about,' he said. 'But Dr Ferris makes me cover them. Cannae let the cheque books see them.'

'Cheque books?'

'Mums and dads,' Hinny told me. 'You're an awful man. But it's true enough. Some of them never even visit.'

'They pay us to care so why would they care too?' Lars said.

'Right.' Hinny drained her cup and put it into the sink. 'Better get the lunches on. Anything special, Larry Lamb?'

'Same as yesterday,' Lars said. 'I reckon Drew could move on, but the doc wants her on replacements till after the next group so that's three.'

I didn't know whether I should pretend to understand, ask what they meant or keep out of it, since I wasn't nursing staff. But Lars saw me trying to look invisible and, after Hinny had gone, he gave me another smile. He wasn't a bad-looking man, if he'd see a dentist.

'The doc's a great believer in hi-cal replacements,' he said. 'She'd keep the girls on shakes till discharge if she had her own way. I reckon they need to get back to solids and eat in the dining room before we say goodbye.'

I didn't know if I should have an opinion so I said nothing.

'But your head must be spinning,' he said. 'Why didn't you come in for the change? If you sit through a change once or twice you'll be all over it. You've got your slots, eh? I saw them on the master. It's a well-oiled machine. Say what you like about Dr F, he can weave a chart.' I felt as if I was going to cry. This was insane. I didn't have a clue what anyone was talking about, and when someone worked that out, I'd be arrested. 'Hey?' said Lars, solemn suddenly. 'Are you okay?' I plastered a smile on and nodded. 'Shite you are,' he said. 'What's up?'

'Nothing, I'm fine.' He waited. 'Dr Ferris was just a bit intrusive.'

'Dr F,' he said. 'Else we'd never know who you were on about. You'd think they'd go first names but, oh, no.'

'Right,' I said. 'Dr Ferris and Dr F. Got it.'

'And what is it that's wrong again?' he said. His eyes were the sort of no colour at all, like most people's eyes, but they had something.

I looked away. 'Wow,' I said. 'I'd forgotten what it was like, hanging around psychiatric professionals.' My voice was shaking but I managed to make it sound careless enough to pass.

'You'll have to try a bit harder than that.' I pretended I didn't know what he meant but when he carried on, 'Look over there, a squirrel,' I gave up and laughed.

'Rough time at home, to be honest,' I said. 'We live right where that body was found.'

'The remains?'

'I suppose that's more accurate,' I said. 'Or maybe it's just bones.'

'It's not,' said Lars. 'I've got a pal on the force. On the team. What else?'

I shrugged but those no-colour eyes kept staring at me. 'Ocht, I think I've been that wound up looking for work I can't unwind even now I've got some,' I said. 'And there's money worries, and a teenage kid . . . You name it.'

'That's four good reasons right enough,' Lars said. 'What's *wrong*, though? I'm not making chit-chat, Ali. I'm really asking.'

I wondered if my face was changing colour. For sure, I could feel a prickle of sweat on the back of my neck and my top lip. He was going to keep picking and picking until I gave in.

'This job,' I said at last. 'My experience is ten years ago in Australia and I've forgotten everything. What slots? What's a change?'

Finally he seemed to believe me. He sat back. 'Just ask,' he said. 'Time slots are your appointments. And shift-change meetings. The daily catch-up. Nothing mysterious and nobody thinks you'll know before you're told.'

'And what's a PVG?' I said. 'Dr Ferris talked about it.'

Lars frowned at me. 'You've done that, though. The doc said it was in and it'd be back any day.'

'Right.' It must have been one of the forms I'd filled. There had been a sheaf of them. 'And the chart?'

His frown cleared. 'Just the timetable. Who's at Group,

who's at indies – individual therapy sessions. Who's at relaxation, activity, off-site, structured tasks, and now you – personal care and art. The doc's a genius at getting twenty people in the right place at the right time.'

'Twenty-three, isn't it?' I said. 'Twenty-three beds?'

'We hold two for emergency admissions. Pretty much keeps the rest of the ship afloat, what we can charge the local authority to let them use an acute bed when they're overloaded.' He put a hand on his heart, while snapping the bandage back into place on top of the swastika. 'God bless the NHS,' he said.

'So that's twenty-two,' I said.

He snapped the other bandage back and smiled, his sharp eyes softening. 'And Miss Boswell, of course.' I frowned and shrugged. 'Sylvie.'

———————

Alone in the staff toilet, I wiped a paper towel over my face and it came away dark with sweat. I had thought Dr Ferris was the worst of it, smirking and hinting but Dr F's interrogation had caught me completely by surprise. And then there was Lars, his X-ray eyes and his soft voice asking me over and over what was wrong. I held the paper towel under the cold tap, squeezed it out, then pressed it against my neck, cheeks, forehead.

I wanted to run, but I had spent three hundred pounds now, on this and that, and Marco had told me what he was getting at the builder's yard. Minimum wage for fifteen hours a week, time and a half if he did Sundays.

I lugged my mobile table into the little room that was going to be mine. Dr Ferris had called it the flower room. I could live with that. It had a sink and nearly enough plugs; I could bring in a rug and a humidifier, and put in some pink bulbs. There were bars on the window but I'd cover them with something. I was scared that my kit would have dried up but I'd forgotten how careful I was when I packed it up that last day at Face Value. I'd screwed the lids on so tight I could hardly shift them now and I'd pressed Blu Tack over all the nozzles. Some of the cosmetics looked tired, but I blotted them off with a tissue, and in the end it was only a few of the cream blushers I had to admit were past using.

As I spread the bed with a towel and a knee roll, then laid a blanket over the foot end, I even started to feel a bit of excitement burbling inside me. This was something I knew how to do, and the patients of Howell Hall needed it more than most of the lunching ladies that used to fill my books. I took a look round before I left and could almost kid myself that things were going to be okay.

And then there was the art. The room I'd been told I could use wasn't so far from the flower room but it wasn't all mine. It had 'group' in it in the morning, Dr Ferris had told me. 'Group'. They all said it. Like 'church' or 'school', like everyone should know what it meant. But it was free in the afternoons, if I could set myself up over lunchtime. I pushed the door open and slipped inside.

My pulse lifted just a little, like a kite with a sudden breeze getting under it. It was unmistakable. A ring of seats marooned in the middle of an ocean of beige carpet, the chairs low and square, no arms, upholstered in the kind of two-tone weave that doesn't show stains. Around the walls there were 'break-out spaces'. The phrase came back from nowhere and jolted me. In one corner beanbags; in another two upright chairs facing each other inches apart; in a third there was a pile of vinyl mats, like gymnasts land on, at least a dozen, maybe with a pea underneath. A screen was pulled over the last corner. I didn't want to think about what was behind it. I had never heard of any kind of 'group' where someone went away and hid behind a screen.

There were no cupboards, I noticed. I would have to ask Dr Ferris where I was supposed to keep the art supplies between classes. If she said my treatment room had to be for storage too I'd need a trolley to ferry things back and forth. Would my thousand pounds have to cover it, or could I ask for one? Surely there would be trolleys. This was a hospital, after all. Tiny, stuck out in the middle of an army training range and staffed by people as weird as the patients, but a hospital.

The police were still at the abbey. They had set up a kind of a canopy, dark green like from a garden centre, and a few of them were trying to huddle underneath it for shelter, shoulders rounded and heads ducked. But the rain was coming in sheets from the side, cold and merciless, and they might as well have been out in the open along with the press that had gathered. A couple of them, TV types, had golf umbrellas up over their hairdos but the spokes were bent like drawn bows and the nylon segments bowed, like boat sails and, as I watched, one of the crew sheltering a cameraman lifted the brolly too high, trying to peek out from under it, and suddenly it was gone. Inside out, tugged from his hand, and careering away across the ground, dodging the police tent and cartwheeling over to where the hard-hatted cops and docs were busy at the base of the walls.

A policeman followed it, clapping on his own hard-hat with one hand and leaning back as the wind carried him faster than he'd bargained for, every step making a splash. The water was rising again.

I felt like laughing. The umbrella had blossomed, I couldn't help thinking, gone from a bud to a bloom and got free. Then the policeman caught up with it and stamped down, cracking the handle. He shouted something back to the press, waving his arms, his face screwed up in anger, or maybe just from the rain.

I gave up waiting for a break and got out of the car to scurry up the path. Stupid. It never even occurred to me that any of the press would give me a second glance, but I'd only just closed the front door when the first of them hammered on it.

'Mrs McGovern?' came a woman's voice. And still I didn't twig. I thought it must be someone who knew me. I opened the door and peered out. There were four, all drenched, one with a kind of plastic tent over a camera and three with mikes covered with sandwich bags and recorders under their Gore-Tex jackets.

'Have you got a quote, love?'

'Did you see the body?'

'Do you know who it is?'

'How's your son?'

That came from the only woman in the bunch. Tall and trim, she was wearing the wreck of a perfect blow-dry and her face was streaked black and pink as mascara and blusher coursed down. But what melted me was the state of her feet. Good patent shoes ruined and mud splattered up her ankles.

'Jane Brown,' she said. '*Record.*'

'Who do you think it is?'

'How did you feel when you heard?'

'Did you see it being buried?'

'Is he in or has he managed to stay at school?' Jane Brown shouted, over the voices of the other three.

And the rest were on their way over the road too, splashing and skidding in the muddy ruts of the track.

'How do you know my name?' I said to her, over their heads. 'How do you know my son?'

I ignored the other three, who were jeering and whining as she pushed her way to the front. 'Can I come in?' she said.

'Why are you asking about An— about my son?'

'Angelo?' she said. 'You can let me in or I can tell you out here.' She slid her eyes to the side. The other reporters, even more of them now, had quietened to listen.

I stood back and she nipped inside, like a little terrier down a rabbit hole, before I could change my mind.

'Bloody Nora!' she said. She took off her coat, kicked her shoes onto the plastic mat, and before I knew what was happening she had stripped off her tights. 'Don't suppose I could hang these over a radiator?'

'Mantelpiece in front of the gas fire,' I said, determined not to apologize for the lack of proper heating. 'How did you know my son's name?'

'I'm a good reporter,' she said. Then she shivered hard. She wasn't acting: I saw the goose pimples pop up on her arms where she'd pushed her sleeves back.

'I'll put the kettle on,' I said.

'Any chance of a Bovril or something?'

'So what's all this about Angelo?' I said, when I came back through from the kitchen.

She had been trying to get the gas fire lit, making herself right at home, but at my words she straightened and turned.

'Don't you know?' she said. 'You sit down. I'll do the drinks. Seriously, you don't know?'

'Tell me right now or I'll put you out, bare feet and all,' I told her, trying to make it sound like a joke.

'He reported the body,' she said. 'You're seriously telling me you didn't know?'

I dropped down onto the couch and stared at her. 'Angelo?'

'Reported the body. The polis have been at the school. Your husband took him to the station. Alison, are you trying to say your husband didn't tell you? Didn't tell the boy's own mother?'

I whipped out my phone and stared at it. Nothing. Not a word. But as she – what was her name? – as she edged towards me I had the sense, dredged up from somewhere, to hide the screen. I pressed it against my chest.

'Fifteen messages,' I said. 'First day at a new job! I had it on silent and never switched it back again. Oh, my God! Look, I need to call them. Do yourself a Cup-a-Soup. Top shelf by the window.' I stood shakily and made my way upstairs, shutting my door and going right to the back of the room before I hit Marco's number.

He answered after half a ring. 'Als!' he said. 'Hiya, babe.'

'Is it true?' I said. 'Did Angelo go to the police station?'

'Calm down, pal,' he said. I could hear him walking and the sound changed as he went from one room to another. 'There's no need to ups—'

'Marco, for once in your life, will you listen to me? Tell me what is happening or, so help me, I'll—'

'See, this is exactly—'

'Marco, if my son is at the police station and I didn't know—'

'He's not. Ali, will you calm the hell down?' Marco started

talking as if each word was a sentence all on its own. As if I was a drunk or a moron. 'He is at school. I am in at my work filling in forms. Everything is all right.'

Finally, I took a breath. 'There's reporters here.'

'At the hospital? How did they get past—'

'At the house, Marco. Someone from the *Record* said Angel was the one who found the body. Where did they get that from, if nothing's wrong?'

He was silent for so long I thought the call had dropped. Bloody Galloway and its dark skies. Great for seeing the Milky Way, useless for mobile connection.

'Marco?'

'It was all a big misunderstanding,' he said.

I had been quiet, thinking of the woman downstairs, but at that I forgot to whisper. 'What? You just told me nothing happened.'

'The report about the remains came from Angel's phone. Don't interrupt me. Just listen. The police contacted me and we went to the school together and spoke to him. Then we all went to the police station so he could identify his phone.'

'I can't—' I said. Then I threw the phone hard against the sloping wall of the bedroom. The back sprang off and the battery fell out, thudding to the floor. The phone bounced back and landed on the bed.

'Ali?' shouted the *Record* woman up the stairs. 'You okay?'

It took that long for Marco's words to sink in. The news of Angel, my son, my little boy, in a police station and me not knowing had drowned them out. But now the truth hit me. I scrabbled the three pieces back together – phone, battery, back cover – and when I powered it up it was already ringing.

'Fine!' I called down. 'Won't be a minute!' I jabbed the green

70

button and whispered, 'Why was his phone at the police station?'

'Ta-dah!' said Marco. 'Exactly. It was stolen three days ago. He's been working up to telling us.' I tried to speak but didn't have the breath for it. 'I know what you're thinking,' Marco said. 'Why didn't he tell us when he found out about our new jobs? Well, get this: because the wee toerag reckoned he'd get an upgrade out of us without us finding out he'd lost the old one. Talk about cheek, eh?'

'And where is he now?' I said.

'I told you,' said Marco. 'He's back at school. He's fine, Als. Don't worry.'

This time I hung up gently.

'Everything okay?' the woman said, when I got downstairs again. She hadn't just found the Cup-a-Soups and boiled a kettle, she'd stuffed her shoes with newspaper and set them in front of the gas fire. And she must travel with a spare pair of tights in her bag. She'd pulled them on. I could see the perfect little red cups of her pedicured toes through them. And she had wiped her face too.

'Fine. Thank God.' All I wanted was to get her out of my house. 'Just a misunderstanding. It was nothing to do with him, after all. He's back at school and he wants smoked-sausage baguettes for his tea.'

'You've spoken to him, then?' she said. 'I thought you were talking to your husband, what with the shouting.' Her voice didn't change and her face didn't change, but all of a sudden she made me think of Dr Ferris.

'He gave the message to his dad,' I said, hoping I wasn't blushing. I'm a terrible liar. 'You can't phone kids in school hours. Don't you have any?'

71

'I don't have any ties with the local education authority,' she said. 'I'm not familiar with their rules.' Trying to make me think she had six rosy-cheeked geniuses in a private school, but not actually saying it.

'Anyway, so keep the mug, if you like,' I said, 'but I'll have to ask you to go, I'm afraid. I wasn't thinking straight when I asked you in. I'm sure you understand.'

She pretended she didn't. 'You – you're putting me back out in the rain?'

'There's no story in here,' I told her.

'We'll see.' She tipped the soup into the sink and shuddered. Too good for instant, suddenly.

She smiled as she left, far too professional to trash a good contact she might be needing later. She didn't fool me.

Chapter 6

Marco was back. He came in quietly and stood just inside the front door, listening.

'I'm through here,' I shouted at last. I was in Angelo's bedroom, using his laptop to try to find out something, anything, about what had happened. BBC Scotland had a tiny piece, two paragraphs and a photograph of the police under their green shelter. 'Human remains were discovered at Dundrennan Abbey in south-west Scotland last night, after an anonymous report to local police. A high-school student was briefly questioned earlier today in connection with the incident but later released. The abbey, which dates from . . .' and then the usual potted history from Wikipedia. I read and reread the words – 'A high-school student was briefly questioned' – and stared at the picture, the view that greeted me every time I left the house.

Then I went back to the search page and refreshed it, finding a bit more on ITV Border News, which said nearby residents were shaken by the discovery and that the abbey grounds were a well-known meeting place for what they called 'local youths'. One 'local youth' had already been questioned by the police in connection and further enquiries were ongoing. I supposed I was the shaken resident, running away like that. But they were scraping together bits of nothing and making it sound suspicious. Really, it was perfectly innocent.

His phone was stolen.

He didn't tell us.

He'd just come from the abbey.

The police found a body.

I couldn't get his voice out of my head. 'I'd just about given up, as it goes.'

'Hey,' said Marco, appearing round the bedroom doorway. 'What are you doing? Don't be looking at that.'

I closed the laptop lid and spun round on Angelo's desk chair to face him. 'You didn't call me,' I said.

'I explained that,' Marco said. 'Are you still annoyed?' He put his head on one side and crinkled his eyes at me, then started forward, coming to kiss me, I was sure. That was our way. A kiss hello and a kiss goodbye. A kiss goodnight and one in the morning. It was my parents' way, my dad stooping to kiss my mum – thank you for a lovely dinner; welcome back from the supermarket – and it had got to be our way too.

I held up a hand, with my arm straight. 'No,' I said, trying to make sure my voice stayed level. 'No and no. You didn't explain. You said things and I left it. But you haven't explained, Marco, because there's no possible explanation in the world. My son was at the police station being questioned and you didn't tell me.'

'I didn't want to upset you,' he said. He had stopped advancing but the smile was still on his face.

'Well, that was a big fat failure, then, wasn't it? Because I'm very upset.'

'Yeah, but—' Marco stopped himself, literally biting down on his tongue. I could see it glistening between his teeth. 'Right then. The boy's had a shit day so I'm going to fire up the frying pan and give him a treat. Come through and keep me company.'

It took me a few breaths to get myself off the chair and through to the kitchen. By the time I got there, he was whistling. I stared at his back. He had put on his apron and rolled up his sleeves and, as he rummaged in the deep cupboard for the plug-in fryer, he was *whistling*.

'How long was he there for?' I said. 'Did they put him in an interview room? Did you leave him alone at any time? What did they ask him? Did he sign a statement? And "Yeah, but" what, by the way?'

Marco poured oil into the fryer, a whole new bottle of pale golden rapeseed oil, glugging out in rhythmic convulsions, making me think of someone vomiting. I looked away.

'Twenty minutes. Yes, he was in an interview room and they gave him a bottle of Fanta. No, I didn't leave him. They asked him where he lost his phone and got him to ID it. And, yes, he signed something and I counter-signed it. And "Yeah, but" nothing.' He had got a packet of bacon out of the fridge and a bag of sausages out of the freezer, beans from the tins cupboard. He looked at his watch and spun the dial of the fryer.

'What did it say?' I said. 'The thing you signed.'

'I didn't read it, Als. I think the cops might have taken it as a bit of an insult if I'd read it, don't you?'

'I don't care,' I said. 'And why are you putting the fryer on now? It's . . .' I looked at my watch and blinked. It was just leaving twenty to four. I turned and checked the clock on the

75

cooker, which confirmed: 3:43. What the hell? I'd left Howell Hall before they served lunch, come back here, let the journo in, kicked her out, looked at the news sites and now, somehow, it was nearly tea-time.

'I'm making doughnuts for when he gets in,' Marco said. 'Okay?'

I said nothing. The Cup-a-Soup the woman had made for me was still sitting on the counter near the sink. I reached out and touched it. There wasn't a trace of warmth left.

'I'll zap that for you, if you want,' Marco said, 'but there's doughnuts in twenty.'

'I've lost some time,' I said. I was still angry, angrier with him than I had ever been, but there he was and he'd been there for a long time, and when you're frightened you reach out to the nearest person. I saw it once on a plane when it hit the worst patch of sudden turbulence anyone had ever seen, the plane walloping up and down, like a speedboat. All up and down the aisles, complete strangers were clutching each other, digging their fingers into each other's arms and staring into each other's eyes. Marco and I locked arms over Angel's head, pressing him between our bodies, so his voice was muffled when he squealed, 'Wheeeee! Again, Mummy! Again!' Then, with a final lurch, it was over and everyone was laughing shakily, and apologizing.

Marco was holding me again now. 'I'm sorry,' he said. 'I got it wrong. But . . .'

I leaned into him, my full weight falling on him. He wrapped his arms tight around me, mine pressed inside his. 'But what?'

'Nothing. And don't worry about the time. It doesn't mean anything. You've had a rough couple of days and you had a shock. Don't worry. At least you were here at home, eh?'

76

His voice always lulled me. He's got this way of talking to me, like he talked to Angelo when he was a baby and like he talked to his grandma when she was old and used to get scared, not knowing where she was and who was in the room. Then his words hit.

'But *what*?' I said, struggling out of his grip. 'Yeah, but *what*?' I braced my arms and pushed against him. 'Is that why you didn't tell me when it was happening? Because you didn't want me freaking out at Howell Hall?'

'No!' Marco said. 'Are you kidding? They'd be the last people to act weird about anyone getting upset. They'd have helped you.'

'Oh, come off it!' I said. 'They help patients but they need the staff to be . . . not getting calls saying their kid's been taken out of school by the police.'

'I think you're wrong about them,' Marco said. He wasn't looking at me. He was staring into the fryer as the oil started to shimmer.

'I'm going for a bath,' I said. 'I'm cold. And don't bother frying bloody doughnuts. I'm taking Angel into Dumfries when he gets off the school bus. He needs a new phone.'

'Fair enough,' Marco said. 'Oh, hey, I printed you out some stuff that looked good. You know how you were worried about the art therapy side of it? It's by your side of the bed. Read it in the bath and tell me what you think.'

———

But I didn't. I locked the door and ran the water blistering hot into the iron bath. It was rough with soap scum from the three of us having showers every morning and there was a line of

77

black at the bottom of the tiles, but once the air filled with steam I could lie there and stare straight up and let it all melt away. I could tell myself nothing had happened. I was just engrossed in looking at news. Everyone said the internet ate your life if you sat in front of it, clicking. And, anyway, the brain is the strongest organ in the body. I refused to be ill again just like I refused to stay ill last time. I got better and I had stayed better for ten years. I didn't even wobble when we lost everything. No way I was going back down now, when I finally had a job and when Angel needed me.

I put my head back and let myself sink deeper into the water, letting it creep up into my ears and steal around my face, like a wimple. My breath was loud in my head and the heat made my blood pulse. I took a deep gulp of air and pulled myself right under so that everything was gone. Ruins and bones, job, car, house, husband and son, phones and print-outs and treatment menus, art supplies and checkpoints, clothes and rooms, words and deeds and life. It was all gone and I floated in warmth again, like we all do in our perfect beginnings. 'Hello,' I said, inside my head. 'Are you still here? I'm back.'

Then I stood up, scrubbed myself down with a mitt and a dollop of vanilla body wash, rinsed under the shower with the plug out and stepped out to dry myself. I was absolutely fine.

I wrapped myself in a bath sheet and scampered upstairs. Angelo was due any minute and he hated to see me in anything less than a neck-to-ankle dressing-gown, these days. I had an ear cocked for him as I dressed but when I started back down again Marco was standing in the living room, looking at the front door.

'The bus is late,' I said.

'The bus has been,' said Marco. 'He wasn't on it.'

I flew down the rest of the stairs and straight out, blew through the gate and stood looking both ways into the sinking light. The rain had stopped but the day was beyond hope, chilled and damp and murky. The police and reporters had gone. There wasn't a soul to be seen in either direction and not a sound to be heard, except the dripping of the trees and the distant downshift of the school bus's diesel engine as it rounded some corner out of sight.

I heard the door shut behind me and Marco was advancing with a coat for me and his own hooked on his head by the hood. 'Come on,' he said. 'We'll go looking.'

'One of us should stay here,' I said. 'In case he comes back.'

'Serve him right to come back to an empty house,' Marco said. 'I'm not leaving you on your own to work yourself up. And no way am I letting you drive.'

'Trouble?' said a voice.

The neighbour. Of course.

I rounded on him. 'You should know. You made it.'

He stood his ground, turning his head to one side to peer at me, like a bird watching grubs. 'Me?' He did look harmless, standing there in his shirt collar and zip-up cardigan, slippers on his feet and his Sta-Prest trousers bagged at the knees.

'Why did you tell the news that kids meet over there?' I demanded.

Marco had laid a hand on my arm and was pulling me gently away. 'Let's get going, Als. Sooner the better, eh?'

'Me?' said the neighbour again. 'I never said a word.'

'What did you tell the cops?' I said, shaking off Marco's hand and taking a step forward.

'I'll tell them about *that*!' he said, pointing a wavering finger.

I thought he was showing me something behind my head and I turned.

That was when I saw my own arm, fist clenched, raised above my head.

'Ali!' Marco called. He was over by the car with the passenger door open.

'I'm sorry,' I said to the neighbour. 'I don't know what came over me. Our son is missing.'

'That's none of my doing,' the old man said. 'We brought up three of our own and never had any of this.'

'Ali!' Marco shouted again. 'Come on!'

———————

'He'll have missed the bus and set off walking. That's all it'll be,' Marco said. He turned the car and set off in the direction of the school, back the way I had come.

He couldn't have made it this far already, ten miles on a twisting road, but still I wound down the windows and scoured the darkness at the edge of the lane, already black in the dying light. We passed the checkpoint gate at the turn to Howell Hall, the soldier's head just visible over the messy windowsills. From there on the trees met above our heads, still dripping, swallowing the last of the daylight. Marco flicked the lights to full beam.

'What's he wearing?' I said.

'In case you don't recognize him in the crowd?'

'In case he's walking up the wrong side of the road.'

'You look out your side and I'll look out mine,' Marco said.

Why couldn't I remember what he was wearing? I had seen him that morning. Black, probably. Black hoodie, black trousers, black shoes. And a black jacket on top. He didn't have to wear reflectors catching the bus from home to the school door. I imagined him jumping into the verge as a lorry came up behind him. He wasn't a country boy. He didn't know to walk into the traffic so you could see what was coming. And he probably had his earbuds in too.

But there weren't lorries on this road. Cars and the odd small delivery van. I trained my eyes into the trees at my side of the car, starting to feel my head spin as they whipped past, and past, and past.

'Slow down,' I said.

'Don't you want to find him as soon as we can?'

I said no more, just kept watching.

We traced the bus route all the way into town, past the trim bungalows and into the quiet streets of stone terraces, right to the school gates, and parked there.

'I'll go in,' I said, unbuckling my seatbelt.

'Ali, he's already been hauled out of school by the cops today,' Marco said. 'He doesn't need another red face. He's probably just gone to a pal's house. He's probably phoned us when he got there and we missed the call because we're sitting here.'

'He'd call one of the mobiles,' I said. A couple of teachers' cars came out of the school gateway. If I didn't go in soon they'd all be gone.

'Get away!' said Marco. 'If he's gone somewhere without asking or telling he'll be chuffed as mince we didn't pick up. Come on, eh?'

I managed to give half a smile. He was right. It was a teenage art-form, getting voicemail instead of your actual parent.

'Let's go back home, eh?'

I looked at every shadow on the way, once asking Marco to reverse because I thought I saw someone at the bus shelter by the Mutehill turn. But it was just a patch of denser shade and the poster of bus times at head height looking like someone's pale face.

'Bet he's back,' Marco said and, when we rounded the last corner and saw the row of lights shining out from the cottages, I believed him. But the small window to the left of our front door, Angelo's room, was in darkness. And he hadn't turned off a light since he could first reach the switches. I felt my breath quicken.

'Okay, okay,' Marco said. 'If he's not there—'

'He's not there!'

'If he's not there, I'll start phoning round.' I opened my mouth to protest. 'I've got most of the numbers,' he said. 'And the ones I haven't I'll get.'

But how did we know who Angelo was hanging out with? For the last six months he'd been getting off the bus on his own and hadn't spoken ten words together. When we'd lived in our real house, he'd arrive with five or six extra and I'd have to make sure their mums knew where they were. Except their mums always knew where they were. They were at ours, with the pool table and the fridge in the playroom.

But these days he just slunk off the bus and . . .

'Oh, my God!' I said, leaping out of the car before it had quite stopped moving. 'How stupid can we be?'

I set off down the track to the abbey, fumbling my phone until the torch app set a tiny yellow cone glowing ahead of me. There was police tape strung up blocking off all the passages through the ruins and the ground around it was churned into muddy ridges and deep pools, as if it had been ploughed, with sprays of liquid mud splatting out for yards across the grass where the cars had struggled to get moving. The flood had been bad enough, but this? The greenkeeper would break his heart. Were there still greenkeepers? Or was it just a crew from the council maintenance team who got stuck with it in the rotation and moaned about coming all the way out here with nowhere to buy a coffee?

'Angel?' I shouted. I lifted the police tape and walked into the belly of the abbey, feeling the cold and darkness thicken. I could have sworn I'd heard him. The air was dead in there, but I could have sworn I'd heard a soft 'Mum?'

'Angel, I'm not angry,' I said. 'I don't care what you're doing, what you're smoking or drinking. Dad and me just freaked out a bit. Because you didn't drop off your bag in the house first. And because of earlier, I suppose. I just want to know you're okay.' I rounded the corner of a buttress into the ruins of a dining room or a chapel or something. The walls were pocked with little niches that could have been shrines, or maybe just salt cupboards and bread ovens.

'Mum?' I heard it again. It was coming from behind the back wall and it sounded low down.

'Angel, have you fallen?' I said, springing forward. I clambered out through what was once a window before the wall below had collapsed and turned it into an awkward kind of door. I shone my light about and finally I saw something.

The mud was churned up even worse there, with footprints and whole square sections cut out, like peat from a bog, and in the middle of it all was a piece of board as big as a door laid flat on the ground.

'Angel?' I said, dropping to my knees and trying to get my fingers under the edge of it. 'What are you doing? Who did this? Are you hurt?'

But now at last I heard it clearly. It wasn't him and it wasn't 'Mum' I was hearing.

'Mmmm,' it cried, on a higher note, now I was near. 'Mmmhmmm.'

―――――――

'Now, don't upset your—' Marco began as I threw myself in at the front door. 'Jesus, Ali. What happened?'

'I fell,' I said. 'It's muddy. Did you find him?'

'Don't panic,' said Marco. 'I'm homing in on him. He's not at Paddy's, Gordo's or Mark's, but they've given me about half a million new numbers to try. We'll get there. Why don't you fire up his laptop and see if he's on one of the . . . God knows. Is it still Snapchat?'

'Yikyak,' I said. 'But I'm phoning the school before everyone leaves.'

'Ali, don't. You'll piss him off and it'll only make it harder next time.'

'I'm phoning the school and then I'm going back out,' I said. 'You can stay here and wait for him, if you like, but I need to be doing something or I'll go mad. And don't tell me you won't let me. I'm not asking your permission.'

I saw him struggle and decide not to argue. His breath came out in a long hiss. 'If you drop me off at Jimbo's I'll borrow his car and we can both look,' he said. That made me turn back. It had taken months to get used to having only one car. One of us was forever just taking off and leaving the other stranded in the house. But eventually we'd worked out a system, like me dropping him off in Dalbeattie before my interview.

'How did you get in to T&C to do your paperwork today?'

I said. 'And how did you get to the school when the cops called you?'

'They picked me up,' said Marco. 'Swung round on the way, then took me back again.'

'But how . . .' I began, then glanced at my watch. I had never believed the way teachers talked about their long hours. They were always coming in for four o'clock appointments at Face Value. I needed to get on it if I wanted to catch them.

The assistant head was cold, firm and procedural. He said Angelo had left the school grounds and their liability ended there. The private company that ran the coaches didn't take a register and we had signed a waiver at the start of the year.

'Mr Munro?' I said. 'You've got kids in the primary, haven't you?'

'This isn't about me, Mrs McGovern.'

'My son has had a rough couple of days,' I said. 'You know where we live, don't you? You must have seen the news. And you know what happened today?'

'I'm not likely to forget the police showing up.'

'Well, could you act like a human being, then? I'm not going to sue you. I just want to find him.'

There was a long silence at the other end of the phone, then he cleared his throat. 'If you would like to come in for a conference at any time, Mrs McGovern,' he said, 'the guidance staff have a lot of useful advice for communication techniques that might avoid this sort of—'

I put the phone down and listened to Marco in the other room. He was saying goodbye to someone and telling them not to worry.

He didn't try to stop me leaving. He hadn't done that for years and only twice even back when I was ill.

It was black as death out there now and cold as an old grave. It wasn't even raining. Raindrops would have cheered it up a bit, sparkling in the headlights and pattering on the roof of the car, but this was like driving through the belly of a beast, the close chill pressing in around me and the sound damped down. I kept the window open and shouted his name out into the night: 'Angelo? *An*gelo!' I drove the main road, and the loops and the dead-end lanes, bumping through farmyards and splashing along in the ruts of tractor tyres. Tors and Balmae, the signs said. Netherlaw and Fagra. Drumgans and Screel and Knockmult, as if I had left the real world behind and fallen into a place of giants and trolls where Angel had been dragged and chained up somewhere.

Then suddenly the lights of the town. I crept along every street in Kirkcudbright, shining my headlamps into the parks where kids sat scuffing on the swings and hiding their cigarettes. All of them lanky and hooded and scowling, but none of them Angelo. I took the main road back to Dalbeattie, made it in twenty, then crept around every side-street there too, even parked in front of his friends' houses. even sounded my horn. If he was inside, he'd look out, wouldn't he?

But all that happened was one of the mums coming to the doorstep with her arms folded tight against the cold. She peered in, then told me to wind down my window. 'I told Marco, Ali. He's not been here. And Gordon's not been out either.'

So I drove away. This time I'd go to the police, I told myself. And if they sent me home to wait until twenty-four hours had passed, I'd take their names and I'd have their badges.

I slowed down at the house as I passed it, but Angelo's bedroom was still in darkness and Marco hadn't called me so I didn't stop. And when I'd got back up to speed I flew along.

I wasn't checking the hedgerows and shouting this time. I took the corners as fast I could on the wet road and flashed past farm entries and the checkpoint gate, the kiosk closed and dark now. I was focused ahead, planning what I'd tell the cops. It was a miracle I noticed it, really.

It took a moment for my brain to make sense of what my eyes had seen. I hit the brakes and reversed until I could back into a field entrance and turn round. Then I crawled back, telling myself it couldn't be, wouldn't be, that it was a trick of the light. But when I nosed my headlights in towards the base of the fence just beyond the checkpoint, there it really was: Angelo's backpack, red and black but with the silver decals that had flashed as I passed them.

It couldn't have been there earlier. Even if I'd been looking the other way when I went past on my own, Marco was watching this side when we came out together. He'd have seen it. Unless it was better hidden in the dusk when the decals didn't reflect so brightly. Anyway. I got out of the car and went over, dreading what I might see. But it was just the backpack, dumped at the bottom of the fence. I looked up and thought I could trace, in the stretched-out sections of chain link, where he had pushed in to make toeholds as he climbed and at the top a scrap of black nylon caught on one of the barbs.

Why would my son have climbed into an army base? Or was he climbing into a hospital? Did he think I was in there? Or was he fleeing someone out here?

I made it up about four feet before I admitted it was beyond me. Then, taking a minute to think, I realized there must be another way. You couldn't have people living behind a gate with no way to open it if the fire brigade or an ambulance needed in. I remembered Lars saying the two acute beds for emergency admissions were a money-spinner. So I went back to the car for my phone.

Dr Ferris herself answered, which surprised me.

'I think my son is in the grounds,' I said. 'I think he climbed over the fence. Can you . . . Is there any way to let me in?'

'The gate should be open, Alison,' said Dr Ferris, in that same cool voice, as if nothing ever surprised her. 'Unless there are night manoeuvres the gates open at dusk when the training centre closes. We're not *captives* here . . .' I didn't hear the rest because I was running to the car and skidding as I turned it into the driveway.

She was right. The gate was closed but not even latched, never mind locked, and it swung wide as I nosed my bumper against it. I left it hanging and drove on, yearning forward in my seat, so much energy I felt as if I was pulling the car along behind me.

And after the second turn, my lights found a shape in the middle of the drive, and I surged forward and there he was. Shaking, white-faced and soaked to his skin, but standing there and looking back at me. I turned the heat up as high as it would go and flipped all the vents to open and then I got out, slowly, as if a wild animal was injured and needed me but might still run away. I put my arms around him and let him sag against me.

Chapter 7

'Where have you been?'

'Nowhere.'

'What are you doing *here*?'

'Nothing.'

We were back in the car. I was sweating from the hot air pouring out of the vents, but Angelo couldn't stop shuddering, deep spasms that made his voice quake and his legs jump as if someone was hitting him, testing his reflexes. He had put his head back and his eyes were closed but tears leaked out from under his lashes, Marco's lashes, long and sweeping.

'What's wrong, Angel-boy?' I said. I didn't think even a fifteen-year-old, with his mum asking, would say, 'Nothing,' when he'd been found soaked and sobbing miles from home, but the answer he did give was worse.

'I can't tell you.'

My stomach lurched up into my chest and stuck there as if it was barbed. 'You can tell me anything,' I said. 'It doesn't matter what you've done. I will always love you and I will fight to my last breath for you.'

He just shook his head. 'See? You think I've *done* something. You've hanged me already.' He lifted one hand and wiped his nose with the inside of his cuff, like he hadn't done since he was tiny.

He was right and it shamed me. A girl in tears, you think she's been hurt. 'Or what you know,' I said. 'Do you know who took your phone and used it? Are you shielding someone? Just tell me. At least tell me how to help you.'

'There's nothing you can do,' he said, and his voice was juddering even harder. He put his arm up over his eyes to hide his face, or maybe to block the light. I reached up and clicked the courtesy light through all its settings until the car was in darkness. 'And it's nothing to do with my bloody phone.'

'Okay,' I said. 'But try me.'

'You could let me leave school,' he said. 'I'm sixteen in three months. Say I've got glandular fever so I never need to go back again. Or we could move house.'

'Tell me what happened.'

'I can't!' he said again. 'I don't want to upset you. I don't want to make you ill as well as everything.'

I sat back, stunned to a lead lump. That was something my granny used to say and she was right. Those were Marco's words coming at me. Not to get upset. Not to risk getting ill. Had he been loading Angel with worry over me?

'I'm stronger than I've ever been in my life,' I said, squashing down the memory of the voice calling from under the muddy boards, the missing slab of time today. 'I was spitting mad with your dad for keeping quiet. I'm your mum, Angel. You'll understand when you've got kids of your own.'

He had been gulping and gasping, getting on top of himself, but now he bent forward and let go, his curled back bucking as a sob came out of him, like a thunderclap. I rubbed him and shushed him and after a minute he swivelled over and rested his head in my lap. I stroked his wet hair back from his face and looked down at him: the sheen of snot on his lip like when he was a toddler playing out in the cold, but also the wisps of hair darkening in front of his ears and the little paintbrush swipes of it at the corners of his mouth. Those scabbed spots he'd been picking in the crease of his chin.

'I won't have kids,' he said.

I kept stroking but stopped shushing. Was that all it was? Was he coming out?

'Nobody's going to want *me*,' he said. 'After *this*.'

'After what?'

'Mum, I can't tell you!' But then, as if he hadn't said it or as if the words meant something else, he did. Honking and spluttering, he did.

'I met someone. We kind of hung out a few times. And then we met up. And then we went on an actual date. Last night.'

'Last night?' I said, thinking back over the evening: the sirens, the neighbours, the cops coming in. 'Wait, you mean online?'

'You said I could tell you anything,' he reminded me. 'No, I mean later. I went out once you and Dad were upstairs.'

'I didn't hear the—'

'I climbed out the window.'

'Where did you go?' Any other night I'd assume he was over at the abbey but there had still been police around.

'She picked me up and we went to the beach round at Ross Bay.'

'What do you mean she picked you up?' I said. 'Jesus Christ, Angel, how old is she?' I could see her, thirty-eight, a teacher at his school.

'Fuck sake, Mum. She's still at school but she's old enough to drive. She got her provisional on her birthday and passed in ten lessons. She's . . . That's what she's like.'

'Okay,' I said.

'And then we were supposed to hook up again today after school. Her school got out early for teachers' training or something. I don't know. She said she'd meet me at the cross.'

The Mercat Cross in Kirkcudbright was just outside the high-school gates. I didn't know kids still met there, like they did when it was me and six or seven other girls, all cheap scent and blue mascara, perched on the steps at its base.

'Did she stand you up?'

He nodded, and I could see his lip start to tremble again.

'Maybe it was a misunderstanding. Have you phoned her?'

'She wasn't there,' he said. 'But she'd sent all her friends. There was, like, fifty of them. Or you know, like, twelve. And they all sat there and watched me walking up and I didn't even *know* till I was right there. And one of them laughed like she couldn't keep it in any more, and then this one girl, she was scrolling through her texts and she just sort of looked up and said: "Are you Angelo? I've got a message for you. The date's off."'

'Oh, Angel. She's doesn't sound—'

'Don't,' he said, suddenly going rigid. He sat up and gave me one of those withering looks. I couldn't have imagined it on his face when he was a little boy and I fixed his dumper truck when the wheels came off or found his shoe he'd lost, and I was some kind of magical genius who made his boiled egg just how he wanted it every time. 'Don't say she's not worth it or I'm better

92

off without her. She's great, and I blew it because I'm such a loser and she had to get rid of me. And everyone saw me, all the girls from her class and half the folk from my class, and people out the bus window. They were all laughing and I tried to walk away and I fell. I tripped and *fell*, Mum.'

'Right,' I said. 'Well, you're chilled to the bone and you need a couple of days to tuck up and make sure you're not ill with a cold. So you're not going back to school in the morning and you're not going on Friday either. Let's see how it looks on Sunday night. About moving house or home-schooling or whatever.'

'Are you laughing at me?'

And of course I was because when he was my age he'd laugh too. Not about the girl – wee bitch that she was – but about the conviction that he was finished for ever. Luckily, before I could answer, I saw headlights beginning to glow ahead of us on the drive and then we were blinded as the car came round the bend and hit us with the full-beams. It slid to an easy stop and I heard a door open and bang shut, saw Dr Ferris emerge from behind the dazzle and come towards us. She was all togged up in a long, fitted coat, with another of her scarves tied in some complicated knot at its collar. She bent and peered in at the driver's side window, waiting until I wound it down.

'You found him, then?' she said. 'Jolly good.'

Angelo slung one look sideways at me, then stared straight ahead, dropping until his coat collar covered half his face.

'No harm done!' I said, too brightly to sound even halfway sane.

'Were you coming to see someone?' Dr Ferris said, looking past me at him. She was wearing slim-fitting driving gloves and they squeaked as she gripped the bottom of the open window. 'Do you need to talk to someone?'

Angelo shrank further down.

'*What*?' I said.

'You'd be surprised,' said Dr Ferris. 'Quite often people just come and knock on the door seeking sanctuary when things go terribly wrong. We can't often admit them, but we always listen.'

'He's not—' I said. 'He's fine. He's just— He was walking and he was getting sick of the cars going past so he turned off onto the quiet lane. Right? Angel?'

'Ah,' said Dr Ferris. 'No climbing after all, then? Good. Oh, Alison, I forgot to mention: your PVG came through. If you want to come in tomorrow.'

'Great,' I said. The woman had a kid of her own. Why did she think I'd care about work right this minute?

'Well, then,' she said, 'if you'd pull over to one side. It's been rather a long day.'

When the car, big as a liner passing us, had swept away he climbed out, and looked after it up the drive. 'What did you tell her, Mum?' he said. 'And don't bother lying cos she just busted you.'

'She's used to people's troubles,' I said. 'There's no need to worry.'

'Right,' he said, dripping sarcasm. I didn't even know why. 'So she knows all about *you*, does she?'

It was a shot in the dark. Angelo knew nothing about me. I ignored him. 'Let's get you home,' I said.

———

Marco came to the door as we were walking up the path.

'Hey!' He stumbled down the steps, tripping over his slippers, and wrapped Angelo in a bear hug. 'You're soaking!

You're freezing. Go and start a bath and I'll bring you a hot—'
But Angelo fought him off and kept walking. He slammed the
bathroom door behind him and shot the lock home. Then,
finally, Marco looked at me. 'You didn't call me,' he said.

'Well, that makes two of us, doesn't it?' I said.

'Oh, come on, Ali. I didn't *worry* you. You didn't stop me
worrying.'

I opened my mouth to argue then nodded. 'Fair point,'
I said.

'Was it just the cops and all that?' he said, slinging an arm
around my neck and turning me towards the house.

I thought before I answered. He was Daddy's boy, but he'd
confided in me this time. 'Yeah, just all a bit much,' I said. 'Oh,
hey,' I added. 'Did I get any post? Something dead official?'

'Likes of what?' he said.

'Everyone keeps talking about something called PVG I'm
supposed to fill in.'

'Protecting Vulnerable Groups,' said Marco. 'New name for
the police check. I did it for you when I was doing all the other
forms. You signed it.'

'Huh,' I said. And then: 'Thank you.'

———————

Does it make me a bad mother that I was glad to know he was
staying at home in his bed for a day? That for one day I'd know
where he was and what he was doing? Probably.

I took his temperature at seven o'clock when I went in with
a cup of tea and I told him it was high and I'd phone the school
and tell them he'd caught a chill from missing the bus and
walking home.

'They'll know,' he said. 'Mrs Thing in the office has got a kid in the fifth year. They'll all know by now.' He turned over to face the wall and pulled the covers so high all I could see was a spout of hair.

'Don't put soup spoons in the microwave,' I said.

'I'm not hungry.'

'Are you going out?' I asked Marco, when I was back in the kitchen. He was making sandwiches, grating the cheese instead of just cutting slices so that little shards of it were landing on the worktop and dropping onto the floor.

He grimaced. 'I said yesterday I'd go in and shadow for a few hours. Get up to speed, learn some product codes.'

'But now Angel's in such a bad way . . .'

'Why don't you take the day off?' Marco said. 'You need some R and R after all the upset.'

'I can't just take sick leave because my son's in his bed,' I said. Then I hoisted a smile onto my face. 'Oh, well. A couple of hours won't do any harm. He'll still be in his bed when you get back.'

'Except once I'm in town I'm stuck till the next bus,' Marco said.

I glanced at Angelo's bedroom door. What would he think if he heard us arguing about who was going to get stuck with him and who was going to get away?

'It's rough not being able to come and go, isn't it?' I said. 'I'll ask if anyone else goes past here. When we're in a routine, I could cadge lifts and you could take the car.'

———

I'd have to get here the same time as the rest of the day shift if I wanted a lift, I thought, when I got to Howell Hall and saw the long row of cars parked on the gravel beside Dr Ferris's BMW. But then I'd have to get here in time for the 'change' anyway. After a bit, I might even chip in. I could tell them things that came out in the art therapy or share what I thought about my clients' general health because you can tell a lot from hair and nails. As I trotted up the steps and let myself in the front door, I was imagining six months' time, when I wasn't scared and new any more, when I was a valued member of the care team and I had got the gist of the Ferris vibe so the pair of them didn't freak me. And in six months' time Angel would be over this blip and Marco would maybe be picking up extra hours and life would be . . . What was the thing my dad used to say? Set fair and making headway.

We'd all have forgotten that strange couple of days when they found the remains and we got jobs, and for some reason the good news turned us sour instead of sweet. In six months' time when we were ourselves again—

I was lost in the daydream when a pink flash came at me and she'd raked her nails down my cheek before I even got an arm up. 'Get me out of here!' she hissed.

'Jesus!' I said. My cheek was throbbing. 'Julia! What was that for?'

Julia looked at her nails, then tucked them against her palm, flicking away the little rolls of skin – my skin! She clamped her other hand on my arm. 'I've got to get out of here!' she said. She was naked under the pink bathrobe today and her heavy breasts swung as she shook me.

'Well, you're going the wrong way about it,' I said. 'Assaulting staff might get a transfer to a jail cell but it's not going to get you home.'

'There's no such place as home, you moron,' she said. 'I killed my father!'

'Is that right?' I said. 'Mine's alive and well and still living on the back of the turnip truck.' I had turned her round and, with an arm across her back, I walked her towards the bottom of the stairs.

'Ha!' she said, a bark of nicotined laughter. She needed to floss her teeth and drink more water. Her breath was rank. 'It's true, you know,' she said. 'I killed him and buried him and left him to rot.'

'Have you told the police?' I said.

'They didn't believe me.'

'Bastards,' I said. 'Typical.'

'I like you, Ali McGovern,' she said, then she broke away and bounded up the stairs.

'Lucky me,' I said, looking after her. I blinked. Dr Ferris was standing on the landing looking down at me, not even glancing as Julia swept by. She couldn't have done a better Mrs Danvers if she'd bought a costume.

'Now, what was the thinking behind your choice there, Alison?' she said, coming down the stairs. 'I'm not admonishing you, but could you talk me through it?'

'I didn't believe her but I didn't want to argue,' I said. 'Sorry.'

'Consistency,' she said, taking my arm and pulling me along in much the same way I had just been steering Julia. 'Consistency is key. The turnip truck or the innocent questions. Not both. You see?'

'I'm sorry,' I said again. 'Where are we going?'

'To get antiseptic ointment for your face,' she said. 'For choice, the turnip truck. We don't want to be reinforcing Julia's flights of fancy. We don't want to be bestowing any legitimacy on them.'

I wondered what had happened to not discussing patients' private business in the hallways, but before I could think of a way to ask we were in her office anyway.

'I thought the new thinking was that you did just that,' I said. 'You listen and don't try to tamper with the—'

'Psychosis,' said Dr Ferris. 'For schizophrenics, certainly. Great strides in that quarter. You're quite right, if rather puzzlingly well-informed. But Julia is not schizoid.'

'So what *is* wrong with her?' I said.

'Histrionic personality disorder,' said Dr Ferris. 'Julia has a new set of symptoms every time she gets her hands on Google, I'm afraid. Her mother handed her over to us when she started flirting with psychopathy.'

I had been standing in front of the desk while Dr Ferris sorted through paperwork, but at that I sank into one of the chairs. 'Psychopathy? She didn't *really* kill her father, did she?'

Dr Ferris looked up. 'Good grief, no. We don't have the security for that. No, of course not.'

'Only people do die and sometimes they do get buried and stay buried, don't they? You know what's happened at the abbey, I'll bet.'

'Now, we don't want to be talking about such matters in Julia's hearing,' said Dr Ferris. 'Heavens, if she got her teeth into it! No, the patricide is just one of her many confabulations. Her mental health took a sharp downturn when her father left, you see.'

'It would, the wee soul,' I said, as if my cheek wasn't still throbbing from her clawing at me.

'And her "psychopathy" was the holy trinity. Performed to a T.'

She was doing it again. Her back was to the window so I couldn't see her features but she had gone very still. She was waiting for me to admit I didn't know what the holy trinity of psychopathy was.

'Histrionic personality disorder,' I said. 'That's a new one on me. I don't think I've had dealings with that particular diagnosis before. I'll have to read up on it.'

'I can send you some references,' Dr Ferris said. 'But for now, don't let me keep you.'

I stood and went towards the door. She had forgotten about the ointment and I didn't want to whinge. 'Sorry I missed the shift change,' I said. 'What time is it usually?'

'Eight,' said Dr Ferris. 'Monday to Friday. Noon at the weekend. I'll give you a residents list with short notes and you can get up to speed before tomorrow.'

'Only I stayed back to get my son settled after his rough night.'

She nodded, but she was reading something on her desk.

'Sorry about that, by the way,' I added.

She shook her head absently. 'Teenagers!'

Maybe someone who had anorexics and cutters and junkies all round her every day didn't think a boy walking about alone in the wet and cold was worrisome. I wondered briefly about her daughter. Then I left the room, closing the door softly, and made my way to Sylvie.

Chapter 8

She didn't even look up when I wheeled my mobile table into her room. Not a flicker. She was sitting where she had been the last time, sunk into her chair, her hands lying in her lap and her legs splayed. One of her ankles had rolled over. I crouched and righted it, pulling her slipper straight. The oedema still bothered me and her skin was cold. Just like that I decided the manicure could wait.

I took all the pillows off her bed and the cushions from the other chair too. Then I stood in front of her and brushed her hands. 'Come on, sweetheart,' I said. 'Upsy-daisy.' She let me pull her to her feet, lead her to the treatment table and push her down until she was sitting. After that I had to lift and swivel her, using my own strength, until her head was nestled in the neck pillow and her legs were raised on the pile of cushions, well above her heart. I took her slippers off and pulled a breath in over my teeth. Her feet were blotched purple under thick yellow rinds of dead skin, the nails long and dirty in the corners.

'Oh, Sylvie,' I said.

Sylvie gazed at the ceiling with that same distant look on her face.

I wrapped her legs in hot towels, dunked in her bathroom sink, and started massaging her feet, gently at first, wondering how she'd be. But even when I traced a finger up and down her instep there was nothing. Not a jerk, not a gasp, not even a twitch, and I knew how strange that was. I'd got good at ducking out of the way of kicks when I went in hard on the soles with my scraper. But Sylvie was like one of the dummies we trained on. So I got my clippers and cracked off a quarter-inch of yellow-grey horn from each toe, cleaned under what was left and lathered them in cuticle oil, while I took a brush to her legs.

I even shaved them. I'd never shaved someone else's legs before. I'd never tried to do a pedicure on feet that were up in the air either. But I managed, with a bit of water-spillage and using every towel in my collection and hers. By the time I was smoothing lotion on, long strokes all the way from her toes to her knees I was sure she was looking better, less purple, and certainly warmer. I covered her with a blanket and went to the head of the table.

She was asleep. Her breaths were slow and deep and, under her eyelids – thin as silk – her eyes were moving. She must dream like other people, I thought. Did she remember, when she woke up again, that she'd been dreaming?

I stroked her hair back and we stayed like that for ten minutes, her sleeping and me stroking, until, with a small sigh, she opened her eyes and smiled at me.

'There,' I said. 'Isn't that better? Now I'm going to sit you back in your chair and do your hands.'

I couldn't bear to put her smooth feet into her old slippers again, so I chose two pairs of loose socks from her underwear drawer and cosied her into them. I kept checking all the time I did her manicure, and I was almost sure her feet were a better colour.

Sylvie showed no interest in anything that was happening. Even when I held her hands up in front of her face – her nails now pale ovals and her skin gleaming with lotion – her pupils didn't shift. She kept gazing straight through to that middle distance she was always watching.

'Well, then,' I said, laying them in her lap again. 'I better go and get this lot in the laundry system before your next shower, eh?' I jerked my head at the heap of wet towels. 'Or you'll have to shake like a dog. Eh?' I shook her hands in mine, swinging them, then pumping them back and forward as if we were jiving. And it might have been my imagination but I was sure they weren't quite lifeless in mine. I was almost sure she pushed and pulled a little, too.

'I've trashed all Sylvie's towels giving her a pedicure,' I said, coming into the staff kitchenette and finding Hinny there, as I had the day before. 'How does the washing work? Can I run them through or is there somewhere we put them? And where can I get clean ones to go in her bathroom?'

Hinny looked at me over the rim of her coffee cup and flashed a look of mock horror. I hoped it was mock horror. 'You're brave,' she said.

'How d'you mean?'

'Mucking up Dr Ferris's housekeeping routine. She's got us

103

all told about how much life you can get out of a towel before it goes out for a wash.'

'Oh,' I said, looking at the bale I was cradling in my arms. 'I'll take these home and do them, maybe. Keep my nose clean seeing I'm new. Unless she'd mind me removing hospital property?'

'She'd mind you saying "hospital",' Hinny said. 'Are you stopping for a cuppa?' I looked at my watch and nodded. 'Mine's an Earl Grey, then,' she added, and winked at me.

'I was sorry to miss the meeting,' I said, once I was settled opposite her. 'Actually, I'm feeling a bit at sea all round.'

'You'll get there,' she said.

'How long have you worked here?'

'Since Dalbeattie Primary went to Central Catering,' Hinny said. 'No scope. I was bored shitless. At least here I still get to cook.'

'Are you from Dalbeattie, then?' I said, thinking about getting lifts to work.

Hinny waggled her eyebrows. 'Oh, aye. I know you, even if you don't know me. Born and bred I am.'

I dipped my head and took a drink of tea to get some thinking time. Earl Grey always sickened me a bit with its perfume and I hated how pale it stayed no matter how hard you squeezed the bag. And maybe it was sitting there, in a new place, in a new job, drinking tea I didn't like that girded me. I could do this right, right from the start, if I just got a bit of courage up this minute.

'Yep, we were the talk of the town for a bit there, weren't we?' I said.

'You know what they called you? In the King's Arms?'

'Fur coat and no knickers?' I guessed. 'Pair of bloody idiots?'

'Not the both of you,' said Hinny. 'I mean what they called *you*.' She took a beat. 'Tammy Wynette. Get it? Standing by your man?'

I got it. Before my silence became too odd, Lars appeared with another nurse, green-tunicked and harassed.

'Any more hot in the kettle?' he said. 'Ali, this is Marion. She's the deputy charge. Usually on backs if I'm on days, but you know.'

If I was going for it, I'd better really go for it. 'Know what?' I said. 'You might as well be speaking Klingon.'

'Are you a Trekkie?' Marion said

'Mum with a son,' I told her. 'But seriously, know what?'

'Ohhhhh,' said Lars, swinging back on his seat and giving me a big grin that showed all the gaps around the back of his mouth. 'She didn't tell you, eh?'

'Of course not,' said Hinny. She put the last bite of her ginger snap on her saucer and folded her hands. 'The expansion of our team to include a para-therapist specializing in personal care and recreational activities is part of the ongoing development of Howell Hall's services, the next step in the programme of all-round blah-bah-blah.'

'They got all "fair and satisfactory" in their CC assessment,' Lars said. 'No goods and no excellents. And the report goes public . . . When is it, Hin?'

'End of the month.'

'So it's battle stations for the next inspection. Which will be unannounced and anytime.'

I hoped I didn't look guilty, but I was sure I did: all those lies and tall tales on my CV.

'What's up?' said Marion. She was the kind of nurse I had come to recognize at ten paces. Neat and brisk and no time for nonsense. She was in her fifties and she must have gone into nursing when it was all tidy wards and bed baths.

'Right enough,' I said. 'We didn't talk about contracts. I thought it was long-term. I didn't think I was just in to make the place look good for a few weeks and then I'd be out again.'

'Depends,' said Hinny. 'If you attract enough new business.'

'How the hell would I do that?' I said.

'Well, Julia's never off her phone,' said Lars. 'I'd keep in with her.'

'That reminds me,' I said. 'Something Dr Ferris said about Julia. What's the holy trinity of psychopathy?'

'Julia's no psychopath,' said Marion. 'She's been bunged in here so's she doesn't disrupt Mummy's bridge club.' Maybe I was wrong about the woman: that sounded like sympathy after all.

'Oh, no, I know what *this* is,' Lars said. 'It was before she was admitted. She peed the bed, set a fire and killed a squirrel.'

Hinny laughed through her last mouthful of ginger-snap crumbs. 'God, I'd forgotten about that.' Now Marion was laughing too, half at the memory but half at my face, eyes wide and mouth open.

Lars brought his front chair legs down with a thump. 'Let me explain,' he said. 'Fire-setting, bedwetting, animal cruelty: the three predictors of psychopathy. Watch any Hollywood film and you'll see. So Julia hit them all. Trouble is, it's all total bollocks. If she really was psycho, yeah, sure, there'd be a shit-ton of signs. But that's not three of them.'

'And she wouldn't dump them when they got boring and go all out for depression instead,' Marion added.

'Ah, right,' I said. 'Got it. Histrionic personality disorder.'

'With a touch of Munchausen's sprinkled on top, we reckon,'

said Lars. 'Her mum just got to the end of her rope. Well, I mean she wears *us* out some days.' His watch pinged and he choked on the mouthful of tea he was swallowing. 'Shit! Forgot!' he said, standing. He fished his phone out of a back pocket and started thumbing the buttons. 'Midday news,' he said. 'I'm dying to hear if they've got an ID. My pal said there was going to be a briefing.'

'The body in the monastery!' said Hinny. 'Disnae sound real, does it?' She stooped to look over Lars's shoulder and Marion crowded in at his other side as the familiar music sounded.

I sat where I was but I could hear it clearly, the tinny little voice squawking, '. . . preliminary results from Glasgow University, where forensic pathologists have examined the remains found in the grounds of Dundrennan Abbey. The body is that of a man, aged between twenty and forty, who died at least twelve years ago. There is no surviving identification. The remains are now being transferred to the Centre for Anatomy and Human Identification in Dundee for further investigations. Missing-person reports from all parts of Scotland and the north of England are being reviewed by Dumfries and Galloway police, who had this to say.'

The sound feed changed to the hubbub of an outside press conference and Lars clicked his phone.

'Aw!' said Hinny.

'Ex-father-in-law,' Lars said. 'I've spent enough time listening to that gobshite.'

'Well, at least we know it was a man,' said Hinny. And then to Lars: 'Don't look at me like that. You know what I mean.'

Lars was gathering the cups and running hot water into the sink. 'Aye, aye,' he said. 'It's not some wee girl that was taken away and kept alive till she gave out. Or some poor cow that got beaten once too often.'

His words were so bleak that only silence followed them.

'Histrionic personality disorder,' I said, when I thought I'd been quiet long enough and wouldn't sound heartless. 'What causes that?'

The two nurses looked at one another and Marion shrugged. 'Same as everything,' she said. 'The usual suspects and nobody knows.'

I waited to see if one of them would say more.

In the end it was Hinny, the dinner lady, who explained. 'Abuse, neglect, abandonment.'

'There's no evidence,' said Lars. 'But yeah.'

'Or is that for borderline and anti-social?' Hinny added, as if she was trying to remember the Latin names for her favourite flower.

'The boys go bad and the girls go mad,' said Marion, sadly. Then she took a deep breath and shook the thought away. 'Bloody hell! How did we get on to this? We were having a nice wee chat about mouldering bones. And now we're neck deep in shoptalk.'

'My fault,' I said. 'I was just wondering. About Julia's father, actually. You know how she says she killed her father? I mean, if he was abusing her, who'd blame her?'

There was a moment of stunned silence in the tea room, then Lars whistled. 'Oh, my God! Ali, you'll have to grow a thicker skin than that and pretty fast.'

'More like a better bullshit detector,' Marion said. She laughed at my face again.

'Don't listen to her,' said Lars. He was drying the cups now, screwing the tea-towel hard into them and twisting until they squeaked. Maybe it was because he was a nurse, with hygiene hammered into him, like how Marco couldn't slice a carrot slowly but had to act like a chef every time.

'It's not bullshit,' Lars said. 'It's just not . . . See, the thing is, the pain's real. The terror – it's all real. And the causes never sound bad enough. So they kind of . . . sex them up. Dad's never just an arsehole that sat behind his newspaper and wouldn't say he was proud of them, ken? He turns into a mixture of Hitler and Hannibal that beat them with a strap and kept them in the cellar.'

I gave a little laugh, even though his words stung. Sometimes life really was as bad as you felt. Sometimes the strap and the cellar were surely true.

'Ask her to do a house-tree-person, if you don't believe me,' Lars said. 'Julia, I mean. When are you seeing her?'

I shrugged. I hadn't drawn up any kind of schedule at all. Tomorrow, after the meeting, I'd have to look for the chart they all talked about and try to slot myself into it somewhere. And as for 'a house-tree-person' – I had no idea what he was on about. Again.

'This afternoon if she's free,' I said. Marion laughed again as she stood.

'Oh, she's free,' she said. 'She's got her one-on-ones with the doc first thing. Then she's free to cut about in that bloody goonie till the sun goes down. Come, and I'll show you where to find her.'

Julia's room was one of the best in the house, I guessed. Certainly the equal of the empty room Dr Ferris had displayed at my interview. The window was a square bay, big enough for a chaise-longue and an ornate mantelpiece with a real oil painting above it. The furniture was white and gold, the chair legs fluted like columns, little swags and urns picked out around the dressing-table mirror and on the bed head.

So it could have been lovely. But the loveliness was hidden under a layer of crap that took my breath away. There were more clothes than I could believe anyone owned lying about on the chairs and strewn on the floor. And there were shoes, some still in their boxes with labels attached. And empty boxes, too, and thick bags ripped open and invoices screwed up and scattered around.

'Is this all new?' I said.

'Not the socks,' said Marion, pointing. Dirty white socks lay all around the edges of the room where they'd been thrown, looking like tennis balls at the end of a long set with no one clearing. 'But everything else is. She shops. The gate's never done ringing to say there's a van trying to deliver.'

'Can't you stop her?'

'Not my decision,' Marion said grimly. 'I'd have her over my knee. But then I'd have this place bankrupt in a month if I put everyone over my knee that belongs there.'

I didn't know what to say to that. I've always believed a little kindness can go a long way myself but Marion was in another league. 'I wonder where she is,' I settled for. 'I'll just scout about. Track her down. Maybe in the garden?'

'I'm needing to go and do a flush on the acute side anyway,' Marion said. I didn't want to know what she meant so I went the other way, then ducked into a staff toilet at the bottom of the stairs, using the swipe card Dr Ferris had given me.

I locked myself in and sat on the toilet lid to Google 'House Tree Person'.

My blood ran cold when the page came up. There was no

chance I could get away with this. If I had *really* done any art therapy, I would have heard of it and I'd only been an inch away from asking Lars what he meant and blowing my cover. I skimmed the Wikipedia page, then chose a link at random. Another couple of minutes and I thought I was ready. I slipped out of the toilet, checking in both directions, then went to the side door to search for Julia in the garden.

There she was right enough, back in the gazebo with a cigarette, but she was in a very different mood from that first morning. She'd been crying. She wasn't a pretty crier. Her nose was swollen and the skin around her eyes was crumpled and pink while the rest of her face was pale. It was a look forward to how she'd be at forty, I thought, as I approached her. Or thirty, if she didn't stop smoking.

'Hiya,' I said, sitting down beside her. 'I've been looking for you. How d'you fancy a facial?'

She took a drag of her cigarette, then looked first at the glowing tip and next at the bare skin of my arm below my short tunic sleeve. I stood up and took a step away from her. But she just shook her head and gave a weary laugh. 'Don't worry,' she said. 'I can't be arsed.'

'Good to know,' I told her. 'Come on, eh? You can lie down nice and warm with your eyes closed and I'll give you a lovely facial. Help your wee face recover from all those tears.'

'Wee face?' she said. 'Am I nine?'

'Just an express—' I began.

'I don't have a wee face,' Julia said. 'I don't have a wee anything. I've got a face like the arse of a cow and an arse like the arse of another one.'

'You've got a hell of a way with words,' I said, but she only scowled harder.

111

'Of course,' she said. 'I'm the funny one. Plug-ugly fat arse but I can make 'em laugh.'

I wanted to disagree but she wasn't a pretty girl. She was tall and broad, with frizzy hair and a nose that hooked round to meet her chin. Her eyes had lids under them as large the lids above and she had gaps between all her teeth. She was plain now, and when she was an old lady she would be truly ugly.

'People can be very cruel,' I said, taking a wild guess. She was eighteen, and I knew how eighteen-year-old girls aspired to look: a sheet of hair; bodies like willow wands; that way of gliding around as if they were on runners. I remembered Julia stomping up the stairs with her elbows going and a wave of pity surged in me. I sat down again.

'The trick is,' I said, and I felt her go still, 'to live inside your body.' She snorted. 'I know it sounds like claptrap, but it's not. Listen.' I leaned back and let my arm rest against hers. That was another thing I learned when I was ill. Sitting touching, not talking, not looking. They do it in Africa, in one of those tribes where everyone's happy even though they've all got nothing. 'So many girls your age live inside other people's heads looking back at themselves. You need to live inside yourself and look out. Come and lie down and let me relax you. Try to visit Julia for a while and see what she sees. Bugger the rest of them.'

She took another drag of her cigarette, then pinged it with thumb and forefinger, sending it sailing in a bright coral-blue arc onto the grass where the damp doused it. 'Do you pop blackheads?'

'You haven't got any,' I told her. 'Stop being so awkward.'

'What about my bikini line?'

'I'm not touching you with a bargepole till you've had a bath,' I said.

She opened the neck of her nightie and stuck her head down, sniffing hard. 'You've got a point.'

'That's the second time you've smelt yourself and pretended to be surprised,' I said. 'You're not fooling me this time, Julia.'

She gave me the look I knew so well from Angelo, the look of outraged injustice: this time there really was a wolf and the villagers down the mountain should learn to tell the difference.

'I'm not trying to fool you!' she said. 'I forgot. I drift. They're still trying to get my meds right and they keep changing the balance. I forgot where I fucking was yesterday morning. I thought I was in a hotel. Thought I had a hangover.'

'A facial, and then we'll sit together and do something lovely and relaxing, eh?' I said. I stood and held out my hand to her. For a minute I thought she was going to take it and then she rolled her eyes and got to her feet, brushing past me.

———

She was quiet, as quiet as Sylvie, while I worked on her. And gradually she relaxed, her face smoothing to serenity. I dug my hands in under her head and worked on the knots in her neck.

'You've got a good skull,' I said. 'Nice neck and jaw.' She said nothing. 'You would suit your hair cut close. Like Halle Berry.'

'Or Julius Caesar,' she murmured, and I laughed softly.

'You would, though.' What I really meant was that the frizzy hair bushing out round her face, along with the hooked nose, made her look like a clown. But if she went all out for bone structure – wore that nose proudly – she'd be magnificent instead of ridiculous.

'Do you cut hair?'

'I could take you into town to a salon,' I said. 'Do you get days out?' She didn't answer. 'Course, you'd have to lose the dressing-gown and actually put on some of these new clothes you keep buying.' I looked again at the heaps of shopping littering her room.

'I don't think my fairy godmother would be very happy about me going off the reservation,' she said. Her voice was slack and gravelly, either from the massage or from the meds she was taking.

'Dr Ferris?' I asked. 'I'm just going to masque you now.'

'Pretty sure the deal with my mum was to keep me bricked up in the tower so I can't do any more damage,' she said, hardly moving her mouth as I smeared the warm paste over her face and down her neck.

'What did you really do, Julia?' I said softly.

'I hurt my daddy,' she answered even softer.

'Hurt him how?'

'I hurt his middle.'

'That doesn't sound like the end of the world.'

Her voice was no more than a whisper now. 'I killed my father?'

'Ssh,' I said, and I listened as her breaths grew deeper and slower and then I listened to her sleeping.

Chapter 9

The words bothered me. Kids make up their own minds what words mean. When Angelo was tiny, just before he threw up like Vesuvius one time, he said his waist was hurting. Not his tummy, which might have warned us: his waist. And then another time when he was toddling along beside me on our way to the shops he heard me wincing and turned his face up, squinting through the hair he wouldn't let me cut. 'What a matter, Mummy?'

'Nothing,' I said. 'I've just got a crick in my neck.' I was all aches and pains that summer, couldn't get comfy to sleep no matter what I tried.

He stopped dead and gazed, as if at some undreamed-of wonder. 'You swallow it?' he said.

'What?'

'It fly in your mouth?'

'*What?*'

'Jimmy Cricket,' he said.

'Not my throat, Angel-boy,' I said. 'My neck. Here.' I touched him under the curling ends of his mop of hair, tickling him, making him shriek and scoot away from me. And, of course, we all said 'a cricket in your neck' from that day on. Until Angelo started rolling his eyes and snorting anyway.

So 'I hurt his middle' could mean anything. She might have elbowed him in the ribs when she got into her parents' bed in the morning for a cuddle. Or maybe she was on his lap and she trampled him and he yelled and frightened her. But I knew what I thought it meant. I could think of ways a little girl could hurt her daddy's 'middle' and then years later would fantasize that she'd killed him to make the memory go away.

If he was even dead. He might be living with her mother, happy and clueless. Or, like Lars said, maybe he'd left his family for pastures new and his daughter made up a more dramatic story. I would ask at the staff meeting if he was still alive.

As quietly as I could, I drew a folder of paperwork out from the tray under the table, my face so close to Julia's that I could hear the little popping sounds she made as each breath out made her lips part.

I moved a bale of clothes, still in their plastic wrappers from the mail order, keeping my movements slow and soft. Then I sat down to study my resident list and start to plan.

Six boys, three junkies and three alkies, and seven girls, four ana-mias, two alkies and Julia. A handful of women with various depressions, although I'd have to study the difference between chronic, acute and major, which all sounded pretty bad. One with late-stage terminal dementia and, of course, Sylvie.

I tapped my pen against my cheek and thought about it. There's not much that massage doesn't help. Even the woman dying of Alzheimer's would no doubt appreciate a bit of gentle effleurage. It would calm the alkies and reinvigorate the junkies.

As for the girls who were scared to eat? I could tell them I'd strip toxins and excess water and they'd be queuing up. And depression was made for it.

Touch is a problem for British people, maybe Scots most of all. We're not huggers. But gentle touch can do wonders for someone feeling the ache of loss or loneliness. Gentle touch, fresh air and exercise is what did it for me. That and determination. I made a note to ask Dr Ferris whether they insisted on residents going outside and walking every day. Maybe they had a physio with her own ideas – I didn't want to step on any toes – but there were still footpaths all over this land, despite the army, and any day they weren't firing live rounds we could all be out there, getting good-tired; so different from the bad-tired you got from staying inside rooms and thinking too much. I lifted my head and looked out of Julia's bedroom window. All I could see was a square of grey sky, the wind strong enough to fling the seagulls where it chose, making me think of ice-skaters, pushing off, then suddenly wheeling away. I closed my eyes and listened to the soft snores and the faint shushing that came through the closed window.

I was drifting when I heard it. 'Mmmhmmm.'

I leaped up. The chair tipped and hit the floor.

'Mmmmhmmm-ah!' Julia said. 'This fucking face masque has set like concrete. I can't move!'

I picked up the chair and put the bale of wrapped clothes back on it. 'Ssh,' I said. 'You're supposed to be relaxing.'

'Look who's talking,' she said, glaring up at me. 'You look like you've seen a ghost.'

'Shush while I wash you,' I said. 'I left it a bit longer than I would have because you were so peaceful. Sorry it freaked you out.'

117

'Take more than that,' she said, through the hot towel I had laid over her face.

'Ssh,' I said again, as I pressed it down.

'Have you got kids?' she said, squinting up at me, once I had wiped away every trace of the masque and was holding my hands cupped over her ears. I always do that as part of a facial, just gently.

'I do. Why?'

'Wish you were *my* mum.' She closed her eyes again and didn't say another word, through toning, serum and deep moisture, until I was taking the band off her hair and telling her to sit up slowly.

'So what's on the cards for the rest of your day?' I asked her. She shrugged. 'Would you do something for me then?' She shrugged the other shoulder. 'Just to start things off,' I said. 'It'll only take twenty minutes.'

I took her into the room with the circle of chairs, settled her at a table in front of the window and spread out a big sheet of paper. I handed her a soft pencil. 'They said you've already drawn a house, a tree and a person,' I told her, 'but would you draw them for me?'

'This again,' she said, but the pencil was moving already. I put my chin into my hand and watched the lines come spilling out of its tip. Her house was a tiny roof hidden in the distance in a mountain range, only recognizable because of a smoking chimney. Her tree was leafless and jagged, more like a gibbet or a radio antenna than a living thing. And her person was a sack tied with a chain, just one eye peering out of a hole that one finger was holding open.

'Is that you?' I said, pointing at the eye.

'Your turn,' she told me, turning the paper over and shoving the pencil at me point first.

I drew a proper house: a door in the middle and four windows. One face in each window, everyone waving. I drew two chimneys and a garden gate with a welcome sign on it. Behind the gate, I drew a cartoon tree with an Afro of fluffy leaves and a swing hanging down. I drew an apple in it, just one, and a bird with its beak open. I was trying to make it look like it was chirping. I drew grass round the bottom of the tree trunk and a rabbit sniffing a flower. And I drew my person on the swing. A little girl with a big ribbon tied in a bow on the top of her head. I gave her a pinafore and scalloped edges to her socks, buttons on the straps of her shoes. I couldn't draw her hands on the swing chains so I folded them in her lap. I worked hard on it but when I looked up at Julia she had stopped watching me. She was staring out of the window.

I rolled the paper up and touched her arm. 'I'd better get a move on now,' I said. 'Don't wash your face again today and try not to touch it. I'll bring some samples of the scrub in tomorrow, if you liked it.'

She nodded. 'Are you sure you couldn't cut my hair?' she said. 'Now you've started me thinking about it, it's like a dead dog hanging on my neck. It's disgusting.'

'Wash it,' I said to her, joke-nagging.

'And you'll cut it tomorrow?'

'I'll ask Dr Ferris if we can get a hairdresser in,' I promised her. 'You staying here or going back to your room? You could tidy up a bit, just so the chairs don't actually fall over backwards from the weight of all the stuff, you know.'

'God, I was wrong. You *are* my mum,' she said.

———

119

There was no one in the staff kitchen, so I went on a round of the lounge where the two women were at their jigsaw again. Harriet and Jo, their names were, although I wasn't entirely sure which was which. I sat and helped them for a bit, then asked them what they'd like to have done as their introduction.

'I'm just saying hello by giving out treats,' I said, hoping they didn't think I was making them sound like dogs. 'Manicure, pedicure, massage, facial. Anything you like.'

'Can you do that hot stones?' said one, looking up with the first glint of life I had seen in her eyes.

'Certainly can,' I said, wondering where in the eaves I had stuffed my stones and heater. 'Have you had that before?'

'Had it at a hotel on a mini-break,' she said. 'She had this great big stone she put on the base of my back, so heavy I could hardly move. I could feel it drawing out all the poison. God help the next one they put it on after me.'

'We detox the stones between clients,' I said. 'Anyway, they're more like conduits than receptacles. The poison passes through.'

The other woman was watching me out of the corner of her eye. 'I don't want you burying me under heavy stones,' she said.

'Aromatherapy massage,' I suggested. 'Light as a feather. And you choose the aroma. Geranium, lavender, citrus. Depends whether you want to be soothed or pepped up. I'll help you decide.'

'Have you got nightshade?' she said. 'That's all *I* want, love. Lie down, close my eyes and never open them again. No more. That'll do me.'

I couldn't answer her for a few moments. The way she put it, it was hard to argue. 'It's my first proper day,' I said eventually. 'You'll get me the sack.'

Her friend gave a short laugh, then bent lower over the jigsaw, but the nightshade woman just stared at me out of her blank eyes. 'You'll fit right in,' she said.

I couldn't avoid the acute side for ever, so I steeled myself. But on the way through, I met Lars coming back and turned round gladly for a break instead of going to sell my services to the boys being dried out. I could imagine what they'd make of a masseuse and I needed tips about how to handle things if they got cheeky.

'Head smashed in,' Lars said, as a greeting, swiping his card and pushing through.

I felt my eyes widen. 'Through there?' I said, as the door swung and latched behind him.

'The body in the abbey,' he said. 'Head stoved in with a blunt instrument. A shovel, they think. I just got an update.'

'They've put that on the news already?'

Lars waggled his phone. 'Update from Boney. My pal? They said his skull was in smithereens, totally bashed to— Whoa! Whoa! You okay?'

He caught me by the forearms and led me towards a windowsill to let me sit. It was deep from the thickness of the walls but I heard the glass grate in the frame when I leaned back so I bent forward again. Probably best anyway when you're woozy.

'Sorry,' I said. 'It's just so close to my house.' But he was still frowning so I pulled the trump card. 'You got kids?'

'Three, but they live in Malta,' he said. 'Come on. I'll make you a sweet cuppa. And Marion's got a tub of Jaffa Cakes.'

There was no one in the kitchenette, only a lot of mugs draining on paper towels by the sink, as if we'd just missed everyone. Lars tutted and grabbed a tea-towel.

'I got Julia to draw the three things, by the way,' I said.

'This should be good.' He sat down beside me as I spread the sheet of paper. After a long hard look, he shook his head, laughing. 'Wow,' he said.

I studied it again trying to see one single thing to laugh about in any of it: the tiny house lost in the mountains, the tree of jagged wire, the person in the sack peering out. 'How long have you worked in psychiatric nursing?' I said. 'You're jaded if you think that's funny.'

'She's faking,' said Lars. 'Come on! The tree I'll give you. At least it's a tree. But no one draws a roof like a needle in a haystack when somebody says, "Draw a house", do they? And nobody for sure draws a sack and an eye instead of a person. She did that deliberately to make you worry about how ill she is.'

'So there's nothing to learn from it?' I said.

'Except that she's faking,' he said, and started rolling the paper up again. 'Wait, though. What's this?'

I put my hand out to stop him, then pulled it back just as fast and rubbed my nose, laughing. 'Oh, that was me,' I said. 'Nothing going on there.'

He waggled his eyebrows and unrolled the paper slowly, spreading it out with my drawing face up. 'Let's see what all *your* secrets are then, Alison McGovern.'

'Feel free,' I said. I could feel my cheeks flaming but what was he going to say about a proper house, like everyone draws, and an ordinary tree and a pretty girl with a bow in her hair? I looked back at his face and saw that the smile had gone. He was frowning.

'What?' I said.

'Just winding you up,' he told me, the frown smoothing. 'So what did Pollyanna do to get stuck out in the garden?'

'What?' I said. I glanced between the paper and his face, not sure if he was joking.

'Perfect family all cosy inside,' he said. 'Mum and Dad and two kids, and this wee lassie with the cares of the world on her head, sent out to sit on the naughty step all on her own?'

'What the hell are you on about?' I said. 'It's four people because there's four windows. And there's another one because you have to draw another one. Are you serious?'

Lars bent until his face was close to mine and spoke softly: 'No. I'm not. It's a load of bollocks and you can use it to say anything. That's why we don't use it.'

I sat back and fanned myself, laughing with relief. 'You had me going for a minute there.' I rolled up the paper. 'And that was a bow, by the way. A ribbon. Not the cares of the world.'

'Yeah, I was crap at art, too,' he said. 'But you're wrong about the windows. If you give a kid a picture of a house and say, "Draw the family that lives there", they always draw the people in their family. Pets too.'

'Dogs and cats, though, right?' I said. 'Not hamsters and goldfish?' Lars shrugged. 'What about nits?'

It felt good to make someone laugh. It had been months since Marco had laughed properly, apart from the night of the job advert, and it had been years since Angelo had thought I was funny.

'Right, then,' Lars said, standing. Awkward, suddenly. 'I'd better get back to it. The wee shites won't straighten their own faces, will they?'

As he was leaving, I called him back. 'Why didn't she play games with the tree?' I said. 'Julia. Why just the house and the person? She drew a tree for the tree.'

Lars grunted. 'Good point,' he said. 'If I bought any of this crap – which I do not because nobody does, it's one step up from stage hypnotism – but if I did, I'd say her issues are about herself and her home life, so that's where she plays the games.'

I nodded as if I thought it was a good answer, but when I thought it over, I wasn't so sure. How could anyone have issues with a tree? What would it mean? Unless you were a forester anyway.

_____

By the time I got home at the end of the afternoon I was wiped. I'd forgotten how much stress you can take on when you lay your hands on stressed people all day. It used to make me glad of things like eyebrow tints and lip waxings. They weren't great earners but they didn't leave me with a load on my back like Buckaroo.

The two boys I had caught up with playing ping-pong in the old billiards room had hooted with laughter, of course. I'd thought I'd played it canny – told them all their football heroes got pounded by the physio and nobody would call *them* sissies.

'Ah fucken would,' said the smaller one. He was a classic wee ned, from the over-gelled hair poking downwards in spikes on his spotty brow to the pristine trainers like puffballs at the ends of his skinny legs. Who was paying his bill to be here instead of in a community centre twice a week and drinking in a bus shelter between times?

The bigger one sniggered.

'Different if you did the likes of tatts or piercing,' the little one said.

'I don't think that would go down very well with the doc,' I said. 'Do you . . .?'

'Ryan,' he said. He pointed his bat at the other. 'And Byron.'

'Byron?' I said, and saw the flare of panic in the other boy's eyes. Ryan had no idea who Byron's namesake was and Byron didn't want me blabbing. 'So, if you were getting a tattoo, what would you get? You can design them with my pens and paper if you like and take them to the tattoo parlour when you're out and you're eighteen.'

'Ah *um* eighteen,' Ryan said. 'Cheeky bitch. No offence.'

'I'm sixteen,' Byron said, and I couldn't mistake the pride in his voice. He might have a daft name and a posh voice but he had managed to get himself into rehab two years earlier than the hard man and that counted for something.

'Well, I'll be back to bug you when I've got my timetable sorted,' I said. 'Just giving you warning. You don't need to let me do anything, but we should talk.' I pointed at Byron's fingers. 'I can help you with your nail biting, for instance,' I said. 'And, Ryan, well . . . let's talk.'

'Whit aboot?' he demanded. I stared at the spots that crusted his face from the points of his fringe to his collar, swollen and angry on his cheekbones, big, painful-looking lumps.

'Relaxation,' I lied

'Ha, Pizza-face!' Byron shouted, shaking his floppy locks back from a perfect complexion. Then he ran.

'Ya fucken bastard,' said Ryan, hurling his table tennis bat at the net and setting off in pursuit, both of them clattering along the corridor, whooping like maniacs. From somewhere else in the house an answering wail rose. I was shaking as I trotted after them.

I met Dr F pattering towards me from the direction of Dr Ferris's office. Or maybe they shared it. He took a look at my face and immediately stopped moving. 'Are you all right?' he said. 'Has something happened?'

'That's my fault,' I said, jerking my head towards the noise. 'I was clumsy and upset Ryan. Byron was unkind to him, but it's my fault.'

'Upset?' said Dr F. 'Unkind? Oh, Ali, please. Don't give it a moment's thought. It sounds like high spirits to me. Sounds like two boys being boys. I was only concerned that one of them might have assaulted you.'

I took a step back. 'Their language is a bit much and there was some name-calling, but . . . Is there a danger of assault? With either of those two?'

Dr F glanced over his shoulder before he answered me. 'This is the thing with para-therapy,' he said. 'With *any* of the ancillary staff in a small facility like ours. There are so many moments in any day where a cleaner or Hinny in the kitchen or indeed you might be faced with a situation you're not equipped for.'

'I see,' I said. It made sense of my pay anyway. 'I was kind of surprised how much freedom they have, if I'm honest. Out in the garden, roaming around the house. I suppose I thought it would be more . . . confined. More . . . supervised.'

'Is that how they did things in Australia?' he said. We were walking along in step now. The boys were still shouting somewhere in the other wing, their voices ringing off the bare walls and lino floors. 'I've never been there. I'm always surprised by how comparatively old-fashioned the *American* system seems when you consider that they're at the cutting edge of medicine overall. Hospice care too. But I have no contacts in Australia.'

'Well,' I said. 'It was ten years ago.' I found all my breath leaving my body in a huge huff. 'I was ten years younger too,' I said, exhausted suddenly.

'Why not call it a day for today?' said Dr F. I was sure I could hear the clip-clop of his wife's shoes somewhere on the parquet and I was just as sure his suggestion was connected to him hearing it too. 'I'll take care of sorting all this out,' he added. My table was locked in my room and I had put my washing in the car after Julia, so I nodded and made my escape before those heels could clip-clop their way to finding me.

I thought about it, parked outside the house an hour later. I had wondered why her husband wasn't there for my interview, thinking that maybe he disapproved of me. But maybe he disapproved *for* me. Maybe he worried I wasn't trained enough to handle the patients. There was something funny going on between the pair of them. Then I looked at my own front door. I'd have to sort out what was going on in there too. I gathered my bags and papers and got out, glad at least that there were no press still hanging around. Next Door's door opened as I was walking up the path but I broke into a trot and got inside before he could catch me.

'He's asleep.' Marco met me just inside the door and whispered, nodding towards Angelo's bedroom. 'This thing with the cops and his phone's really knocked him for six.' So, I thought, Angelo hadn't told him about the girl sending her friends to the Mercat Cross.

'Last straw,' I said. 'After everything.'

I could have kicked myself, dragging it up like that. I watched him struggle not to act hurt as he cast about for something kind to say.

'Been treating yourself?' he said, with a look at the DE Shoes bag I was carrying. It wasn't really kind, but it was good-natured. Marco's never been the sly type.

'They're not for me,' I said.

'Pick-me-up for the boy?' Marco said, beaming at me.

'Something I need for work,' I said, turning away. I *should* have got a treat for Angelo, but I'd gone to town and chosen new slippers for Sylvie.

Chapter 10

I always told Marco not to wrap me in cotton wool so I could hardly complain that he had the breakfast news on. I came out of the bathroom and he was already sitting on the couch, cereal bowl just under his chin, scooping it in, glued to the telly. I rubbed my hair. It was so cold up in our bedroom I wanted the worst of the water off it before I went to dress, but the bathroom was so tiny and the window not even a foot square, opening just six inches at the bottom, that if I took my clothes in on a hanger, like I used to in our real house, they'd be damp for the rest of the day.

'Angel awake?' I said.

Marco gulped down a mouthful of milk. 'I've left him sleeping. He put a note out saying he was taking another day off.'

'And are you—'

'I'll be here.'

'I'll make up for it at the weekend . . .' I began, but Marco had seen the TV picture change from the floods, still high at

Carlisle, to a shot of the abbey. He leaned forward and stabbed the volume button up to drown me.

'... match so far with missing-person records from the area, as the search widens. The cause of death has been confirmed as blunt-force trauma to the back of the skull and the case is being treated as murder. There was no identification on the body. Preliminary examination suggests that this was not a vagrant. "This was a man who would be missed," said the chief investigating officer. However, only the belt buckle ...' Here the picture changed to a shot of a silver-coloured Kangol buckle, like you could buy anywhere in the country. It was new and shiny and rested against a pale blue background, with a label underneath saying 'example'. The voice was still droning on: '... the zip from a pair of Asda's own-brand jeans ...' another picture of the top of a pair of jeans against that blue card, as if anyone needed to see what jeans looked like "... and part of the earpiece to a pair of spectacles' no picture 'has survived the years underground.' The picture changed to a plainclothes guy standing outside the offices in Dumfries. He looked cold and tired. 'The wire from the glasses is our big hope for identification. That and the dental work.' He huddled deeper into his coat collar as a squall of rain hit him side on. I tried to think when it must have been filmed to catch weather like that. 'We're working with opticians to try to reconstruct the look of the complete pair of spectacles and we're very hopeful that this might lead to an ID.'

'Makes sense,' Marco said. 'Every photo's going to have his specs in it. Not like his belt or his flies.'

Back in the studio the newsreader was staring out at us with the solemn look they keep for tragedy, then ditch for the weather five minutes later. 'Police have asked for the public's help in compiling a full list of males, aged twenty-five to forty-five at the time they went missing, between 1990 and 2010. Any additional photographs to add to missing-person documents already filed might be of value.'

'Aye, right,' said Marco, stretching forward and dumping his bowl on the coffee table. 'Damn sure the cops are dying for everybody's aunty to go rootling through the photo album and come clogging up the office.' He pointed at the newsreader. 'She'll get her arse handed to her for that.'

———————

Lars and Hinny were full of it too.

'What does that mean then, "not a vagrant"?' Hinny was saying, when I ducked into the kitchen. It was only half past seven and I needed one more cup of coffee to be ready for the 'change'. It was starting to loom over me, I'd thought about it so much – telling myself that after it I'd be up to speed and ready for anything.

'That's what I wondered,' said Lars. 'A dirt-cheap pair of jeans and a Kangol belt? It's not as if some jakey dressing out the charity shop couldn't have them.

'Teeth, maybe,' Hinny said. 'Veneers or posh crowns and that.'

I shot a swift look at Lars to see if mention of good teeth and social standing might hurt his feelings. But he was shaking his head, his mind on the question and no sign of upset.

'Aye, but anyone can hit the streets at any time,' he said. 'Things I saw in the big wards in Glasgow, you wouldn't believe. Guys still with their Beamer key rings, no keys, no car anymore, but they kept it to remind themselves what they'd had once.'

'That's tragic,' Hinny said. I was sure she looked at my bag as she spoke. My Coach bag that I'd got in the duty-free on our last trip to Orlando.

'You know what I don't understand,' I said, trying to move the conversation on. 'How could somebody be killed and moved and buried and still have one of his specs legs hooked round his ear?'

'Moved?' Lars said. 'Have they let that out, like? Do they know it wasn't done there where they found him?'

'I just assumed,' I said. 'I mean, it's a public place. It doesn't seem that likely.'

'Aye, but it's digging a hole and filling it up that takes all the time,' said Hinny. 'A bash on the head with a shovel's the least of it.'

I shook my head. I knew something about that bothered me and it wasn't just the notion of it happening so close to where we lived. It was years ago and we hadn't been there.

Lars clicked his finger and winked at Hinny. 'Genius,' he said. 'That's how come he's still wearing half his specs, isn't it? The blow from the shovel smashed them into the wound and then all the blood made them stick. Eh? Do you not think?'

'I don't *want* to think,' said Hinny. 'And Ali's gone as white as a ghostie. Never mind him, hen.'

'We're getting late anyway,' Lars said. 'Come and share the joy and love of the shift change, Ali. That'll put you right.'

'Is it okay to bring my coffee?' I said. I needed sugar as well as the caffeine now. My lips felt thick and numb from the blood leaving them.

'Christ, aye,' said Hinny. 'Dr F practically wheels his in on a drip stand.'

We met Marion coming downstairs, yawning and rubbing her face with her palms.

'I know what it is,' I whispered to Lars, as we waited outside Dr Ferris's office door. She was on the phone and she held up a hand like a traffic cop to stop us trooping in. 'Why I don't think he was killed right there where they found him.'

'Is this the bones in the monk house?' said Marion.

'It's because— What are the chances of having an argument that got out of hand and made you bash someone with a shovel exactly in a place where you could just start digging a grave? I mean, fights happen in pubs and car parks, don't they? Not at historic monuments.'

'Unless you asked the person to meet you there,' Hinny said. 'Had it all planned, like.'

'Or,' said Lars, 'unless you had the shovel there for digging anyway and then you used it to kill him. Because that was bothering me too. Kind of handy, eh, no? Getting away with just one tool for both jobs?'

'But digging what, though?' I said. 'You mean maybe it was two archaeologists? People who were there officially? If a historian went missing actually from the site, they'd have ID-ed him already, wouldn't they? They'd have looked for him there and seen the earth disturbed right away.'

'That's actually— How *didn't* they see it?' said Marion. 'Someone. There's tourists all over that place all the time.'

'Depends on the time of year,' I said.

'Leaf litter,' said Lars. 'There's letters in the *News* about the council works department every week. Leaves lying, graves all dandelions, but never mind that. I didn't mean Indiana Jones digging up monks – they don't use shovels anyway. They scrape away with toothpicks. That's how come it takes them so long. I was thinking of someone digging a grave to put a body in and someone strolling up and seeing it. Then bash bang wallop.

Two graves instead of one. I'm surprised they're not digging the whole place up, checking.'

'Or maybe it's a serial killer,' Marion said. 'Yeah, you're right. They should be checking.'

It hadn't even crossed my mind. One grave, one body – and Angelo's phone mixed up in it all – was horrendous enough. Imagination had been silenced. That voice that had been dripping poison into my ear since the first positive pee-test ('What if, but what if, but if you're not careful') had for once been reduced to a grinning goblin just sitting on my shoulder, watching the show.

'Don't say that!' I said. 'I live right across the road, you know. My front windows look out at it. I'll never sleep again.'

'Is that right?' said Lars. 'You stay in the row at Dundrennan?'

'I was meaning to say, actually,' I began, 'if anyone goes past, I'd chip in for petrol.'

But Dr Ferris was winding up her phone call, clicking her fingers at us to tell us to come in. 'It'll blow over, sweetheart. Don't worry about it, and don't text everyone under the sun, for heaven's sake. Everything dies eventually if you don't feed it . . . I know . . . I know. But listen to your mother.' She smiled fondly at her desktop, listening to the quacking from the phone. 'Urchin,' she said. 'Wretched child. Home at the usual. Lots of love. Lots and lots.' And she hung up and clicked her phone a few times, turning it to mute. 'My daughter Dido,' she said to me. 'The usual drama,' she said to the others, with a rueful smile around the room, as if asking the other parents to share the moment with her. I couldn't get her words to stop echoing – *Everything dies eventually if you don't feed it.* It wasn't my idea of comfort.

More staff were filing in, but not many. I had thought on my visits that the life of Howell Hall was going on somewhere else, that I was managing to find the quiet corners. But was this it? Lars and Marion, four more nurses in different colour-coded uniforms that I couldn't decipher, Hinny and another woman in the same white overall as hers, the two doctors, a man in a tracksuit who must be the physio. And me.

'And we're missing . . . Oonagh and I've had a long string of texts from John,' Dr Ferris was saying, as I started listening again.

'Who are they?' I said. It would be easy to sit shtum but I had promised myself I would be the squeaky wheel and leave the room feeling like I knew enough to get through the rest of the day.

'Oonagh is Marion's opposite number and John's our current bank night nurse,' said Dr F. I scribbled it down. Eight nurses, at least one hired by the shift from an employment agency. 'And speaking of which, let's do a round of introductions, shall we?'

'I've got Lars, Marion and Hinny,' I said. I turned to the other kitchen worker who had taken the seat next to mine. 'I'm Ali McGovern, beauty and art therapist.' I stuck my hand out and the woman shook it, her eyes so wide I could see the whites all round, but she said nothing.

'Thank you, Alison,' said Dr Ferris, as sour as a pickled lime. 'I think I can handle this. This is Alison, everyone. She's a beautician who's joining us to do some para-therapeutic work on personal care and some recreational art. And from left to right: Amana is a kitchen assistant, Yvonne an enrolled nurse. Dick is a registered nurse. They're both usually on the acute side so you'll have few dealings with them. Belle and Surraya are registered and enrolled on the open side. Marion is the

135

deputy charge nurse. Lars is the charge nurse. And then there's Dr Ferris, who's deputy director, and at the top, of course, me. You should direct all questions to me.'

'And this is Jed, our trainer and fitness expert,' Dr F added. 'You'll probably be working quite closely with Jed so you should—'

'Darling?' said Dr Ferris. 'Perhaps we could start the meeting.'

Dr F clamped his lips shut so quickly they actually made a smacking noise and I could see Lars bite his cheeks trying not to laugh. Surraya was wearing a hijab and she put her head on one side so it swung forward hiding her face from the doctors. She looked right at me, crossed her eyes and mouthed, *Bitch*, so I had to bite my cheeks too and couldn't look at Lars for the rest of the meeting.

Anyway, there was plenty to do. I scribbled furious notes, cross-referring to my patient list, as the departing night shift rattled off reports of meds and checks and hours.

'And apart from that I spent the shift sitting with Rosa,' Marion finished up.

'*You* did?' said Dr Ferris, turning a sharp eye on one of the other nurses. One in a dark green uniform. Yvonne, maybe. I would have got them all if she'd let them say their own names.

'I did,' Marion said. 'We can have a review of nursing practice, if you like, Doctor.'

There was a long moment of stillness. Then Dr Ferris spoke again, in a voice like liquid nitrogen: 'Moving along, then. Lars?'

I had only heard him gossiping and joking so far, but as he laid out the patient plan for the day he was a different man: rattling off the appointments for the 'substance dependents', the one-on-one schedule, the drug regimes and changes. I filled in my list, blocking out who was free and when among it all. My days could have been filled four times over. He finished up with the group he called simply 'Drew, Posy, Roisin, and the new admission'. I guessed from the vintage of the names that they were the anorexics. 'I'll take Drew for breakfast and lunch today and see if it goes better. If we're right in thinking it's gender that's the problem with the mealtime supervision, I'll text John and get him in early for tea and supper. Okay, Belle?'

Belle snorted and shook her head, making that 'mp-mp-mm' noise that only very large black ladies can make without sounding daft. 'Thanks for the kind words, Lars,' she said, in a West Indian accent that sounded like honey dropping off a spoon into a bowl of cream. 'But I think we know it's not *gender*!'

There was a burst of tittering that lasted until Dr Ferris killed it. 'Before we degenerate into a book club . . .' she said, and I saw a couple of people frown as they tried to follow the thread. *Book club*? '. . . does anyone have any questions?'

I put my hand up and heard the tittering break out again.

'This isn't a classroom, Alison,' she said.

I pulled my hand down again. 'I've got some,' I said. 'But I don't want to waste everyone's time. Maybe I should just ask you.'

'Oh?' said Dr Ferris. 'My time not being as valuable as, say, Amana's.'

Bitch, mouthed Surraya again, on another hijab swing.

'Of course not,' I said. 'Only you said to bring things to you.'

'In the meeting, naturally,' said Dr Ferris.

'Don't worry, Ali,' said Dr F. 'What is it you want to know?'

'Couple of things,' I said. 'One, can I group people together willy-nilly? I mean, if three patients are all free at the one time, can I get them together for a class or do I have to check that they want to or are allowed to?'

Dr F began, 'That's a very g—'

'Of course you can,' said Dr Ferris. 'With permission, of course. But there's no overtime available simply because you try to eke out your work by over-focusing.'

'Great,' I said. I saw Surraya move her head yet again and it boosted me, even though I didn't look. 'And two. Is Julia's dad actually dead?'

This time the silence was more like a freeze-frame.

'I beg your pardon?' said Dr Ferris.

'Off the back of what you were saying before,' I ploughed on, 'about not . . . what was it? Bolstering her confabulations? Well, I kind of didn't know what to say because I didn't know if he was dead of natural causes and she just pretends she killed him or if he's not even dead and she's confabulating the whole shebang.'

'Patients' confidential personal circumstances should have no reason to come up in the course of any of the services you offer,' Dr Ferris said.

'He walked out shortly before her admittance,' Dr F said.

I was pleased, in a nasty way, to see that *she* could change colour too. Dr Ferris was in salmon, coral and brown today, and as her face turned an angry pink with suppressed annoyance, the scarf and cardie clashed pretty badly.

'Thanks,' I said.

'Anything else?' said Dr Ferris.

I smiled at her. 'I know where to find you.'

Then the nurses and the rest of them started folding the

seats that were set out and stashing them on a trolley that Amana the kitchen assistant rolled away.

'Bloody Nora, Ali!' Lars said, once the office door had been shut smartly at our heels.

'Bloody Nora, yourself,' I said. 'She's hellish. How long have you worked here? How can you stand it?'

'It's a laugh,' said Marion. 'It doesn't get in the way as long as you're firm. She doesn't even know she's doing it.'

'But what's she like with the patients?' I said. 'I can't imagine turning to her and telling her all my worries. And her daughter!'

'The ice princess can't get frozen by the ice queen,' said Surraya, who was coming along behind us. 'It's a fair fight. Oh, hey, good challenge in there, by the way, Marion.'

'Oh, yeah,' I said, remembering. 'Why shouldn't you be sitting with Rosa?'

'Shift charge nurse should be doing admin and leaving the grunt to the greenies,' Marion said. 'But I've been here the whole time Rosa's been in and she knows me.'

'She'd moan if we were doing it too,' said another – one of the 'greenies'? – who was walking along arm in arm with Surraya. 'I'll never forget her saying it straight out that time when it was old Ted.'

'Yvonne, isn't it?' I said, pleased when she nodded.

'She said,' Yvonne went on, 'that sitting by the bedside of an unconscious patient waiting for them to die was a waste of staff resources.'

She was watching me carefully but I didn't have to act my shock. 'Seriously?' I said. 'She reckoned someone in here could just lie there and die alone?'

Yvonne gave me a smile. I had passed the test. 'She said, "What is the benefit of this use of a nurse's time?"'

'What did *you* say?' I asked.

Yvonne drew herself up. 'I said, "Anyone who has to ask that question probably wouldn't understand the answer." Said it loud and clear. In my head. Nah, I said I'd wait to hear the new protocol from Lars and Marion. That shut her up.'

'You know what else I didn't understand,' I said. We had got to my treatment room now and I stopped at the door. 'What's she got against book clubs?'

'No clue,' said Marion.

But Belle, who hadn't spoken yet, let out a deep chuckle. 'That was all my fault, sweetness.' I looked around but it seemed that 'sweetness' was me. 'Book clubs were in her mind on account of Oprah. Because she was looking at me. Because she can't look at me and see a nurse. She looks at me and sees B-L-A-C-K.'

I gave that nervous laugh you do when you don't know whether you can laugh or not. Then another thought struck me. 'Is that what's wrong with the patient too? The one that won't let you . . . whatever it is?'

Now they were all laughing.

'Lord! No, that's not the problem with little Miss Drew. She only just came in – six stone and eating tissues – and who does Dr F get to sit with her at mealtimes and make sure she gets her shake down and keeps it there?' Belle spread her arms and displayed herself. She really was pretty impressive. 'Only her worst living nightmare!'

'You're a beautiful woman, Belladonna,' said Lars.

'I'm two beautiful women,' Belle said, and sashayed off along the corridor, swinging her hips so hard they shivered, still laughing.

'Bloody wish I came from somewhere where fat was

fabulous,' Yvonne said. 'Wait till you see Belle's husband, Ali. He's drop-dead gorgeous. And guess what mine got me last Valentine's Day? A free month's intro at Ballantyne's. Bloody gym membership. Bastard.'

I looked at Lars, wondering if he minded being the only man, listening to women bitch up their husbands all day.

He read my mind. 'It's training. When I get my hands on another woman I'm gonny be an expert. "She's too thin, love. You're younger than her too. Let's go and see the new Jane Austen, then get a bottle of wine to take home."'

'Hey,' I said. 'Some men actually like historical drama.'

'Oh, yeah, so they do,' said Lars. 'Except, no, they don't. How long have you been married?'

'Twenty years.'

'Poor sod. That's four films and the six-hour BBC thing he's had to sit through.'

'Don't listen to him, Ali,' said Marion. 'But don't make your man watch Jane Austen, eh?'

I was happy. As I let myself into my room to pick up Sylvie's slippers and take them to her, planning an art class that would make the boys laugh and help Jo and Harriet smile if I was lucky, the last six months faded. I was wearing my whites again with my hair scraped back and I was joking with my workmates. I was in a big, warm, clean house, even if I only worked there. There was a master-chart and an integrated schedule, and I was part of it. Even the last three days seemed more like a bad dream now. My husband was a kind man who watched my soppy films. My kid was a good boy who only rolled his eyes because he didn't know how lucky he was to have me. Yes, at that minute of that day, I was actually feeling happy.

Chapter 11

Sylvie was in bed. I had to fight the thought that she was stuck there to keep her feet warm because I'd binned her slippers, but two minutes after I arrived, Yvonne came trotting in after me, already talking.

'Sorry, pet. Big mess over on the acute. Did you think I'd run away and joined the . . .' Then she saw me. I had taken Sylvie's hands and held them up as she swung her legs out and got to her feet. We were standing like two dancers about to start a minuet. Me in my whites and Sylvie in a poly-cotton nightie that fell to mid-calf, washed out and pilled. 'How did you get her up?' she said.

I shrugged. Walking slowly backwards, I led Sylvie towards her bathroom door. She was gazing through me at about the level of my collarbone but she moved smoothly, no shuffling. She didn't react when her bare feet left the carpet and hit the bathroom lino.

'Well, I've seen everything now,' Yvonne said. 'Ali, I don't

142

suppose you'd get her washed and changed, would you? I'm already dead late.'

'I'd love to,' I said, and I meant it.

'On the quiet, like?'

'My PVG's through.'

'Eh?' said Yvonne. 'That was quick. No, I mean don't tell Lars. I've got my appraisal coming.'

'Lars?' I said, taking my eye off Sylvie for the first time and looking over my shoulder.

'Aye, aye, but he's not your boss,' Yvonne said. 'I'll swing back. Case you get in a fankle.' But she was already walking away.

I led Sylvie to the toilet and pushed on her shoulder until she sank down onto the closed lid. Then I moved close and cradled her head against my stomach, stroking her hair back, trying to work out what to do with her.

'This is a new one on me too, darlin',' I said. I thought I could feel her resting against me, but maybe that was the way of it. Maybe she'd slump against any object close enough. I leaned over and felt around her waist, through the nightie. She wasn't wearing a nappy so presumably she used the loo. 'Upsy,' I said. I held both her hands in one and got her nightie hitched up and her knickers pulled down. Then I opened the lid and guided her down again. 'You needed that,' I said, listening to her peeing. 'You must have been busting.' When the trickle turned to drops and then to silence, I waited. Then I whirled a big wad of paper off the roll and looked at her. I didn't fancy my chances of coping with the nightie, the loo roll and Sylvie herself, so I grabbed the hem and said, 'Hands up!' Nothing happened. I tugged gently upwards pulling her arms into the tent of fabric. They fell hard when I had it clear of them but landed harmlessly in her lap.

She was as pale as a candle, her skin so soft and crumpled, it made me think of newspaper after a bonfire, burned away to a billowing grey gossamer, too fragile to touch. And she was thin. Her shoulder bones showed through and her ribs. Even her hip bones poked out on either side of the small drooping pouch of her stomach. I needed to speak to that physio: Sylvie should be working her muscles. I wondered if she could cope with a swimming-pool. If I could lead her around by her hands, neck-deep in water, working against the resistance. Or would she sink?

I ran a basin of hot water and soaked the flannel that was screwed in a knot behind the taps. I soaped it, nasty supermarket liquid soap in a pump bottle but it would do until I could bring her something better. I started with her face. And when I drew the flannel away to rinse it, what I saw made my heart leap. She had closed her eyes to stop the soap getting into them.

'You're still in there somewhere, Sylvie, aren't you?'

I rubbed her neck, ears, arms and hands, everything coming back to me. Rinsing the soap out of hairy armpits was new, but I couldn't see shaving them without making her uncomfy. 'Your feet'll do since they had a major wash yesterday,' I said. 'Now what about the fiddly bits?' That's what I used to say to Angelo. A big bath meant hair and back and arms and legs all scrubbed pink. In between times if he wasn't mucky it was feet, pits and fiddly bits. But this was a thirty-year-old woman.

While I was trying to decide, Sylvie started shivering and goose pimples broke out on her arms. 'Right,' I said. 'That's that decided.' I took the bathrobe off the back of the door and wrapped it round her while I brushed her hair and, just to entertain myself more than anything, twisted it into a French plait. I always had scrunchies on my wrists when I was working, ready to scrape clients' hair out of the way of my products and I worked one onto the tiny tail of thistledown left at the end of the plait.

Her wardrobe had day clothes in it, even though I had only ever seen her in night things. Slouchy socks that were easy to pull on and wide linen trousers with elastic waists. She had soft cosy camisoles instead of bras – I couldn't imagine getting a bra onto her – and a selection of chenille jumpers with wide necks and flared sleeves. Even so, I was panting by the time I had her in her chair.

'You look fantastic, Sylvie,' I said. The trousers were pink and the jumper was green with pink flecks. I changed the scrunchie for a yellow one to match her socks and put her new slippers on. I took out my phone and snapped a picture. Either of her or of all my hard work, it was hard to say. It was probably against a hundred and fifty regulations but I wasn't going to show anyone. It was just for me. She looked about seventeen, in the bad light with the flash off. Like a bookish seventeen-year-old, who studied for piano exams and didn't smoke.

'Is that who you are?' I asked her. 'Is that who you were when you came in?'

She breathed in and out and stared at a spot behind me.

'Well, what will we do now?' I asked her. 'I can't go till Yvonne's been back and checked my handiwork. What do you fancy?'

I didn't have any of my kit with me, even if I'd wanted to make Sylvie sit through any more of my efforts after I'd just learned on the job, washing her. I looked in my bag.

'Oh, here's a thought. Draw me something, eh?' I took out my pad of paper and a black marker pen. I thought she could do with all the help she could get and it was a good size to put

145

in her hand. I printed 'SYLVIE' at the top of the sheet, then wrapped her fingers round the pen until she held it in her fist like a kid with a crayon. I put the paper under the tip and held it steady. 'Sylvie? Can you draw me a house, a tree and a person? Can you do that for me?'

The pen was leaking ink in a spreading blot as she held it pressed against the paper. Then her hand relaxed and it trailed away in faint jags and dots towards the corner.

'Come on, eh?' I said. 'A house. A tree. And a person.' I lifted her hand back into place again. 'Come on, Sylvie. You can walk and sit and eat and hold your pee, even when your nurse is late. Come on, sweetheart.'

The blot spread again, so I grabbed the paper and started to move it away. But as I did so a thick black line started to spool out across the white and – I wasn't imagining this – Sylvie was watching it. And I wasn't imagining *this* either. When the line was three inches long, she took a tighter grip on the pen and pushed it. The line turned a corner and then another and a third until she had made a square. A very small square in the top left-hand corner of the paper but she had done it.

'Is that a house?' I said. 'Can you put a roof on it? A door? How about some windows?' And I held my breath as Sylvie lifted the pen and set it down a quarter-inch above the little shape. She pulled the pen down until she had made a slash right through it. Then she lifted her hand and slashed through it again, left to right. She let the pen drop out of her grasp and I bent and snatched it up before the ink could bleed into her pale-green carpet.

'Sorry,' I said. 'I didn't mean to nag you. I'm really sorry, sweet girl. Here, let me take that paper away.' I had got it hidden, the pen capped and stowed, when Yvonne came back.

'Hey, look at you!' she said, chucking Sylvie under the chin. 'It's been a while since I've seen her in anything but her nightie.'

'Yeah, sorry,' I said. 'Bit of a nerve, waltzing in here thinking I know better than folk that've been here years.'

Yvonne turned to me with her mouth hanging open. She had a weak chin and small eyes behind her narrow glasses and the expression made her look vacant. She was anything but. 'What the hell did you just hear, Ali?' she asked me. 'Because what I *said* was meant to be a compliment.'

'Sorry,' I said again.

She walked over and put her hand on my arm. 'Get your chin up,' she said. 'You'll need it.' It sounded like a threat but I didn't want to do it again – hear something that hadn't been said. 'Did Dr F get a chance to talk to you?' she asked me. She moved her hand down to under my elbow and drew me away, right out of the room.

'What about?' I said.

'Standard,' said Yvonne. 'New staff get a counselling session. Kind of like a vaccination more than anything. There's some pretty manipulative individuals wind up in here, you know. The ana-mias can have you tied round yourself if you're not careful.'

'Counselling?' I said. 'I don't need counselling. There's nothing wrong with me.'

'Just so the doc can see where your sore spots are,' said Yvonne.

'I don't have any "sore spots",' I said. 'And I need to go back to Sylvie's room. I've left my bag in there.'

Yvonne finally let go of my arm and stopped dragging me. Where was she taking me anyway? Straight to Dr F's office to be put under the microscope? 'Just as a matter of interest,' she said, 'how old were you when it happened?'

I couldn't speak. There was no way she could know that anything had ever happened to me.

'Was it your mum or your dad?' she said. 'That abandoned you.'

'It was both,' I said. 'But I was in my thirties.'

'Can't be that, then,' she said. 'What is it, Ali? What are you so sorry for?'

I was never going to answer her but, still, the clip-clop of Dr Ferris approaching filled me with relief. She came round the corner of the dining-room corridor and stopped two paces before she bumped into us.

'At last,' she said. 'Yvonne, you should be in Group. Alison, you need to go to Julia and see what you can do. I can't even speak to you yet. I'll try to calm down and you can come to see me before lunch. Twelve fifteen in my office.'

'What's happened?' I said.

'You and I need to have a long conversation about boundaries,' she said quietly. 'I thought, given your experience, that you could be trusted to work independently but perhaps it would be more suitable for me to draw up a rota and set some targets for you.'

'I don't know what you're—' I said.

'Go to Julia now,' said Dr Ferris. 'I'll talk to you later.'

I bounded up the stairs with my heart a high, painful lump and my face red with the shame of it. I hadn't been spoken to like that since I was at school. And if I was so useless and had made Julia worse, I was the last one she should be sending to fix whatever it was. I gave a quick rap on the door and went in.

'Oh, Jesus!' I said.

She was sitting on her bed, with a pair of scissors in her hand and a lapful of her bushy orange hair. She had hacked it

148

off in handfuls, all over her head, only missing the odd tuft at the nape of her neck where she couldn't quite reach. She'd made no attempt to follow the curve of her skull either. Some of it was down to the scalp and some of it was an inch long.

'What do you think?' she said.

I didn't know whether it was tears or laughter burbling up inside me, only that if I let it go, it would come out in hysterical shrieks. 'I was right,' I said. 'It's better. You need some blusher but you're halfway there.'

'What the actual fuck are you on about?' Julia said, scrambling to her feet. 'This face needs all the camouflage it can get.' She stalked into her bathroom. 'Oh! Oh, fuck, no!' she screamed. 'Stupid ugly shit!' I heard a sound I was pretty sure was the scissors hitting the mirror. She had covered her face with both hands by the time I came up behind her and took her in my arms.

'What have I *done*?' She was sobbing into my neck. She had had a bath anyway. She smelt of lemon and coconut.

'Sit down on the bog seat,' I said, 'and give me ten minutes. I promise you I can make it okay.'

I'm not a hairdresser but some of it rubbed off, all those years in Face Value, and I set to with as much confidence as I could scrape together, knowing she needed it, knowing that the sight of her bald head had touched something that lay deep under whatever was wrong with her – her histrionic personality: it touched a wee girl that just wanted to be pretty. See, that's the thing that used to bug me about Marco. He never said it but he always believed that what I did was shallow. 'Because you care so much what things look like, Ali,' he said to me once, like it made me less than him, who cared so much what things tasted like instead.

'Now, who told you you were ugly?' I asked her, as I clipped away, taking off the long hanks and ruffling up what was left. I was only making conversation. I wasn't aware of Yvonne's words still rattling around in my head.

'Who didn't?' she said. 'My mum, my granny, teachers at school.'

'Get away!' I said. 'What the hell school was this, then?'

'Don't try to make me laugh,' she said. 'They didn't say it as such, but we did *The Boy Friend* and I wanted to be a flapper, but they cast me as Madame Dubonnet.'

'Is she ugly? I've never seen it.'

'She's old. Then we did *Macbeth*. And I was a witch.'

'Well, there's hardly any parts for girls in—'

'And the other two who were witches had fake noses and warts and blacked-out teeth. But the drama teacher just backcombed my hair and said I'd do.'

'What a bitch!' I said. 'But see? I'm right about your hair.' She said nothing. I was clipping away at the back of her neck now. It was a shame, really, because it was the only place there was any length left at all, but an extreme mullet wouldn't help her, and I had meant what I'd said the day before: she had a lovely head and her hair grew in a perfect butterfly over the tendons on her nape. Mine grows like a crash helmet so I always notice. 'And at least you're not called Dido,' I said. My heart swelled when she rewarded me with a soft chuckle.

'Right, then. Where's your make-up?' I asked her, when I was done. I knew she'd have some. No way she'd ignore the potential to spend so much money online. But I was surprised when she bent and hauled the basket out from under her basin.

'Half of Boots in here,' I said, rummaging. 'I'm confiscating the green eye shadow. And this lipstick's hellish. Shut your eyes and don't argue.'

When she turned her face up to me I thought of Angelo when he was little and needed a nose-blow. He had never minded it. Never fought me like some I'd seen, twisting away from their mums and leaving trails over their cheeks.

'I'm plucking your eyebrows,' I told her. She winced like clockwork at every pinch but she let me. And she was biddable about looking down and then up as I turned her lashes black.

'Tilda Swinton doesn't wear mascara,' was all she said.

'Tilda Swinton is freakishly beautiful,' I told her, 'and even she's touch and go. Ordinary mortals like you and me need all the help we can get.'

I went to town with the contour and the highlight, and by the time I was choosing a lipstick I had surprised myself. Her beautiful head, her jaw and her temples, her huge eyes with the privet-hedge eyebrows gone, her razor's edge cheekbones and, yes, yes, her glorious haughty nose were astonishing now they were out from inside that flaming nest where they'd been hiding.

'You have no idea on this earth what lipstick suits you, do you?' I said, throwing out a purple nightmare and a crimson shimmering lip-gloss. I mixed some peach blusher with a slick of balm, just to give her the idea and stroked it on with a brush.

'Okay,' I said, raking my fingers through her hair one last time. 'You ready? You will never be a pretty girl, Julia, because you're stunning and magnificent. So much better than pretty any day. Bloom fades. But bones like you've got last for ever. You'll be even more gorgeous when you're sixty than you are now.'

'Are you ever going to shut up and show me?' she said.

I looked behind the mirror above the basin and saw it was only hanging on a cord, so I lifted it off and held it in front and slightly above her.

She said nothing. She turned this way and that. She ran her fingers over her head. Then she leaned forward and looked at what I had done to her eyes.

'I look like a drag act,' she said. 'You're a bitch for getting my hopes up.' She stood up and was suddenly so close to me that I took a step back, holding the mirror like a shield. 'Put that bloody mirror down before I smash it.'

When I lowered it, leaning it against the wall and stepping away, she pounced, wrapping her arms around me and squeezing me so hard my bra squeaked. 'I'm joking, you moron,' she said. 'I look fantastic. I'm going to *kill* my mum.'

'I can't actually breathe,' I said, and she let go, laughing.

'*And* my granny. Telling me I was ugly! Will you come in every morning and fix me?'

'No, but I'll teach you,' I said. 'Now get dressed and come downstairs, eh?'

'Can I have the first lesson today?'

'I've got a full morning and Dr Ferris before lunch,' I said, but Dr Ferris was already on her way towards me as I spoke, stalking through the corridors on her high heels. Both of us heard the smack-smack-smack of her climbing the stairs, then listened to the soft thump-thump of her coming along the corridor.

'Bye-bye, gotta go, catch you soon,' Julia said, and then the doctor was crossing her bedroom floor and sweeping the bathroom door wide. I stood in front of Julia, without thinking.

'Alison. My office. Now.' She was even angrier than before. I stepped to one side and put my arm on Julia's shoulder. I knew I was beaming.

The doctor registered the transformation with a flash of her eyes. I saw it. I saw her pupils dilate.

Then Julia spoke. 'She cut the rest of it off. She cut it all off. She's scalped me. It's all gone. She cut it off.' She was rocking back and forward on the toilet seat. Rocking so far back that her head banged off the wall behind the cistern and the cistern lid scraped and clanked every time her shoulders hit it.

Dr Ferris turned away. She pulled a mobile from her back pocket and spoke into it, very calmly. 'Lars, urgent to Julia's room, please.'

I cupped the back of Julia's head so it was my fingers taking the brunt. Now my wedding ring was hurting us both but I couldn't move. I was frozen. Because in her other hand Dr Ferris held my sketchpad, open at Sylvie's drawing, her fingers white and her nails red with the strain of how hard she clutched it.

———————

Lars was there within a minute and, soundlessly, he got Julia on her feet and away from all the hard edges of the bathroom. She pulled her head back as if to butt him in the face but he changed his hold and tsk-tsked at her.

'I like your hair,' he said. 'But you've wrecked your mascara.'

'Alison!' said Dr Ferris, once she was sure Lars had it in hand. 'Outside.' She stood four square in front of me and held the sketchpad up against her chest. 'What's the meaning of this?'

'I'm not with you, Doc,' I said.

'My husband is "Doc",' she said, as if the word was a slur. 'And don't buy time. Why did you write Sylvie's name on this doodle and leave it in her room?'

'Actually, I left it in my bag,' I said. 'And my bag was zipped shut.'

'Until I opened it to see whom it belonged to.' That was reasonable enough, I supposed. If it had been me I'd have taken it to the staff kitchen and got a witness to watch me opening it but she was the boss. 'I shall repeat my question for the final time: why did you write Sylvie's name on your doodle?'

I searched her face but I was sure she wasn't being clever-clever, trying to catch me out. She genuinely had not the slightest suspicion that Sylvie's name was on there for the reason people's names are always on pictures, from handprints bound for the front of the fridge to Rembrandt's last self-portrait.

'I meant to write notes on the page,' I said. 'But I never got round to it. The doodle doesn't mean anything.'

'Informal private notes about a patient?' she said, in the same tone as she'd said 'Doc'.

'Sylvie's not my patient,' I said. 'She's my client. Like you said at the meeting, I'm not a therapist.'

'Sylvie and the other residents are under my care,' said Dr Ferris, 'and you are in my employment. Any "notes" you make must be entered into the patients' files after proper cross-signing by a member of the medical team.'

'But how would I get them out again?'

'Why would you want to?'

I frowned at her. I didn't try to tell her *her* job. 'To check back what products I used or what tint mix had worked or not worked,' I said. 'To see when I'd done the last treatment and when it'd fall due again. To be able to tell you all that I'd done to help.'

'What are you talking about? Help what?'

'If you said someone had slept through the night and I'd

154

given them an aromatherapy massage, or if someone was upset and I'd—'

'Told her to cut off all her hair?' She turned and walked away from me. 'Ask one of the enrolled nurses to give you the Bible and you can spend the rest of today trying to bring yourself to a better understanding of what goes on here and what the true scope of your role really is.' She turned back and threw the sketchpad at me, like a Frisbee. Or a Chinese star, maybe. Unfortunately for her mood, I caught it. 'After you clean the hair from Julia's room. I need to go and make a written report to deliver to her parents about the incident.'

'Her parents?' I said. 'Did her dad come back then?'

'Be very careful,' Dr Ferris said.

As I watched her walk away, her perfectly cut trousers winking at the knee with each stride, the hems lifting to show the polished tips of her heels and the pale leather of her insteps then falling free again, I said to myself, 'If I start being very careful, that'll make one of us, Missus. Because you are all over the place. What the hell – what, as Julia would say, the actual fuck – is going on here?'

Chapter 12

The 'Bible' was four ring binders of Care Scotland protocols, NHS guidelines, Best Practice reports from NICE, Howell Hall house rules and leaflet after leaflet tucked into plastic sleeves about everything from alcohol-abuse warning signs to dealing with dementia. Between the bleeding obvious that an alien landing from Mars wouldn't need to be told and the total codswallop that nobody – not even the pen-pusher who wrote it – could explain if their life depended on it, it made for a long day.

Lars brought me a cup of tea and a huge cupcake halfway through the afternoon. 'It's the anniversary of Hinny's divorce,' he said. 'She always pushes the boat out.'

'Tell me what's going on out there in the real world,' I said. 'I feel like I've been stuck in here for a week.'

'This is for telling Julia to cut her hair, is it?'

I didn't think so. I was pretty sure this was for whatever rule Dr Ferris reckoned I'd broken by writing 'Sylvie' on a piece of paper with a square and two lines drawn on it in marker pen.

But I didn't want to say that. Not even to Lars. I wanted to take it home and google the life out of it first.

So I shrugged. 'For one,' I said, 'I didn't tell her to cut her hair. I suggested she get a haircut. And for two she liked it. She bloody *liked* it until Fanny Ice Arse came. Then she created blue murder.'

'What did I tell you?' he said, but everyone had told me so much I had no idea what he meant. I shrugged again. 'Watch out for the personality disorders. Julia's very sick. She'll manipulate you any way she can. Of course, she pretended she hated her hair and made out you'd traumatized her.'

'She was fine,' I said, 'when I was doing it. She was absolutely fine.'

'Of course she was,' said Lars. 'She had all your attention, all your focus. She'd have loved it.'

'Yeah, but . . .' I began, and managed to stop myself. He was a psychiatric nurse and I'd blagged my way into this job. If he thought it was a sign of illness to want a bit of pampering, I shouldn't argue.

'And as for what's going on out in the world,' he said. 'There's another update from the pathologist. We know he's not a vagrant because he'd had about a million pounds' worth of dentistry done just before he died. Hadn't even finished it. He still had a temporary crown on one side.' He gave a huge grin, showing off the empty gums where his molars should have been.

I could feel my colour rising, flustered as I was by his lack of discomfort. I changed the subject before he could ask me what was wrong. 'Can I ask your advice about something?' He nodded and I plunged on: 'My kid, my son. He's fifteen and he's had a bit of a knock. Some girl asked him out, then sent all her

157

friends along to laugh when he turned up for the date.' Lars whistled. 'He's taking it really badly.'

'First ever rejection?' said Lars. 'And no Morrissey to help like I had.' I laughed. 'It *is* his first ever rejection, isn't it?' he said. 'You're still married to his dad, eh? No losses?'

'Grandparents,' I said. I blurted it out so hard that Lars cocked his head, interested.

'Recent?' he said. 'Sorry, if it was one of yours.'

'Oh, no, it was ten years ago,' I said. 'But it was complicated. That's all.' I took a breath and tried to get hold of the conversation again, tried to steer it away. 'And he was pretty low anyway yesterday.'

'Oh?'

'He had his phone stolen and it was the one that was used to call the cops about the body.'

It was out before I'd decided to say it.

Lars had been nodding along, but it took a couple of blinks for him to take that in.

'This is just between you and me, right?' I said. 'Except I'm surprised you haven't had it from your pal already. Whatsisname.'

'Boney,' said Lars. 'What makes you think it was stolen?'

I thought back over everything and couldn't remember who had said that or why we'd thought it.

'Because you live there, right?' Lars went on. 'Across the road? Does your son ever go to the abbey? Because it said on the news it was a hang-out.'

'What are you getting at?'

'What? Oh, come off it, Ali! I'm not saying anything about your boy! Just that, if you live there and he goes there, maybe he dropped it. And if someone was over there and saw something

158

suspicious and spotted a phone just lying . . . Well, of course they'd want to use the lost phone and keep it anonymous. Wouldn't you?'

Relief rushed in and filled me until I felt I might start floating. 'Oh!' I said. 'Oh, my God, you've no idea the nightmares I've been having. I thought he was *lying* about it being lost. I thought he was lying to the police and he *knew* something about the bones.'

'Why would you think that?'

I stared at him. Because he looked at the police lights that night and said, 'I'd just about given up, as it goes.' But I didn't say it. And I didn't even say, 'Because he's too upset for it to be a stand-up from a girl he hardly knew,' either. What I did say – changing the subject again – was 'Something suspicious? Like what?'

'Bones breaking the surface when the flood went down,' Lars said. 'That's the obvious thing. You're right, though. Nobody's ever said it. We've no idea how the person who made the call knew the body was there, have we?'

'Kind of gets in the way of saying they found Angel's phone lying there and grabbed it,' I said.

'Angel's your boy?' said Lars.

'Angelo.'

'Unless . . .' He looked at his watch and started. 'Bugger it, I'm late.'

'Unless what?' I asked him.

'Unless it was the killer,' he said. 'Unless the killer's been visiting the grave all the time the bones were in there, knowing he'd have to report them sometime, and then he sees a phone and thinks it's a sign. TTFN, Ali.'

And he was gone, just leaving me with it. A killer coming to

159

gloat over the site of his crime. Bones breaking the surface. Angelo over there all those nights on his own.

'How you feeling?' I asked, as I edged round his bedroom door.

'Shit, thanks. You?' he said, from under his duvet.

The room was beyond stale. It was foetid. My fingers itched to open the window. I sat down on the end of his bed and he snatched his feet away as if the touch of my hip had burned them. 'What have you got planned for the weekend?' I said.

'Skiing,' Angelo muttered. 'Surfing. Scuba-diving. Might go to the opera.'

'You're a cheeky wee toerag,' I said, grabbing an ankle through the bedclothes and squeezing it. 'Do you want us to take you to get a new phone or will I just give you cash and you go yourself?'

'I don't need a phone,' he said. 'I've got no one I want to talk to.'

'Now, look, Angel,' I said. 'I'm sorry you got hurt. I'd like to track her down and tan her arse for her, if you'd tell me her name.'

'Her arse is tanned already,' Angelo said. 'She's got a sunbed.'

'That's more like it,' I said. 'That sounds more like you. And I'm going to choose to think that was a guess, by the way, and you've never seen her arse.' But I made a note to tell Marco to buy some condoms and hand them over. 'I'm not here to talk about that, anyway. I want to talk about the abbey. The times you were over at the abbey.'

'I'm not going back,' he said, 'if that's what's bothering you.'

'But when you *were* there. Did you ever see anyone hanging around? I mean, did you ever see the same person twice?'

'Mum, just *leave* it!' he said, nearly shouting. 'I'm not going back. I don't want a phone. I'm not asking you for anything. Just leave me *alone*.'

'Oh, okay, I'll leave you alone,' I said. 'Except for this one thing: I'm never going to leave you alone, Angel. You're my son. I'm your mother. You are stuck with me asking you stuff and worrying about you and being right in your face whether you want me there or not until the day I pop my clogs. Me *and* your dad. Sorry, kid. That's a family.'

'Aye, right,' he said. 'Our perfect family.'

I let go of his ankle and laid a hand instead on his arm. He swatted me away. 'Is this about Gran and Granddad?' I was casting around wildly now, but I hadn't forgotten him saying that Billie had been in their swimming pool. 'Just because they reckoned they'd done their job and I'd graduated, you have to believe I'd never do that to you.'

He was moving. He sat up and shook back damp hair. 'You haven't got a bloody clue, Mum, have you? And you think I'm as clueless as you are.'

'What does that mean?' I stared at him, his red eyes and his picked spots.

'If you have to ask the question . . .' he said.

'Yeah, yeah. I wouldn't understand the answer. That's the second time I've heard that today. Okay, answer this question instead. Why weren't you surprised when the cops found the bones?'

'Bones?' he said. He shook his head and did that breathing-out laugh. 'Not a clue.'

So I left him, shut the door on the stale air and misery, went into the kitchen and pulled the magnetic notepad down off the fridge door.

So many notes, over the years. The early ones had love hearts and kisses on them, then they were dashed off in shorthand code as we juggled our jobs and the baby: *ETA? Defrost 8 mins*. Lately I'd been careful to compose them just right: kisses again and nothing too breezy. Still, I had never hesitated this long. I could text Marco, but he'd call back. He always did. And for some reason I couldn't fathom, I didn't want to talk to him. 'Gone to big T,' I wrote in the end. 'Need to PaT. KO. Love you, Ax'.

That should do it. It would make him happy to see me back to my old ways, off to the big Tesco to push a trolley, always my cure for a rough day. And he'd know what I meant by KO, not OK. He was always better at talking to Angel than I was. Loved his daddy's boy.

It shone out across the dark like a mega-church and I could feel myself unwinding as soon as I bumped the trolley over the corded mat between the double doors and into the Technicolor burst of flowers and magazines and the pumped-out scent of cinnamon rolls. I took my coat off and stowed it in the baby seat, checked there were plenty of hot chicken portions in the display for when I'd finished and headed for the books.

I didn't even need to buy anything, just touch and wonder. Seven quid for two good paperbacks, like the bras and pants for a tenner a set. A client bored me to death once about why I should shop local and sign some online petition, but nowhere else made me quite as happy in quite the same way. And it was guaranteed to keep Marco and Angelo away, too, so it was all mine for the taking.

I put pâté, raisin loaf and coconut milk in my trolley, feeling a little bit of the last six months shake loose and lift away from me in flakes, like the dark grease from a roasting pan when it's plunged into deep hot water. I could even face the cosmetics aisle again. At first, after I'd lost my wholesale supplier, I couldn't stand trawling up and down buying this mass-produced muck, then I couldn't afford it and I was buying litre bottles of body lotion, putting it on my face and pressing a flannel over it before bed. When I got up to the toilet one time, Marco, sitting in the living room with a bottle of beer half drunk, said, 'Why's your face so shiny? You not feeling well?' I said nothing. It was shiny every night, as he'd know if he ever came to bed, because I was saving the money he spent on beer.

There was another woman in the make-up aisle with me. I walked past her, then something about her face made me turn back. She was testing lipsticks on the back of her hand, opening tubes and drawing stripes on herself. She had a phone crooked against her shoulder.

'Calm down,' she was saying. A haughty voice, plenty tobacco in it. 'I shall hang up if you don't calm down and talk properly.' She found a shade she liked and smeared it over her mouth, then looked around for a mirror. I was sure I knew her, I thought, as she wheeled briefly to face me. I pretended to read the back of the night-cream box I was holding and kept listening.

'How short is short?' she said. 'You haven't shaved it off, have you?'

Her face was definitely familiar, strong and ugly, and the way she stood, knees locked in that over-straight way and her high bosom thrown out.

'Julius Caesar?' she said, with a smoky laugh. 'That's supposed to be a reasonable stylistic choice, is it?'

I turned away and picked up another pot of cream from a higher shelf, jumping when the censor went off. This was one of the expensive ones.

'What?' said the woman. 'I didn't hear you. I'm in the middle of a supermarket with God knows what going on.' I could feel her eyes on my back. 'Oh, don't be ridiculous. It'll grow Ju-ju. God knows, it can't look worse. No, of course I won't sue them. You must learn to act with a little more— . . . I shan't stay on the line if you're going to be silly. I'm hanging up. Goodbye.'

I gave her a minute, then turned round. She was still twisting this way and that, looking for the mirror she wanted. I scrabbled in my bag and held out a vanity compact to her. A pretty embellished thing Angelo had got me for Christmas. I knew he had probably pocketed it in some accessories shop but I treasured it anyway.

'Ha,' said the woman. 'Very civil of you. These places used to have mirrors and tissues, didn't they? Gad! Horrific. I look like a tart.'

I was sure now. This was Julia's mother.

'Did one of your girlfriends get the haircut from hell?' I said. 'Sorry. I couldn't help overhearing.'

'My daughter,' she said. 'She's boarding and there seems to have been a sort of pyjama party that got out of hand. She's done a bit of a DIY Samson job, apparently.'

'Oh dear,' I said. I couldn't think of a single way to keep this conversation going.

'No loss. She had perpetrated a hideous home dye job anyway and she takes after her late lamented father in the follicular department.'

I hoped I'd managed to hide the leap of interest in my face. 'I'm very sorry for your loss,' I said.

'What?' She was raking through the lipsticks again.

'Late father, you said.'

'Oh!' she said. 'Not a bit of it. He left no will so I scooped the lot. No loss at all.'

'And your daughter's away at boarding school, is she?' I said. 'That must be difficult at such a time.'

'What?' she said again. She was just about to tell me to get lost and stop pestering her. I knew it.

'You're working from the wrong palette, you know,' I said, moving closer. 'You should be steering clear of bluish reds and pinks, with your colouring. A tomato-red would be much more flattering.'

'Tomato?' she said, with another rasping laugh. 'Bet they don't call it that!'

I handed her a tissue and started riffling through the stand, ignoring the ones she'd broken open, looking for what I wanted. 'Here you go,' I said, seizing one and handing it over. 'Try this.'

'November Sunset,' she said. 'See what I mean? Not a tomato in sight.' But she cracked the seal and smeared it on her lips, rubbing them together to spread it. She peered in my mirror and grunted. 'You've done me a favour,' she said. 'I look almost human.'

'You look very striking,' I said. The yellow-red was better against her drinker's complexion and her tombstone teeth. She really was a remarkably unattractive woman. So much so that she had come out the other end somehow and I couldn't take my eyes off her.

'Well, thank you,' she said. She gave me a little nod of dismissal and started to move away.

'You could say it with coffee,' I said. 'I'm going up to the caff for a sit-down.'

She frowned. Maybe she thought I was trying to pick her up. I smiled and walked away, then held my grin in check as I heard her coming after me.

'I'm headed that way myself,' she said. 'Meeting someone, but I'm early. So why not? Why ever not?' She had pocketed the lipstick, I saw. I left my trolley at the bottom of the stairs for when I came back.

'What did you say your daughter's name was?' I said, when we sat down with our coffees. 'Sorry. I wasn't really eavesdropping, but being a hairdresser, I couldn't help pricking up my ears.'

'Ah,' she said. 'And I suppose you do all the paint and powder too, do you?'

'Busted,' I said. 'Jo-jo? That's my sister's name.' The lies were pouring out of me.

'Juju,' she said. 'Short for Julia.'

'How old is she?' I said. 'You never think when they're toddling that they'll ever be more trouble, do you?'

'Julia gives trouble a new meaning,' the woman said. 'Hence a meeting, out of hours, with her bloody headmistress. If I go in during office hours I'm liable to break things. We meet on neutral territory.'

I nodded. She was really going for this 'boarding school' story. Odd. Women like her were usually immune from shame. They let it all hang out and stared down anyone who had an opinion. 'Private school?' I said. 'No way you'd get this service otherwise.'

'I pay for it and more, believe me. *And* she's late.' She took a draught of her coffee as if it was a pint of cider on a hot summer's day and left half the colour from her bottom lip on the cup. 'Ugh,' she said, swiping at it with her thumb. 'That's why I don't usually paint myself like the whore of Babylon. But this bloody woman I'm meeting is always so perfect. With her scarves matching her shoes and her bloody tailored—'

I was gone. I shouted over my shoulder about my pager going off on vibrate, as if a hairdresser would ever have to break into a run, and then I was gone. I left the trolley where it stood and took a wide swerve towards the front door, checking for Dr Ferris before I darted out of the double doors and across the car park, my stomach roiling. Not until I was sitting in my car did I let my breath out.

No way. It was strange for a school headmistress to meet one of the mums at half seven in Tesco's café. It was bizarre for Dr Ferris to do the same. Which one of them didn't want Julia's mum at the hall? And why?

I couldn't make sense of it, but one thing was clear. That woman had said her husband was dead. Dr F had told me he'd walked out. Someone was lying.

Chapter 13

The weekend laboured past, an angry wind hurling rain at the windows and the three of us sealed in our separate little spheres.

Angelo stayed in his room, silent and plugged in, refusing to answer any of my enquiries or even respond to my smiles. His MP3 and earbuds were so tiny it seemed worse, somehow, than a big box on his desk and a cushiony pair of headphones that dwarfed his face, like a bonnet. Now he was just absent, and until you looked closely, it was hard to see why. 'You know where I am, if you need me,' I mouthed at him.

Marco was on the couch, his phone on the armrest chirping at him. He had a ring binder of his own, a grubby blue plastic thing mended with insulating tape, and he flipped through it, pretending to be learning the stock, but with golf and football both on the split screen.

I should have tried harder to get through to them, either of them, but I stayed upstairs, under the covers, drawing up treatment plans, trying to learn names. There were three junkies called Ron, Trish and Cate: three women in their twenties, with the same over-dyed, over-straightened hair and the same dark shadows round their eyes, and with histories so identical I knew I'd never learn which was which. I wondered if it mattered. Unless I got the name of one of their kids wrong, they'd never know. The new ana-mia joining Drew, Posy and Roisin was called Beryl. Her photo didn't tell me if she dated from when 'Beryl' was a common name and she'd been ill for years or if 'Beryl' was coming round again and she just looked old from starving. I studied her picture and wondered if I would dare to touch her, if her scabbed skin and skeletal frame could actually stand up to anything I could offer.

That was *my* split screen of golf and footy. What I was really drinking from, as Marco drank from the beeps of his phone, was the picture Sylvie had drawn for me. I gazed at it for long spells and spun them into tales. It hadn't even occurred to Dr Ferris that Sylvie had put those marks on the paper, I thought again. And she'd been thunderstruck that Sylvie met my gaze that first day. She hadn't seen the smile or heard the echoed whisper, 'Better.' Maybe I was getting through to Sylvie like no one had in all those long years.

Once, just once, I tried to get the three of us back together again.

'Do me a favour?' I asked them, when they were standing in the kitchen waiting for the Chinese carry-out to reheat in the microwave. Marco, clearly, wasn't in a cooking mood. I held out a sheet of paper and a black marker to each of them. 'Take this and draw me a house, a tree and a person.'

'Mu-um,' said Angelo.

'What?' Marco said.

'It's for work. I want some examples to show the patients

169

who might have trouble with it. Come on, ten minutes, eh? I'll dish the food up when it's ready.'

'Don't give me any mushrooms,' said Angelo, as he threw himself down at one end of the couch.

Marco took the other end and uncapped the pen, then stared back at me through the open kitchen door. 'Examples,' he said. 'Not a test?'

'A test of what?' I asked him.

I couldn't resist watching over their shoulders as they worked. Marco drew our house, our old house, as detailed as the elevation we'd pored over when it was being built, double garage and all. He drew a Christmas tree covered with decorations, baubles filled in with black except for a bit left white to look like a highlight, and endless interlocking circles for the paper chains we used to make when Angel was tiny. The person he drew was me: hair scraped up in a ponytail like for work and dressed in my short-sleeved tunic and my flat, comfy shoes. I ruffled his hair, then turned to check on Angelo.

He had drawn a child's house, four windows and a smoking chimney, an apple tree in the garden, heavy with fruit, and under it, a baby. Swaddled like a little lozenge with its eyes shut and its lashes sweeping its cheeks, it was cuddled into the roots of the tree.

'Cheat!' said Marco. 'Draw another one with hands and feet, you lazy get!'

'That's fine, Angel,' I said. 'Don't listen to him.' I twitched both sheets away and rolled them up.

'If you did that in the likes of Afghanistan,' Angel said, 'would you just get those big blue blobs? What are they called?'

'Burkhas?' I said. 'I suppose so.'

'You wouldn't do it,' Marco said. 'You're not allowed pictures of people. It's against their religion.'

'Why?' Angel said. 'What harm does it do?'

'Same as eating steak on a Friday,' said Marco. 'Zero.'

Then the microwave pinged and, as if it signalled the end of a game, the moment of closeness was over. Angelo took his plate to his room. Marco turned up the volume on three angry pundits arguing strategy and I ate standing in the kitchen, both drawings spread before me, wondering. Maybe it wasn't a swaddled baby at all. Maybe it was supposed to be a mummy in bandages. Maybe he was thinking of the long-dead monks over the road, buried among the tree roots, wrapped in their winding sheets. But I had told them it wasn't a test so I could hardly start poking around asking questions.

We made it to the shore of Monday morning somehow. At seven o'clock, Marco and I were doing our usual dance, reaching past each other on the landing to get our clothes out, skirting round each other to get dressed in the one spot in the bedroom you could stand upright at the bottom of the bed, then bumping into each other in the kitchen where you couldn't open the fridge all the way if someone was bending over the grill to see how the toast was doing. It had never occurred to me when we lived in our own house that some of the ease and affection was because we could all get away from each other. I didn't want to face what that might mean.

When the bell rang, I wondered if Lars had come miles early and felt myself flush. I hadn't mentioned him yet. I told myself Marco – burly, handsome Marco with his great smile and his great hair – wouldn't think Lars was worth mentioning. So why was I red, I asked myself. I went to the door to distract myself from the answer.

It was the police. The same sergeant with a different WPC, just as eager as the last one to show her boss she wasn't soft. She looked at me as if I'd come in on her shoe.

'It's just too much of a coincidence, you see, Mrs McGovern,' the sergeant said, once he was inside, settling himself. 'Your lad. He hangs out at the abbey every night after school, fair weather or foul. *But* he doesn't tell you anything about the body. *But* the report comes from his phone. *But* he says it's been stolen. *But* he hasn't told you that either. You see the problem, don't you?'

'I see a lot of "but" on show,' I said. What was wrong with me? It was stupid to piss off an overweight cop. And it was probably Marco I was angry with, really, because for some insane reason he had gone and blabbed to the cops that the stolen phone was news to us. Maybe he had even confirmed the neighbour's muckraking about where Angelo hung out too.

Then the rest of the sergeant's words sank in and I came back from inside the cloud of rage and dread and really looked at him. 'Doesn't tell us anything about the body?' I echoed. 'Likes of what? Is that right enough what they're saying about the flood washing it up then? Was it visible?'

The sergeant stared back blankly. Too blankly. He had slipped up and given me information he hadn't meant to. The young girl at his side raised an eyebrow with perfect cool disdain. She didn't respect this guy, even while she sucked up to him.

'So here we are, back to talk to him again,' the sergeant said. 'Last chance, I think, before we take him in. We can't be having this, see?'

172

'He's not here,' I said. I wasn't lying. Or not exactly. I had got up a bit late and hadn't looked in his room. If push came to shove I could say I was mistaken.

'Ali,' said Marco, a warning note in his voice.

'Away to school already?' the sergeant said. 'It's early, surely.'

'Not that early,' Marco said. 'In fact, I need to be getting going, if that's okay.'

The young girl turned her head a little, intrigued by this, but she kept her eyes on me and her thoughts were on her face. I'd settled for not very much, in her opinion. This little house and a man who'd walk away and leave me to deal with cops on my own. Not to mention the mess I'd made of bringing up my son.

'You can have the car,' I told Marco. 'I'm getting a lift. So you don't need to go belting off.'

Marco eased himself back down onto the windowsill where he'd been perching. I was on the footstool, the two police side by side on the couch. I couldn't help it: I was ashamed of the way we were living. I wanted to explain it to them, except I was sure they'd already know. Local cops, they'd know everything.

'You can't honestly think my son knows anything about the murder,' I said, deciding not just to take it. Whatever 'it' was. 'It said on the news he'd been there for years and years. I mean, have you even identified him yet? Are you round here bugging us because you can't think what else to do? Because we've only been here six months. Him next door that was so happy to point you our way? He's in with the bricks. He'd have been here when the body was buried. Have you just taken *him* at his word?'

'Ali,' Marco said again. His face was a picture of something I couldn't name but it wasn't husbandly concern. Maybe I was talking louder than I realized. He turned to the cops and gave

173

them a grimacing kind of smile. 'You need to excuse my wife,' he said. 'She's been under a lot of strain recently and she sometimes doesn't keep very well, you know.'

'What sort of strain would that be?' the sergeant said. He'd been sitting back against the cushions but he bent forward now. 'Do you spend much time over there, Mrs McGovern?'

'I never go near the place!' I said. 'I've just started a new job, so I've been busy. If that's what you mean, Marco? As to not keeping well, I haven't had so much as a cold for ten years, so I've no idea what you're on about.'

The young cop was exploring one of her molars and staring down at her notebook.

'Oh, we're not dinosaurs in the police service,' the sergeant said. 'We understand there's more to good health than colds and cholesterol. So, would you say your child inherited any of your problems, Mrs McGovern? Is that the cause of you being so very protective?'

I stared at him. 'I don't have any problems,' I said. 'And Angelo doesn't have any problems either. No more than every other teenager.'

He must have been standing right behind his door listening, because I didn't hear a single footfall before his door blatted open and Angelo came out, walking in a strange, stiff-legged gait around the little living room, hopping over everyone's legs. 'For fuck's sake, Mum!' he said. 'What is wrong with you? What's wrong with both of you? You're not fine. I'm not fine. I never was. What's the point of saying it when everyone knows it's not true?'

'That's more like it,' the sergeant said. 'Now we might get somewhere.' I wanted to hit him. I wanted to pick up the stupid glass bowl we kept in the middle of the coffee table and run at him with it, drive it into his stupid face for sounding so pleased when my boy was in this state.

'I saw it,' Angelo said. 'I was over there on the Sunday night after the flood drained and there was a hand sticking up out of the ground. But I thought it was a monk. I thought it was funny.'

'Funny?' said the girl. She hadn't learned the poker face yet, new to the job of not reacting.

'Harmless,' Angelo said. 'Gross but harmless. Like mummies or that. I never knew it was a real person from now.'

'And your phone?' said the sergeant.

Angelo stopped stalking around and stood panting. 'It. Got. Stolen,' he said.

'Not lost,' said the sergeant. 'How can you be so sure?'

'Because it was in my back pocket and then it wasn't,' Angel said. 'Like I told you. At the school and the police station. Over and over and over again.'

'Yes, I remember,' the sergeant said. 'Stolen from your back pocket while you walked through the Loreburne Shopping Centre on the afternoon of Monday, the fifteenth of February.' He was watching me as he spoke and I'm sure he saw the quick tug at my eyebrows. *Had* Angelo been in Dumfries that day? He could get there easy enough. He just had to stay on the school bus all the way, but then he was stuck. He had to phone one of us to get back again. Had he? The day before my interview at Howell Hall. *Had* he?

'Quite a coincidence,' the sergeant was saying. 'A phone's stolen all that way away, then used to report a body right across from where its owner happens to stay. Twenty-four hours after the owner admits he saw the body.'

Angelo said nothing.

'Well, son,' said the cop, 'I'm afraid I'm going to have to ask you to come back with us again. Sorry and all that, but since your story has changed so much I think we need to take a different statement.'

'After school,' I said. I wanted some good to come of this, and getting Angelo back in the classroom would be something to be thankful for. 'After your school and our work. We'll all come in tonight.'

'This is a murder enquiry, Mrs McGovern,' said the sergeant. 'We make the timetable.'

'Did you not just hear me saying I've got a new job?' I said. 'And my husband too? What do you think's going to happen if we start taking time off already?'

'Ali, Ali,' Marco said. 'It's okay. I can take a bit of time off this morning.'

I didn't want to argue, but I didn't see how that could be true. It was one thing walking out of training days, but it was something else on the first real shift. Marco had never worked for anyone but his dad and then himself: he had no clue.

'Don't look like that,' he was saying to me. 'Honest, Als, I'll take Angel in and then get him back to school after. It's no problem at all.'

'Can we say we'll meet you there within the hour, Mr McGovern?' the sergeant said. 'We've got more enquiries to make but we'll see you when we get back.'

Marco went out with them, God knows why. Angelo and I stood staring at one another across the coffee table. I couldn't read his expression.

'At least put some decent clothes on and have a wash, eh?'

'Behind my ears and under my fingernails?'

'But not your black waterproof. I'm borrowing it because it's teeming down and you're getting lifts.'

'You're getting lifts too,' Angelo said.

I took his coat down from the peg, hoping he would protest, tell me I was a weirdo for wearing his clothes and if I got perfume on it he'd never wear it again and I'd have to buy him a new one. But he knew I was goading him and he didn't rise.

'Aye, okay, whatever,' he said. 'Go to work and stop worrying.'

'We've gone over this,' I said, trying to sound light. 'I'll stop worrying about you when I'm dead, oka—?' but I cut myself off when a sort of yelp escaped him.

'Don't,' he said. 'Stop being brave and stop trying to be funny. For God's sake, just try to be okay. Okay?'

'What are you talking about?' I said. 'Of course I'm okay. I'm worried about *you*. And I'm pissed off with you too. Why didn't you tell someone about the monk?'

He opened his mouth to speak but the door opened and Marco was back. 'Your lift's here,' he said. His voice was flat and his face was blank, but as he turned to Angelo he managed a smile. 'Right then, my wee gangster! Here we go again, eh?' So it looked like the flat words and dead look were just for me.

Lars was parked outside the gate with his engine running but he had stepped out of the car into the last heavy splats at the end of the rain to get a better look at the abbey. And he had attracted attention, standing there in his hoodie. The neighbour was just closing his door when I came out of mine. 'Here! You!' he said. 'You can't just stop there and gawp. That's a crime scene.'

I was at the little hedge before I knew I was moving. 'Leave him alone,' I shouted. 'He's a friend of mine and it's none of your bloody business who parks where on a public road or who looks at what. If you would keep your nose out, and stop spreading lies about other people to cover your own arse, the police might actually find this murderer. Unless there's some reason you don't want them to. Eh? Eh?' I could feel a bulge of sour heat rising up inside me.

The man was shrinking back against his front door, like my words were darts. 'What's that supposed—' he said. He put a tremulous hand up to his mouth. 'What lies? Cover what?'

'Lies about my son,' I said, in a fierce whisper. I knew my face was red. Maybe my eyes were red too. Maybe my hair was smoking. 'And I don't know *what* you're covering, do I? I don't go sneaking around in everybody's business to find out.'

'Ali.' Lars put a hand on my arm. I flinched at his touch but just before I jerked to shrug him off, some bit of me registered the warm, firm grip and the steady sound of his voice. 'Come on, come away, come and sit down. Sorry, pal,' he said to the neighbour.

'I've never been spoken to like that in my life!' the man said. He had misted up behind his bottle-bottom glasses, either from fear or anger, it was hard to say.

'Well, this has been a nice change for you, then,' Lars said, guiding me over to his car and helping me in. He did up my seatbelt, then hopped in at the driver's side and drew gently away. 'Want to tell me what that was all about?' he said, so reasonable.

I bent over at my waist and pressed my face into the fabric of my white uniform trousers, not caring if I was covering them in tears and snot. At least I never wore make-up for work. I thought it was better to be bare-faced and show my clients the benefit of a good cleansing routine. That was me: nothing to hide.

'Angel knew about the body,' I said at last, sitting up and letting my head fall back against the headrest. It was hammering. 'He lied to the police.'

Lars had just slowed to turn off at the checkpoint. He tooted and waved to the soldier on duty and then, when we were out of sight, he pulled off the track and turned to me.

'You mean he was lying about the phone being stolen?' he said. 'Why?' I just shook my head. It wouldn't sound any more sensible to Lars than it had to the sergeant. 'And what's the problem with your neighbour?' I shook my head again. 'I thought you were going to lamp him. And I'm not the only one. He was shaking like a Chihuahua.' He was almost laughing now. I tried to join in but it came out like a sob so I bit it back again.

'What else is it, though, Ali?' he said. 'Is it this place?'

'Else?' I asked him. 'Isn't that enough?'

'Plenty, but I can tell the difference between massive trouble hitting you like a frying pan when you're basically okay and massive trouble coming along like one last thing and finishing you off.'

'I'm basically okay,' I said.

'Sure?' said Lars. 'Because that would mean I can't tell the difference at all.'

I nodded. I sat forward, flipped open his sun-blind mirror and looked at my face. 'Bloody hell. I'm getting too old to cry. I'll look like shit for days now.'

'So you're not going to tell me what's wrong?' Lars said.

'Right now, what's wrong is that if Dr Ferris sees me looking like this she'll think I'm too flaky to be doing my job and she'll sack me.' But again my voice let me down. It shook towards the end.

'Look in that bag on the back seat,' Lars said. 'If you can reach it. I know it sounds daft but it helps.'

He wouldn't say any more so, as he started up and got going again, I twisted round and grabbed a big hospital laundry bag,

179

sturdy blue plastic and a toggle with a drawstring. I peered inside, no idea what I thought I'd be seeing.

'It's a dolly,' he said. 'We use them for regression. I took it home to put it on the gentle cycle, after it got cried on on Friday.'

'What am I supposed to do with it?' I said, still peering into the bag. I could see the checked pinafore and round white legs of a Raggedy Ann.

'Seriously? You're supposed to cuddle it. What else would you do with a dolly?'

'This is your idea of therapy?' I said. 'Cuddling a doll?'

'Cuddling a doll,' Lars said. 'Going for a walk, baking a tray of fairy cakes.'

I had no idea what had happened to my dolls after I was grown-up and left home. Maybe they were still in the eaves of my parents' attic. Or maybe my sister-in-law had chucked them. But I had been a good mum to my plastic Tiny Tears, changing her clothes every day, going up to my bedroom after school and getting her out of her pram to sit and watch me doing my sums and my reading.

I didn't see what good it could do me, but because I agreed about the walks and the baking, I reached into the bag and grabbed the rag doll.

'There you go,' Lars said.

I pulled it out and turned it to face me. Then everything slowed down and turned to sludge as I pushed the woollen hair back off the disc of white and saw the blankness ripple and bulge and heard the moaning start – 'Mmmhmmm.'

And I was out of the car and running, running as fast as I had ever run in my life, gasping the cold air down into my burning lungs, stumbling over the rough grass towards the sea.

Chapter 14

He caught me easily, pinned my arms to my sides and held me hard in a deft professional grip that kicked me back ten years, like falling down a well into blackness. I could hear my breath, half-sobs, half-gasps.

'Please,' I said. 'No.'

'Sorry,' said Lars, 'but it's a live ammo day. Didn't you see the flags at the gate? Red means you can't be out here, Ali.'

'I need to go home,' I said. But not to the house I'd just left. Not even to our real house. I wanted to go to the house I was born in. To my room with the high narrow bed and the skirted dressing-table. I shook my head to take the picture away.

I had wanted to go there when I was ill too. I had wanted my old room and my mum bringing me soup on a tray and a comic to read. Marco had made me sushi, hand-rolled and perfect, like little mosaic medallions, and he'd bought me a box-set to play on the flatscreen at the bottom of our bed. He'd told me ever so gently that my parents weren't coming, that my mum was busy in France with her new house and her olive harvest.

His voice had been hypnotic as he spoke so I didn't throw the square plate against the wall. I didn't smash the DVDs and pull the covers over my head. And I was better in six months, start to finish. Fine for a decade after.

Lars let me go, in slow careful stages in case I ran again, then took my hand and started walking me back to the car. He had left it sitting in the middle of the track, both its doors hanging open, like Dumbo's ears. I peered at it but wherever the dolly had fallen I couldn't see it. I stopped walking anyway. 'I can't get back in,' I said. 'But I really need to go home.'

'I can't take you home,' said Lars. 'I need to run the meeting.'

'I can't go to the meeting!' I heard myself yelp. 'Dr Ferris would—'

'Ssh,' Lars said. 'She's not in. Dr F texted me first thing to say she got called away last night and I'm in charge.'

'I just need to go,' I said. 'I thought I could do this and I need the money but I can't cope and I want to go home. My kid needs me. Oh, Jesus!'

As if humiliating myself in front of Lars wasn't enough, now another car was bumping over the track. He waved at it to slow down and it crunched to a stop a foot behind his bumper. Belle leaned out of the driver's side and I could see Surraya bending forward to crane out at us.

'Didn't you see the flags?' Belle shouted. 'Live day, Lars. What are you doing?'

'Ali had a funny turn,' Lars said. 'All okay now.' He had let go of my hand.

'You shouldn't be in if you're coming down with a bug, sweetness,' Belle said.

I hung my head and said nothing.

'Not that kind of turn,' Lars said. 'I was being my usual brilliant self and I upset her.'

'I'm fine,' I said at last, looking up. 'I'm really fine.'

But all three of them gazed back at me so shrewdly that I felt myself shrivel.

'I can't get back in that car,' I said, nodding at the open doors. 'Will you two take me up the road so I can . . .' hand in my notice and call a taxi, was what I was thinking.

Belle gave Lars a hard stare, then turned to me with a smile, her eyes crinkled. 'Happy to.'

Once I was in, Surraya twisted round and put a hand on my knee. 'So,' she said. 'You're fine, eh?' I nodded, pretending to fiddle with my seatbelt so I didn't have to look at her. 'Ali,' she went on, 'nobody "fine" comes to work here.' Belle muttered agreement under her breath as she started the engine again and followed Lars's car.

'From Dr Ferris down,' Surraya went on, 'no one's fine. We're all walking wounded.'

She appeared so untroubled. Maybe it was the hijab, reminding me of nuns, women who lived in serenity. 'What do you mean?' I said.

'It's what makes the Ferrises such a good team. She only cares about the bottom line and he's a big softie but, by amazing coincidence, that means they want the same things. Dr Ferris gives people second chances because it keeps them grateful and makes sure they can't walk away. And Dr F really and truly believes that staff with problems help clients with problems.'

'Problems,' I said. I didn't ask, but they told me anyway.

'I got sacked from the NHS,' Belle said, 'for stepping over professional boundaries.'

'And I'm a veiled Muslim,' said Surraya. Belle snorted. 'Yeah, okay,' Surraya added. 'Who's done a bit of time.'

'And Lars? And Marion?'

'You'd need to ask them,' Belle said.

'Do you think he's right?' I asked her. 'Dr F?'

'Course he is,' said Surraya. 'Some wee Pollyanna with a Dolly Dimple life would be no bloody good whatsoever when our nutters go the full woo-woo.' Belle laughed softly, as Surraya cleared her throat. 'I mean, when the clients enter episodes of low-function.'

'So I really can just go and tell my brand-new employer that I'm one scream off a breakdown?' I said. 'While I'm on probation?' It was the stupidest thing I'd ever heard.

'I bet he already knows,' Surraya said. 'Did nothing come up at your interview?'

'He wasn't there,' I said. 'It was Dr Ferris on her own.'

Neither of them said anything. Belle didn't even make her mp-mp-mm noise and Surraya's eyebrows stayed level all the time she was looking at me and only rose to a peak as she shared a glance with Belle, turning to face the front again.

'What?' I said.

'Probably nothing,' Belle told me. We had got to the staff car park and she stopped.

'Go and talk to him,' Surraya said again.

We climbed out and Lars walked over to join us. We stood staring at one another over the roof of the car as if it was a ping-pong table and we were psyching each other out before a match.

'Belle and Surraya think I can just go to Dr F and say I'm having panic attacks,' I told Lars.

'You could if you were having panic attacks,' Surraya said. 'Are you?'

'Well, I got out of a moving car and ran onto a firing range,' I said. 'I'm having something.'

After a moment Lars shivered. 'Come on, Ali. I'm freezing my buns off standing out here in my tunic.'

'Because you don't have any meat on your bones,' said Belle. 'You need a woman to feed you up and put some flesh on you.'

Just like that the atmosphere was broken, the strange moment of tension gone. And somehow it seemed to have been decided that I wasn't calling a taxi and going home. I was going to lay myself bare to Dr F and listen to whatever he had to tell me.

I even got through the staff meeting. I sat in the back row of folding chairs, sunk inside Angelo's coat. It was a different world without Dr Ferris watching everyone and trying to trip them up. The night shift reported a quiet twelve hours.

'Except for Julia,' Marion said. 'She was on the phone again, saying she was being held against her will.'

Dr F clucked and tutted but the rest of the staff were ready to laugh.

'Samaritans?' said Lars. 'With that bloody centralized number? At least with the local office they knew where the call came from.'

'It wasn't the Samaritans,' Marion said. 'It was a phone-in show on WestSound. They pulled her off at the first F-bomb but the producer kept her talking and called the polis on another line. She was not a very happy bunny when the good old D and G constabulary said Julia had been yanking them. I think the poor lassie thought she'd just broken the story of her life.'

'Ali,' said Dr F, suddenly, 'you seem to have established a rapport with her. Can you dream up something to keep her busy today? We've got too many groups and off-site visits going on to be at action stations all shift. Thank you, by the way, Marion.'

He didn't seem to want an answer from me, just assumed I'd do his bidding.

'Speaking of groups,' Lars said, 'I was looking at the rota and wondering if we could collapse the two sets of substance or if there's a good reason I'm not seeing to keep them both going. I know Ryan can be a bit lively and I thought maybe he'd be better in solo and the others can all meet at the one time.'

The nursing staff all had something to say about what seemed like ten different permutations of two groups and Ryan, and eventually I drifted off, looking at my own diary and planning what else I could offer Julia that would keep her quiet.

I stayed behind at the end, as the rest of the staff filed out, the night shift hurrying to their cars and the day shift, much slower, off to do the meds round and start the morning's clinics.

'Dr . . . F?' I said. It still seemed cheeky to call him that. 'Can I ask you something? Is now a good time?'

He looked up from his phone and beamed at me. 'One moment. I'm attempting to hold a conversation with my daughter. But I'm falling behind.'

I smiled. I could see her in my mind's eye: a younger version of her mother with the same swan neck and sharp cheekbones, the same drawling voice.

'Thank God she only ever texts me when my wife is unavailable,' Dr F said, still frantically jabbing at his phone. 'Oh, I give up!' He lifted it to his ear and motioned me to take the chair opposite the desk.

'It's quicker,' he said, into the phone. 'Well, walk away so they *can't* hear. Look, I'm sure that's not tr— . . . Don't be so hard on yourse— . . . I'm sure you're overreac—' He listened for a moment. 'Oh. Well, another time you'll know better. Who suggested— . . . Oh? Well, look, I'm sure it'll all blow over soon enough. Least said, soonest mended. I'd leave it be, Dido, truly.'

He didn't sound like a psychiatrist. *Least said, soonest mended?*

He hung up and put the phone down with a groan. 'I can't keep up,' he said. 'Another day, another drama! But what can I do for *you*?'

'I'm having second thoughts,' I told the top of his head. He was scrolling back over his texts. 'Not sure this job is right for me, after all. And I reckoned it was best to come to you because you're not . . .' He cocked his head. 'Well, because it wasn't your idea to have me here so you'll tell me straight.'

He finally stopped rereading what his daughter had told him and looked up. 'I hope I haven't given the impression that you're not welcome, Ali.'

'I just don't think I'm doing what's expected,' I blurted out. 'I can't see why I'm being paid so much to do so little, do you understand? And so I think I'm not actually getting what it is I'm really meant to do.' I sat back, feeling as if I'd put down a huge bulky burden now that the fears were words and the words were out of me. 'And,' I went on, 'it's really stressing me out.' If I could blame the new job for my – what had Lars called them? – funny turns, they'd be a lot less worrying.

He nodded slowly a few times before speaking. 'My wife is the businesswoman, Ali,' he said. 'It would be more worrying if *I* had employed a para-therapist without *her* say-so. Rest assured, if Tammy feels you're needed, you're needed. And she would never make a poor financial decision. She's a strategist as well as a fine doctor.'

Tammy, was all I could think. It didn't suit her. That, and 'strategist' was a funny way to talk about the love of your life.

'So,' he went on, 'there's no need to be stressed. None at all.'

'Right,' I said. 'Good. Well, I'll take your word for it. I had no idea rehab was so— I mean, I thought it would all be on a bit more of a shoestring.'

'Howell Hall isn't our only enterprise,' he said. 'Although it's where we started. Managing to get this property for a song was what convinced us we could open our own place, when we were both at the infirmary, juggling childcare and shift-work. So I suppose you could say it's our flagship, but we've got Rowan House in Dumfries. That's mostly contract work from the local authority, more focused on through-put, and the same at Fairview in Stranraer. And my wife's family business is still very much a going concern.'

'Childcare?' I said. 'So Howell Hall hasn't really been open that long, then? I mean if your daughter's still a teenager.' He shrugged. 'Sorry, didn't mean to be nosy.'

'We do try to keep Dido away from our professional lives, I admit,' he said. 'We send her up to Wellington's so she's not in a geography class with the child of a patient, and so forth. You have children yourself, Ali. I'm sure you'll understand.'

I understood perfectly. They might be making their money off of Fairview and Rowan House, off of junkies and alkies from the housing schemes in the region's greyest towns, but they spent their days here on polished floors behind graceful windows. And their daughter was the Queen of Sheba. For devilment I asked: 'What's Dr Ferris's family business, then? Does it take up much of your time?'

'I never go near the place from one year's end to the next,' said Dr F. 'Our manager runs everything, and since he's getting close to retirement, she's grooming another.'

But he hadn't said what it was. I kind of hoped it was an undertaker's or a waste recycler, something grubby that it bugged her to think about whenever she remembered.

'Can I ask you one more thing?' I said. He glanced at his watch and grimaced but he nodded. 'What will I say to Julia if she starts on again about killing her dad?'

'Human kindness goes a long way,' he said. Then he echoed what Marion had told me that first day. 'The pain is real even if the words are false. Something is troubling Julia so very deeply that she makes shocking claims to try to express it.'

'So . . . it's really not that she might actually have killed him, then?' I said.

'Not a chance,' Dr F said. 'Garran Swain is alive and well and currently golfing in Portugal. He sent us a postcard.' He must have seen my start of surprise. 'Galloway is a small place,' he told me, 'and the Swains are friends of ours from years back. In fact, we bought Howell Hall from them. Well, from Mona, when she got tired of the family ghosts and moved to the splendid new digs across the way. It's an architectural gem. Been in all the glossy magazines.'

'So why does Julia keep saying she killed him?' I said. I couldn't care less about how posh the family were or what their house looked like, although I suppose the connection made sense of why Julia got to stay when she was such a pain in the arse every day.

'Julia has a personality disorder,' he said. 'Her wild tales are a symptom.'

'Yeah, but . . .' He glanced at his watch again and I knew I

189

was losing him. 'Why does she say her dad? Why not her mum? If she's trying to think of the worst thing she could say, wouldn't she say she killed her mum?'

Dr F opened his eyes so wide that his straggly brows curved forward over them. 'Well, Mona Swain is very much alive, you see.' I thought of her wrenching the cellophane off lipsticks in Tesco and smearing them on her big lips. 'And Garran has gone away. But you make an interesting point and I don't take offence. Much as I love my daughter and know she loves me, I agree that the central relationship, the strongest bond, is that between mother and child. Only . . . Are you all right?' he asked suddenly, in a different voice. 'Have I said something to upset you?'

'My son is closer to my husband,' I said. 'It's hard not be jealous sometimes.' I knew that my face had drained and now I felt it flood. I must look like a maniac sitting there. 'Thanks for helping me. About Julia, I mean. It makes sense.'

'She's doing her very best to give voice to fear and pain the only way she knows how,' Dr F said. 'It doesn't matter how deeply you bury something, Ali, it comes to the surface eventually. Good grief, like that body at the abbey, eh!'

'A hand,' I said. 'That's what the police are saying now. A hand broke through the ground after all the flooding.'

Dr F sat forward in his seat and stared at me. 'I hadn't heard that.'

'Well, to be honest' – I hoped I wasn't blushing – 'I heard on the grapevine. Not officially. I live across the street from the abbey and the whole row of neighbours is pretty much talking about nothing else.'

'I can imagine!'

'My son has taken it very badly,' I told him. 'I'm really worried about him.'

'Is that his coat?' Dr F asked, smiling. I smiled back. I hadn't realized it, but I'd snuggled further into it when I'd mentioned him.

'And it's kicked up some old stuff for me too,' I said, brave inside Angelo's jacket. 'Nightmares and things. And, actually, *that*'s really why I'm here. Lars and Belle and Surraya reckoned I should tell you I'm having a few . . . they told me not to call them panic attacks so I don't really know what to call them. Flashbacks?'

'To what?' His voice was gentle and his face soft, with the faintest smile.

'A bad time. Ten years ago.'

Now he smiled widely. Beamed at me. 'Ten years ago?' he said. 'And your son's a teenager? And you're married to his father? Well, there's nothing to worry about at all then.' He laughed a little at my confusion but not unkindly. 'Ten years ago you were grown-up, Ali. You were formed by your family long before then. Ten years ago you'd formed your adult bonds and you'd made your own family. Anything that happens when our life is made can be remedied.'

'Even if something happens that . . . unmakes it?' I said. That was as far as I was willing to go.

He sat forward a little further in his seat. 'Unmakes it?' he said. 'You mean . . . you found out your life was not what you thought it was?'

I nodded, thinking, no way I was going to speak, then found myself speaking anyway. 'I was really low,' I said, the words coming out on one little breath each. 'And I needed my mum. Like you said. My mum. The central . . . like you said. And she wouldn't come. She lives in France and she wouldn't come back.' I sniffed and swallowed the gulp of air. 'And so I got better anyway, without her.'

'That seems very unlikely,' Dr F said. Then he flapped his hands at the expression on my face. 'I don't doubt that you're better. Of course you are, although a scab's not a scar, Ali. We need to heal to scars if we're going to carry on.'

'Scars.'

'Being realistic. But that's not what I meant was unlikely. I mean that you asked her to come and she wouldn't. Children learn very quickly how much they can lean on their parents. It's one of the tragedies of poor parenting, actually. How quickly a little one learns not to look for help.' I flashed on Angel that morning saying, 'Just be okay, Mum,' and I found myself nodding. 'So my best guess is that it was a misunderstanding. A miscommunication?'

'I don't think so,' I said.

'Check,' he told me. 'And then let's talk again.'

———

I walked out as if I had springs under me. He really was a good doctor. He'd given me more hope than I'd ever had. He'd made it sound so easy. I was on the phone to Marco before I was ten paces down the corridor. 'Where are you?' I asked him.

'Where do you think? Cooling our heels at the police station, waiting for Sergeant Fat Arse to show up.'

'Is Angel okay? Put him on.'

There was a kerfuffle of sound while the phone got passed over and then silence.

'Ange?'

'What?'

'Just tell them the truth, the whole truth this time, and answer all their questions. You've got nothing to hide and they'll understand why you said what you said last time. Okay? Listen to me and trust me.'

'Tell the whole truth,' he said. 'Okay. You first.'

'I don't know what that's supposed to mean,' I said.

'Yeah, that's what I thought,' he told me, his voice cold as roadkill, and then the phone rustled again.

'What did you just say to him?' Marco's voice sounded amused, like this was all just teenage stuff.

'We can't go on like this,' I said. '*I* can't go on like this. I need to get things straightened out.'

'What things?' said Marco. ''Uck's sake, Ali, I'm sitting in a police station. It's not the time.'

'Things with my mum and dad,' I said. 'And we need to tell Angelo.'

'Tell him *what*?' Marco had forgotten to be quiet. 'There's nothing to tell him except ancient history. And as for your parents? Ali, I can't go back through that again. I cannot watch you go downhill again. And I sure as hell can't watch you reach out to them again and get smacked down. How can you even— How can you think *this* is a good time to start raking things over?'

'*This*?' I said. 'What time is "this"? We've both got jobs again at long last and we've had a bloody big wake-up call. Our son didn't turn to us because he thinks we're not strong enough to help him. He shouldn't be protecting us and going it alone, Marco, he's fifteen.'

'Us?' Marco was nearly shouting now. 'What do you mean "us"? It's not "us", Ali. It's Angel and me trying not to let anything knock *you*.'

'Well, it shouldn't be,' I said. 'It should be you and me looking after him. And it's going to be. I'm going to phone my parents and have it out with them.'

'What the bloody hell does that have to do with Angelo?' Marco whispered down the phone.

'Everything,' I said. 'Because I'm thinking there must be some kind of mistake. I can't believe there's no misunderstanding or miscommunication.' I knew I was parroting Dr F, but Marco didn't, and it lent me some swagger. 'At the very least, I need to tell them how I feel and see if maybe they'll just say sorry and we can put it behind us. Then Angel'll stop thinking I'm some kind of orchid that can't be breathed on and he'll be okay too. Because there's no way he should be in this mess.'

'Ali,' said Marco. I could hear his footsteps and the sound of a door squeaking. 'Right. I'm outside,' he said. 'Standing outside the police station for the world to see. Are you happy now? Ali, please. Your parents told me that they didn't see the point of coming all the way back and that you shouldn't make a drama out of a misfortune.'

'Yes,' I said. 'Yes, you told me. But what had you said to them? I don't think you ever told me exactly what everyone said to everyone.'

'I told you over and *over* again,' said Marco. 'But you were off your head on tranquillizers and painkillers and those sleeping tablets that made you feel so sick. Ali, don't go back there.'

'I'm still there!' I said. 'I never left. I'm stuck there. I need to pick the scab off and let it heal to a good strong scar instead. So tell me. What did you say?'

'I told them you needed them, that there was a funeral planned, and asked them when I could pick them up at the airport.'

'And who were you talking to? My mum or my dad?'

'Both,' Marco said. 'Skype. And they said they were really

busy with the builders and it was ridiculous to have a funeral. Mawkish, your mum said, whatever the hell that means.' It was the kind of word my mum would use right enough. 'She said to tell you to get back in touch when you were on your feet again and we could all go over and have a break in the sun.'

For a long time I said nothing. It still hurt but, poking at it, I thought maybe it hurt a bit less than before. Maybe it was the kindness of Dr F, his wise words telling me I'd formed my own bonds and made my family. Or maybe it was that his words were true. Angelo needed me to be the mum now.

'Okay,' I said, 'you've convinced me. But I still need to tell Angel.' He started to speak. 'I'm not asking you, Marco. This is between Angel and me. I need to tell him and he needs to know. We should have told him years ago.'

'I'd better go back in,' was all Marco said. 'I need to be there if they call him through. And I've been on the bloody phone too much already. There's a big sign telling you to switch them off and I've been sitting right under it yakking for the last half-hour.'

'Bit of an exaggeration.'

'Not to you, Ali. To work. I've got some good news. Just got a call to say I'm going full-time. I'm moving up to supervisor.'

'That was quick. Did somebody leave?' I couldn't quite swallow anyone leaving a job the way things were just now.

'The harder you hit the bottom, the higher you bounce,' said Marco. 'You know me.' I bit my lip on the answer. I knew that he had killed a family business stone-dead trying to turn it into something it wasn't, as if Dalbeattie was some southern foodie heaven. And I knew he'd tanked Face Value trying to stay afloat. I knew he watched *Dragons' Den* and had an opinion about every nervous hopeful. I had had to stop watching with him, startled by his unkindness and his short memory, not recognizing him.

'You'll be the boss by Christmas, eh?' I said at last. Marco gave an awkward laugh I couldn't quite decipher. 'Give Angelo a kiss and tell him to shame the devil,' I said.

I put the phone in my pocket, then cuddled down into the coat again, smelling his body spray on the lining and marvelling that my baby boy filled these long sleeves, that the flaps I could wrap right round me only just met and zipped up his front.

From habit, I dug my fingers into the corners of the pockets and pulled out all the detritus. No cigarette ends, no Rizla papers, no beer-can ring pulls. Just hard lumps of chewing gum rewrapped in twists of silver paper. That and the usual receipts. I spread one flat and checked it: 88p from after school on the twelfth. A can of Coke on the way to the bus. And another: £1.76 from the same shop, likely for two. I wondered if this was the day of his big date, if he'd treated the girl, like a gentleman. Then I looked at the date again. The fifteenth. And the time was 3:48. That was the day when he had sworn he was in the Loreburne Centre in Dumfries having his phone stolen. How could he have been in the corner shop in Kirkcudbright buying two cans?

I tried Marco's phone again but it was switched off. Maybe that meant they were already in the interview room. I looked up the number for the police station and tried it but got lost in a warren of options and pre-records. If I called 999, could I ask to speak to them? There must be some way to get in touch before Angelo repeated the lie in a formal statement and signed it.

Then it hit me. Like a meteor. Thinking about how much we'd come to expect that everyone was accessible all the time these days, it hit me. Ten years ago, no one Skyped anyone, did they?

Chapter 15

'Hello, sweetheart,' I said, cupping her cheek in my hand and lifting her chin so I could look into her eyes. 'How are you today?'

Sylvie rested her head in the curve of my palm and breathed out. I felt it like the ache in my chest when tears were close. Dr Ferris had been so clear but she was wrong. There was communication in everything Sylvie did, like the way a cat tells you what it thinks if you pay attention. Maybe Dr Ferris was a dog person.

'We're going outside,' I told her. 'Look.' I had brought along a wheelchair and a knee blanket that usually sat in the corner of one of the lounges. Jo had looked up from her jigsaw and said, 'Someone taken a tumble?'

Sylvie stood up with her hands in mine, then sat down in the wheelchair, lifting her eyes in surprise when it rolled a little because, of course, I had forgotten to put the brake on. I tucked the knee blanket over her and threw a shawl round her shoulders too, lifting it up the back of her head so her cloud of colourless hair was mussed into a ruff.

'Let's get some colour in those cheeks,' I said, and started pushing.

Julia was waiting at the bottom of the stairs, swinging her feet and kicking at the rail of an antique chair. She was dressed, booted and coated. She already had an unlit cigarette in her mouth and her Bic lighter in her mittened hand. 'It's supposed to be *fresh* air,' I told her. She rolled her eyes. 'Well, at least blow it away from Sylvie.'

Julia frowned at me, then flicked her first glance towards the wheelchair. So self-absorbed, like all youngsters. Even without the diagnosis. 'You're bringing Grandma?'

'She's thirty.'

'Why's she here?' she insisted, ignoring me.

I ignored her back. Once I'd negotiated the ramp at the side of the front steps, and faced exactly how hard it was to get the chair to roll over the gravel, I had no breath left for chatting. And when we reached the start of the grass it got worse. The tyres made deep ruts and I had to put one hip against the back rest to keep the chair moving at all. If it hadn't been for the way Sylvie raised her face, letting the breeze blow her hair back, I'd have packed it in.

'Jesus fucking Christ,' Julia said. 'She looks like a dog hanging out the back window of a Transit van. You'd think she'd never been outside before.'

'Transit. Vans. Don't. Have back windows,' I said, finally getting going on a slight down slope. 'And it probably *has* been a while since she was outside so don't spoil it.'

Julia threw her head back and gave a Tarzan roar, beating her chest so hard she must have been leaving bruises. Then she lodged her ciggie in the corner of her mouth and seized one of the handles.

'Come on, then, Sylvia! Let's see what this baby can do!' She started running and when I skidded on the wet grass, she elbowed me aside and grasped the other handle too. Then she was off. Sylvie's shawl came untucked and flew like a flag behind them, as I stumbled in their wake.

'Slow down!' I shouted. 'Julia, be careful!'

'She's hanging on,' Julia shouted over her shoulder. 'She's fine.' And they were at the gazebo before I caught them. 'Skid finish!' Julia yelled, then screeched like the brakes of a racing car and pulled Sylvie hard round to the left so she was facing me.

She was smiling. Clutching the arm-rests hard, she was pink-cheeked and smiling with her mouth open.

'Jesus, I'm a fat pig,' Julia said, throwing herself down on one of the steps and hawking hard to spit up the result of running in the cold air with her smoker's chest. 'Just as well it's not Sylvia pushing *me*.'

'Sylvie,' I said. Julia spat again, then turned to face her.

'Good name for a sylph,' she said. 'I should be called Bertha.'

'Oh, now!' I said. 'Okay, well, what about me, then?'

Julia pretended to take a good long look at me while lighting up and delivered the verdict with a curling smile. 'Can't decide between Priscilla and Prudence,' she said. 'How can you bear to be such a Goody Two Shoes with your perfect nails and your perfect hair?'

But I was barely listening. I was watching Sylvie. She was smiling again, even wider this time.

'Oh, you think that's funny, do you?' I said. 'Priscilla? Prudence?'

But that was too much attention to be taken from Julia. She flicked her cigarette into the grass where it fizzled out in the

200

damp tussocks, then lifted herself to the side and farted long and loud. 'So, what's the programme?' she said.

'Art,' I told her. 'Look at all the leaves on the ground. I want you to gather them and write a message on the grass with them.'

'You've got it,' Julia said. 'Is douchebag one word or two?'

'Seriously,' I said. 'First you need to decide who you're writing it to and then you need to decide what to say.'

'Are we even on a flight path?' said Julia, lying back on the steps and squinting up into the sky. 'And how is that art, anyway? How's it not just writing?'

'Well, make a collage,' I said. 'I'm not the boss. I just looked out the window and saw all the leaves.'

'And what's Sissy going to do?' Julia said.

'*Sylvie.*'

'Can I use her in the collage? Lie her on the grass and stick twigs in her?'

'Do you have family photos on your phone?' I asked. 'You could try to copy one of them.' Was it too obvious? Was it dangerous to make her think about her family when there were no nursing staff anywhere near?

She was scrolling, Sylvie watching her. I wondered if Sylvie had ever seen a smart phone, then thought she must have when her family visited. If her family visited. I laid a hand on her arm, then perched myself on the wheelchair to hold her. 'Warm enough?' I said. Again, she settled into me and I snuggled her closer.

But Julia had noticed and leaped up, shoving her phone into my face. 'Here's one of my dad,' she said. 'Before I beat his head in with a cast-iron frying pan and shovelled up the jelly.'

Sylvie kept watching Julia but I glanced at the photograph,

201

seeing a smiling man I could easily believe was golfing somewhere warm. He wore a pink cashmere jersey and had dazzling
teeth in his brown face. It made me think, for a minute, of the
man in the abbey grounds, 'definitely not a vagrant'. But the
man in the picture had a Bluetooth in his ear. He hadn't been
dead all those years.

'And here's one of my new dad,' Julia said, flashing me
another shot, this time of a middle-aged man in a dinner jacket
and black bow-tie, a cigar in his mouth and his face shining
with drink and laughter. He was sitting with his back to a wall
of glass and the camera flash had bounced and dazzled, so that
something about it looked supernatural.

'And then there's my first dad.' A snaggle-toothed man,
clearly upper-class, and possibly also drunk. Red-eyed anyway.
He was dressed for hunting, hard hat and everything, standing
by a loose-box door with a horse nuzzling at him, spreading snot
on the red of his jacket. 'With my dear mother,' Julia said, and I
laughed because, thinking of Mona Swain, it was so nearly true.

Sylvie started at my laughter. As quick as that, she had fallen
back into her stupor.

'So, forget family,' I said to Julia. 'Just make a picture.'

'House-tree-person again?'

'Anything you fancy,' I said.

She got to her feet and went off skipping and lurching in a
way I didn't understand until, leaping to one side and stamping
hard, she shouted, 'Bastard worms. Take that, you slimy little
fuck!'

'Don't stamp on worms,' I called over to her.

'Oh, God. Save the Worms! Print me a T-shirt,' she yelled
back. But she had reached the canopy of one of the sycamore
trees and bent to start collecting the leaves instead.

'And how about you, Sylvie?' I said softly, when I was sure Julia was engrossed. 'Would you like to try to draw a picture again?' Sylvie said nothing and didn't look at me, but her fingers twitched. Maybe they did. I pulled the pad out of my bag and put the thick marker in her hand.

'Awright?' The voice made me jump.

It was Ryan. He'd come up over the bank behind us from the lower, wilder area of the grounds and stood staring at me.

'Aren't you at Substance Group?' I said, throwing a glance back towards the house, hoping one of the nurses was passing a window.

'Got expelled,' he said. Like Julia, he hawked and spat, but unlike Julia he glanced at Sylvie, then rubbed his spit into the grass.

'What for?' I asked him.

'I'm a disruptive influence,' he said, the pride unmistakable. 'I told some lame cunt she was kidding herself.'

'That is a really horrible way to talk about someone, Ryan,' I said. 'But . . . kidding herself how?'

'She was all up to ninety over a few wee glasses of sherry. She's got nae record, nae cautions. She's just giving her mind a treat. Looking for attention.'

'So she's in and you're out?' I said. 'Well, you can join us if you like. We're a right wee bunch of misfits. The more the merrier.'

Ryan gave one scathing look at Julia's bottom, really quite prominent as she bent double picking up leaves, then threw another glance Sylvie's way. 'Who's this?' he said.

I knew Julia was new, but if Ryan didn't know Sylvie either, maybe it had been some time since she'd left her room. I maybe should have checked, I told myself, shifting uncomfortably. But she seemed fine. Better, I'd say.

'Sylvie,' I told him. 'Catatonic but understands everything. So no more C-words, okay?'

'And what are youse doing? Are you no' the slap wifie?'

'Slap and art,' I said. 'It's art today. Autumn leaf collage on the grass or you can draw me a picture. Hey, actually, has anyone ever asked you to draw a house, a tree and a person? It's something I'm doing with everyone.'

He lit the inevitable cigarette and settled down with a torn-off sheet and a black marker pen, while I tried again with Sylvie.

'A house,' I said. She stared ahead and then once again she drew the tiny square in the corner of the paper. 'I'm sorry, sweetheart,' I said. 'Never mind, then.'

'Fucken impossible to draw a flat,' Ryan said. 'I'll draw the whole block and then I'll just put an arrow, right? And a tree, eh?'

Sylvie, as she had before, scored through the square, top to bottom.

'A tree, yes,' I said to Ryan.

'That'll do,' he said, viewing his sheet. 'And a person.' He turned away to stop me watching. I only had eyes for Sylvie. She drew a slash through the square making a cross. Just as before. Except this time I knew she wasn't protesting. She was drawing. She was trying to tell me something.

'Ta-dah!' Ryan said and held up the sheet. The block of flats and tree were sketched in well enough but the person was a crude depiction of a woman with her legs open and her genitals huge and detailed. He threw it at me, then walked off, laughing.

'House, tree, person, darling,' I said to Sylvie, as I tucked Ryan's effort into the back of the pad.

She did it again. The square. And the two lines.

I put my finger on all three, one after the other. 'This is a

204

house?' She didn't nod or smile but I was sure she was trying to say yes. There was a softening about her. So I checked. I touched the vertical line. 'This is a person standing in the house?' And she didn't frown and she didn't shake her head but she was saying no to me. She really was. I touched the horizontal line. 'Is the tree dead?' I asked her. This time there was nothing.

'Ta-dah!' said Julia, just as Ryan had, which should have warned me. She was standing quite close to us and on the grass was a dazzling litter of leaves. How had she done so much in such a short time? She blew on her hands, then beamed at me. 'What do you think?'

I stood up, surprised at how creaky I felt. Then the thought hit me. I touched Sylvie's hand and it was icy-cold. Her face was pale and the light had changed and the guns had started without me noticing. As I pulled the blanket closer around Sylvie there was a long barrage and then a single louder crack. How long had I been sitting there after Ryan left? Had it happened again?

'What is it?' I said to Julia. 'I can't tell what it is.'

'Best viewed from up in the house,' she told me. 'Jesus, it's cold. Dr Deville will have a great view.'

'Oh, Julia, what *is* it?' I said. 'Do I need to kick it over before she sees?'

But it was too late. Dr Ferris was on her way already. As we watched she let herself out of the French window in her office and came powering across the grass, her spike heels sinking in but not slowing her.

'Alison, what exactly do you think you're doing?' she said, when she was close enough to speak loudly but not have to shout.

'Art,' I said. Julia snorted.

'What's Sylvie doing out of her room?'

'A-art?' I said.

'Who gave you permission to form a group?'

'A group?'

'These two patients are not—' She bit the words off.

'Ryan was here too for a bit,' I said

'And she's frozen!' Dr Ferris exclaimed, reaching us and immediately bundling Sylvie back into her shawl, hands and all. 'She's chilled to the bone. How long have you been out here? What were you thinking?'

'Dr Ferris – the other Dr Ferris – asked me to take care of Julia this morning,' I said.

'Oh, I see!' Julia said. 'You drew the short straw, did you? You got landed with me? Well, fuck you very much.'

'I didn't mean it that way,' I said. 'Stop stirring the shit, will you? And I thought Sylvie could do with some fresh air.'

'Alison,' said Dr Ferris, speaking low and cold as she grasped the handles of Sylvie's wheelchair, 'that is extremely unprofessional language to use to a client.'

'I don't care,' Julia said.

But Dr Ferris ignored her. 'And Sylvie's care is not your concern, beyond the cosmetic and aesthetic matters you were employed to cater to.'

'I was catering to them,' I said. 'Fresh air is essential to good skin. I was absolutely—'

'I'm afraid I'm going to have to—'

'And, anyway,' I went on, 'it's working. Julia took her for a hurl and made her smile. And look!'

I held out the notepad to show her Sylvie's drawing but she didn't so much as glance at it.

'Julia *took* her?' she repeated, voice even colder. 'Are you suggesting that you left one vulnerable patient in the charge of another, unsupervised, patient? A patient still under initial assessment?'

'Standing. Right. Here,' Julia said. 'And look at what she's showing you, at least.'

Dr Ferris did flick a glance at the notepad then. Then she stared at Sylvie. She had grown very still and her heels were sinking further into the wet ground the longer she stood there so that she looked as if she was deflating. 'Are you trying to tell me that Sylvie . . . made those marks?'

'She was trying to draw a house, a tree and a person,' I said. 'I don't think she's as far gone as you thought, actually.'

'And you – you guided her hand?' said Dr Ferris. 'To – to make those marks?'

'No,' I said. 'She did it herself.'

Dr Ferris held out her hand for the pad and I gave it to her. 'It's not helpful to concoct fanciful interpretations,' she said. 'And *this* would be Ryan's, would it?'

Julia went to stand beside her and look over her shoulder, giving a thunderclap of a laugh – '*Ha!*' – at the drawing. Dr Ferris snapped the top sheet back over.

'Jesus Christ!' said Julia, staring at the paper and then at me. 'You're right, though. It's not fanciful at all. The square's a house and the line's a tree, right? That is spooky. That is *seriously* creepy.'

'My office, ten minutes.' Dr Ferris folded the whole pad in half, cracking the cardboard backing, then put it under her arm like a soldier's baton. She tugged her feet free, kicked the brake off Sylvie's chair and struggled off across the grass with her, sinking and shoving, so grimly set on getting away from me that I don't think she even noticed one of Sylvie's hands creeping out of the folds of the shawl and wagging gently at her side, as if she was saying goodbye.

'So . . . why's she so pissed off?' Julia said. 'Isn't it good news if Whatshername's better? And why the hell shouldn't I be allowed to hang out with her? Everyone else gets together and plays ping-pong if they feel like it. What makes me so toxic?'

'Apart from nearly bouncing a frail woman out of her wheelchair onto wet grass?' I said.

'She's less frail now than she was at breakfast. Like you said. So why isn't Dr Frosty glad of it?'

I shrugged and it turned into a huge shudder that left my teeth chattering. Without speaking, we started across the grass towards the house again. When we were halfway there, Julia heaved a huge sigh. 'Oh, God,' she said. 'It's Monday, isn't it? I tell you what, Ali, I'll swap you. I'll go to get bollocked by the ice queen and you can go to my one-on-one with Gummy Boy and think up something new to shock him with.'

'Gummy Boy?'

Julia stretched her lips over her teeth and mugged. 'Lars. He creeps me out. I want to ask him what's going on. Same with that whale Bella. What a fucking cheek they've got letting her talk to the skinny minnies about body image. But Gummy Lars is worse. Hey, listen! I don't suppose you know what tats he's got under those stretchy bandages, do you?'

'Belle,' I said. 'Not Bella. What do you mean, "think up something new to shock him"?'

'Go on. Ask him to show you and then you tell me. I'm dying to know, but when I made a grab for him and tried to rip one off he was too quick for me. He had my arms pinned and the help bell going off before I could blink.'

I nodded, remembering my own run-in with him on the range that morning. As another bout of gunfire split the air, I found myself wondering what Mona Swain was playing at, and asking myself what sort of mother would send her daughter here. With the Ferrises, and all the staff taken on after they'd been fired from somewhere else. I'd never let Angelo within ten miles of it even if he peed himself every night for a year, killed all the wildlife in the county – and what else was it?

'Why don't you tell Lars the truth instead of making up stories to shock him?' I said. 'He might be able to help you.'

'I can't,' said Julia. 'I can't remember the truth. I can't remember anything. But I know it's real. It happened even if nobody will admit it.'

'Any of what? Who won't?'

'I don't *know*!' she bellowed. Then she shook a cigarette out of the packet and lit it with shaking fingers. 'So here I am, trying to find out.'

'By talking crap to the people trying to help you?'

'Oh, for fuck's sake!' she said. 'I'm not exploring my inner *turmoil*. Jesus! I'm *here*. Back in the ancestral pile my bloody parents offloaded to the docs, because I'm trying to find out what the fuck's going *on*. Because *here* is where it's happening. Whatever it is.'

I stopped walking and stared at her. After a few paces, she realized I'd fallen behind and turned to scowl at me. 'What?' she said. 'Or are you farting? Waft it away, will you?'

'You've fooled them all,' I said. 'You haven't got any kind of personality disorder, have you?' She opened her eyes very wide. Marion had said it and so had Lars. Dr F had touched on it too. The pain under the fairytales was real. 'You're as sane as I am, aren't you?'

She regarded me for a long slug of dead time before she spoke again. 'As sane as you are? Oh, Ali, how much does *that* say?'

Chapter 16

I stretched the ten minutes as far as I dared, taking the time to check in with Angelo, via Marco.

'*Fine*, Mum. Jeez!' was all I could get out of him and it soothed me. He sounded back to his old self. I could almost hear his eyes rolling.

'Dad'll pick you up after school, if you like,' I said. 'Spare you the bus.'

'I'm not going in,' Angelo said. 'Dad's dropping me at home.'

I wanted to argue but I was ten paces from Dr Ferris's office door so I just told him I loved him and he should text me what he wanted for tea. Then I put the phone away, smoothed my hair back into a tighter ponytail and squared my shoulders.

I had my hand back to rap on the door when I heard their voices.

'. . . absolutely adequate to the requirements,' Dr Ferris was saying.

'We should have had a shortlist and interviewed candidates together, Tam,' her husband said, in the same kind voice he had used talking to me. I put my head closer to the door and held my breath.

'For God's sake, she's washing their faces and letting them paint pretty pictures! It's not worth all this.'

'That's my point,' Dr F said. 'We could have had a nutritionist, another physio, a drama therapist. If we really wanted to make this level of investment in para-therapies, we—'

'There's another consideration,' said Dr Ferris.

'Isn't there always? What are you up to this time?'

I heard a chair move and the unmistakable sound of Dr Ferris's heels on the parquet. She was pacing. One, two, three, and turn. Back, two, three, and turn. She was literally pacing.

'Oh, you know me,' she said at last. 'Protecting our investment, securing our future. The usual donkey work. But by all means you carry on listening to their whining and patting their heads.'

'That's what makes us such a great team,' said Dr F. 'I'll plod on doing the work we have to do and you play your games and see what you can cheat your way into this time.'

The pacing stopped. I put my ear against the wood of the door and only then noticed Hinny, in her kitchen whites, standing at the far end of the corridor watching me. I jerked up and away, cheeks flaming. Hinny flitted towards me and breathed in my ear. 'Share it if it's good stuff,' she whispered, then glided off again, silent in her soft shoes. I cleared my throat, rapped on the door and, at a word from Dr Ferris, sidled in.

'You're late,' she said.

'I had to call my kid but I'm here now and I'm ready to learn where I went wrong and make sure not to do it again. I really hope Sylvie didn't catch a chill.'

211

'She's minty.' Dr Ferris said, her voice biting at the word. She sniffed. 'As all the kids are saying these days, apparently.'

She had got so far under my skin I suspected she was using that stupid slang word to prove that she was better at talking to teenagers than me, that she didn't need to phone her kid, because her kid phoned her. Paranoia. I shook it away. 'Good,' I said. 'I really am—'

'My husband is going to deal with you,' she said, cutting me off and, without another word, she swept out, leaving a ringing silence behind her.

'So,' I said, after an awkward moment, 'you'll have heard that I screwed up, I suppose. I let one patient meet another and I took one outside to do some art with the— Oh, actually, can I have a look at it from this window?'

'Feast your eyes,' said Dr F. 'I'll need to get out there with a rake before this afternoon. Posy's mum and dad are coming for a visit and family therapy session.'

Julia's handiwork was an enormous penis. Of course. It was made of dull yellow sycamore leaves, topped with bright red maple leaves and finished with a little heap of brown birch leaves for pubic hair.

'It's actually quite well done,' said Dr F, joining me to look at it. 'But even saying that to you is sexual harassment so I'll need to get rid of it.'

'And do you need to get rid of me too?' I said. 'I really didn't mean to let Sylvie get cold.'

'Sylvie?' said Dr F. 'You took *Sylvie* out? With Julia?'

'I thought she needed the fresh air. I'm sorry.'

'Well, she's so inactive. We have to be careful. Pneumonia's a constant concern when someone moves as little as she does.'

'Shouldn't she move more, then? Sorry.'

'Her case is very complex,' Dr F said.

'But shouldn't she be getting physiotherapy or something? In a swimming pool if she's too wobbly to be on her own two feet. Although, you know, she walked about quite the thing when I was holding her hands. And outside today, she was smiling!'

'We've been taking care of Sylvie for a long time,' Dr F said. 'You don't need to worry.'

'Maybe you're right,' I said. 'Maybe it is a waste of money having me instead of someone else who could—' I stopped when his eyebrows had risen high enough to be lost in his untidy hair. 'I might just have caught a bit of what you were saying,' I admitted.

'Have you heard of transference, Ali?' said Dr F. I shrugged. 'Where a patient in therapy imagines a close relationship – a love connection or a family bond – with their therapist?' I nodded, waiting. 'And then of course there's counter-transference, where a professional in a caring role can reflect that imaginary bond and start to project a relationship onto a patient. Typically a patient who offers a way back to unresolved relationships in the therapist's own past.' I nodded again, maybe with a bit less certainty now. 'Sylvie is absent but she is not your mother,' he said. 'She is within age-range for it but she is not your sister.' I nodded very fast. I wanted him to stop talking. 'And although she is very helpless and very appealing, she is not your child.'

'Thank you,' I said. 'Thank you, yes. I see that. I get that. Absolutely. Thanks.' I breathed in deep and managed to stop talking. 'But I really helped Sylvie. Why would Dr Ferris mind that?'

'It's complicated,' he said.

'She's not jealous, is she?' It was a stupid idea, that someone so polished and perfect could be jealous of me.

Dr Ferris considered me for a long time before he spoke again. 'Jealousy is not in my wife's repertoire,' he said. 'Look, absolutely off the record, do you really need this job?'

I answered what lay under the words instead of the words themselves. 'There's something wrong, isn't there? You don't need a beautician for twenty-odd patients and it's not worth forty-five thou even if you do.'

'Forty-*five*?' he said. 'Look, Ali, it's easy to think things are calm and you can cope when the nursing staff are on hand in case of trouble. But it takes real training to manage a crisis. Especially at night when staffing levels are reduced.'

Was he warning me off the night shift I'd agreed to?

'I had better go and rake up Julia's leaves,' he said and, without another word, we left together.

———

Gales of laughter were gusting out of the staff kitchenette, like sweet puffs of air from a bakery, and I felt myself smiling and walking faster. Surraya was in there with Hinny and Lars today. She was holding a tissue under each eye and crying with laughter.

'Oh, stop!' she said. 'Stop it. I'm losing my lenses. My eyes'll be killing me the rest of the shift if I need to lick them and put them back in.'

'Ali, you're a wee smasher,' Lars said. 'I've got it on my phone. Look.'

I nodded at the photograph of Julia's leaf collage taken from an upstairs window but I couldn't laugh.

'Aw, come on!' Hinny said, slapping a tea mug down in front of me. 'It's the best laugh we've had here since Rosa went streaking through the dining hall.'

'Rosa who's dying?' I said.

'A while back this was,' Hinny said.

'I'm in big trouble,' I said. 'I've maybe given Sylvie a chill that might turn into pneumonia and I've formed a group without permission and I've just had a lecture from Dr F about counter-transference and he's asked me to think hard about if I really need this job.'

I was expecting more knee-jerk sympathy but, to my surprise, they exchanged a look, like a snooker ball kissing off three cushions before it disappeared.

'Aye, he gives everyone that warning,' Lars said at last. 'He knows her better than she knows herself.'

'I have no idea what you mean,' I told him.

'Hard to explain,' Surraya said.

'Dr Ferris trades in loyalties,' Hinny said. 'Dr F is just loyal.'

Lars whistled through his teeth and Surraya gave a short laugh. 'Coming to something when the cook can say it better than the psychiatric nurses, eh?' she said. 'Anyway. Ali, thank you for calming us down. I get red eyes if I cry with my lenses in and that wee bitch Roisin's wrecked my specs. So thanks, pal.' She stood, threw her tissues into the bin and clapped her hands. 'Right. I'm doing the new alkie's drink diary with him. I'd better get going.'

'And I've got three pork shoulders to whack apart for a casserole,' Hinny said. 'Bloody local-sourced butcher meat. A catering pack from Reid's, you just open the plastic and tip it in. None of this Hannibal Lecter shite. You'll do the cups, eh, no, Lars?'

'I'll get dishpan hands,' said Lars, 'but for you, anything.'

'Tell her about the specs,' Hinny said, over her shoulder, as she was leaving.

'Surraya's specs?' I said. 'What did Roisin do? She's one of the . . .?'

'Aye, that's her.' Lars stood, peered into my mug, hoping I'd finished, then started washing up the rest. 'Grabbed them and snapped them. No, though. The specs on the corpse, this is. Ken how they found a bit of one of the leg bits? Still there even though the nose and ear was gone? Like, totally smashed into the skull?'

I said nothing and he craned over his shoulder to see if I was listening. 'Specs, right,' I said.

'Armani.'

'Get out.'

'It's on the BBC feed. They released it so fast Boney couldn't even leak it to me. Designer glasses by Giorgio Armani. No word of a lie.'

'And a Kangol belt and Asda's own-make jeans?'

'Weird, eh? The polis are saying it's bound to help narrow it down, get something to run the DNA against. The "intersection of the two sets" is going to be likes of one guy, right?'

I wondered who he was quoting, but before I could ask him he told me anyway. 'Lola. My middle one. I asked her how school was going last night and she talked about maths for forty minutes. She gets it from her mum.'

'You must miss them,' I said. In answer, he did what everyone always does these days. He reached into his tunic pocket and took out his phone, scrolled and passed it over to me. I looked at the picture of the three girls sitting on a stone wall squinting into strong light. One was still chubby, her belly pushing out

216

the skirt of her sundress and the ruched bodice dead flat against her chest. The middle one was long and gangly, one of her thin legs bent up so her knee was by her ear. The oldest was a beauty, burnished skin and tumbling curls. She sat with her littlest sister hugged on her lap, smiling widely. No sulks or pouting.

'They're gorgeous,' I said. 'And they look like good kids too.'

'How about you?' said Lars. 'You got any photos?'

His voice was soft and it made me look up at him. 'Of my son?' I said. 'Only about a million.'

But he shook his head. 'Or a footprint maybe? Her handprint?'

I stared at him and felt my eyes fill, and the tears start to fall. 'No,' I said. 'There's no pictures. Because she wasn't even— I never really—'

'Aye, but she was, wasn't she?' Lars said. 'And you still are.'

The tears were so hot, I felt them spike as they came up out of me, stinging my cheeks as they fell.

'You need a wee hug?' Lars said.

I shook my head hard. 'How did you know?'

'What?' he said. 'You're kidding. You might as well walk about with a sign round your neck, Ali.'

'Stop it,' I said. 'You've no idea. It was a terrible time and I got through it and I'm fine.'

'Aye, right,' he said. 'You *look* fine. So what's the scoop with the rag doll?' He put a hand out and covered mine. His felt warm because mine was icy. 'Ask Belle,' he said. 'It was Maternity she got the sack from, you know. She retrained for this place. *She*'ll tell you how to get fine.'

'Oh, Belle will, will she? Belle that got the sack for . . . What was it?'

'Too much kindness and not enough rules.' Belle spoke

217

suddenly from the door. For such a large woman she moved softly.

'Boundary issues!' I said, the phrase coming back to me. 'You've all got bloody boundary issues. You're all bloody freaks! And let go of my hand too.' I wrenched free of him and, clattering my chair over backwards, I was up and out of there.

Of course I remembered as soon as I was in the front hall that I couldn't storm out because I'd got a lift in. But I'd rather walk home than sit and listen to any more of their pity. Condescending, patronizing . . . And then, rounding a corner, I ran into Dr Ferris again.

'Alison?' she said.

'Oh, don't start,' I said. 'And don't worry. I'm leaving.'

'I was coming to talk to you,' she said. 'It appears that my husband forgot to tell you something during your debriefing.' Her voice was clipped and she seemed to be standing even more ramrod-straight than usual, although it was hard to see how that could be since she was like a poker at the best of times. 'The drawing. The little doodle that Sylvie made?'

'So you do believe she drew it, then,' I said. 'Because why would I lie about something like that?'

'It's a worrying sign,' said Dr Ferris. 'The very last thing we want to do is to let Sylvie regress to the trauma that brought her here.'

'Really?' I said. 'Even if going back there would maybe set her off on a different path? I mean, it's not as though she's getting better as she is.'

'Alison,' said Dr Ferris, taking a step closer, 'you are a beautician. I am a psychiatrist.'

'What was it that happened to her anyway? The trauma that landed her in here? That makes her draw that weird cross?'

'Cross?' said Dr Ferris. 'Is that what you see?'

The light was low and the house was quiet, and standing there, with her two steps closer than any normal person would come, close enough that I could smell her perfume and even the coffee on her breath, it seemed suddenly as if we were all alone. It was hard to believe there were twenty patients in the house and a shift of nurses too, with the back-shift due any minute. Maybe that was why she was talking in the corridor, private business, like she'd told me not to do. I tried to take a step away but I was pressed against the edge of a thin hall table already. I put my hand back and gripped it to steady myself, tried to talk lightly.

'Cross, square, whatever,' I said. 'It's not a house, is it?'

'Popular culture has led to a belief that mental illness is triggered by one horrific event,' said Dr Ferris. The words were cool and measured, but she was still speaking in that urgent, breathy way. I put the other hand round behind me and gripped the table tighter. 'Sylvie's descent into her illness was triggered by something you or I would fully expect a young woman to take in her stride.'

'Well,' I said, 'they do feel things very deeply at that age.'

'She was hurt,' said Dr Ferris, 'and she withdrew to save herself from being hurt again. A total withdrawal from all relationships – her family, friends, all human contact.'

'But today she was smiling,' I said. 'And drawing that . . . whatever it is.'

'It's the Mercat Cross,' said Dr Ferris. 'In Kirkcudbright. The square base and the cross on top. You probably know it.'

'Of course,' I said, 'In fact . . .' But Angelo wouldn't want me blabbing his business at work so I bit my lip.

'She was stood up,' Dr Ferris said. 'Well, not just stood up.

Asked out on a date by a boy she liked when she was a schoolgirl. They were to meet at the Mercat Cross. But when she got there, he had sent a pack of his friends to mock and jeer at her. She ran away, boorish laughter ringing in her ears, and she started that very day to shut down. She came here shortly afterwards and she's been here ever since.'

I said nothing. I couldn't blame the low light and the quiet now. Now I felt as if the two of us were wrapped in a black sack together, like puppies for drowning, no air and no escape, just her voice and her coffee breath and the glint in her eyes.

'So, you see, it's not a good sign at all that she's drawing it.'

'I see,' I managed to say.

'What's wrong?' said Dr Ferris, rearing back to get a clearer look at me, breaking the black sack and letting the air in. I gasped at it. 'What's wrong with you?' she said again.

'Just shocked,' I got out. 'Years of illness from something so small? It's frightening. Makes it feel like anyone could go wrong.'

'But you've actually gone white,' she said. 'Are you ill?'

'I am feeling a bit stomachy, actually,' I said. 'Have been all day. And Belle said first thing I shouldn't really be in contact with patients if I've got a bug.'

'Belle is right,' she said. She had taken another step away and she swiped at her face as if to get my germs off her. 'You should go home and don't come in tomorrow if you have symptoms.'

'It might be something I ate,' I said. 'But, yes, I'll go. I'll phone my husband.'

She frowned at that. 'How long will it take him to get here?'

'I'll start walking and meet him,' I told her. 'I need the air.'

Chapter 17

At least the firing had stopped. If I had walked up the drive to the checkpoint with guns going off I might have lost my mind. I would have been in the next room to Sylvie, staring out at the emptiness along with her. As it was, there was just the cold light of a sinking fog and the dark sparkle of the wet road disappearing under my feet as I pitched myself forward.

'But you've got to come!' I said to Marco, pressing the phone so hard to the side of my head that the ridges of my ear ached. 'I'm walking to meet you. I need to get home.'

'Has something happened?' said Marco. In the background I could hear voices and the beep-beep of someone ringing things through a till.

'Yes!' I said. Shouted, really, only the day was so close and damp it swallowed my voice. 'Yes, something has happened and I need to get home. Now.'

'Okay, Ali. Promise me you won't overreact,' Marco said, 'but this thing that's happened. Is it real? Is it outside your head or are you just upset?'

'Yes, for God's sake, it's real,' I told him. 'I heard something, Marco. Something I can't explain. And I need to get home right now.'

His sigh came across the line as a long buzz. 'You heard something,' he said. 'Did anyone else hear it?'

'What? What are you asking? Why aren't you in the car already?'

'I'm at work,' he said, soft but fierce. Then he spoke louder 'Eh? Naw. Fine. Just the wife.' Then quietly to me again, 'Ali, come on, eh? There's no need to go back down that way again. You're finished with all that.'

'I don't know what you're talking about.'

'Running out of the pictures bawling your head off? Chucking presents straight in the bin? Walking out and leaving the shop hanging open that night? None of us needs to go back there, do we?'

'When did I leave the shop open?' I said. He had stung me. I didn't know he had noticed the faceless angel gone from the mantelpiece the morning after the Christmas party and I thought he had believed me when I said I had rushed out of *Harry Potter* to throw up from too much popcorn. I had never read it to Angelo and I didn't know until it was right there in front of me and everyone was laughing. Nearly Headless Nick. Even Marco was laughing and Angelo all lit up and his eyes shining. I couldn't hear anything, not the film or the audience, except the moan that seemed to come from all around me. 'Mmmhmmm.'

'That time one of the girls saw you running down the street in the rain in your shirtsleeves and phoned me and I went in and locked up for you,' Marco said.

I had never wondered why the shop was locked up when I'd got back in the morning.

'One time,' I said.

'And you used to hear it at night and get up out your bed and go looking for where it came from.'

I had no memory of doing that. Except maybe, now he'd reminded me, there were nights when I checked the house, sure I could hear a tiny humming noise, and was never able to find it, even when the telly was unplugged and all the digital clocks switched off, everything needing resetting in the morning. 'I've never said a word about it for ten long years,' I whispered into the phone. 'Why would I start now?'

'That's my girl,' Marco said. 'Go back to work, eh? And I'll see you at tea-time.'

'I'm talking about something someone *told* me, Marco,' I said. 'I'm talking about something Dr Ferris just told me. Something I don't even know how to begin to understand.'

'I'm on my way,' he said. He was walking as he talked now and his voice was all business suddenly. 'I'll just tell them I'm taking a break and I'll come and meet you.'

'Stop in on the way past the house and check Angel's okay,' I said. 'Five more minutes won't hurt me.'

'Christ, make your bloody mind up,' he said. 'Of course Angel's okay. The wee toerag's in his jammies watching videos.'

'Just don't drive past the door without at least saying hiya,' I said. 'Give him a cuddle, then come and meet me.'

I clicked off, stowed the phone, then put my head down and really started moving.

The man on the checkpoint shouted to me, 'Getting a lift, hen? You want to wait in here for it?' but I ignored him and swung out onto the road for home.

Angelo was on the drive to Howell Hall. He hadn't just stepped off the road onto the verge or gone looking for

223

somewhere to pee. He had put his backpack down and set off down the drive towards the hall. There had to be a reason. But he wasn't coming to find me, because he knew I'd be at home. There was only one other explanation and it made sense of how he could tell me the story about the Mercat Cross. The story that was Sylvie's.

Lars had even said it: Howell Hall took referrals from the NHS. Angelo, my Angelo, must have gone to the GP all on his own and got himself signed up with someone to talk to. My son needed someone so badly he was talking to a psychiatrist without me even knowing. Dr Ferris. A cool, collected professional who wouldn't touch him and nag him and call it love. And part of what she had done to help him was share a story about the most extreme case she knew of another kid not dealing well with trouble.

And, that dreadful night, he tried to get *more* help from her. Her, not me. Walking through the rain to reach her instead of sitting on the bus to come home.

It even made sense of her reaction to his name the day of the interview. She'd covered it with that nasty jibe about which babies get called 'Angel', but really she must have been surprised to find that the parent of one of her patients was sitting there having an interview. Conflict of interest kind of thing, jeopardizing confidentiality. But he was fifteen. I didn't understand how he could be her patient without my say-so.

Had I neglected him? Calling him daddy's boy, trying so hard to keep myself together I never noticed my son – my only child – falling apart. *My only child.* I never let that thought into my head. I had a hundred different ways of dodging it. 'Do you have kids?' people would ask, and I'd say, 'I do. My son is . . .' Clever. I kept all my truth in the spaces between the words.

'How many kids you got?'

'Well, there's Angelo, my boy . . .' hugging my precious truth in the sneaky wee gaps in the meaning.

Barrelling along the road, the hawthorns in the high hedge dripping on my head and the foggy air creeping into my bones, I said it aloud for the first time ever: 'Angelo is my only child. I've got one kid. His name is Angelo.'

As soon as the words left my lips, I heard her louder than I'd ever heard her before. It was coming from my right, the other side of the hedge.

'Mmmhmmmm.'

'No!' I screamed. 'I'm sorry! I'm coming. I'm sorry!'

'Mmmmmmhhmmmmmm.'

I started running flat out, searching for a break in the hedge, a gate, a fence, anything.

'Mmmmhhuuhhmmmm,' she said, clearer than she'd ever said it.

'I'm coming!' I yelled, and suddenly there was a chorus, bellowing, a crowd of voices, and there was a gate and I threw myself at it and scrambled over.

Then I saw them.

Seven mothers and their calves, hoofs deep in the mud, all huddled for warmth against the hedge and lowing their alarm, scared of the rushing feet in the lane and the stupid woman shouting her mouth off.

I sank back against the gate and let it take my weight. 'I'm sorry,' I told them. 'Sorry. I'm not going to hurt your babies. You're okay.' The one nearest to me swished her tail, then put her head down and tugged up a mouthful of grass. Slowly, as my breath settled, all of them turned away from me.

'You've got the right idea,' I said. 'Keep them close.'

I was down on my hunkers now, my bum getting soaked on the wet ground, but I could no more move than I could laugh or even cry. And that was where Marco found me.

The car went past, then I heard it slow and stop, and the whine of the reverse gear as he came carefully back and hitched up into the gateway. The door opened.

'Ali?' He clambered over and crouched beside me. 'What's up, pal?' He put an arm round me. 'What did that doctor tell you that's got you in this state, eh?'

I leaned into him, feeling his warmth begin to spread to me even through all our clothes. 'I don't think I can tell you,' I said. 'Not yet anyway.'

'You can tell me anything,' Marco said. He put his lips against the side of my head and pressed hard.

'It's just it's nothing to do with you,' I said. 'It's a secret and it's not mine to tell. Sorry.'

His arm fell away and he stopped pressing his lips to my hair. I looked up to see if he was angry, but he gave me a smile and shook his head, as if in wonder. 'Someone else's secret?' he said. 'All this and it's not you and me? It's not even Angel? So . . . you've heard a sad story from one of the nutters and you've got me stopping and landing smoochies on the boy and you're zooming home to knit a onesie for him?'

I didn't say anything. So technically I didn't lie.

———————

It was when I got into the car that the lightning bolt hit me. I pulled a carrier bag off the back seat to spread under my muddy trousers and remembered picking Angel up that night, soaked and shivering, the damp patch on the car seat after. *Of course* a fifteen-year-old kid couldn't get referred to a psychiatrist without a parent's consent. But they *had* a parent's consent.

I shot a sideways look at Marco. That one parent had decided not to worry the other. He trusted the doctors. But he didn't know what I knew.

'Something's wrong at Howell Hall,' I said, when we were under way.

'I thought you weren't going to tell me,' Marco said. 'Someone else's secret and all that?'

I almost laughed. That *was* it. That was what he thought I'd heard – that my son was an outpatient at a nuthouse and his dad had kept it from me. That was what got him out of work and belting over here to pick me up.

'Not that,' I said. 'Not only that. There's something off about the whole place. Did you know that all the staff there have been chucked out of somewhere else? Dr Ferris takes them on. Why would she do that?'

'Don't put yourself down,' Marco said. 'Not *all* the staff. Not you.'

I said nothing. Of *course* there was something wrong with me. My CV was a joke. But Dr Ferris had employed me anyway. And her own husband had warned me off the night shift. Practically.

'I don't know what all the parents and relatives would think if they knew their posh rehab place was staffed by rejects.'

'They can't be that bad,' Marco said. Defending the place he'd agreed Angelo could go to. 'They need to have clearance and accreditation and all that.'

'I don't think the clearance procedure is much cop,' I said. 'Mine came through on the nod. Dead quick.' Marco said nothing and I found myself turning to him. 'When was it you got

227

me to sign the PVG exactly?' I said. 'Everyone seems surprised how quick it came back.'

Marco shrugged. 'Bit of efficiency in the system,' he said. 'Don't knock it. And don't do yourself down. Saying Howell Hall must be crap if they've settled for you.'

'They're hanging by a thread,' I told him, remembering what Lars had told me. 'Didn't get a great rating last time the inspectors came, and they're trying to clean up their act before the next sneak raid.'

'Sneak raid?'

'Surprise inspection. That's why I'm in there, actually. To make the place look good and bump up the marks.'

For a while Marco didn't say anything. When he spoke again his voice sounded strained. 'That's what you've been told?' he said. 'Or that's what you've decided out of your own head?'

'I'm just glad *your* thing's going so well,' I said. 'Hang in, eh? Because I'll bet you as soon as the next CC's been I'll be out on my ear.'

'You shouldn't be so cynical,' Marco said. 'You're not even doing clinical care, are you? It wouldn't make any difference. You're dead wrong about why you're there, Ali.'

I didn't argue. I'd found out what I wanted to know. Because why would Marco know that 'CC' stood for 'clinical care' unless he'd been looking at Howell Hall's credentials? Like a parent would. Then we were slowing at the gate and I was out and up the path. When the engine didn't go off I turned round and bent to look in at him.

'I'm going back to work,' he said, as the window went down. 'Hanging in, like you said. See you tea-time.'

I stared. He'd found me crouched in a cow field crying and

he knew I was demented with worry about our son, not to mention that he knew Angelo was in all kinds of pain and trouble too, but he was going back to work? On the other hand it suited me. I didn't want him listening in when I talked to Angelo. I nodded and turned to put my key in the door.

———————

He was lying on his bed. Of course. The same trackie bums and baggy sweatshirt he'd worn all weekend. Earbuds in, curtains closed, the little room fugged with his sweat and farts and the snacks he'd been living on. For once, I said nothing. I'd rather live with my head in his armpit than have him sitting in a hospital, silent for decades.

'Hiya,' I said, sitting.

He plucked out one of the earbuds and regarded me stonily. 'Your turn, is it?' he said. 'Dad's already been in and had a go at me.'

'I want to talk to you.' I ignored the eye-roll. 'I need to hear what happened, Angelo.' I ignored the sigh that was almost a groan. 'I know what you said about the day at the Mercat Cross isn't the . . .' truth, I wanted to say '. . . whole story,' I settled for.

Out came the other earbud and he switched off the iPod. 'What is your *problem*?' he said. 'I told you that like you were a *friend*. And now you turn round and— What is *wrong* with you?'

He pulled his legs up, knees to chest, so fast I thought he was going to kick out at me to get me off his bed but he was only preparing to spring up and make for the door.

'Angel, I'm talking to you!' I said. 'Don't you dare walk out on me.'

'I'm going for a *piss*, Mum,' he said. 'Is that okay?'

'Was I supposed to know that?' I said.

But he had slammed the door. By the time he came back I had got a hold of myself again. *The stories are crap but the pain is real.*

'You've got a point,' I told him. 'I'm sorry. I really am grateful you opened up to me that night. But I've got to know everything that's going on, Angel. I'm your mum and I want to protect you. I can't protect you if I don't know what's happening. Can I?'

'Protect me from what?' He sat down at the head of his bed and put his feet up on the end of his desk, joggling it, piece of flat-pack crap that it was, so his laptop stirred to life.

'Look,' I said. 'Your dad loves you and he's trying to do his best for you. And for me. But he doesn't always *know* best.'

Angelo snorted. 'No shit!'

'So,' I said, treading carefully, 'why not tell me what really happened?'

'You first,' Angel said. And then, after the silence had gone on so long that the air had turned dead between us, he added, 'Yeah, I thought so.' He stood up again. 'I need a shower,' he said. 'I need to think. Let me go and have a shower and maybe I'll tell you when I get back. Okay?'

And he was gone. I heard the bathroom door lock, then the water turning on. His laptop went back to standby, turning the dim room almost to darkness. I reached out to shake the desk and bring it life again. For the light. Swear on my life, swear to God, it was only for the light. It never occurred to me until after I'd done it that he was logged in to his messages.

The shower was running. I stood up and bent over the

230

lighted screen. There was nothing. Not a single message in his inbox and nothing saved. Nothing in the sent file and the trash was empty. My heart was cantering. He had cut himself off from everyone.

Was this really happening? My son had started hanging out all alone at a deserted ruin and he'd seen a human hand sticking up out of the ground and instead of coming to me he turned to a psychiatrist. And the story she'd told him about the dangers of letting little things loom large was what he served up to me as a sop. To make me stop asking him questions.

Could this really be true?

I stared at the screen. Something was wrong with a teenage kid who didn't contact anyone for days on end. I hadn't seen his thumbs at rest for three years before we left our real house and came here. Then a simpler explanation hit me. He might have been using the landline when he was in the house on his own. The shower water was still running, so sitting quickly in his desk chair I called up the browser, found the British Telecom homepage and entered our details. It loaded slowly and I heard the water go off before the first page of itemized calls was complete, but it covered more than a week and I scanned them, noting incoming from 0800 numbers and one or two back and forth from Marco's mobile, one or two back and forth to mine. There was only one number I didn't recognize and there were five calls to it, the last one just today, not even an hour ago. I whipped out my phone and dialled it with one hand, shutting down our account and paging back to Angel's message page with the other.

It rang three times and then the familiar voice answered with a recorded message: 'You have reached Tamara Ferris's out-of-hours line. If you wish—' I killed the call.

By the time he opened the door again, bringing a wave of Lynx and warmth in with him, the laptop had gone back to standby.

'Right,' he said, sitting down. 'Here goes.'

'No,' I said. 'You're right, darlin'. I need to go first. What is it you want me to tell you? I don't know where to start and I don't want to overload you, but ask me anything. What is it you want to know?'

'Just . . .' he said. 'Why do you never talk about it to me? That's all, really. I'm supposed to be a part of this family too. But you and Dad never even mention it in front of me. It's like your private . . . Is it too special? Is it like I'd spoil your memories?'

I stood, opened the curtains, then the window. If I didn't let some air in, I'd faint. He had no idea who we were, Marco and me. How long had he spent thinking we were this tight little unit of two sharing everything, keeping him outside?

'Angelo,' I said, 'I swear to God, I didn't think you knew. We decided not to tell you.'

'What the fuck, Mum?' I could see the pale disc of his face and the gleam of his eyes in the light coming through the window. 'Of course I know. What are you talking about?'

'When did Dad tell you?' I said.

'What are you *on* about?' said Angelo. 'Dad didn't have to tell me. I was there. I *remember*.'

'What?' My voice was no more than a whisper.

'I remember your fat belly and the room with horses on the mobile and the bed that was even smaller than my bed. And then you were away and I bought a present and brought it to the hospital but you were asleep. Then . . . then Dad said I wasn't supposed to talk about it because it would make you cry. And you did cry. I remember that. Every night you cried. And then we were at the beach and it was sunny every day.'

'Australia,' I said. 'But you were three. You were a baby. Wait, you're saying you came to the hospital?'

'But you were asleep,' he said again.

'I didn't even know you'd been.'

'And then you just kept it all to yourselves. Like I wasn't even . . .'

'No,' I said. 'That's not right.'

'Fuck's sake, Mum,' he said. 'How can you deny it? I don't even know if it was a boy or a girl. I don't even know if I had a brother or a sister.'

'Oh, Angel,' I said. 'You never had either. There wasn't a baby. But . . . yes, if things had been different she would have been your sister. But she never was.'

Angelo's voice was a breath of breeze in the room between us. 'I don't even know her name.'

You and me both, I wanted to tell him. Her 'name' was Baby Girl McGovern. We hadn't chosen one in advance and then there was no point. 'Sylvie,' I said, for no reason at all except that I couldn't tell him something so cold and make him think I didn't love her.

For a long moment, we sat and looked at each other, then Angelo nodded, slowly and rhythmically, more as if he was bobbing his head to music than trying to communicate something. When he finally spoke again I couldn't make any sense of it.

'I knew it was someone from now,' he said.

'Sylvie?' I said, panic flaring in me.

Angelo frowned. 'What? No. I knew it wasn't a monk, over there, in the ground.'

233

'Huh. Right. Sorry,' I said. Then: 'How?'

'Because he had a watch on,' said Angelo. 'But the police don't know that.'

Now I was doing the rhythmic nodding and it helped me like it had helped him. It helped me swallow what he was telling me, like it helped him swallow his sister's name, suddenly.

'Where is it?' I said at last. 'You need to get rid of it, Angel.'

His breath was a thin gasp. 'I haven't *got* it!' he said. 'I didn't take it. I didn't even touch it. It was too weird and minging. I just saw it.'

'So . . .' I said. 'Maybe the police do know and they're holding it back. So they can sift the time-wasters from the serious witnesses.'

'What?'

Of course, he didn't watch drama or read novels: he wasn't as up on all the tricks as me. 'Yeah, that's what they do, see?' I said. 'If someone comes along and says their brother had that belt and those jeans and Armani specs and he's been missing for years on end, they'll ask about the watch to double check.'

But Angelo was shaking his head. 'I don't think so. They'd want to ID him, wouldn't they?'

Plus, I thought, Lars's friend hadn't leaked the watch either.

'So what kind was it?' I asked him. 'Could you tell?'

'No,' he said. 'But I took a photo.'

My blood seemed to clench inside me, thick and sticky. 'There's a photograph of the hand on your phone? Angel, that phone's at the police station. They're bound to go through what's on it eventually.'

'It's not on my phone,' he said. 'I'm not an idiot, Mum. I emailed it to myself and downloaded it.'

I glanced over at his laptop. 'Why?'

234

'It was the coolest freak show I'd ever seen,' he said, with a shrug. 'It was a laugh.'

My hand shot out and grabbed his arm without me willing it. 'Angel, who has seen the photo? Who have you shown it to?'

'What?' he said, shaking my hand off and giving me the look of wounded outrage I knew so well. I've *done* my homework; you *said* I could borrow it; everyone *else* is getting to go. But this wasn't kids' stuff now.

'Don't even try playing the daftie,' I told him. 'How is it a laugh if you don't show someone? How is it cool if no one knows you've got it?'

He was staring at me, his eyes darting around my face and his jaw clamped so tight that a muscle was flickering in his cheek. 'How can I show anyone a picture on my laptop in my bedroom?' he said.

'Email. You think I zip up the back?'

'Mum, I haven't shown anyone the *picture*!' he said. 'I swear on . . . What do you want me to swear on? Sylvie's grave?'

'She hasn't got a grave,' I said.

'Fine, well, her memory then. I swear on—'

'Don't,' I said. I didn't know whether I hated the thought of the real Sylvie sitting calmly in her room or my faceless angel, gone before she was ever called anything. I didn't want either of them mixed up in this. 'You don't need to swear. I believe you. Now, let me see it, eh?'

I saw his shoulders sag as he relaxed. He'd got away with something. He'd managed not to lie to me. Technically.

Chapter 18

There were three pictures. One dark from the flash failing, one fuzzy from the phone shaking, and one, like Goldilocks, just right. I thought I was ready but still I gasped when Angelo clicked it onto the screen in front of me.

It was nothing like the skeleton hands from medical models, white and shining. This one was streaked dark, with leathery twists of gristle still in its joints and jagged tags of fingernail still hanging from the thumb and the middle finger. And the watch, of course. It had fallen down the arm as the flesh rotted away from around it so it was half submerged in the soup of mud that the bone stood up from. I clicked and zoomed in, too close at first so the details were gone, then too far out, then – Goldilocks again – just right, the watch clear and huge on the screen and all of the body out of the shot except two brown lines that could be anything. I swallowed hard, then squinted at the letters visible under the glass, half of them lost in the flash but three of them as plain as day. MEX.

'Timex?' I said, turning to Angelo. 'Does any other kind of watch end with M-E-X?'

'No way,' he said. 'We did this in Design and Tech. It's not a prestige brand so nobody would want to make knock-offs.'

'Yeah,' I said. 'Timex, then.'

'Kind of makes you wonder why the cops kept the watch quiet instead of the specs,' said Angelo. 'There's got to be tons more men wore Timex watches than . . . what was it specs? Dolce and Gabbana?'

'Armani,' I said. 'And I really don't think they did.' I tested the idea and it didn't break. 'I think someone was there after you took the picture but before the police came. And that person took the watch away. Angel, when did you take the photo?'

'Two nights before the cops came. I told you.'

'The Sunday, right,' I said. 'And did you look on the Monday after school? On the Tuesday?'

'I didn't go over on the Monday. I was in Dumfries getting my phone stolen, remember?'

I fingered the receipt in the pocket of his coat. Why was he lying to me? Then I felt a flood of relief. 'She's got a car!' I said. 'She picked you up after school in her car and took you to the Centre. And brought you back here later. And you bought her a Coke.'

'Have you been *spying* on me?' he said.

'No,' I blurted. 'Else I'd know if you went back and saw the hand again, wouldn't I?'

'Well, stop nagging me about drinking Coke and let's talk about the – you know – *murder.*'

'Good scheme. Right. Sorry. Okay, then.' I clicked the zoom back out again until we could see everything. 'What else? Is that a left hand or a right hand? It's a left hand, so the guy was right-handed. And can we tell if he bit his nails?' I moved the cursor, then clicked in again. 'Hard to say. Ange? What do you think?' He was silent, so I turned again, to find him staring at me.

'What are you doing?' he said. 'Why are you getting all Sherlock?'

'What do you think I'm doing? Even if you didn't see anyone, I think someone was over there and took the watch. And the sooner this guy's identified the sooner the cops will stop bugging you as if you've got something to do with it. So here's what I'm thinking. Can you print this out with no marks on the paper that would show that it came from your computer?'

'What marks?' Angelo said. 'It's a piece of paper. What are you on about?'

'Good,' I said. 'And then we can send it to the cops. Anonymously.'

'What's the point of that? Mum, what are you playing at? This is getting daft.' His voice had risen and there was a faint flush on his cheeks too.

'We need to wipe the paper in case there's prints on it from when you filled the tray,' I said. 'And wipe the envelope. And for sure not lick the stamp. Then we send it to the cops from somewhere in town and they'll never know it came from us. Will they?'

'You can't be serious. You don't think they'll be able to work it out? After I've admitted that I saw a hand? They'll be round here with a warrant for my printer quicker than—'

'Well, put it on a flash drive and I'll print it somewhere else,' I said. 'At the library.' He snorted, which I deserved. 'Or at work.'

238

'At work!' Angelo's eyes were as round as when I'd read him bedtime stories about the tea-time tiger or the Gruffalo; like two little roasted hazelnuts, I used to tell him. 'You can't get them mixed up in this, Mum.'

Protecting his doctor from the trouble I'd cause her. I reached out and brushed the hair back from his forehead. It had almost dried after his shower, soft black silk lying in feathers. 'Okay,' I told him. 'Sorry. But I've got to say this, Angel. I don't think you should see her again. At least not until all this is—'

'I'm *not*,' he said. 'And I don't want to talk about it.'

'Of course you don't,' I said. 'Put it on a flash drive for me, I'll print it out, give it to the cops, and we'll never talk about any of it again.'

———

Of course the neighbour was getting off the bus, on his way home from Kirkcudbright, and we could hardly ignore each other. In fact, I couldn't help putting out a hand to help him get down the last big step and steady on his feet on the pavement. The look he gave me, wary but ready to fight, brought a flush of shame.

'Hiya,' I said. 'Sorry about earlier. I think we're all feeling a bit tense.'

'*My* conscience is clear,' he said.

'Oh, for God's sake,' I said. 'That was an olive branch. Did you have to crack it over your knee?'

'I've no idea what you mean,' he said, his voice beginning to sound thin as his temper flared.

'Hey, Missus!' the bus driver shouted, leaning forward and peering out at me. 'Are you getting in or no'?'

'Sorry, pal, I'm just coming.' I stepped round the neighbour and boarded. Then, at the last minute, as the thought struck me, I leaned back out and asked him softly, 'Have you got a watch on?'

'Eh?'

'I wanted to know the time. But I haven't got my watch on. Have you got a watch on by any chance?'

He gave me a look of such blank bewilderment that I just waved a hand at him and turned to scrabble out my bus fare. No one who'd snatched a watch from a corpse's hand in the last week could have pulled off that innocent face. So, even though the guy lived as close as we did, and had it in for Angel, and pissed me off every time I clapped eyes on him, I didn't think he was guilty.

————

I hadn't been in T&C's builder's merchants since the early days in our real house when we were still hanging pictures and spreading gravel. It had grown since then. The outside yard had displays of decorative paving, birdbaths and sundials, and inside, as well as the saw blades and nails by the pound, there were alcoves with bathrooms set up and bigger alcoves with kitchens laid out, fruit bowls, wine racks and all. For the first time, it struck me that Marco getting his foot in the door here was more than just a bit of casual money and a way to save his face while he looked for a proper job. This *was* a proper job.

'Ali?' I looked at the girl behind the counter and just about recognized her. She'd definitely been at school with me, anyway. 'You looking for Marco?'

'I was in town and thought I'd stop by,' I said. 'See if I could cadge a lift home with him. What time does he finish?'

She shrugged. 'He's the boss. He can finish when he likes. Go through.' She nodded at a half-glass door to the side of the counter and I opened it after a quick knock to find Marco behind a desk covered with invoices and sample books. He was on the phone and he was smiling round the stick of a lollipop held between his teeth. As he saw me, he sat up and spat the lolly out all in one smooth move. I had time to wonder who he was talking to, with his eyes dancing that way. The same brown eyes as Angel, of course, since that was where Angel had got them, but Marco's were bigger, big enough to shine tawny in sunlight, not like those two wee roasted hazelnuts that spiked my heart every time I really looked at them.

'I'll phone you back in a bit,' Marco said. 'My wife's just walked in . . . Eh? . . . Aye . . . Oh, aye, probably.'

'Who was that?' I said, when the phone was down and Marco had wrapped the lolly in a twist of paper and dropped it in the wastebasket. He stood up and wiped his hands on his trouser-fronts.

'Pete Muirhead,' he said, just a bit too loud. 'You know he got divorced, right? Aye, well, he's been at that online dating. Jesus Christ, don't ever leave me, Als. It's a jungle.' He laughed, and that was loud as well.

'Whose office is this?' I asked him.

'Shared,' he said. 'The two supervisors and the manager all share it, depending on who's in. But never mind that. Are you okay? What are you doing? Not that— Listen, do you want a cuppa now you're here? I'm gasping. I'll shoot over to the Whistlin' Kettle, eh? Tea? Latte?'

I had meant to tell him about the photograph of the watch and ask him what he thought. Double-checking, relying as I always had on his rough-and-ready good sense. The same bluff common sense that got me better quick after I was ill and had got him a supervisor's job ten minutes after he'd started working here.

But three things got in the way. One, I didn't believe for a minute that Pete Muirhead had put those lights in Marco's eyes, and two, that common sense hadn't stopped him bringing a three-year-old child to a hospital and letting him see his mum pure white and flaked out with compression boots on and needles in the backs of her hands. There was too much else going on for me to think about that right now, but it was in there waiting. And three, it never occurred to me how strange it would strike him, me turning up like this. He should be worried, like maybe I wasn't okay. He shouldn't be stuttering and stumbling, trying to say the right thing and not quite making it. Covering up with offers of tea.

But even while I tried to unpick all that, I saw something that distracted me. On the cabinet behind him there was a colour printer, its red standby light flashing at me. 'Cup of tea would be great,' I said. 'And a coconut cake if they still do them.'

'Oh, aye,' said Marco, standing up and patting his back pocket to check his wallet. 'Ice caps melt and empires fall but the Whistlin' Kettle's coconut cakes are for ever.'

He gave me a kiss on the cheek as he passed me and I heard him shout to whatever her name was behind the till did she want a coffee. Hail fellow well met, I thought. And he hadn't asked about Angelo. I walked round the desk and sat down, hoping the guy who really belonged here didn't show up suddenly. Marco's claim that the office was shared hadn't fooled me for a minute. Then I saw something that puzzled me. There was a silver picture frame on the desk, incongruous there in that scruffy little room with the order books and invoices. It belonged on a bank manager's polished mahogany or even on the top of a piano in a grand drawing room. But that wasn't what bothered me. It was the picture. It was a photograph from a year ago, when Angelo had dabbled, so briefly, in after-school rugby. He had hated the dirt and the endless bruises as much as I had and he'd dropped out again. But there, on the manager's desk at Marco's new job, was a picture of him, hot and muddy, laughing into the camera with some other boy's leg behind his head and some third boy's hand tugging his jersey.

I didn't know whether to laugh or cry. Did two supervisors and the manager himself 'hot-desk' this grubby little office, even to the length of swapping their family photos shift by shift? And who was Marco trying to impress, picking a photo of Angel from a short-lived and out-of-character sporting career, instead of the honest truth of him scowling out from under his hoodie?

But I was wasting time. I kissed the photo – he was my boy, after all – then looked for where to stick in the flash drive.

The picture printed and the envelope sealed with a squirt of hand sanitizer, I pushed it up my sleeve and went back out to the shop floor.

'Melanie!' I said, happy finally to have remembered.

'What?' she said, startled.

'Can you tell Marco I'll be back in a minute?' I said. 'And don't let him eat my cake. I just need to nip out to the post.'

'Away and get,' Mel said. She nodded to a wire basket on a

shelf behind the till. 'Stick it in there and I'll bung it in with my post office run at the back of five.'

'Oh, but I haven't got a stamp on it yet,' I said. 'I'm not going to give Marco a bad name, pilfering the petty cash on his first week.'

Mel frowned at me. 'Who's going to know?' she said.

'The other supervisor?' I said. 'The big boss?' This was why I didn't lie. I tripped myself up. I could have said anything, but because I had an envelope up my sleeve I had to mention posting something.

'The supervisors don't care,' Mel said. 'And the big boss thinks the sun shines out Marco's hm-hm. Take a bloody stamp, Ali. This is me you're talking to.'

And I knew what she meant. Her and me and Elaine Malcolm had swiped all the cooking chocolate from the home-economics department store cupboard one day when we were going to an athletics tournament and made ourselves as sick as pigs in the back of the bus.

She dinged open the till and peeled a stamp off a sheet, holding it out stuck to the tip of one finger. I stared at it. If I stuck that stamp on the envelope her print would be on it. If prints can survive the glue. Never mind that she'd wonder why I put gloves on before I shook my letter down from up my sleeve.

'I'll just nip out to the post if that's okay,' I said. 'Keep things ship-shape.'

Mel's face closed, like a flytrap, and she jerked her chin up once before she unpeeled the stamp and stuck it back to the book again. 'Good to know,' she said. 'Spot me this one for old times' sake, eh? And I'll watch it from now on. Never had Marco down as a jobsworth.'

I gave her the best smile I could muster, then headed out, trying to make sense of the drop in temperature. Just because I didn't want to nick a stamp, why would I go clyping to Marco? And how big a numpty would he have to be to carry tales from his wife to the manager about somebody who'd worked there longer than he had?

I could just see the back of his head in the queue inside the Kettle so I turned away and nipped up the side-street, headed the long way round to the post office.

'Well, there's a sight for sore eyes,' a voice said, as I came out of the next street down. I lifted my head. It was Muriel, one of the hairdressers who'd rented a chair from me and then gone in as co-owner when I left. 'How are you? Where have you been? How come you've not been in to see us all?'

'Oh, you know,' I said.

'What? You're not waiting for an invite, are you?'

She had never been the sharpest tack on the stair carpet. Maybe she really couldn't imagine why I didn't want to come back in and visit the place that used to be mine now it was nothing to do with me. I gave her a smile and hoped my thoughts didn't show through it, because I was thinking that it was pretty great to work with people who had a clue about how brains work. But as well as that I was thinking I couldn't go into the post office now because clearly meeting me was a big deal in Muriel's day and she wouldn't forget it in a hurry.

And just like that I came to my senses. I was mad to think I could hand it over on the down low. The cops would check Marco's work printer as quick as they'd check Angelo's home one. There was a much better way to do it. As long as my nerve didn't fail me.

Five minutes later I marched into the police station, all set to tell them someone had pushed the sealed envelope through our door and I had brought it to them before I even opened it in case it was something to do with the investigation. I sat down under the posters about needle disposal and drink-driving, waiting for the person in front of me to finish up. It was an elderly woman, well dressed and so ashamed of what had brought her there that she was leaning right over the desk, whispering to the secretary. I tried to sink back into myself so's not to hear whatever it was she was so desperate to keep quiet. Her voice shook with emotion and the low responses she was getting didn't seem to be soothing her.

I shifted on the hard bench and moved the envelope to my other hand. The more of my prints on the outside the better, since the inside was clean. I read the poster about home safety again. I could feel sweat trickling down the insides of my arms. I was sitting so rigidly that, when my phone rang, I let go of the envelope, then dropped my phone when I bent down to swipe it up again.

'Mum?' It was Angel, his voice stretched harsh. 'Where are you?'

'I'm in the waiting room at the poli—' I said.

The secretary stood up and looked round the embarrassed woman at the desk. 'No mobiles in here, madam,' she said.

'Mum, you need to get out of there.'

'I'm just leaving,' I said, standing up. I waved the phone at them. 'He found it so I don't need to make the theft report. Typical male!' The secretary gave the ghost of a smile. I think she believed me. The old woman didn't even turn round.

'What is it?' I said to Angel, once I was outside.

'Were you really going to hand over a flash drive to the cops?' he said.

246

'I printed it out.'

'They'd still know it came from my phone.'

'How?' My voice was a whisper as faint as that poor woman inside the station.

'Okay, well, not my phone but one the same as mine. A Nokia. Not an iPhone. They can tell what make and model it was taken on.'

I swallowed hard. 'They'd be able to tell that from a printed-out copy? Not just from a file?' I had the buzzing feeling in my lips that I knew went along with my face draining. I had got so close to doing something so stupid. 'Why didn't you tell me?' I said, turning my fright into temper, unable to help it. 'Jeez, Angel. Why didn't you say that right away?'

'I didn't know! I – I looked it up.'

But I had heard the break in his voice. 'Don't lie to me, Angelo. What did you key in?'

'What?'

'Don't mess with me. If you looked it up, what did you Google?'

'I can't remember,' he said. He was always a terrible liar. Not much better now than when he'd say he didn't know what had happened to the choc ices when he was standing there with a mask of melted chocolate six inches wide all round his mouth.

'Who did you phone?' I asked him. 'The same person you showed the picture to?'

'I didn't show the picture to anyone,' he said, full of umbrage, covered by his technicality.

But *what* technicality?

I almost laughed as it hit me. He had practically told me. He'd said they 'hung out' a few times before they met up and before their 'real date'.

'You weren't alone,' I said. 'You didn't have to show someone the photo because someone was right there with you to see the real thing. And that same someone just told you about identifying the phone from the printed photo.'

'Mum, for God's sake,' was his reply. 'No one was with me when I took the photo!' There was that same grievance and outrage again.

'Angelo, this isn't a game and she's not trustworthy. She's proved that to you.'

'Never mind that,' he said. 'I just want to forget all about it. Listen, I've worked out why the specs are posher than the rest of his stuff. At least, I think so.'

'Okay,' I said. 'Convince me.'

'The cheap belt and jeans and watch, right?' he said.

'Yeah.'

'Whoever stashed the body knew they'd be found, right?'

'Yeah.'

'Exactly. Whoever it was took his Gucci belt and Ferragamo suit and Hublot watch off him and disguised him as an ordinary Asda kind of guy. And they took his posh specs off him too. His smashed specs. Only they didn't know they'd left a bit behind. They had no idea they'd left behind a clue that he was rich.'

'God Almighty, you're right!' I said. 'Yeah, you're right. Did you think of that all on your own? Do you really know all those designers' names? Ferra-who?'

He didn't answer me. But before I could wonder why, I saw the sergeant coming round the corner with one of his wee WPCs trotting at his side. 'I need to go, Angel,' I said, and switched off the phone.

'Mrs McGovern,' the sergeant said, twinkle-eyed and beaming, standing right in front of me that way that policemen do.

He wasn't tall but he was wide with big shoulders and thick short legs. The overall effect was someone you wouldn't mess with.

'I was waiting to see you,' I said, 'but my phone rang so I had to come out.'

'And what's brought you all the way in here from the wilds of Dundrennan to ask me?' he said.

'*Tell* you actually,' I corrected, which he didn't think much of. 'It's about the Armani specs and how they don't go with the—' my lips had rounded to say 'watch' before I managed to stop and change it to '—own-make jeans and cheap belt.'

'Oh, uh-huh?' he said. 'You think you've considered some angle that's outwitted the plods, do you?'

'I wouldn't put it that way,' I said. 'It's just it occurred to me, you know, chewing it over, that the cheap stuff was deliberately put on him to make you think you were looking for that kind of guy. An ordinary type. And whoever it was that bashed his head in didn't notice that a bit of his fancy glasses got left behind when they stripped him. So I reckon you're looking for a Flash Harry and they didn't want you to know that. See?'

The look of scorn didn't even flicker on his face as he answered me. 'Very good, Mrs McGovern. Yes, we've been working on that basis for eight days now. And I'd be grateful if you'd not gossip about your theory. Okay?'

But the WPC blew it. Her eyes flashed and a little grin crept onto her lips. She even half turned towards the door of the station as if she was champing to get in and see what they could make of the new information.

'Really?' I said. 'I'd have thought you'd want to spread the news. Help with the ID.'

'But you're not a trained detective,' the sergeant said. His poker face was a thing of wonder. There wasn't the slightest sign on it that he was talking shite, but his eyes had lost the twinkle.

'Right, then,' I said. 'I better get round to T&C, see if that man of mine's ready to hit the road.'

'Oh, yes, that's right,' the sergeant said. 'The McGovern family is well in *there*, all of a sudden.'

I nodded and left them. I wondered if he had always liked being a know-all and if that's what made the police service seem like such a tempting idea, or if being the one who got to ask the questions and didn't have to answer any had turned him into what he was.

Marco was back in the manager's office with my lukewarm tea and the coconut cake turning the bag greasy.

'You can use a stamp, Ali,' he said. When I didn't answer he went on, 'I didn't go bankrupt over stationery.'

'What?' I said. 'I never said a word.'

'Yeah, and it nearly deafened me.'

So I never said a word about the decoy watch, belt and jeans theory and how the specs had scuppered it either. We drove home in silence and he didn't turn the car round to get the passenger side into the kerb, like he usually did when it was raining. He just pulled in, climbed out and slammed the door, leaving me to scrabble for my own key to dink the car locked, then hurry up the path as the wind threw the cold rods of rain at the side of my head until my hair was dripping.

Chapter 19

But I told Lars all about it in the car the next morning, and he told Belle and Hinny in the staff kitchenette, where they were setting themselves up with coffee for the change.

'Lord, you're right, Ali,' Belle said, thinking it over and nodding. 'Did all of that just come to you?'

'To my kid,' I said, squashing down the memory of Angel saying, Gucci, Ferra-something and Hublot. Unless they made trainers, how could he possibly know?

'Bright spark,' said Hinny. I flashed on the picture of him that morning, a mound under the duvet, refusing to budge, missing another day of school.

'Wasted effort, though,' Lars said. 'He's been in the ground over a decade. Whoever killed him, and chavved him up away back when, couldn't have dreamed what was going to happen in between then and now, eh?'

'What's that?' Hinny said.

'Computers,' said Lars. 'The skull's getting sent to Dundee to have the face reconstructed. All the cheap disguise in the world's not going to help when they put his face back on, is it?'

'Egads, just the skull?' Hinny said. She shuddered and put a third spoonful of sugar in her coffee. 'That's not nice, whacking his head off and taking it . . . What are we saying? They take it up on the train in a biscuit tin?'

'Ali?' said Belle, her voice a soft stroke. 'Are you okay? Are you still feeling poorly?'

I took a few deep breaths, in and out, and felt my pulse begin to settle again, the humming that had started as faint as a breeze in tall grasses already dying away. Belle's face was puckered with concern. Lars, leaning against the sink twitching the stretchy bandages over his nasty tattoos, gave me half a smile, just one side of his mouth hooking up and his eyes as sad as Sundays.

Hinny checked both of them before she glanced back at me. 'Tell us,' she said. The kitchen worker as wise as the nurses, like before. Although I couldn't remember what we'd been on about that time.

One more deep breath, right down into the pit of my stomach, and held until my fingers tingled. I had never said it. I never even said it when I was ill. There was no point dwelling on what was past unless you could change it.

'I had a stillbirth,' I told them.

'Oh, love,' Belle said. 'I'm sorry. When was this?'

'Oh!' I said. 'No, don't worry. It was years ago. It was ten years ago.'

Lars and Hinny shared a look. 'It doesn't matter if it was fifty years ago,' Hinny said. 'Your baby died.'

'Not really,' I said. I knew something was coming. I thought it was a howl but when I let it out and heard it I could almost think I was laughing. 'It wasn't a baby and she didn't die. It was

252

tissue. It was . . . I never saw it. I mean, they could tell it would have been a girl but it wasn't a girl. It wasn't a baby.'

'Like a miscarriage, you mean?' Lars said. 'How early?'

'A week,' I said.

I thought I saw all of their shoulders drop.

'How could they tell it was female after just a week?' Hinny said, glancing at the nurses.

'Oh,' I said. 'No, I mean she was a week early. But so deformed, you know. She had anencephaly. Severe anencephaly. She never lived. Couldn't have lived. Wasn't. Didn't.' I wrapped my fingers, icy suddenly, round the cup Lars had handed me and felt the good solid burn of the hot tea through its side.

After a silence, Hinny spoke up. 'Sorry, Ali, I'm just the cook: what's anencephaly?'

'She didn't have a head.' Again the cry that came out with these never-spoken words sounded more like laughter than I could believe. 'She had no brain. She had no *face*.'

'Aw, shite, the rag dolls!' Lars said.

'Yeah, I'm a basket-case but not a very complicated one,' I said. 'My baby had no head to put a face on and faceless things just . . . headless things just . . .'

'You must bloody hate those poxy china angels,' said Lars. And why would that make the tears start to fall? But here they came, surging up and dashing down my cheeks and, with the first sob, snot bubbles too. I roared. I sounded like a sea lion, but Belle put her warm hand on my knee and Lars stood behind my chair and put both hands on my shoulders and held me tight like that and I didn't care. I blew my nose on the tea-towel Hinny handed me and I didn't care one single shit.

'That actually feels a lot better,' I said.

'Do you think you can do the change?' said Hinny.

'And do you think you could answer a question?' Belle said.

I nodded, meaning it to cover both of them.

'Because that's very severe anencephaly,' Belle said.

I blinked a couple of times and blew my nose again. 'Eh? Well, it's okay. I had my tubes tied. We decided it was best. There's no danger.'

'Ten years ago?' Belle said. 'At Dumfries?'

Lars had let go of my shoulders and walked round so he could see me. 'That was a big decision to make at a time like that,' he said.

I nodded, but it hadn't felt that way. I barely remembered it, except that it was one more thing my mum could have helped me through if she'd been willing to. I couldn't even remember, now I thought about it, where the idea had come from. Marco, probably. He was thinking for both of us back then.

'Can I ask *you* a question?' I said. 'You used to work in Maternity, didn't you?' Belle grew very still. 'Sorry. I know it wasn't very happy when you left. Lars said it was kind of hard at the end. But you might be able to tell me.' Now it seemed that all of them were still. A drip fell from the cold tap into the shallow basin of bleachy water Lars had laid the dishcloth in and the plink sounded like someone hitting a triangle, a pure note in the silence. 'It was just this,' I said. 'Is there any way I can name her? Now. We didn't name her because of how she was and now I wish we had. Can we do that? Is that something people ever do?'

'I don't know if people ever do,' said Belle, speaking slowly, 'but I think it sounds like a good idea. Where is she? Is she buried or did you scatter her ashes?'

'We didn't do anything. She just got . . . It wasn't like that,' I said. 'Hospital waste.'

'You could put a bench somewhere nice that you like to go,' Lars said, jumping in. 'You could put her name on a nice bench or a picnic table. Even if you can't register a name. What's to stop you?'

'So what were you going to call her?' Hinny said. 'What would you put on the plaque on the picnic table?'

But there was only one name I could even think of and I couldn't say it to them. So I just shook my head. 'I don't think I can face the staff meeting, actually,' I said. 'If you think it would be okay for me to skip it, I'll go and see how Sylvie's doing today.'

She was in bed, propped up on her pillows with her eyes closed. I crossed the room quietly and looked down at her, at the thin, colourless hair and the pale, dry skin, feeling my heart go out to her. It's a strange expression until you've felt it, but after the first time it happens nothing else can sum it up so perfectly. My heart left my body, slipping in wisps from between my ribs, and drifted over to settle on Sylvie. As if she had felt it, she opened her eyes and smiled at me.

Now I could hear the hirstle in her chest as she breathed. She had caught a cold out there in the gardens. I put the back of my hand to her head and thought I could feel a fever, her skin clammy.

'Next time we go outside, I'll wrap you up better,' I said. 'And we'll wait for a sunny day.'

She closed her eyes in that way that does for nodding, like a cat.

'But we had a good time, didn't we?' I said. 'It was good to see you smiling, Sylvie.'

Still with her eyes shut, she pursed her lips, then let them fall loose again. 'Ju,' she said. And again, 'Ju.'

'That's right!' I said. 'Julia was there. Oh, you clever girl. You met someone called Julia yesterday. You clever, clever girl. They've all made a big mistake about you.'

'Ju,' whispered Sylvie. 'Ju.'

'Do you want to see her?' I said.

Sylvie only breathed out but something about the way her mouth relaxed sounded like a yes to me. 'I won't be long,' I said, dropped a kiss on her damp brow and left.

Julia was in the shower, which was a step forward. Her room was littered deeper than ever with discarded clothes and ripped-open mail-order. I skidded on a slippery bag and had to grab at the top of her chest of drawers to stop myself falling.

'Who the fuck's that?' Julia shouted. 'Ryan, if that's you again you can fuck the fuck off. Byron, if it's you, you can join me.'

'No luck,' I said. 'It's Ali. And you're joking, aren't you? The boys don't come waltzing in and out of your room?'

The water turned off and Julia opened the shower screen. She was bright red down her front as if the water had been too hot or she'd stood under it too long. 'Fling me a towel if you've finished gawping, pervy.'

'You'll get thread veins if you blast yourself with scorching water like that every day,' I told her. 'And you shouldn't be using that apricot scrub either. It's far too harsh. If you could look at your skin under a microscope you'd see it's lacerated. All those shards of apricot stone are like little daggers.'

'Oh, I see. You think we should let all the sea life fill their bellies with plastic micro beads just in case we ever see our skin under a microscope? Pretty goddamn shallow, if you ask me.'

I smiled. It was good to hear her sounding eighteen for a change. For some reason teenage girls always cared a lot about sea life. I blamed *The Little Mermaid*.

'What do you want, anyway? Have you come to rub my naked flesh again? What team do you play for anyway, Ali? Your husband's pretty tasty for a geriatric but you don't half like to get your hands on the girlies.'

'I've come to see if you'd like to visit Sylvie again,' I said.

'And how the hell do you know what my husband looks like?'

'Small world,' said Julia. 'Why would I want another thrill-a-minute visit to Sissy?'

'Sylvie,' I said. 'She's asking for you.'

Julia had been bent over towelling her head but when she heard that she straightened up. 'The zombie's asking for me?' she said. 'I thought she was supposed to be lobotomized.'

'Catatonic,' I said. 'You don't have to bend double to dry your hair now it's short, you know. In case that hadn't occurred to you.'

She gave me a screwball look, then let out a shout of laughter. 'Ha! You're right.' Being told she'd done something stupid seemed to cheer her up in a way that didn't seem like a teenager. I thought of how Angelo grew red and mulish if I caught him out in the slightest dip in his cool.

'Yeah, okay, then,' she said. 'Why not? I've got nothing better to fill the aching void today. Sissy and Juju ride again. 'Let's go.' She marched out of the bathroom. Then, halfway across her bedroom, she looked over her shoulder and winked at me. 'Ha!' she said again. 'You win the game of chicken. Well played. I'll put some clothes on, shall I?'

The shift change was finished. From the landing window as we made our way downstairs, I saw Yvonne and Marion tramp wearily over the gravel to Marion's car and watched Yvonne unbutton the waistband of her uniform trousers before she dropped into the passenger seat. The door to the acute side opened and closed with a beep from the keypad and a soft swish of its pneumatic hinge. Then silence.

'This place,' I said to Julia, 'isn't at all how I thought it would be.'

'It's exactly how I thought it would be,' she said. 'It's a joke and I knew it was a joke. I just don't know why.'

'Why what?' I asked her.

'I don't know that either,' she said. 'Do you?'

'Me?' I turned and searched her face. The strong morning light was streaming through the high window at our side. 'Why would I know anything?'

'Well, what are you *doing* here?' said Julia. 'I had to say I'd killed a squirrel to freak my mother out enough to put me in. How did you talk your way past the bouncer?'

'I answered a job advert,' I said. 'I don't know what you're on about.'

'Christ, you're gullible,' said Julia. 'You really think they're paying you to scoof about with me and squeeze Ryan's blackheads all day?'

'What else?' I said.

'Exactly,' said Julia. 'What else?'

Even as late as that, though, I couldn't take the final step to admitting it was real so I deflected her. 'You didn't kill the squirrel?'

Julia took my arm and started barrelling me down the half-flight to the ground floor, cackling. 'It was roadkill. I just bashed it about a bit more, then stuck it through with some of my granny's earrings and hid it in a shoebox under my bed till the smell brought my dear mama. Then the smell of piss in the bed hit her when she knelt down to drag the shoebox out. And when she went into the en suite to puke, she saw my little bonfire in the bath.'

'Nicely done,' I said. 'And with an eye on safety, doing it in the bath like that. What did you burn?'

'Family photographs,' Julia said. 'My birth certificate, my passport, that sort of thing.'

'Photographs?' I couldn't help the note in my voice. That was a meanness I hadn't expected.

'It's all shit anyway,' she said. '*So* much bullshit in my mother's version of our saintly family. And anyway I made copies. Why do you think I've got snaps of my various stepfathers all over my phone? I made copies first and the rest of it you can get new ones, can't you? Register House?'

We had arrived at Sylvie's room and I shushed her before we entered. Thankfully, as it turned out, because Sylvie was deeply asleep. Someone had been in and taken one of the pillows out from behind her head and she was lying flatter and snoring gently.

'Another action-packed morning coming up,' said Julia, but she said it softly.

'Come and sit in the armchair,' I said, beckoning her. 'Let me do a scalp massage and you can talk to me. How about that, eh?'

I really hadn't done too bad a job with her hair, considering what I had had to work with. I lifted it, half dried, and let it run through my fingers, thinking no one would know it was a fix-it number unless you told them.

'So you didn't kill your father?' I said, once I had settled into rubbing small circles over her scalp with the tips of my fingers. I watched her shoulders drop and heard her breathing slow.

'Honestly?' she said. 'I don't know. My mum says he left but I know he died. What I don't know is why she would lie about it.'

I nodded, even though she couldn't see me. Why *would* she lie about it? When I bumped into Julia's mother in Tesco, the redoubtable Mona Swain, she had said 'late lamented' and told me he'd left her his whole estate in his will. Why would she lie to a stranger she'd never meet again?

Then suddenly I wondered if there was a simple explanation after all.

'Which one of them are you talking about, though?' I said. 'Show me the pictures again.'

Julia fished out her phone and started scrolling. 'I sprang from *his* loins,' she said, showing me the red-eyed, snaggle-toothed man holding the horse's nose. 'Ralph. But he left when I was tiny. He got a fancy woman and started spiffing himself up for her. He'd already begun when this was taken, actually. He'd scrapped his Coke-bottle specs and was trying contacts but they made him look like even more of a drunk than he really was so he gave them up. But that was what alerted my mother to the fact of him getting ready to dump her. Going to the optician and all the rest of it. Suddenly taking more baths and clipping his horny toenails.' She shuddered. 'So you can imagine what she thought of Garran's gym membership and tooth-polishing regime?' She flicked the screen until the tanned man in the pink cashmere appeared. 'Poor Mother. They keep deciding that all her money isn't worth waking up to her face on the pillow beside them every day. Well, maybe she's wise to settle for this grunter. Good old Perry Uving.' Another swipe and the red-faced man in front of the wall of glass was laughing out at us around his cigar again. 'Can you actually think of a more bogus P. G. Wodehouse name than Peregrine Uving? I think he must have made it up. I bet he was Keith McGurk before.'

'But it really is her money?' I said. 'Is she an heiress or something?'

'Uuuh,' said Julia. 'Jesus, I don't know. It's se-ew *terribly* vulg-ah to talk about money, you know.'

'Humour me,' I said. 'I'm the vulgar sort, in case you hadn't noticed.'

'Well, I know the *land* was my dad's,' Julia said. 'My real dad, I mean. Ralph. It was his family estate, before the army got their finger in the pie. So I suppose she just got it in the divorce. The new place and what's left in the way of policies and all that. I've never thought about it.'

It was a different world. She was probably speaking no more than the truth; she really hadn't ever questioned the fact that she lived in a posh house on a huge chunk of land that used to be even huger before they sold it off for a hospital and army training. I raked my fingers back from her forehead to the nape of her neck – once, twice, three times – and felt the last bit of tension leave her. The phone dropped into her lap and went to standby.

'Julia?' I said very softly. 'Do you remember saying to me that you hurt your daddy's middle?'

'No,' she said. She sounded drowsy. 'His middle? What does that mean? His stomach?'

'I don't know. You said it one night when you were almost asleep.'

'No, that's not right. I *heard* it one night when I was almost asleep. I didn't *say* it.'

Maybe that was how it seemed to her, if she was groggy. Maybe the words didn't feel as if they'd come from her. I had never taken the drugs Dr Ferris had her on and I couldn't say what they might do to perception.

'Which daddy was it, though?' I said. 'Ralph or Garran or Perry?'

'Ralph,' she said, without a moment's hesitation. Then she jerked upright in the chair and turned to face me. 'Are you fucking hypnotizing me? I didn't say you could hypnotize me.'

'I'm not,' I said. I put out a hand towards her shoulder but she made a fist and knocked my arm away, hard enough to bruise me.

'I'm not doing some bullshit regression to a past life,' she said. 'It's bad enough pretending to be a nutter. I've got no intention of going off my rocker for real.'

'I've no idea why you're so upset,' I told her. 'I'm not trying to regress you to anything.' I flashed on Angelo telling me he remembered seeing me in the hospital. 'You said it yourself, you were a toddler when your dad left. You were old enough to remember.'

And, of course, we had woken Sylvie. She didn't sit up but she turned her head and blinked slowly. 'Ju,' she whispered. 'Ju.'

Julia shot to her feet and screamed, a long, whistling scream of pure terror. Sylvie bent her head and drew her knees up, curling herself into a tiny ball under her covers.

'You!' Julia said, sticking a finger into my face close enough to make me draw back. 'Leave me alone. Don't you dare mess with me any more or I'll fucking kill you. I'll stick a knife in your belly and fucking kill you.' She slammed out of the room, taking a swipe at a little side table as she went and sending it flying, scattering a bowl of potpourri and smashing a glass lamp-base into tiny shards on the pale carpet.

I couldn't speak. I couldn't go to comfort Sylvie, or follow Julia to stop her harming herself or anyone else who might get in her way. I was turned to stone. I was still just standing there when Lars put his head round the door, his eyes like saucers, and found me. 'What the fudge, Ali?' he said. He hurried over to Sylvie's bed and laid a hand on the highest point of the quivering mound under the covers. 'Ssh-ssh,' he said. Then he looked back over at me. 'Seriously, what happened?'

'I don't know,' I told him. 'I can't explain it.' But at last the spell that had locked my knees and glued my feet to the floor was fading and I went over and folded the covers back from Sylvie's head, stroked her hair and kissed her brow.

She took a deep breath in, her bottom lip wuthering twice against her teeth as she sucked the air, then shifted onto her back, pushing her legs down the bed, and turned to look at Lars. She smiled at him.

Lars's eyes fell wide and his mouth dropped open. 'Hel-lo!' he said. He glanced up at me, then back at Sylvie, a grin spreading over his face. 'Sylvie, I'm Lars. We've not exactly met.'

'La-la,' Sylvie breathed, touching the tip of her tongue very precisely to her teeth. She rolled her head on the pillow until her eyes met mine. 'La-li,' she said, with the same two careful flicks of movement.

'Well, well, well,' said Lars. 'We need to get the doc in here to see this.'

'No,' I blurted.

Lars frowned and turned his head to one side, as if he could see me clearer from the corner of his eye or as if he was maybe listening to something only he could hear. 'What's going on?' he said.

'I have no clue,' I told him. 'Yet. So let's just keep this to ourselves until I get one.'

I'm not sure if he would ever have agreed to it if it was only me but he couldn't argue with both of us, and Sylvie was right behind me. She rolled her head again, fixed Lars with the clearest look I had ever seen on her face and said, 'Ssh.'

Chapter 20

'Can I ask you something?' I said to Lars, when we were out of Sylvie's room. He glanced at his watch but nodded. 'How easy would it be for a patient to fool you?'

'Make out they're better and get out?' he said. 'It happens. If someone's sectioned in, but they're determined, they can give us all the right answers and get home again.'

'I meant the other way, actually,' I said. 'Malingering, I suppose you'd say.'

'Even easier,' he said. 'Doesn't happen so much here where somebody's got to pay a bill. But it's part of the game in the NHS. In for five weeks and six days, touch and go, then miraculously better on day seven when the benefits dry up. You get used to it.'

'But you'd know what they're at,' I said. 'What I'm asking is, can people really make you believe they're seriously ill if they're not? If they're just maybe hiding out here. Or they've got some reason they want to be here.'

'Are we talking about Sylvie?' Lars said. 'No. No one could keep that up for fifteen years.'

'Not Sylvie,' I said. 'Julia.'

Lars considered it before he answered. Then he shook his head. 'Naw. She's a troubled wee soul. The diagnosis might change depending on where she is in her mood-cycle, but there's no chance she's having us on. Why would she?' He glanced at his watch again and started walking, speaking over his shoulder: 'Sorry, Ali. I've got to run. Catch you later, eh?'

I walked out the front door and across the grass to the gazebo. I should be working. I should be wrapping Posy in seaweed or threading Jo's eyebrows up into cheerful arches, see if I could lift her depression face-first.

And I would. If I couldn't put my finger on what was wrong in twenty minutes sitting thinking, I would let it go for good. I was practised at that, after all.

But first I'd let it rip. What were my worst fears whispering to me? I was there as a stooge. I was going to be planted there one night shift to take the blame for something, my faked credentials and my medical history all doing their bit to bring me down. As I tramped over the wet grass, my work shoes squeaking and squelching, I tried to throw my mind back over everything that had happened, every word and look, to see if there were any clues about what that something might be.

Julia. What else, if not Julia? The job advert went out not long after she arrived there. And we'd been thrown together from my first day. And Lars hadn't answered the question I'd asked him. I wanted to know how someone could fool the staff and he'd come back with 'Why *would* she?'.

But if Julia was in here on the trail of something she knew – that same something I almost knew if I half shut my eyes and half turned away – then the why was answered and only the how remained.

I had reached the gazebo. Its inside was littered with cigarette ends and it stank of pee in a way it hadn't the day before. Had one of the boys, caught short, saved himself a trip? Had Julia squatted here, too lazy to go back to the house? I turned and looked back. The French window in Dr Ferris's office overlooked this bit of the garden, but her desk faced the other way. In fact, I could see the back of her head as she sat there now. She'd have to stand up and walk to the glass to see me.

Still, and despite the reek, I went inside and sat down right at the back, in the shadows, on the wooden bench that lined the wall.

Dr Ferris had employed me. If something rotten was going on at Howell Hall, some corruption or abuse of power, fiddling the council or bilking the parents, she knew about it. Her own husband said she was the businesswoman, and all he wanted to do was help patients get well.

Dr Ferris wouldn't wonder 'why' Julia had got herself committed, not if she was hiding something. So Dr Ferris might be able to see through the act: the shouting and swearing, the shopping, the tantrums, even the chopping off of all that frizzy hair. Maybe she'd met Mrs Swain in Tesco that night to try to persuade her to take Julia away. Did that make any sense, I asked myself. Honestly? I didn't think so. Why wouldn't Dr Ferris just call Mrs Swain, or email her, or even ask both parents to come in for a meeting?

I tried to think it through. Maybe Dr F wouldn't let Mrs Swain come to the hall so soon after Julia had been admitted in case seeing her mother got in the way of her official treatment plan. I knew that was the sort of thing places like this went in for. Like a cult. Certainly, if Dr F believed Julia was really ill, he wouldn't approve of his wife trying to get Mrs Swain to take the girl home.

But if Julia really was here to spy on the Ferrises and Dr Ferris knew that, she'd have to find a way to deal with the girl. Finally, I saw a glimmer of a reason for me being employed there. Dr Ferris was going to accuse Julia of doing something so dreadful that the hall couldn't keep her. Something dreadful that needed a patsy, although I didn't understand why the patsy couldn't be Belle or Surraya or one of the others.

Until suddenly I could. *They* were valuable members of the team. The hospital couldn't function without its nurses. I was expendable. If something happened when a beauty therapist was taking a turn of the night shift, and it came out after that she'd lied her way into the job, everyone would blame her – blame *me*! – and once the hospital had got rid of them both, the framed patient and the disgraced staff member, Howell Hall would carry on the same as ever.

If this was real, I needed to warn Mrs Swain that Julia was in trouble, maybe even in danger, try to persuade her to get the girl away.

If it was real. And how could I warn her when I didn't know what the trouble or the danger actually was? What *was* the rottenness at the heart of Howell Hall? What *was* the secret Julia had got herself in here to ferret out?

I went as far inside my head as I could get and found . . . nothing. I had to let this go.

So. A bench. Except the park I sat in when I was pregnant with her was Angelo's park. The swings had plastic beads set into the safety rails that he used to spin round endlessly with one cold little pink finger, his mitten pulled off and held bunched in his other hand. He didn't want me to push him.

More than that, he would wail and wave me away if I *tried* to push him, the movement spoiling his concentration on the fascinating little beads as he spun them and spun them. Once or twice, I even felt a shift of unease in me. This was how autism started: obsessively repeated behaviours, unnatural focus and a pulling away from others. But he was always happy enough to come away when I said it was tea-time, taking my hand and chatting to me about how much he loved sausages and where Daddy was and why trees stopped holding on to leaves.

If not Angel's park, how about the hospital? People sometimes donated couches to the antenatal-clinic waiting room, or the neonatal-unit family room, but no one wanted a memorial to a baby in there. I wouldn't have wanted to sit on a dead baby's couch when it was my time.

Anyway, first we'd have to have a name to put on the brass plaque of the bench or embroider on scatter cushions for the couch. I lifted my head and looked through the fretted-wood lintel above the gazebo door at the grey sky and the bare branches. *Skye. Leaf. Pearl. Dawn.* I began to understand what Dr Ferris had said about 'Angel'. But I kept thinking 'Sylvie'. It was perfect for her. She was a sylph, only ever seen as a silvery fish on the early scans before she slipped away. Sylvie, over there in her room, with her unmoving bookmark in her Maya Angelou, was another one. Silvery and slipping away. I wondered if Julia called her Sissy just to be mean, or to pay Sylvie back for 'Juju'. But then she was used to Juju. That was what Mona called her too.

Mona! Whose daughter knew it was real, no matter what I was telling myself, sitting here trying to name a child who'd never been and picking out imaginary furniture I knew I'd never buy.

I'd never buy it because Marco would never agree.

The memories of our whispered words that night in the side-ward were burned into me. I'd been taken away from all the other mums, and I didn't know why. Maybe my stark face and empty arms would frighten them, or maybe their sleepy smiles and milky warmth would send me raving. Whatever. I was in a side-ward, curtains closed across the glass front wall and lights dim. Marco had taken away the flowers I'd brought in with me. The girls at work had bought them for me, a huge burst of orange and red gerbera, freesia and gladioli, like a firework going off, and a balloon bobbing above them – *You can do it!*

Afterwards, when I opened my eyes, shuffled to the toilet, brushed my teeth, shuffled back, choked down a cup of weak tea and finally looked around, there were no cards, no teddies, no ribboned parcels of tiny dresses.

The nurses just outside at their station were speaking in low voices at first, no laughter. But by the end of the night they were back to normal, clucking and cooing at the other babies and giggling about what one of the dads had done. But by that time I was dressed and sitting on the side of the bed. I just needed the doctor to sign off on me and I was ready to go.

'I know we can't take her home,' I said to Marco. 'I get that. I really do.'

'Take . . . *home*?'

'But I want to hold her. Just once.'

'Ali.'

'Or even just see her. I want to see her face.'

'*Face?*' Marco said, so sharply that the nurses' conversation outside dipped a little. 'Ali, I thought you were awake when they told you. Didn't you hear what they said?'

270

'Anencephaly,' I said. 'I heard.'

'So why . . .?' he said. His voice was gravelly with exhaustion, his face grey-yellow under long stubble and his breath sour from a night of coffee out of the machine. 'You can't see a face, Ally-pal. There's nothing to see.'

'I keep thinking I can hear her crying,' I said. 'I hear her calling for me.'

'We need to get you out of here,' Marco said. 'They've given you the furthest-away room but of course you can still hear them. You need to come home.'

But it wasn't the other babies I could hear. I mean, of course I heard them: their reedy voices lifted high in hunger or grunting rustily as the fumbling new mums tried to get them dressed and comfy. But I could hear something else besides. All the way home from the hospital I kept straining to see if I could still hear it over the stretching miles and then I slumped into the emptiness when I was finally sure it was gone. That first night when I heard her in my dreams, 'Mmmhmmm', I felt no fear at all, only a wash of pure relief that she was still with me.

It was the six months in the day-clinic, three days a week, that turned her voice into a problem, a symptom, something to be recovered from. I went in furred over with sleeplessness and loss and there, in group, in class, in session, I killed her all over again. I unpeeled her gripping fingers from around my heart and brushed her off me. I left her there and walked away without a backward glance, all the way to Australia and the perfect silence of being far too far away for her to find me.

After that, any time I heard her voice my pulse rattled like dice in a cup and my mouth flooded bitter. If your head hurts, you take an aspirin. If your leg's broken you put a cast on. If your dead daughter calls your name, you ignore her.

271

If, on the other hand, someone else's daughter, eighteen years old, is in the kind of trouble I suspected Julia was in, you pay attention. But was she? Or was it all smoke and shadows?

I squeezed my eyes tight, then lifted my head to look out, past the fretted woodwork of the gazebo this time, all the way to the far trees, trying to clear my brain. As I gazed out over the gardens, starting to feel my certainty drain away, getting the first whiff of the foolishness coming along at its back, I saw a sudden movement.

Dr Ferris was standing at the French window looking out into the garden. I thought she had a hand clapped to her head in a parody of shock or outrage but when I saw her lips move, then saw her throw her head back and shake her hair, I knew she was on the phone to someone. And I knew it was someone who made her happy. She was laughing and, with her free hand, she smoothed the front of her throat and let one finger catch on the string of pearls at her collarbone. If it had been anyone else, I would have thought she was flirting. At least I could be sure she couldn't see me sitting there in the shadows: she would never have carried on that way if she knew someone, the likes of me, was watching.

After another minute she hung up but kept her eyes on her phone and her thumbs busy. She lifted it to her ear. And gazed out. She seemed to be looking right at me when my phone started vibrating in my pocket. My fingers felt numb as I plucked it out and swiped the call to life.

'Hello?'

'Alison,' came Dr Ferris's voice, clipped and sure, down the line. I watched her turn away from the window and heard through the phone the woodpecker pock-pock-pock of her heels on the floor as she paced while she was speaking. 'I think we talked about this but I didn't expect to have to call on you quite so soon. Would it be at all possible for you to take a night shift tonight?'

'Tonight?' I said. It was on the tip of my tongue to say, 'Of course not.' To ask her on what planet a woman with a family can do an overnight away from home at the drop of a hat, but I managed to stop in time. 'What exactly would I have to do?' I said.

'Sleep in Sylvie's room with her,' Dr Ferris said.

'*Sylvie?*' I knew it had come out as a squawk.

'Didn't you know?' she said. She was back at the window again. 'We always have someone sleep in Sylvie's room. You haven't been paying attention at shift change, have you?'

'I thought the night shift stayed awake.' I *had* been paying attention at shift change, taking notes even. This was pure fantasy.

'Of course,' said Dr Ferris. 'The night shift has three awake and one on call. The one on call sleeps in Sylvie's room.'

She sounded so sure that she almost had me believing her. If I hadn't been able to see her I might have swallowed it whole. As it was, I saw her take the phone away from her ear and stare at it, annoyed to have a pawn in her game not simply agree to go where she placed it.

'Well?' she said, putting the phone back.

'Okay,' I said. 'I'll need to slip home and get some things, but yes. Okay. Who should I ask what to do? Lars?'

'No!' It was slightly too loud. 'Come to my office. I'm busy just now but I'll be there all afternoon. Come before eight o'clock and I'll go over things with you.'

'Right-oh,' I said. 'And it's double-time, right? Even though I'm just on call and not actually working?'

'Yes, yes, good grief,' she said. 'I'll see you this evening.' The line went dead and I saw her go back to worrying over her phone with her thumbs again. There was another short phone call to the same person as before. At least, I would have put money on it, because she laughed and stroked her throat again. But I wasn't really watching closely now.

Sylvie.

Not Julia. Sylvie.

Or not just Julia, but Sylvie too.

And it made sense. After all, it was Sylvie that Dr Ferris took me to see that very first day. It was Sylvie looking at me, making contact with me, that had unsettled her so. It was the thought of Sylvie drawing the Mercat Cross that rattled her. And then me taking Julia and Sylvie out together had enraged her. As it would if, somehow, I was scuppering some carefully laid plan.

What careful plan? I asked myself, as I sat there.

There was only one thing I could think of that would get rid of Julia, involved Sylvie and could be laid at my door. I couldn't even let myself think it, though. And I had to stop it.

The French window was opening. As I watched, Dr Ferris slipped out through a slim gap, her head still turned to the inside, leaving the door ajar. She stepped very softly down the three stone steps and, keeping close to the house wall, she hurried to the front corner and peeped round it. Seeing no one, she put her head down and scurried across the gravel to the last parking space, right under the trees, puddles all around, where she had left her car. She got in, closed the door without a sound and then, taking the brake off, she used the little slope on the drive to roll silently away, not starting the engine until she was round the first bend. Even straining to catch it, I could hardly hear it.

It might have been nothing. Even watching her, I thought maybe she was having an affair or maybe she'd heard the arrival of some heart-sink visitor she couldn't face. I knew all about them. There was a woman who 'dropped in' to Face Value whenever she was in town and wouldn't take no for an answer, always sure I could squeeze her in if I tried. I used to get Reception to buzz up and I'd leave by the fire escape.

So Dr Ferris's sneak getaway might be nothing to do with my night shift but sometimes it's good to listen to your gut and my gut was telling me it was a sign written in red letters, three feet high. I needed to tell the Swains to get Julia away, tell the – oh, what was Sylvie's name? – well, her family that she was in danger. Hope they believed me.

But I couldn't ask Julia for her mum's number. She might be faking her disorder but she was just a bit too good at it for me to trust her. And she was only eighteen. There must be another way. It had to be close. The new house Julia had spoken about was built on some remaining corner of the estate they'd sold to the army. But I couldn't just drive around knocking on doors. There must be some way.

I put my chin up and my shoulders back and walked towards the front corner of the house as I had every right to do. Then, when I was in the lee of the walls and invisible to anyone looking out, I darted round the side, up the stone steps and in at the French window.

I went over to the hall door first to see if I could lock it against anyone trying to get in, but Dr Ferris had had the same idea and the door was already bolted on the inside. I put my back against it and looked around. There was nothing so old-school as filing cabinets, and they'd have been locked anyway, full of confidential patient information. There was a new phone book, still in its plastic wrapper, wedged into the top shelf of a low bookcase, but that pretty much summed it up. No one's in the phone book, these days. I unwrapped it anyway and checked, but Mona Swain certainly wasn't and neither was Peregrine Uving. And *what* was Sylvie's family's name?

Dr Ferris didn't have anything so handy as a Rolodex or a fat Filofax on her desk top either.

So far, all I had done was walk through an open door, look in a phone book and cast my eyes over the surfaces of a room. It was when I stepped around the desk and tugged the handle of the top drawer that I crossed the line. I don't even know what I was looking for. Maybe that Filofax after all, or one of Mona Swain's business cards. If she would even have business cards when she had no business. A little frog of hope leaped into my throat when the drawer opened and another joined it when I recognized what I was looking at in there: invoices, some of them with cheques stapled to the tops. But there was no SWAIN among them.

I tried the next drawer down but it was full of highlighter pens and Post-it notes, boxes of paperclips, and cartridges for a colour printer. Losing hope, I opened the bottom drawer.

It took a long moment for the sight that met my eyes to make sense to my brain. I blinked twice, half expecting it to disappear. But when I reached my hand out, it was as real under my touch as the warm polished wood of the desk top where I put my other hand to steady myself in case I fell in a faint to the floor.

It was in a plastic sandwich bag, sealed shut with that zip thing that I can never get to work, either unable to shut it or unable to prise it open. It was filthy, crusted with grit and rusted, the glass crazed and missing some shards that had gathered in the bottom of the bag, but it was unmistakable. A Timex watch with its bracelet still closed. It had been wrenched from the skeletal hand of a long dead man without being opened.

I slipped back out of the French window and ran round to go in the front door, not caring this time who saw me.

Chapter 21

Angelo came first. I hurried into my little treatment room and phoned home. It took three calls to rouse him. The first one got kicked to the answering machine; the second one let me switch the automatic answer off. With the third call I let the bell ring out for a solid two minutes until, at last, enraged, Angel swiped up the phone and shouted, 'Sod off, will you? The fuck is wrong with you?'

'Angel, it's Mum,' I said. 'And I need you to listen to me. I don't have time to go into it all just now, but I need you to promise me something. If Dr Ferris gets in touch with you, hang up. If she comes to the door, don't answer.'

'Dr Ferris?' he said. 'Your boss? Why would she want to be phoning me?'

'Dr Ferris, your therapist,' I said. 'Promise me.'

'Mum,' said Angelo in his 'duh' voice. 'I haven't got a therapist. What the hell are you talking about?'

I said nothing for a minute, then the words tumbled out so fast even *I* couldn't make sense of them. 'Angelo, don't lie to me.

It's too important. I know you spoke to her and I know she told you about Sylvie and the Mercat Cross.'

'Told me about *Sylvie*?' he said.

I bludgeoned on. I should never have told him his sister was called that name but now wasn't the time to fix it. 'I know you've phoned her from our landline, Angel. And, for God's sake, I met you halfway down the drive that night you were so upset. Stop fannying about and start talking straight to me, right? You've told me you didn't show the picture of the watch to anyone, but answer me this: was she there with you when you took it?'

His breath was a long fuzzy blast down the line as he let it go.

'Was Dr Tamara Ferris at the abbey with me when I saw the hand?' he said. 'Eh, no, Mum. What have you been smoking?'

'Okay, okay,' I said, then my breath caught. 'How do you know her first name?'

'*What?*'

'Never mind,' I said. 'My brain's fizzing, that's all. Listen, email me the picture of the hand, eh?'

'Why?'

'Because I know for sure the watch wasn't on the hand when the cops turned up.'

'How?' he said. 'Who told you that?'

'Because I found it. It's at Howell Hall.'

'*What?*'

'And, Angel, I really need to you to be honest with me. Did you take it off the corpse and give it to the doctor?'

'What? No! Fuck sake. What is it with you trying to make out I'm in cahoots with Dr bloody Ferris?'

'Okay, okay,' I said. 'I believe you. Angel, I don't know what this means but if she comes to the door, don't let her in and, for God's sake, don't go anywhere with her. Okay?'

'I promise I won't go anywhere with Dr Ferris,' Angel said. 'Or let her in the house.'

'And email me the—'

'I have,' he said and, right enough, I heard the plink of an email landing.

'And stop talking to me as if I'm some kind of moron, eh?' I said. 'You don't know everything, Angelo.'

'That makes two of us, then,' he said, and was gone.

I opened the email and looked at the picture to make sure, but I knew already. There was no doubt of what I'd found. As to what it meant, that was a different question and one my brain couldn't even take the first nibble at.

I tried Marco's phone, but it went to voicemail. So I tried T&C and got Mel, who hadn't forgiven me for making her feel bad about a pilfered stamp and was in no mood to help me.

'He's out,' she said.

'Can you tell me when he'll be back?'

'If he's not answering his phone . . .' Mel said. 'Your marriage is your business.'

'If he's not answering his phone it means he's driving,' I said. 'If he gets back can you tell him to call me? Or – here's a thought – do you know where he's going? To a job? A wholesaler? Can you give me a number?'

'I've got no more idea where your husband is than you have, Ali,' Mel said. 'I might not be the employee of the month in your opinion but I know more than to grill my new boss about his doings.'

'Well, can you maybe put me on to the manager?' I said.

'Chrissake, how many different ways have I got to tell you?' she said. 'Are you away to La-la Land again, likes of?'

280

I hung up and stared at the phone. La-la Land? How did Melanie from school know that I'd been . . . a 'mental-health-service user' was what it was called, these days. The rest of her words were lost under that and didn't hit me until much, much later. Didn't even graze me as they went whooshing by.

———————

Surraya was in the big meeting room with her depression group, Jo and Harriet, dragged away from their jigsaw for once, and two more I didn't recognize. One of them was crying softly into a crumpled tissue.

'I'm so sorry,' I said, hovering at the door, 'but can I have a quick word?'

Surraya's eyebrows lowered and her eyes were like chips of granite as she glared at me. 'One minute,' she said to the group, and she laid a hand on the shoulder of the crying woman, patting her as she passed.

'Ali, you can't do this,' she whispered, when we were outside in the corridor. 'Group's sacrosanct.'

'I know,' I said. 'I'm sorry. I just need two things. I need you to beep Lars for me and I need you to— Actually, can you just beep Lars and I'll ask him?'

Surraya had already keyed the number into her phone. She waited, then said, 'Don't start. It's not me. Ali needs you in the main hall . . . Lars, I know. I'm in *Group*. Oh, for f—' She hung up and glared harder than ever. 'He's coming,' she told me. 'You'd better think up something good before he gets here.' Then she disappeared back inside and shut the door smartly.

I heard Lars in less than another minute but that didn't stop me kicking myself for not asking Surraya the other question and getting a jump on it. I was already asking as I ran up the stairs to meet him, my phone all ready in my hand.

'What's Sylvie's surname?' I said, as we met on the half landing.

'You're kidding?' said Lars. 'You got me out of a one-to-one for this?'

'No, I got you out of a one-to-one to get your car keys,' I told him, holding out my hand, 'but while we're at it, what's Sylvie's surname?'

'Bos—' Lars began.

'Boswell!' I chimed in. 'It was right on the tip of my tongue. I don't suppose you know the address or phone number offhand, do you? Well, can I borrow your car?'

'Ali, what's going on?' said Lars. 'If you've had another breakthrough with Sylvie you've got to tell Dr Ferris. You can't go piling off to her parents like a maniac. Look, I need to get back.'

'Lars,' I said. 'Can I trust you?'

'You're starting to worry me,' he answered. 'But aye.'

I stared at him, hardly knowing where to start. 'Picture speaks a thousand words,' I muttered, woke my phone, scrolled to the email and hit the attachment, handing it to him as the picture started loading.

'What am I looking at?' he said, pinching his fingers and flicking them wide to zoom in.

'That's the hand that was sticking up out of the ground at the abbey,' I said.

Lars lifted his eyes to mine, then dropped them back to the picture. He stepped back and rested his bum on the landing windowsill behind him. 'It's got a watch on,' he said. 'The cops never said anything about a watch.'

'They didn't know,' I said. 'It was gone before they got there.'

'Wait,' he said. 'How do you know that? How did you get the picture?'

'My kid took the photo,' I said. 'But he didn't take the watch. I just found it in Dr Ferris's desk drawer.'

He stared at me. 'The watch from the corpse at Dundrennan is here?'

'Hidden in Dr Ferris's bottom drawer,' I said. 'You can go and check if you don't believe me. There's no one in the office. But I wish you'd just believe me.'

'And you didn't put it there?' he said. 'You didn't get it from your kid and plant it there?'

'I didn't,' I said. 'It's your choice whether or not you believe me. And my kid didn't take it and give it to her. He says he didn't and I can tell when he's lying.'

The silence lasted until I could hear the blood screaming in my ears, like a train in a tunnel.

'I believe you,' he said at last. 'But, Ali, what the fuck's going on?'

Relief stopped me talking until I had taken three or four big gulping breaths. Then: 'I think Dr Ferris is going to . . . harm Sylvie. And possibly say Julia did it, but definitely blame the whole mess on me. Tonight.'

'*What?*' Lars shook his head, as if he had water in his ears. 'Ali, I'm trying to accept what you're telling me. I want to, but you sound paranoid. And what's it got to do with the hand and the watch?'

'Nothing that I can see,' I said. 'Except maybe it's evidence that she's "harmed" someone before.' I nodded at the phone. 'So, again, do you know how I can contact Sylvie's family?'

'Not a clue,' said Lars. 'Her bills get paid by a trust and no one ever visits. Not in the time I've been here anyway.'

283

'Boswell,' I said. 'Are they local?'

'No idea,' Lars said. 'But I can tell you the trust money comes from a solicitor with offices in Dumfries. So probably, eh?'

'I'd never get a solicitor to give anything away,' I said. 'But, come on – it's Galloway.'

'Right?' said Lars. 'Naebody here except three old farmers and a dead sheep.'

'Can't be that many Boswells anyway.'

'Why not go to the poli— Oh, yeah,' Lars said.

'Yeah,' I said. 'Angelo.' We were silent for a moment. 'Hey, you never said what your other two girls were called. As well as Lola.'

'Maddie, Lola and Saran,' he said. He smiled. He knew I had mentioned his girls to get under his skin, make him think like a dad. 'You reckon something's set for tonight, eh?'

I smiled back to tell him I knew he knew. 'Will you stay on? Watch Sylvie?'

'Course I will,' he said. 'Who wouldn't?' He gave me a grin, one that showed the black caves in his mouth where his molars should have been and for some reason I hugged him.

'You're not going to do anything daft,' he said, into my hair. 'You'll take care, eh?'

'I'm only going to find Sylvie's family and tell them . . . Well, tell them she's talking for a start and tell them I'm worried she's not safe.'

'We could all lose our jobs,' Lars said, letting me go and stepping back. 'But if you're right enough about Dr Ferris being mixed up with the corpse, we're all going to lose our jobs anyway.'

When he lifted the chain from round his neck and held it

out to me I thought he was giving me a good-luck charm, a blessing on my quest. 'My car keys are in my locker,' he told me.

———————

The soldier in the kiosk lifted a hand and gave a lazy wave as I went by. I answered with a bib on the horn as I slowed, wondering which way to go: Kirkcudbright was closest, Castle Douglas was biggest, Dalbeattie was where I knew people well enough to march up and start asking who remembered a family called Boswell. Then, cursing myself for a fool, I threw the car into reverse, pulled back to the kiosk again and climbed out.

'La— Oh, I thought it was Lars,' the soldier said.

'I borrowed his car,' I explained. 'And I was wondering if I could borrow something of yours too.' He stood up – stood to attention, really. He made me think of a gundog, a-quiver from his crew cut to the toes of his shiny boots to give me whatever it was I wanted from him. 'Can I look up a number in one of your phone books there?'

He gave them a glance as if seeing them for the first time. 'They're all out of date,' he said.

'Out of date's what I'm after,' I told him. 'Fifteen years out of date, if possible.'

We both set to, rummaging through them two by two – a phone book and a *Yellow Pages* for each year. The oldest one was from thirteen years back. I plucked it out of the pile and stifled a sneeze at the dust it let go. 'If you don't mind me asking,' I said, 'why have you got these?'

'Never got an order to discard them,' the soldier said.

I busied myself looking for the start of the Bs so he couldn't see the look on my face. And there it was! *Boswell, Col. & Mrs. R., White Bay House, Kirkcudbrightshire.* And a number.

'Found what you were looking for?'

'I'll just put this number in my phone,' I said.

'Or just . . .' said the soldier, ripping out the page and handing it to me. I really didn't get the army.

———————

White Bay was round the estuary down towards the next headland. These little lanes, there was no way you could afford to take your attention off the road but I couldn't resist it: I put the number in and put my phone in the stand on speaker when I heard it ringing out.

'Hello?' said a voice, after the fifth ring. A stern-sounding voice, posh and confident. Another one.

'Ah, hello,' I said. 'Is that Mrs Boswell, by any chance?'

There was a hesitation, long enough for me to think that of course the family had moved on. That this was whoever bought White Bay House from them. Then the woman said, 'Yes? Who is it?'

I shot my hand out and killed the call. I couldn't do it on the phone.

Pulling over into a driveway I got my satnav up and punched in 'White Bay House', then stared dumbly, with a chill creeping over me, when the answer came. White Bay House wasn't at White Bay on the next headland. It had got that name because it looked *across* the estuary at White Bay. My map app told me my destination was 0.3 of a mile away and in current traffic conditions my journey would take one minute. I was actually parked at the mouth of the drive to Sylvie's house, where her mother still lived, fifteen years of no visits later.

I wiggled Lars's car back and forth so it wasn't blocking the way and then, dinking it locked, I set off on foot. I'd rather have the walk down the tree-lined drive to plan what I was going to say and not bring her out, at the sound of a car, before I was ready.

But what *was* I going to say? I could always just throw Julia under the bus, tell Mrs Boswell that I thought Sylvie was in danger from another patient at the hospital. If I accused Dr Ferris without solid evidence I could end up in court for slander. But what if I told the woman that her daughter had been talking and laughing, had been drawing, revisiting the start of her long illness? What mother wouldn't want to hear that?

I could see something glinting through the tree trunks now. I couldn't work out if it was glass or water. There was a lot of it, if it was glass. I slowed down a little and made sure I was in shadow as I rounded the last corner and looked at the place Sylvie had called home.

My breath stilled in my throat. It was a cube of windows, flat-roofed and featureless, standing on stilts with a spiral staircase leading down to a garage tucked in below. I couldn't even see the door from here. What I could see, though, was a pine tree – or a fir maybe, a Douglas fir? I didn't know many plant names – growing up through the middle of it as if the house had been thrown round the trunk, like a fairground ring.

She had drawn it. A square for the house and a line for the tree it was built round. That sketch was nothing to do with the Mercat Cross. I leaned against the nearest trunk, trying to make sense of it all. I had accused Angelo of lying to me, rehashing a story he had heard in his doctor's consulting room instead of telling me what had really happened. But maybe the truth was he had told Dr Ferris and she had rehashed the story to me, telling me it was Sylvie's tale, using it to explain the sketch, so I wouldn't know the truth of what she was trying to draw.

The cube of a house and the line of a tree growing through it.

And, of course, the person. I traced it on the shiny banded bark beside my head. A square and a line up and down and a line straight across. There was only one way I could think of a person being a horizontal line in the middle of a house. Finally, I thought I knew what Sylvie was trying to tell me.

The sound of a slamming door sent me darting behind the birch tree to hide in its shade and peer round it. Someone had come out of the house and was walking across the deck towards the spiral staircase. The woman, lumbering down the stairs, leaned over the banister and clicked a key fob to start one of the garage doors opening. I pulled further back into the shadows.

I would know her anywhere, from her walk, her bulk, her haughty profile and her frizz of hair. It was Mona Swain. It was Julia's mother. She squeezed up the space at the side of the garage and wriggled herself into the driving seat of a scuffed BMW. Once she was out on the drive she hit her buttons again to close the garage door and put the outside lights on, for later, then she drove away.

Chapter 22

Memories burst like flour bombs in my head as I stood there: Dr Ferris saying, 'Now, Sylvie really *has* been here for ten years. Well, goodness me, almost fifteen now.' Julia screeching, 'I killed my father,' then mumbling, 'I didn't say it. I heard it.' And Angelo's voice was in there too: 'No one *told* me, Mum. I was *there*.' And Sylvie's face breaking into such a wide grin as she bumped across the rough grass, then whispering 'Ju,' and, again, 'Ju.'

But remembering is something you can do anywhere. You can only look for a body in its grave.

I was certain the house was empty, but I rang the number again to make doubly sure, and heard it in both ears, from my phone and through the glass walls of the cube. It would be a cheerless place to live in a typical winter if the windows were flimsy enough to let the sound of a ringing phone through. Stupid sort of house to build in a Scottish forest, whichever way you looked at it. Winters here, you wanted to batten down and sit round a fire, not rattle about in a see-through biscuit tin with the rain hitting it on all four sides and the leaves dropping on the flat roof.

I clicked off and waited a moment. Then, bent at the waist, I scurried over the bit of clear space between the trees and the house and ducked in among the stilts, past the garage, to get to the middle where the pine stood tall and, if I was right, the corpse of . . . someone lay buried at its roots.

It could have been striking if it was in Japan or if Mona Swain was the type who cared what people thought. But the gravel had sunk as the years went by and the tree roots had pulled up into claws, not to mention the mats of soaked leaves blown against the house supports and left to rot there.

God knows what I thought I would see. But if one corpse could rise and reach up out of the ground, why not two? I walked around the tree. Definitely some kind of conifer, I thought, once I was close enough to smell the sharp gin-stink of its fallen greenery under my feet. The litter of leaves was deep and rotten and hadn't been disturbed for years. I looked up into the canopy of the tree, a dizzying cross-hatch of bare branches. Were both lines the tree? Was I making too much of everything?

I stopped and leaned back against the rough bark. Because Lars was right: it did sound insane. It was crazy to think Dr Ferris was mixed up with the corpse at the abbey. Was it possible, I asked myself, that the watch wasn't in the drawer at all? I'd been *hearing* things that weren't there for years. Maybe I had started seeing them too. So scared for Angel, desperate to get all the trouble away from him and onto someone else. Anyone.

I started, stumbled and went over on my ankle hard. My phone was ringing and this stupid ugly house acted like a trumpet so the sound boomed up into the empty air.

'*What?*' I hissed, jabbing at it. 'Jesus!'

'Als?' said Marco's voice. 'What's up?' I took a few breaths to calm myself down. 'Ali, what is it?'

'What the hell?' I said. 'Oh, shit, my foot! What do you mean "what is it"? You phoned me, Marco. What do you want?'

'What's wrong with your foot? And where are you? You sound like you're in a cave. I phoned you *back*, Ali. I missed a call and Mel said you were trying to get me.'

'Where are you?' I said. When he didn't answer, I swept on. 'Listen, go home. I don't want Angel to be on his own.'

'Aw, come *on*,' Marco said. 'Not this agai—'

'I'm not asking,' I said, cutting him off. 'I'm telling you that our son can't be on his own. If you won't go home I'll get someone else.'

'Ali, seriously. What is going on?'

'Well, I'm not going to be home tonight,' I said. 'So there's that.'

'Oho! Open marriage time, is it?' Marco said. I didn't answer. I took the chance to hold out my phone and get a picture of the cube.

'I'm doing a night shift,' I said, with the phone back at my ear. 'You need to take care of Angel while I take care of someone else. And another thing. I need get to the bottom of it all.' I was out from under the house again by the time I got through this little speech, striding up the drive towards Lars's car. I had never felt stronger or surer in my life.

'The bottom of what? Ali, you need to get a gri—'

I hung up. More than half of me thought he was right. I was imagining things and seeing things and there was no way that any of this could really be happening. Surely. I couldn't trust myself, I had learned that years ago.

I slowed and stopped and stood there. I'd been *taught* that years ago. Had I learned my lesson? I put my hands over my face to shut out even the dim light under those glowering trees. I tried to stop the sound of the wind and its cold breath on the backs of my hands, and get myself down to the plain truth inside all the madness. The hard ground under my feet.

I punched Marco's number and he answered after half a ring.

'And I want to name our daughter and have a memorial to her,' I said. 'Just so you know.'

Dr Ferris's car still wasn't back when I arrived at the hall, neither in its usual space nor at the far end chosen for her quiet getaway. I parked and went in, still striding, still sure. Dr F, crossing the main hall with a stack of folders in his arms, stopped and quirked his head at me. 'You seem filled with purpose, Ali,' he said. 'Having a good day?'

'Very,' I said. I walked past him so he had to turn and face the light from the landing window. I needed to watch his face while I said the next bit. I was pretty sure he wasn't a part of whatever his wife was up to but I'd be able to tell from his eyes when I told him what I had to say.

'Sylvie,' I said, 'has been talking.'

He went through a frown, a big blink and a hoick of his eyebrows up into his hair. Then a beaming smile spread over his face. '*Sylvie?*' he said. 'What did she say?'

I gave the grin back to him. 'La-la, Ju-ju, La-li, and ssh,' I said.

'Oh!' He covered his mouth with his hand and I could see his eyes shining. 'Am I the first one you've told?'

'Lars heard some of it.'

'And this was today,' he said, not quite a question. 'Or we'd have heard at the shift change.'

'Right,' I agreed.

'Amazing,' he said. Then he blinked hard again a couple of times. 'I need to get a hold of myself or I'll lose a lens. Such vanity. I should wear my specs and be done with it. Congratulations, Ali. Whatever you did, I applaud you.'

I gave him a tight smile, but I couldn't speak. Flour bombs going off again. Only this time they were more like fireworks, setting light to little dry scraps of memory.

'It was Julia,' I said to Dr F, as I turned to go. 'Not me.'

I bounded up the stairs to her room and walked in, with a cursory couple of raps on the door.

'Ju?' I called.

'I'm having a shit!' she shouted, from behind the half-open bathroom door.

'You sound like you're feeling better again,' I said. 'I know what it is you're here to try and find out. I'm going to help you. But you need to come back to Sylvie's room.'

She blatted the door open and strode out. 'What?' she said. 'How?'

'Aren't you going to wash your hands?' I said. 'Or flush the bog?'

'Oh, FFS! I wasn't shitting. I said that because it's inappropriate and inappropriate is textbook histrionic.' I gave her a look. 'Yeah, I know you've busted me but I've got in the habit. And it's a good laugh too.'

'Well, you're going to have to can it,' I told her. 'You're going to have to sit quietly and let your elders and betters talk about important stuff, okay?'

I watched a few candidate comebacks cross her mind and her face but in the end she nodded. I took her arm and pulled her out of her room and down the stairs.

'Your dad,' I said, once we were in the side-corridor that led to Sylvie. 'Ralph, I mean. Ralph Boswell? You said he tarted himself up for a fancy woman. I'm guessing he got his teeth fixed as well as buying contact lenses. Am I right?'

'He looked like a gameshow host,' Julia said. 'From photos, I mean. I was too young to remember him for real.'

'Yeah, you said,' I told her, squeezing her tight just for a second as I opened the door and ushered her in. 'Stay here until I get back, okay? Give me your phone till I put my number in. If anyone comes, call me. *Anyone*. Okay?'

I made my way to the staff kitchen, sure I would find someone there who could beep Lars. As luck would have it, I found Lars himself. Him, Belle, Hinny, Surraya and Yvonne all turned solemn eyes on me as I came in.

'How much did you tell them?' I said.

'Well, you know, the watch,' Lars said. 'Shoot me.'

'Did anyone else go to look at it?' I said. There were frowns all round. 'Because this is so insane I'm having a hard time believing it's happening.'

'He's your boy and you love him,' Belle said. 'At least Dr Ferris didn't turn him in. He'll get off with a warning.'

I blinked. 'Oh, God,' I said. 'That would be bad enough, Belle. I think whatever's really going on is worse by a mile. Lars, can you come with me back to Sylvie's room?'

'I was going to insist,' Lars said.

It wasn't until we were halfway there that I realized he was coming to guard them from me, not help me guard them.

Julia was already sitting hitched onto Sylvie's bed with her arm around Sylvie's head like a . . . what I thought was a roll-bar. For protection against whatever incoming blows I had brought with me.

'I don't really know where to start,' I said. 'So just promise me you'll keep quiet and let me get through it all? That means you, Julia.'

She nodded but she was looking at Sylvie, and Sylvie was looking back at her, sliding out of focus but then returning.

'There's good news and there's bad news. But most of all, there's answers. Okay?' She nodded. 'Good news first. That's your sister.'

I don't know what I expected, but what I got – as well as 'Jesus! Seriously?' from Lars – was just Julia nodding slowly as she dotted little looks at Sylvie's hair and eyes and lips and hands, like the way a little animal touches down its nose when it's picking up scents from the ground.

'Sissy,' she said. 'Yes, I remember. I really do.'

'You *remember* her?' said Lars.

But it didn't seem strange to me. Angel remembered what happened when he was three. He knew there was someone missing from our family. That trip of a lifetime? Six months in Australia, just the three of us and the dolly he wouldn't let go of? I had lost count of the number of nights he woke up clawing his way out of his little bed, rushing about the strange hotel rooms, opening cupboards and bathroom doors, searching. I had lost count, and then I had taken the memory and buried it down, down deep, like you would bury a battered corpse and build a house on top and plant a tree and let the leaves fall and rot until . . .

'But there's bad news too.'

'She killed him,' said Julia. 'Sylvie killed him.'

'She did,' I agreed.

'Your dad?' said Lars. 'Dr F reckons he's golfing, you know.'

'Garran Swain is golfing,' I said. 'Ralph Boswell is dead.'

'She hurt his middle,' said Julia.

'I think it was his head,' Lars said softly. 'The post-mortem report.'

'Yeah, yeah,' Julia said. 'His head bashed in so bad a bit of his glasses was embedded in his skull. I know. But she "hurt his middle". So, you know, I'd say he had it coming. She should have bitten "his middle" off.'

'Jesus,' said Lars again, and his voice was as thick as a burp, his throat open as bile rose, father of those three beautiful girls.

'So . . .' Julia said. 'Just to make sure I've got this straight. My mother made out he'd left and hid his body. And she sold the Ferrises this place at a knock-down price and in return they kept Sylvie here instead of her going to trial and then to jail? Is that how it goes?'

'That's about the size of it,' I said.

'And she buried him at Dundrennan Abbey,' Julia said. 'Where he rested in peace until the floods came.'

'She tried to disguise him,' I said. 'Cheap watch, cheap belt. No one would think that guy in the Asda jeans was Ralph Boswell, would they?'

'It was definitely Mum who did that bit?' said Julia.

'Definitely,' I said. 'Sylvie couldn't have managed it when she was fifteen. She was too young to drive and far too small to manhandle a man's body. Dig a grave. Your mum did it. To protect her.'

Julia looked down at Sylvie's blank face. 'How did *you* get that?' she asked. 'The bitch wouldn't spit on me if I was burning.' There were tears in her eyes as she looked up again. 'Are you definitely sure Sylvie didn't do it all? They say you get strong when you're scared. Adrenalin and all that. And I was nicking Mum's car when I was fifteen.'

'Yes, but Sylvie doesn't actually know where he was buried. She thought she did but she guessed wrong.'

'What do you mean?' Julia said. 'How the hell do you know what Sylvie *thinks*?'

'She's been drawing it,' I said. 'If you ask her to draw a house and a tree and a person she draws . . .' I rummaged a pen out of my bag and dashed off the few lines, then showed it to Julia.

Lars cleared his throat. 'It's even more certain than that, actually. He wasn't buried at the abbey the whole time. He was actually somewhere else first. He's been moved. A few years ago, while Sylvie was in here.'

'How do they know?' I said.

'The soil,' said Lars. 'Well, not soil . . . what do they call it? Humus. Plant matter. Clinging around him.'

'Was it like a pine tree or a fir tree or something?' I said.

'Aw, man, what did Boney say?' said Lars. '*Cupressus* something. *Cupressus semper* . . . Sounded more like a school motto than a tree to me.' Julia pulled her arm free and squirmed her way up the bed to lean against the bed head. She gathered Sylvie to her and held her tight with both arms. '*Cupressus sempervirens*,' she said. 'It's a kind of juniper. Stinks like a skunk.'

'She buried him there until he was unrecognizable,' I said, speaking more to myself than anything.

'Then she dug him up,' said Julia, taking over, 'gave him some trinkets he wouldn't have touched with a barge pole and

297

shifted him to a public place.' Her words were harsh but the tears were falling. 'My dad's dead. And my mum's going to prison for whatever the hell you call what she did. And my poor sister's obviously never getting out of the loony bin, is she?' She gave a helpless sob. 'I had to meddle, didn't I? I had to kick it all up and now I've got no one.'

'You've got answers,' said Lars.

She nodded. 'Yep,' she said. 'Good point. I got what I said I wanted.' She dropped a kiss on Sylvie's head and lifted her face with a strand of Sylvie's thistledown hair still stuck to her lip. 'I've got the cold, hard truth. Wonderful. I always knew something was . . .'

'Missing?' I said, thinking of Angelo.

'Hidden,' said Julia. 'Not anymore. Lucky me. I've got all the answers now.'

She gathered Sylvie to her again and rocked her. Lars, who was so used to letting people feel like shit, just stood there. But inside me a volcano was rumbling and my breath was coming quicker and quicker. *She* was speaking to me. 'Mmmhmmm.'

'Bullshit!' I said. Sylvie twitched, reacting to the harsh sound. 'That's not the cold, hard truth. That's just a different story.'

It had to be coincidence but, as Julia looked up, Sylvie looked at me too. I saw for the first time that they really were sisters.

'Your sister killed your dad and then just happened to turn catatonic?' I said. I was pacing. I thought it was stagy when Dr Ferris did it, but I couldn't contain the bulge and burst of all the ideas going off inside me. 'That seems a bit convenient, doesn't it? Not to mention the fact that she's suddenly a bit *less* catatonic all of a sudden just exactly as the bones come to the surface again. Doesn't that strike you as odd? Doesn't it strike you as pretty odd, too, that Dr Ferris would suddenly employ a fucked-up beautician, whose PVG comes through miraculously quickly and who gets to look after Sylvie overnight? And – most of all – doesn't it seem a bit odd that your mother would let you come here, Julia?'

Julia searched my face, then Lars's. 'Well, after all the bedwetting and fire-setting she had to put me somewhere, but . . . yes, actually.'

I screwed up my face, trying to think, still marching up and down the little stretch of carpet, not caring how it looked. It was helping. And *she* was helping too. 'Mmmhmmm,' she said. I nodded. She was right. It made no sense. If Mona Swain loved her elder daughter so much that she covered up a murder, and kept her safe and quiet at Howell Hall instead of in prison, she would want her younger daughter well away. You keep your children safe. Like we did with Angelo. Safe from the pain of it, safe from the memories.

'Well,' said Lars, 'Sylvie's been all right here for all these years. It maybe seemed like the best place for you.'

But Julia had caught the fire that was in me. She wasn't going to settle for another story. She shook away the comfort and stared hard at Sylvie, thinking. 'Now, of all times,' she said. 'I mean, if my mother knew the jig was up, the bones washing to the surface, the story bound to break . . . Except – oooh.' She rubbed her head and now she screwed up her eyes too. 'The time's wrong. I was in here before the police found the body, wasn't I?'

'How long would you say you'd been trying to get in here?' I asked her.

Julia stuck out her bottom lip and puffed a breath up her face. 'Couple of years?' she said. 'When my dad left – Garran, I

299

mean – I went snooping. I thought *he* was in here. I found receipts, you know.'

'It doesn't fit,' I said. 'Mona and Sylvie make sense. But you don't, Julia. And I sure as hell don't. And Angelo's phone and the watch . . .' I had ground down into silence when my phone rang. Marco again.

'What?' I said.

'Ali, this is getting ridiculous,' he said. 'I left work early, like you said, I came home, like you said, and the wee toerag's not in.'

'What?' I said. I spoke so sharply that Sylvie jerked out of her drift and whimpered. Julia pulled her closer and glared at me. 'What do you mean, not in? Where is he?'

'He's out on a bloody date,' Marco said. 'Left every towel in the house soaking wet on the bathroom floor, used all the hot water and borrowed my aftershave. See, this is typical you, Als. You buy all his crap, thinking he was broken-hearted, and now she's clicked her fingers again and he's off.'

'*Again?*' I said.

'It's the same lassie from last time! He was never going to go outside and he was finished with school after the way she treated him. Then she phones him up and he's away back for more.'

'The girl who stood him up in front of all her friends and laughed at him?' I said. Lars and Julia were watching my end of the conversation, avidity in their eyes. 'Do you know where they are? Go and get him home and spit in her Coke while you're at it! What's wrong with you?'

'Ocht now,' Marco said. 'She's not a bad lassie. She's got some class. Good family and all that. Bloody stupid name, but that's not her fault.'

As he spoke, I felt a grating and grinding somewhere deep inside me as wheels that were stuck began to turn and slabs of meaning heaved themselves until they hung over cold, black holes and slid home.

'Dido,' I said, my voice parched.

'That's her,' said Marco.

'That bitch!' said Julia.

'Where are they?' I asked Marco. My voice had dried out even more, to a croak.

'Ocht, Als. They're fine,' he said. 'They'll be at the pictures or sitting in a café. Or they'll be parked up somewhere with the seats flat. Nothing we didn't do.'

'Find him and get him away from her,' I rasped at him.

'Ali,' Marco said, 'don't upset yourself. Come on!'

How many times a day did he tell me to 'come on'? How many times in the last week? How many times in the six months I was il— I caught myself. I could almost feel myself reaching for the thought as it formed, taking it by its neck and squeezing it until it hung grey and limp in my hand. I wasn't ill. I was mourning. Or, at least, I was trying to.

'Do what I'm asking, Marco,' I said. 'For once, just listen to me, eh?'

'That could be awkward,' Marco said. 'I don't want to cause trouble. Not when things are finally looking up for us.'

'What are you talking about?' I said. 'You think her mum's going to sack me because my son won't go out with her daughter?'

Marco said nothing and into his silence came memories. His face when he was on the phone; her sharp look when I said his name; the call log on our landline. A great big sack of understanding came swinging in, like a sandbag, and socked me in my guts. I hung up without another word.

'Lars,' I said. 'The Ferrises' other business?'

'Eh?' said Lars. 'What about it? You mean Springview House . . . or wait. You mean her family business?'

'Yeah, that's the one,' I said. 'The builder's yard. T&C, right?'

'What about it?'

I swallowed vomit, leaving a bitter blackness in the back of my mouth. 'Nothing,' I said. 'Julia? How well do you know Dido Ferris? Do you know where she hangs out? Where she'd be likely to go if she was out for a laugh one night?'

Julia shrugged. 'Why?'

'Because she's the missing link and she's got my son.'

She had bewitched him, picked him up in her car, goaded him to photograph the hand and its watch at the abbey. She had stolen his phone and used it to call the police. She had stolen the watch. Then, when she was done with him, she had tossed him aside and broken him. And she'd laughed about it – or at least talked about it – with her mum. Whatever it was she wanted with him now, I had to stop it happening.

'Lars,' I said. 'I have no idea what's going on, but either I need your keys back or I need you to come with me. And I need you to phone your pal and ask him what make and model of car stopped at my door the night the bones were found. Somebody'll have written it down. They were all still at the crime scene when Dido came and Angelo jumped out his window.'

'I can tell you that,' said Julia. 'Roughly. It's like a red Mini or a pink Jeep or some stupid chick car like that. But are you really both going to go shooting off? What about us?'

And then all of us jumped, even Sylvie, at the sound of a voice from the half-open door.

Chapter 23

'I'll take care of you both,' said Dr F. He looked as if he'd been running, his chest heaving up and down and his face shining.

'Nice ambiguity!' Julia said. 'Could you get any creepier? And are you wearing a white coat to look like Dr Frankenstein, by the way? Just for a bit of extra—'

'I'm wearing a white coat because . . .' His voice trailed away. 'Comfort blanket, I suppose you'd say,' he said at last, with an unhappy laugh. 'The SCCE are just off the phone. Today's the day. Two inspectors are on their way from Glasgow as we speak.'

'They won't be here till God knows when,' said Lars, with a glance at his watch.

'It's part of the plan,' said Dr F. 'They start at the fag end of the day shift. The manager I just spoke to said they get the most accurate picture of true protocols and procedures at that time of day.'

'Bastards,' said Lars.

'So,' said Dr F, 'I think it's fair to say that Howell Hall's number is up. My wife is AWOL and she appears to have left her office open to the outside and her computer unprotected.'

'Her *computer* was on?' I said. I hadn't even checked. I almost laughed thinking about the page ripped out of the phone book.

A frown flickered over Dr F's face, but he wasn't really listening to me. 'And so, while the cat's away, the mouse has just reviewed Sylvie's details. Something I've been meaning to do for a while now. Something, if I'm honest, I've always meant to do and never found the courage to.' He sniffed deeply, a rich liquid sniff and a big swallow at the end of it. He walked over to Sylvie's bed and looked down at her, with that same kind smile that had beguiled me. Julia moved her arms more closely around Sylvie's shoulders so that one elbow poked straight at Dr F's chest. 'I'm Paul, Sylvie,' he said. 'I'm going to help your sister take care of you tonight and then tomorrow—'

'Hang on,' I said. 'How—'

'—do you know you can trust me?' said Dr F. 'That's the wrong question. You should be asking yourself, *do* you trust me? And the answer is . . .'

'Yes,' said Lars, without a pause. 'The answer is yes.'

'*My* answer is "What choice have I got?"' I said.

'Pragmatic,' the doc said. 'Practical to a fault. How about you, Julia? What do you say?'

'What happens tomorrow?' said Julia. 'That's all I'm bothered about.'

'I'm going to help you and Sylvie get settled somewhere new. Howell Hall is finished.'

'You don't think you're finished too?' I asked him. 'Seeing as how you knew what was going on?'

He shook his head. 'I didn't know a thing. I put it together

304

when I saw the records just now. I was negligent and I might be reprimanded but it's my wife going down and I'm not going with her.'

'But . . . *tomorrow*?' said Julia. She spoke in a whisper. 'You think they'll take her away as quick as that?' Maybe she hoped Sylvie wouldn't hear her.

'I think either everyone will be leaving tomorrow,' Dr F said, 'or they'll be bringing someone in. I knew my wife had pulled some strings to get us started. And I knew she didn't always play the straight bat. A little collusion here, a convenient assessment there. But I honestly had no idea about Sylvie till I saw it in black and white.'

'She wrote it down in her *records*?' I said.

Dr F raised his chin a little at that. 'Of course she did,' he said. 'She's not completely lost to goodness. She's still a doctor.'

'And what exactly does being a doctor have to do with anything?' said Julia. She was wriggling out from under Sylvie, who had fallen suddenly and deeply asleep, her mouth hanging open and her breath dragging on her palate.

'We're talking about two different things,' Lars said. 'Doc, you're talking about her drug regimen, aren't you?'

'What else?' said Dr F. 'She's been sedated for years. And now the sedation is being lifted. What are *you* talking about?' Something about what he said bothered me. Because I remembered that first day and how disturbed Dr Ferris was when Sylvie looked at me. Well, maybe she just didn't know how quickly the girl would start to come out of the fog when the sedation was lifted.

'Didn't you wonder why?' I asked him. 'Didn't you wonder why a woman would want her daughter tidied away into this room for keeps?'

'I've only *known* for half an hour,' Dr F said. 'But of course I wonder.'

'Julia will tell you,' I said. 'Lars and I have got to go.'

———————

I didn't bother asking him where his daughter might be. No matter how quickly he was willing to stop covering for his wife, a daughter is different. I wouldn't have told *him* anything to help him find Angelo, would I?

Lars and I made our way as fast as we could move and still look casual out of the front door and into his car.

'Did you know about Sylvie's drugs?' I asked, as we moved off up the drive.

His silence told me everything I needed to know but he followed it up with an answer eventually. 'Not out loud,' he said. 'I wondered and I knew wondering would get me out on my ear so I let it go. At least now I know it was that or jail.'

'Catatonic,' I said. 'Oedema in her legs. Years drifting by. She was a kid, Lars. She was fifteen. She might have got a suspended sentence. And she'd have been out by now either way. What kind of mother . . .?'

'Mmmhmmm,' she said.

'But Sylvie *wanted* to take the blame,' Lars said. 'As soon as she came back to life she started trying to draw a flipping treasure map to the body. Her mum was only trying to save her from herself. Where am I going, by the way?'

'Where did you go when you were a kid?' I said, looking both ways as we passed the checkpoint and stopped at the side of the road. 'Did you ever go out with a posh bird? Where would she take you?'

'Wimpy, ice rink, Loreburne Centre. Anywhere the grass was dry,' Lars said. 'And no, there were no posh birds for me. Sharon and Tracy all the way till my wife. And by then we were old enough for pubs.'

I nodded, letting his words wash over me. If it was Angelo, if it was . . . if life had turned out differently and it was my little girl . . . I would have got the best lawyer I could afford, made a stink and tried to get her sentence down, visited her on remand, visited her in prison.

'Mmmmhmmmm,' she said.

'I'm sorry,' I whispered, as I tried to shake her out of my head. Angelo. I needed to concentrate hard on Angelo. My boy. My only one. Why had Dido Ferris picked him up again and where would they be?

'Dumfries, then,' I said, pointing right. 'They went to the Loreburne Centre one . . . time . . . before.'

'Sure?' said Lars. He was a good driver for these roads, sitting well back behind a tractor that was rumbling along in front of us. The farm worker saw us and pulled in, waving us past. Marco always tucked right up in the blind spot, like a fly at a cow's arse, then sat there fuming.

'What?' I said.

'You kind of stopped talking there. Let it out. There's sense there somewhere. You'll find it, Ali.'

'How could she stand it?' I said. 'She lives a mile away as the crow flies and never visits for fifteen years? She lives in that comfortless house – honest to God, Lars, you should see it! – she lives there for years waiting for the flesh to rot from her dead husband's bones so she can move him, and the girl she loves *so* much, the girl she did it all to protect, is silent and softening all alone just out of sight? Something is wrong with that story.'

307

'Mmmhmmm,' she said.

'Okay, forget talking,' said Lars. 'Listen. What does your gut tell you? What does your heart say?'

'Mmmmmmhhhmmmmmm,' she said. 'Mmmmmmhhhh uuuuhhhhmm,' she said, clearer than ever. Then she said something she'd never said before. 'Mhhuuuuhhmmm?'

'Lars, stop the car!'

If he hadn't been the driver he was he'd have skidded off the road at the sound of me. We had reached the row of cottages at Dundrennan and he pulled in a hundred yards from my house.

'What is it?' he said.

'My daughter's voice,' I told him. I knew I sounded insane. But I didn't care. 'I'm listening to my daughter's voice. And Mona's daughter's voice too. Both of them.'

'Ali,' Lars said, 'I know daughters are a difficult thing for you to think about clearly. Especially when you're so ups—'

'Fuck *that*!' I said. 'You can take that fucking shit and fuck the fuck off with it. I am thinking clearly about daughters today for the first fucking time in my fucking life.'

Lars had a light dancing in his eyes but he knew better than to laugh at me. 'Got it,' he said. 'So what are the daughters saying?'

'They're both saying what Julia's been saying ever since she came to Howell Hall.'

'That she killed her father and she hurt his middle.'

'Right,' I agreed. 'But she knows she's not repeating something she *said* all those years back. She's repeating something she *heard*.'

'She heard both things. She heard Sylvie say them.'

'Of course she did. Okay, do your best Julia impersonation. Say it like she says it.' Lars grimaced at me, not understanding. 'Go on.'

308

'I killed my father?' he said, in a high-pitched voice that sounded nothing like Julia except that it was loud and crazy. 'I killed my *father*?'

'You see,' I said softly.

Lars gave a long low whistle. 'She's asking,' he said. 'She heard Sylvie *asking*. Who was she asking?'

'Exactly.'

I could imagine it all now, in that ugly glass cube of a house. A fifteen-year-old girl asking, 'I killed my father?' and the sound carrying into the bedroom of a three-year-old child. 'I killed my father?' she asked.

'Yes,' her mother answered. 'Yes, you did.'

And what kind of mother tries to make her child believe such a thing? The sort of mother who would leave her in an empty room for fifteen years to keep her quiet. The sort of mother who'd rather have her dulled to a shadow by drugs than risk her talking. The sort of mother who'd put her other daughter in the same place, under the thumb of the same people.

'Mona Swain killed her husband,' Lars said.

'Yeah, I think so,' I said. 'He was abusing Sylvie. She "hurt his middle". So once he was dead she was all set to take the blame.'

'But Mona would have stopped her,' Lars said. 'And even Mona – if she killed him in a maternal rage, because of what he was doing to Sylvie, no jury would blame her. She'd probably get a round of applause.'

'Maybe that wasn't the problem,' I said. 'Mothers aren't all saints, you know. Maybe her rage wasn't maternal. Maybe it was jealous so she punished both of them.'

We sat silently and tested it.

'And then the floods came,' Lars said. 'And Mona knew what might happen.'

We had seen it on the news: subsoil washed up, wrecking farmers' fields; corners of coffin lids poking through the dead grey grass of that cemetery on the edge of the South Downs.

'And if it did,' I said, 'the cops would ID him, and they'd want to know where Sylvie was.'

'And once she was in the spotlight, sent to a police psychiatrist for evaluation . . .' Lars fell silent.

'Her oh-so-convenient catatonia would have to stop. They'd have to see her drug list, wouldn't they?'

'And so . . .' Silence again, for even longer this time, but eventually he roused himself. 'How does Julia fit in?'

'You really don't know?'

'The only thing I can think of is so insane I can't believe it. I can't even say it.'

'I'll say it for you,' I told him. 'I've got no trouble believing it. It was going to look like Julia killed Sylvie and then herself while under the care of an unstable woman who lied on her application. Dr Ferris hand-picked me.'

'How the hell did Dr Ferris even know about you?'

'Because she's having an affair with my husband,' I said. It was interesting to say it and feel nothing. True things don't hurt at all when you finally face them. 'She's moved him in and now he moves me out. Three birds, one stone. Dr Ferris gets rid of Sylvie, Mona Swain gets rid of both kids for good, and she can stop worrying about what they know and what they'll say, and as a bonus Marco finally gets rid of me.'

'And Angelo?' said Lars. 'How does he fit in?'

'Marco would never let anyone harm him,' I said. 'I think . . . I think . . . I think Dr Ferris told her daughter to find a stooge with a phone.'

'Just a coincidence that she chose your son?' said Lars.

We stared at each other. We both knew that was too much to swallow.

'Okay, so it wasn't that innocent,' I said. 'Dr Ferris told Dido to get in with my son and steal his phone. But Marco didn't know that bit of the plan.'

'But – but Angelo could have dropped Dido right in it. Told the police she'd made a beeline for him, told them she'd nicked his phone.'

'She'd deny it and her lawyers would say he was trying to protect me.' I wrapped my arms around my body and squeezed. 'He does that. He's been doing it for years.'

'So . . . you're supposed to have just generally gone off your rocker? Is that it?' Lars said.

'I think so.'

'But why are they together again tonight?' said Lars.

'Because she's a teenage girl and Angel's got his dad's eyes?' I said. 'She decided to phone him up again and have some more fun? I think Marco's right. He'll be in by eleven, crunching Tic-Tacs to hide the booze on his breath, all zipped up to the neck if she's a biter.'

Lars nodded. 'Did Marco actually say she phoned him?' he said. 'Is that definitely how they hooked up again today?'

'I think so,' I said. 'I think he phoned her yesterday to talk to her about the photo of the hand. At least, he definitely phoned someone, someone who knows the names of designers, but if it was Dido, she resisted him. He was in all last night.'

'Could he have tried again?' said Lars. 'Did he have anything else to offer? Anything new to tell—'

'Fuck!' I was out of the car and running. 'Of course he did!' I yelled back over my shoulder, as Lars scrambled out and followed me. 'He called her to say the watch was in her mum's desk drawer. When she heard that she couldn't get here fast enough.' I was fumbling with my key but my fingers felt like jelly. 'Oh, Jesus! Dr Ferris is AWOL too. He might be with both of them.'

Lars took the keys from me and fitted one into the lock. 'Say Dido didn't know he took a picture,' I said. 'Say she only found out today there was a way to tie him to the hand. Well that would tie *her* to the hand and that would blow their story sky-high.'

We burst in and both of us were panting. Marco was on the couch, a can of beer in his hand and the telly on.

'Who phoned who?' I fired at him.

'What?' said Marco. He frowned past me. 'Liam? Is it? Ali, shouldn't you be at work?'

'Close enough,' Lars said.

'What's going on?' Marco said. 'Liam, you need to know, pal, my wife can get a bit—'

'Give it up,' I said. 'I know you're at it with Tamara Ferris. I know that's how you got your job and got me mine.' I held up a hand. 'Don't even bother. We're past that. And let me tell you, Marco, I will never forgive you for letting our son get mixed up in all this. Even if we find him safe and sound, I will never forgive you. And if he's come to harm I will kill you.'

'Angelo's fine,' Marco said. 'There's no need to upset yours—'

'NO!' I bellowed it at him. 'You say that over and over like it's some kind of slogan. And I never knew why it made me feel as if I was going mad. I don't "upset myself", Marco. Things "upset me". Things "upset" everyone, unless they're catatonic or drugged to their eyeballs. It's called life.'

'Do you think we could maybe—' said Marco, flicking a glance at Lars.

'He's a friend,' I said. 'I needed one. So we're done. We're over. But I'm going to give you the chance to tell me the truth before I check for myself. Who phoned who?'

'It was a long time ago, Ali,' Marco said. He was shifting from foot to foot and not quite looking at me.

'What the hell are you on about?' I said. I walked up close to him and dipped my head trying to scoop up his gaze. 'It was today. It was this afternoon.'

'What are *you* on about?' Marco said, meeting my eye at last. 'Are you ill again?'

My hand shot out without any particle of me choosing to move. 'I was never ill,' I said, gripping his arm and squeezing. 'That was all you. Now tell me: did Dido Ferris click her fingers and have him come running for a laugh or did Angelo go running back to her with a big piece of bad news? Who phoned who?'

'Ali,' said Lars. 'You said he's not got a mobile at the minute, right?' He sounded unfazed by the mini-drama playing out in front of him. But, then, I supposed a psychiatric nurse would be used to worse than a gripped arm and some hissed words.

I turned to him and let Marco's arm go. 'You're right,' I said. 'It'll be on the log on the landline.'

'Is this Angelo?' Marco said. 'What exactly does my son's priva—'

'Oh, fuck off,' Lars said. 'And try redial too, Ali. Just in case.'

Marco was swaggering over the few feet of carpet towards him. I grabbed the phone from the arm of the couch and punched the buttons. 'It's ringing,' I said.

'Who do you think you are?' Marco said. He was squaring up, taller and heavier, inches away from Lars. 'This is my house and my family.'

313

'And this is my job,' Lars said. He didn't step back and his voice was calm. 'I diagnosed your wife the minute she walked through the door the first day. She's had a chronic case of being married to a man like you. She's on the mend, though.'

Someone answered the phone. 'What *now*?' It was Dr Ferris. Of course it was.

'Tamara?' I said. 'Do you know where your daughter and my son are? I'm fussy about who he hangs out with.'

The silence went on so long I wondered if the call had dropped. When at last she spoke her voice quaked with swallowed rage. 'Alison, shouldn't you be at work?'

'Oh, no,' I said. 'We decided not to go ahead with that . . . project. Your soon-to-be-ex-husband is looking after the Boswell girls and Lars and I are here teaching my soon-to-be-ex-husband a lesson. Okay?'

'Project?' Dr Ferris said.

'We'll never prove it,' I told her. 'So you're probably safe. You'll only get done for . . . Lars, what would you call it? What the doc did to Sylvie?'

'Assault,' said Lars, loud enough for her to hear. 'False imprisonment, actual bodily harm. Maybe grievous bodily harm.'

'You'll never prove anything,' she said.

'Tell me one thing,' I said. 'Did you know my son took a photo of the hand while it had the watch on? Did Dido tell you?'

Her intake of breath was like paper ripping. 'What?' she whispered.

'Oh, yes. He took it off his phone but he kept it on his laptop and I've got it on a flash drive too.'

'A photo? Of the watch?'

'Before it wound up in your desk drawer,' I said. 'Didn't

Dido tell you?' Another sheet of paper ripped and afterwards her breath came rough and ragged.

'Nonsense,' she said. 'My desk drawer?'

'And *I* took a photo of it in there,' I lied. I wished I had, but her thinking I did was almost as good. 'You're telling me you didn't know?'

'Of course I didn't know!' she said. 'Why would I bother taking it off if there was a photo?'

'So you didn't send your daughter to silence my son?' I said.

'What are you talking about?'

'You sound sincere,' I said. 'And I want to believe you. So how about if you tell me where Dido and Angel are?'

'I don't know,' she said. 'I didn't know they were—'

'Or give me her number, at least,' I broke in. 'And we'll help you pretend Sylvie just recovered suddenly. How about that, eh?'

'You're not going to harm her, are you?' she said. The first genuine words I had ever heard drip from her lips.

'Harm her?' I said. 'Harm your daughter?'

And I think she recognized the truth of what I'd said. At any rate, she gave me the number. I relayed it to Lars and he keyed it into my phone. Then, without another word, we left the house. Left Marco just sitting there. The sun was going down behind the abbey, long fingers of yellow light dazzling through the empty sockets where windows should be. I stopped on the doorstep and stared across at it.

'Is this real?' I said. 'Is any of this really happening? Or is this me going off my head like Marco's been ready for, all these years?'

'Wouldn't that be nice?' said Lars. 'Sorry, Ali. This is as real as rat shit in your raisins.'

'Right,' I said, laughing. 'Right then. Looks like I won't be getting a month at Howell Hall in one of the big bedrooms with the good toiletries. Even if I *am* married to the boss's boyfriend.'

'If the doc's right about the SCCE inspectors heading that way this afternoon, nobody'll be in there long,' said Lars. 'I've seen those guys bring the hammer down on a place before. It'll have started already.'

'As quick as that?'

'If getting sued's the other option. Anyway, that's not really the point this minute, is it?'

I nodded, gathering myself up again. 'How are we going to find Angel and Dido? Where will we start? Are you going to try her phone?'

'Speaking of phones,' said Lars, 'what did Marco mean when he said the phone call was a long time ago? What call was he talking about?'

I shook my head, casting my thoughts around, like driftnets. So many phones. Missed calls and logs and messages. It was so much harder, these days, for anyone to miss anyone they wanted to speak to, yet it was just as hard to reach across a chasm once you'd let it open.

'Oh!' I said, as the truth broke over me.

I looked down at the contacts on my phone. I'd kept the number. I'd even transferred it from phone to phone when I upgraded, made sure I had a Euro-roving account. All for that one French phone number I had never rung. I hit the little green icon and listened to it ringing.

'Hello?' she said.

'Mum?' I said. 'It's Ali. Mum, I know this is coming out of nowhere, but . . . all those years ago, what did Marco tell you?'

'He simply made your position clear,' my mum said, that

same snippy voice that used to tell me to sit up straight and clear my own dishes.

'What did he say?' I asked her again.

'He told me you were fine and didn't want a fuss.'

'*He* was fine,' I said. '*He* didn't want a fuss.'

'That there was no funeral planned.'

'That's true. I couldn't have planned a funeral if my— So we didn't have one.'

'He said we'd only upset you if we came over and tried to change your mind. It seemed so cold, Ali. I didn't understand.'

'Me neither.' I took a few big breaths, calming myself, before I tried to speak again.

'We've got a lot of talking to do. When would be a good time?'

'Anytime, Ali,' she told me. 'Day or night, darlin'. I'm your mum.'

I hung up, because the neighbour was twitching at his curtains and because if I said another word I would be sobbing.

Chapter 24

All those years. I'd missed their ruby wedding. They'd missed my fortieth birthday. They hadn't seen Angel on his first day at school or his best day at swimming. They hadn't been there to share the Champagne when Face Value opened or the vodka when it closed. My dad hadn't been around when Marco laid out his plans, and couldn't tell me how muddle-headed they were, help me get him told before we lost everything. And how I had hated them for it. If she'd phoned me, I wouldn't have said *day or night*. But then I wasn't her mum.

'Why?' I said to Lars.

'You want comfort or a diagnosis?' Lars said.

'Comfort!' I said. It came out in a howl.

'He's a shit.'

It wasn't exactly comforting but it made me laugh.

As I shook my head, I noticed that the neighbour was peering at me. Poor old codger. Bloody awful neighbours we'd been since we rocked up, hadn't we? I waved at him and mimed opening the window.

'I don't want another mouthful,' he said, as he leaned out.

'I need your help,' I said. 'I think my son probably got picked up by a friend in a car a wee while ago. Can you tell me which way it went?'

'Went? It didn't go anywhere,' he said. 'That's it sitting right there in my space outside my gate.'

I looked where he was pointing. Julia had said a red Mini or a pink Jeep. It was actually a Volkswagen Beetle in lemon yellow. Same difference: it was a car that screamed spoiled teenage girl.

'You haven't got a car,' I said. 'What harm's it doing you?'

'I could have a taxi coming,' he said, and slammed the window.

Lars was already dialling and, of course – *of course* – when the call went through we heard it both tinny from inside the phone and very faint from all the way across the road in the abbey grounds.

'Where else?' Lars said, and started walking.

'I think she meant it,' I said, scurrying along beside him. 'I don't think Dr Ferris knew about the photo. I don't think she sent Dido to . . . shut Angel up.'

Lars took my arm and broke into a run. 'Let's hurry anyway,' he said grimly.

All the police cars and vans had made a worse mess than the flood. A week before when the water went down, the grass was still grass, even sodden in yellowing clumps, but now the whole bowl of grounds where the ruins sat was a soup of mud, churned up into ropes and clods from the tyres, like piped chocolate icing. It sucked at my feet and splatted up my trouser legs. Lars had to give me his arm to steady me as I lurched and skidded towards where the phone was ringing out, bouncing off the high stones and echoing.

'Why doesn't she answer?' I said, clutching at Lars.

'Angelo?' he shouted. 'Where are you? Are you okay?'

The ringing stopped.

I could see it in my head long before I got to the corner and looked for real. I saw her, tall and haughty, standing over him, looking coldly down, taking a picture for a souvenir. And Angel's face blue with blood, his eyes drying, his tongue pushed out and as black as his lashes. I threw myself at the last of the buttresses and hauled my way round to look at the scene, to grab her and choke the life out of her with my two bare hands.

They were huddled together on a slab of rock, their muddy feet pulled up out of the mess, arms around each other. Angel and a little round girl with a pink flash in the front of her Mohawk.

'Dido?' I said, as the vision of the younger, taller, icier version of her mother melted away.

'Are you Mrs McGovern?' she said.

'Does your mum know where you are?'

'My *mum*?' she said. 'You're kidding. My mum told me I had to dump Angelo. She told me he was trouble.'

'Who's that?' said Angelo. He was glaring at Lars.

I dropped his hand and took a step towards the pair of them. 'Sounds like you made a proper job of the dumping,' I said. 'Did your mum tell you to send your friends to carry out a public shaming?'

'Mu-um!' said Angelo. 'We've sorted all that out.'

Dido had put her head down and when she spoke again her voice was tiny. 'I had to burn my bridges to make myself stick to it,' she said.

'It doesn't seem to have worked,' I said, looking at the way their arms were still wrapped round one another. 'And did your mum tell you to go out with him in the first place?' I said. 'Did your mum tell you to get his phone?'

Angelo took his arms away and stared at her, the shock making his face turn pale. 'Did she?' he said. He turned to me. 'Mum, is that why you've been asking about Dr Ferris on and on?'

'Of course she didn't,' Dido said. 'No! He left the phone in the car, I think. It fell out of his pocket when we were—' She stopped as a blush the colour of a raspberry filled her cold cheeks. That exact colour even as far as the faint blue top note.

'Wow,' said Lars. 'It was a coincidence? Her daughter and your son? His phone?'

'Well,' said Dido, her face still flaming. 'She pointed him out. She— Angel, she pointed you out. One day in Kirkcudbright. You were with your dad and she just said you were handsome.'

I could imagine it. Dr Ferris seeing her fancy man and saying to her daughter, 'He's a looker, isn't he?' not realizing that Dido would look at the boy Dr Ferris barely noticed.

'What's going on, Mum?' Angelo said.

I stared at him. Where would I begin? 'Nothing you need to worry about,' I said. 'A bit of trouble with a couple of patients at work, that's all. But it's going to be okay.'

'Is it Sylvie?' Dido said.

'What do you know about Sylvie?' said Lars.

'Only what my mum says when she's been drinking,' Dido said. 'Is she in trouble?'

'Sylvie and her sister are both in a bit of trouble,' said Lars. 'But, really, it's going to be okay. There might be a lot of changes coming but it'll work out.'

Dido gave a small unhappy laugh. 'I want to live with Dad, not with her.'

321

I smiled at her. I only knew what it was like to be a let-down to my husband. I couldn't imagine how it must be for a girl like Dido to be the kid of a woman like her mother.

'Sylvie and her sister.' Angelo's voice was as flat and cold as a slab of mud.

'What about them?' I said.

'Her *sister*? There's two of them, Mum? Seriously? I've got two sisters living a few miles away and I've never met either of them? What the fuck is wrong with this family? How could you come and live here? No wonder you didn't want to go and work there.'

'Oh, my sweetheart,' I said. 'I'm so sorry. I don't know why I said that. Except I was embarrassed that your sister never had a name. I said the first one that came into my head. Sylvie is over thirty. She's not your sister. Your sister was ... Darlin', I'm sorry, but she was so deformed she wasn't really a baby at all.'

Dido winced at the words but Angelo just frowned at me. 'What are you talking about?' he said. 'Of course, she was a baby. I told you. Dad took me to the hospital. I saw her. She was perfect. She was like a dolly. She was like the dolly I brought for her. You remember that dolly, right? I took it to Australia.'

'Oh, Angelo,' I said. 'That wasn't her. Your dad showed you a different baby so's not to upset you.'

'No,' Angel said. 'That's not right. It was definitely her. She was perfect. But she was dead. Like a dolly.'

The wind had dropped, the way it does, winter afternoons, and when the rain started it fell straight down, like threads of heavy silk. Lars came wading towards me through the mud and put one flap of his jacket around my back. 'We need to get out of here before we all drown,' he said. 'Ali, you're shivering.'

'I don't know where to go,' I said. I didn't even think of what

322

Angelo would make of his mum sounding so lost. He was on his feet, helping Dido down from the slab of stone. She came up to his shoulder, her little pink and black head fitting in close under his chin. He wasn't paying any attention to me. In Angelo's head, the last few days had been about a date and a dumping and now a second chance. The police, and his mum cracking up didn't even register.

'Angelo, take Dido to my place,' Lars said, fishing in his pocket and handing over a set of keys. 'Seventeen Bailey Park.'

'It's my car,' Dido said. 'So I'll be taking him.'

Angelo rolled his eyes but I couldn't help a small smile. I liked her. She took no nonsense from anyone.

'Where are we going?' I said to Lars.

'You need to catch Belle coming off her shift.'

He wouldn't say more.

———

Back at the hall the car park was full.

'What's going on?' I asked Lars, as we drew up.

'I told you,' he said. 'If the doc's chucked his wife under the bus things are going to move pretty quick.' He pointed to a couple hurrying in the front door. 'That's Byron's mum and dad, coming to pick him up and save themselves a fortune.'

I twisted round as an NHS patient-transfer minibus came up the drive behind us. Lars whistled. 'He's really stuck it to her if they're scooping up the *referrals* as quick as this, though.'

'It's too much,' I said. 'What if we're wrong? It's all so unlikely, you know. We can't be responsible for *this* on a crazy hunch about a crazy plot to— I can't—'

'Ali,' Lars said, putting a hand on my arm. 'You need to start

323

trusting yourself again. We're not wrong. You know that really. And . . .'

'And what?' I said, watching Ryan come out of the front door carrying a bulging gym bag, a nurse I didn't know holding him under the elbow.

'And you need to get ready for something else that's going to seem unlikely,' Lars said.

Ryan had seen us and came over, the nurse trotting after him. I wound down the window. 'Fucken hell,' he said, in greeting.

'I couldn't put it better myself,' I said, getting out of the car and giving him a quick hug, expert that I am in getting a hug in before a teenage boy can stop me. 'Take care, eh?' Then I made for the front door.

'Where are you going?' Lars said, once we were inside.

'Sylvie. Where do you think? If Belle really needs to speak to me about this "unlikely thing", bring her there.'

———

Julia was lying on the bed and Sylvie was in her chair facing the window, but she turned her head just a little as she heard me coming.

'It's all kicking off,' Julia said. 'You wouldn't believe how quick the tents are folding. My dad's coming back from Portugal. I told them I was eighteen but back he comes. That'll be fun, won't it? Perry and Garran both fussing over me, like two hens with one chick.'

'And your mum?'

'On the run,' Julia said. 'Cops came. Dr F told them she killed Ralph and kept Sylvie high as a kite. She's for it.'

Her voice was back to the drawl again and she was scrolling through texts and swinging one of her crossed legs with her shoe dangling from a toe-tip. But she didn't fool me.

'You'll get help,' I said. 'You'll get the help you need and you'll be okay. Don't be brave if you feel like bawling, eh?'

Movement at the door told me Belle was there.

'I'll stay with this pair,' Lars said. 'You go.'

Belle took me to the gazebo. The security light was on and it shone like a lantern as we tramped across the grass towards it through the mussed remains of Julia's leaf collage. The inside didn't smell any better and the cold blue tint of the lightbulb made it more cheerless than it would have been in the dark.

'So you remember why I got sacked,' Belle said, once we were settled.

'Boundary issues?'

'You see, the thing is,' said Belle, 'that sometimes the parents of a stillborn child, or even a late mis, sometimes they want to see and hold and love that baby a while. And sometimes they can't. But afterwards they might regret it and it's too late? I always wanted to help them not regret the decision they made.'

She had taken something out of her tunic pocket but she was covering it with her hand.

'Because you can't unsee a horror,' I said, nodding. But Angel's voice was in my head and the words he said were 'perfect' and 'dolly'.

'She wasn't a horror,' Belle said, and uncovered her phone. On the screen was a picture of a sleeping child, a long sweep of lashes from the huge almond eyes, eyes that seemed to reach around her little face. Her mouth was pursed shut and firm lines scored down it, on either side, Queen Victoria, not amused. The hospital blanket that was wound around her like a cocoon covered all but a single sticky spike of jet-black hair.

'So is this what she would have looked like?' I asked. 'Best-case scenario for that condition?'

Belle put her arm round me. 'Ali, my love, this is her. This is your baby girl. I took her picture. To give you the option. I took all their pictures, until they caught me.'

I grabbed the phone out of her hand and star-fished the photo as big as it would go.

'But it's true,' I said. 'She really is perfect.'

'No,' said Belle. 'I puffed up the blanket around the top of her head to make the shape look better. She wasn't perfect, but she was beautiful. Wouldn't you say so?'

'She looks like my mum,' I said, and kept gazing. Her nose was as smooth and round as a seashell washed by endless tides. Her lashes were as neat and soft as if someone had brushed them. And that determined little mouth. Tight shut on all her secrets. If I could have this picture on my bedside table in a silver frame, a little one laminated in my wallet, I knew I'd never hear her crying out for me again.

'She's not who I thought she was,' I said. But then neither was I. Single mum of two kids, the boy more trouble than his sister, close to my family, over my ex.

Well, that wasn't exactly who I was just yet, but I was on my way.

Postscript

Sylvie and Julia sold the cube house. Got a good price for it too from some ghoul who was actually tickled by the thought that a body had been buried there. The girls bought a cottage, other side of the bay, quite near my brother's farm and the annex he rents to me.

The last day I visited, Sylvie was gardening. A cherry tree, newly sunk in a mulched hole. It had three bare branches, gnarled and scaly as chicken's feet, and the dark tips only just beginning to swell where the buds would be. I watched her pour a Coke bottle full of water carefully around its roots, then stand up and watch the puddle seep into the soil.

'There,' she said. 'As long as Julia doesn't back the car into it.'

I sighed. Of the three of them, we never could say who was worst. Dido was teaching Julia to drive. Julia was teaching Dido to drink. I suspected Angelo was teaching both of them things I'd rather not know. I tried to care when the school called me in but, deep down, I reckoned if those three kids wanted some wild time they had my blessing.

Only Lars ever managed to keep them in line. Lars was in from the start with Dr F. Co-owner of the new drop-in clinic, co-chairman of the funding board. It was only his good name that got them accredited at all, since no one quite believed that Dr F knew nothing of what had happened at Howell Hall.

Tamara Ferris got twelve years. Mona Swain just fifteen, with a domestic-abuse defence. If I was a better person I would try never to think about either of them. But, being who I am, I like to imagine them passing in the halls at Cornton Vale, the women's prison. I like to think maybe they work together in the laundry, despising each other and still having to face each other every day.

Angel tells me Marco still lives in the cottage at Dundrennan. Fine by me. I don't suppose I'll ever need to drive down that way again. Howell Hall is closed. The army has the run of the headland now.

I saw Sylvie raise her head and glance over that way. Then she turned resolutely back and watched the last of the water soak away. 'By the time I can sit in its shade,' she said, 'all of this will feel far away.'

I said nothing, but she heard me at it and sighed. 'I don't want to remember any more than I remember already,' she said.

'And you're still sure you don't want someone to talk to?' I asked her. 'Professionally?'

She shook her head with a shudder. 'Just time,' she said. 'I have my new home and you, my good friend, and I have this to take care of and look forward to.'

She had, in other words, a house, a tree and a person.

'And Julia,' I reminded her.

'Mmhmm, mmhmm,' she said. She was new at it, but every time I heard it, it made me happy. The sound of Sylvie laughing.

Facts and Fictions

Galloway is a real place, but . . . something about it is just unreal enough to make it perfect for fiction. This time, Castle Douglas, Dalbeattie, Kirkcudbright and Dundrennan are borrowed whole. The abbey is pretty close but Historic Scotland looks after the real one far too well for any of this to happen there. There is a MoD training area near Dundrennan, but it's not much like mine. Howell Hall is entirely imaginary. Indeed, none of the houses, businesses or individuals in the book are based on real places, institutions or people.

Acknowledgements

I would like to thank:

Martin Fletcher, Krystyna Green, Amanda Keats, Aimee Kitson, Tara Loder, Helen Upton and all at Little, Brown for everything except the car-lift at the office.

Lisa Moylett and all at CMM Literary Agency.

My UK friends and my family: Nancy Balfour, Terri Bischoff, Audrey Ford and the gang, Wendy Keegan and *her* gang, Louise Kelly, Catherine Lepreux, Jean and Jim McPherson, Sheila McPherson (still) and a small but growing gang, Neil McRoberts, Nan McRoberts and *that* gang.